D1547012

MAY 2 4 2022

Herrick's End

Book 1 of The Neath Trilogy

By

T.M. Blanchet

A Tiny Fox Press Book

399 7212

© 2021 T.M. Blanchet

All rights reserved. No part of this book may be reproduced, stored in a retrieval system, or transmitted in any form or by any means, electronic, mechanical, photocopying, recording, or otherwise, without the prior written permission of the publisher, except as provided by U.S.A. copyright law. For information address: Tiny Fox Press, North Port, FL.

This is a work of fiction: Names, places, characters, and events are a product of the author's imagination or used fictitiously. Any resemblance to actual persons, living or dead, locales, or events is purely coincidental.

Cover art by Damonza

Library of Congress Control Number: 2022930682
ISBN: 978-1-946501-47-9

Tiny Fox Press and the book fox logo are all registered trademarks of Tiny Fox Press LLC

Tiny Fox Press LLC
North Port, FL

For Mary Bonfiglio Voner
"faccia bella"

Prologue

Salem Village, Massachusetts Bay Colony
May, 1692

The horses kicked up clouds of dust as they traveled the narrow dirt road, dragging the cart behind them. One driver, three passengers. The women's wailing drowned out every other sound on the grassy hill.

The driver stared straight ahead, snapping the reins with tight precision as his prisoners sobbed and implored him for mercy. They also bellowed prayers and, he suspected, incantations of a more suspicious sort. He paid them no heed. The women had been examined; some had even confessed. Anything they said now surely came from Satan's mouth, designed to deceive. But he would not be fooled. He had work enough to do in this earthly realm, difficult and underpaid, without partaking in the devil's work, as well.

As the cart reached the crest of the hill, the driver gave a start. Something clutched his sleeve. He looked down to see a bony and bent hand, its fingernails caked with dirt. For just a moment, he turned, and the cart slowed.

She had reached for him through the bars, this woman, this unholy creature.

"Unhand me," he ordered.

But her grip did not loosen. "I see you," the woman hissed through blackened, crooked teeth. Her hair was a wild mass. "I know your name."

"Silence, woman," he snapped, tearing her fingers away from his coat sleeve.

She clutched the bars of the crude cage, pressing her face through the narrow opening. Behind her, the two others wept and keened. "Hear me now, afflictor," the woman said, her voice as graveled as the road beneath his wheels. "You cannot hide from this. They see all that you do. And they will know your name."

The driver gave a snort. "You are mad, old woman. Mad, and cursed."

The prisoner's bloodshot eyes widened as her voice rose. "Can you not see it? I am no more a witch than I am a cloud in the sky. You have imprisoned innocents! It is not too late for you to save us, and to save yourself. I beseech you now, open this cage! Stop this injustice! By your own hands, you bring us to death, George Herrick! You bring us to hell!"

The man blinked. He was startled to notice that he'd been leaning toward the crazed woman, as though pulled by an unseen force. Disgusted, he reached forward to shove her face through the bars. "Cease with your tricks!" he spat, spinning around in his seat. "They hold no purchase here." Then he snapped the reins again, urging the horses forward.

The cart continued its arduous journey along the pocked road, jostling its passengers with every rut. The driver, who held the official title of Marshall and Deputy-Sheriff, concentrated on the animals as he navigated a particularly narrow curve. Not far, now: The jail was only a mile or so ahead. Then he would be free of his passengers. Free of the incessant wailing. The wild-eyed woman's insinuations had left a foul taste on his tongue, try as he might to ignore it. He was only doing his job, after all. Earning his wage, supporting his family. As a man should. What happened to the prisoners after that was none of his concern.

With all of his attention focused on the road, the harried driver did not notice the faces peering out through the leaves as he passed.

Five pairs of eyes, following the cart's progress. Taking measure of the man, and of the women trapped inside the traveling, makeshift cell. The unlucky prisoners were not witches, of course, no matter who it had served to call them so.

The real witches watched from the trees. They heard the woman's cry: "By your own hands, you bring us to death, George Herrick! You bring us to hell!"

They watched him on that day, and on all the days that followed in the perilous year of 1692. They observed the transport, and the examinations, and the cold, dank prison cells infested with lice. They

6

saw the pleading, and the starvation, and the lies, and the hatred, and the hubris, and the persecutions, and the bodies jerking and twisting at the ends of knotted ropes.

The real witches watched it all.

And they did not forget.

One

I am not the fattest person in the room.

It was true, if only marginally. Ollie repeated the thought like a feverish prayer, hiding behind the rim of his baseball hat as his eyes jumped from chair to chair. *Fatter. Fatter. Smaller. About the same. Fatter.* He knew he had no right to judge—not here. These people had been nothing but kind to him. But he couldn't seem to stop himself. In this one place, at least, he could look left and right and find someone, anyone, whose girth exceeded his own.

Ollie wanted to feel smug. Or even mildly confident. He would have settled for any emotion, really, other than the usual debilitating humiliation.

I am not the fattest person in the room.

The room in question had tall ceilings, exposed-brick walls, and just enough floor space to accommodate its ten folding chairs. The group sat in a circle, as always. To Ollie's left, Kendra was saying something about her "holiday weight gain," though the holidays were already three months past. The others nodded. "Holiday weight gain" was a popular topic in Lighter Tomorrows meetings, as was "summer weight gain." Kendra, in particular, liked to label her gains, as though assigning them a name made them different, somehow. Less permanent.

8

Ollie was sitting with his arms folded and his right leg bouncing. He needed to crack his knuckles, but knew the sound would be too disruptive. He shifted and sat on his hands instead.

"Kendra makes a good point," said Lorraine. In Lorraine-speak, that meant it was time for someone else to talk. She surveyed the room with a wide, tight-lipped smile. Lorraine was the meeting host, hired to keep the gatherings in check and the members engaged. She had lost 53 pounds—a figure Ollie always found oddly specific—and now served as an enthusiastic ambassador for the LT brand.

"This time of year can be particularly tough, don't you think?" Lorraine prodded. Her thin hair, stung by static, lifted from the tips of her shoulders. "Does anyone else have winter struggles they'd like to share?"

Ollie knew what he was supposed to say. He could have written the script. *My God, yes, it's tough. Snowstorms, comfort food, trapped inside. Darn this weather.* The group would murmur in agreement, and Lorraine would thank him "for sharing."

The truth, the real truth, was uglier. And harder to wrap in a crowd-pleasing soundbite. Yes, winter was challenging. Of course it was. But so was spring, and Halloween, and the third Tuesday in August. Ollie's trials didn't begin or end with any particular season; they began when he opened his eyes in the morning and ended, if only temporarily, when he was unconscious at night. Winter wasn't the problem. Food was the problem. Always had been, always would be. Delicious, wretched food.

Lorraine turned to her left. "How about you, Christine? Are you finding it hard to stay active this winter?"

Christine shared that she was, in fact, finding it quite hard to stay active. Her work hours were long. Her boss was unsupportive. A gym membership was not in her family's budget.

Ollie tried his best to "listen actively," as LT hosts liked to say. But as Christine's monologue morphed, predictably, into a description of her boys' demanding hockey schedules, his gaze drifted to the window. He could almost see the cold air snaking its way past the loose, rattling casing. The building was hundreds of years old—the windows, only slightly younger. From his second-floor vantage point, he could just make out the snow-dusted top of Nina's Bakery across the street. Nina's made the best anise cookies he had ever tasted. Ever, and that was saying something. Perfect domes of spiced dough smothered in a sugary white glaze and sprinkled with multi-colored nonpareils. Soft on the inside, with just the tiniest crisp on the edges. His grandmother had

9

made spectacular anise cookies, as had his mother. But Nina's Bakery made the best.

"Lisa, last week you mentioned you were planning to make a list of trigger foods," Lorraine said. "How did that go?"

Lisa scooted forward in her seat. "Good," she answered, holding up a notebook. "Should I...read it?"

"Of course," Lorraine smiled.

"Okay. Well, the first thing I thought of was birthday cake. Seems like every week we have a birthday in the office. Stupid, right? I mean, why do grown adults need a birthday party at work? And then, for number two, I wrote chips and salsa. I mean, I know the salsa is fine, but..."

The list went on. And on. As Lisa talked, Ollie returned his attention to the scene outside. Two restaurant awnings, one blue and one gold, flanked Nina's doorway. Though Ollie couldn't see the signs, he knew that the blue awning belonged to Andiamo, and the gold to Fioretti's. Anywhere else, both eateries would be considered top-notch. Best in the city, maybe. But this wasn't anywhere else. This was the North End, where cannoli was currency and the smell of simmering tomato wafted down every alley. The neighborhood housed nearly a hundred Italian restaurants, pizzerias, salumerias, bakeries, and cafes within its one-third of one square mile. Vampire hunters used less garlic than the kitchens on Hanover Street, where Andiamo and Fioretti's had to compete with the likes of La Sicilia, Pesco Fresco, and the indomitable Mama Mary's. The tourists and suburbanites descended every Saturday night, eager to walk the cobblestone streets and inhale a week's worth of calories in one meal.

Ollie's neighborhood was a swirling orgy of alfredo and gelato and Pappardelle Bolognese. Or, as he had come to think of it, Fat Quicksand. And he had lived there, sinking slowly day by day, for all of his 19 years.

A deep voice to the left jarred him from his musings. Vince was asking a question: something about the merits of treadmills versus stationary bikes. "Big Vince" was a local cop whose weight was about to cost him his job. He sat through each LT meeting wide-eyed and panicked, as though he had just fallen from a high place and was trying to figure out where he had landed. Every once in a while, Big Vince would interrupt the group discussion with an urgent question: Butter or margarine? Steamed or broiled? Weights or cardio?

Vince is the fattest person in the room, Ollie thought to himself, gripping the edge of the metal folding chair. *Then Audrey, then Jose.*

Next, it was a toss-up between Kendra and Lisa. And then him. He wasn't even in the top five.

But he'd never be the smallest. Not even here. At six-foot-six, Ollie would always be the awkward giant of any gathering. A massive, hovering ghost, complete with pale skin, light hair, watery brown eyes, and undefined edges.

Today, the smallest person at the meeting was Grandma Helen, a cotton-topped eighty-something who came to the meetings mainly for the social interaction; while not thin, per se, she wasn't any rounder than any other *nonna* on the block. Normally, though, the title of Smallest in the Room would have gone to someone else. Ollie's gaze traveled to the empty chair in their little circle. Conspicuously, curiously empty.

"Let's move on to this week's recipe," Lorraine said, rising to hand out sheets of paper. With a note of excitement, she read the top line: "Tandoori Tofu with Brown Rice and Cilantro-Lime Drizzle! Looks yummy. And easy, too."

Ollie took the recipe and sighed. Who drizzled? Nobody drizzled. He didn't even know what that meant. He had dunked, smothered, and poured, plenty of times. But never drizzled. If Nell were there, this would be the moment when she would catch his attention and roll her eyes to mock Lorraine's Tandoori Tofu enthusiasm. And he would smile and nod in silent agreement. But Nell wasn't there. Her seat was empty. Again.

This was the third meeting in a row she had missed. Two Tuesdays, one Saturday. Ollie felt her absence like thumbtack in his shoe.

Antonella "Nell" Cascone wasn't the only reason he came to meetings. Definitely not. But if pressed, he might admit that she was probably the reason he came to this particular location on these particular days. He'd first spotted her in the circle nearly two years prior; since then, she'd been a regular. And so had he.

Nell was 18 years old, voluptuous, sable-haired, and by far the best-looking girl to have ever given him the time of day. So yes, she was pretty. And hell yes, he'd noticed. He'd have to have cataracts the size of quarters not to. But Nell was also just...nice. Nice to him, specifically, in a way that other people were not. Hers was an easy, almost accidental sort of kindness, radiating from her body like steam from a hot bath. She asked him about his college applications. She asked him about his job. She laughed at his jokes, which, he knew, were usually not all that funny. She gave him hugs goodbye, and casually affectionate pats on the arm. To some, these might be small things. But to Ollie, they were mountainous.

Nell had even come to his mother's wake. *And* sent flowers. Most people had done one or the other, but Nell had done both.

So if she was also a bit scatter-brained and stubborn, Ollie could, and did, forgive it all. Whatever her faults, Nell had, day by day, grown to become an outsized figure in his life. Perhaps too outsized. Even the smallest spot of color draws the eye on a blank canvas, and Ollie's canvas, sadly, was nothing if not blank. He knew this. When she invited him for the occasional coffee after a meeting, he had to remind himself that it was just that—a coffee. Not dinner. And certainly not a date.

But coffee was coffee, and Nell was...Nell. He was happy to take what he could get, considering that she already had plenty of options to choose from. Ollie often saw them waiting for her out in the street: blonde athlete types, brunette construction-worker types, bearded emo types. Once, even a woman. Nell had her pick of the city, and there was no way she was wasting a Saturday night on the likes of him. Ollie harbored no delusions about his standing.

And yet, sometimes, when the winter night fell and the loneliness squeezed him like an orange juicer, Ollie liked to tell himself a different story. He liked to tell himself that he and Nell shared a special bond—something those gorgeous, strapping suitors would never understand. Like him, Nell struggled with food. She confided those struggles in him. For all he knew, she confided *only* in him. That had to mean something, right? And he had watched enough rom-coms to know that sometimes the clueless young heroine does, inexplicably, turn around one day to find that the one she was searching for—*cue the swelling symphony*—had been right there all along.

"And how about you, Ollie?"

"Hmm?" He straightened, pushing up the lid on his baseball cap.

Lorraine was staring at him. Everyone was staring at him.

"Any goals for the week ahead?" she asked, in a tone that implied she was repeating herself.

Goals. Goals, goals, goals... His mind spun.

The question wasn't a surprise. At every meeting, Lorraine asked each of them: "What are your goals for the week ahead?" She was talking specifically about weight-loss goals, of course, and the answers were easy: *Extra steps*, maybe. Or: *less carbs, more protein*. Duh. It was Lighter Tomorrows 101.

So why did he never have an answer ready? And why did the question always strike a nerve, as though she were accusing him of something?

What are your goals for the week ahead, Ollie Delgato? For the year? For your future? Anything? Anything at all?

"Less pasta, I guess," Ollie finally said.

"Just do your best. And keep counting those credits."

"Fill up with water before you eat," chimed in Kendra.

Ollie would do all those things. And it wouldn't make one damn bit of difference. That day's weigh-in had been disastrous. Three pounds up, again, despite the fact that he'd been drinking enough water to float a ferry. In the LT program, each food was assigned a "wellness credit," and each member had a daily limit. Ollie was supposed to count his credits each day, and he did. Most days he just counted too high.

As for his other "goals for the week ahead," it was nothing they wanted to hear. Leveling up on his PS4 game, maybe. Restocking the Diet Coke in the fridge. Ten thousand steps per day. Binge-watching superhero movies. Wasting his youth.

Ollie rubbed a hand against his stubbled chin. Down below, in the street, two different car horns were honking: a high *meep meep*, followed by a deeper, aggravated series of bellows.

I am not the fattest person in—

"Okay, that's time, people!" Lorraine said, interrupting his thought with a sudden clap. "Great meeting. I'll see you all on Saturday. In the meantime, let's hear our motto..." She cupped a hand over her ear.

Dutifully, the group chanted in unison: "Here today, lighter tomorrow."

"Here today, lighter tomorrow!" she trilled in response. "Have a great weekend, and keep up the good work!" Lorraine stood up and started the exodus. Chair legs scraped against the floor as people rose to leave.

"See ya, Ollie," Big Vince said, sliding an arm into his coat.

"Bye, Vince. Have a good one."

And off they all went, back to the cold, hard world of judgment and scorn. Ollie watched them leave, then turned back to look at her chair.

Empty.

Did she quit the group? He couldn't imagine it. Nell loved Lighter Tomorrows. Plus, she was doing well. Counting her credits, losing weight. She said it was like a game, the counting, and she wanted to win.

Maybe she was annoyed at him. Maybe she was tired of the meetings. Or maybe she had decided to accept herself the way she was and stop the futile effort of attending a weight-loss support group located steps away from three different pastry shops.

Maybe. Or maybe something was wrong.

If he'd had to guess, this probably had something to do with The Guy. That was how Nell talked about him—capital T, capital G. The latest one. After they started dating a few months ago, the other suitors had disappeared. Ollie got the impression that she'd moved in with him, at least unofficially. Ollie didn't even know the dude's name, or anything about him other than the fact that he apparently liked kielbasa, a lot, and he *didn't* like Nell hanging out with other guys, even if they were "just friends." Which would explain why she hadn't been returning any of Ollie's calls or texts.

Each time he thought about it, a thick weight of dread began to settle on his chest. Heavier every time.

Ollie squirmed in his chair. All these "maybes" and "probablys" and ridiculous invented theories... Maybe Nell had Lyme disease. Maybe she had a sick relative, or a dead relative. Dead relative with a faraway funeral. Cosmetology conference. Habitat for Humanity. Swept away by Mormons. Touring with a band.

Who did he think he was kidding with this shit?

He knew already, didn't he? Hadn't he known it for weeks? He knew, but didn't want to know. He hadn't wanted to believe it. And maybe he had hoped that if he ignored the obvious, it might just go away. But now, in that suddenly empty room full of suddenly empty chairs, the repressed images returned in a sickening series of flashes: Nell's scarf, arranged in an odd way to obscure the purplish discoloration on her jaw. Sunglasses on a cloudy day. Twitchy behavior. Strange isolation. Thick, sometimes cakey makeup.

The last time Ollie had seen her in person, two weeks ago, he and Nell had made a quick stop for cappuccino after a meeting. The weather that day had been brisk: low 20s with a sharp wind. Nell had kept on her coat—a hunter green thrift-store find—even while they were inside. Her lipstick left a ruby smudge on the rim of the white cup.

"You okay?" Ollie had asked.

She was staring over her shoulder, out the window. At the sound of his voice, Nell had spun and flashed an unconvincing smile. "Yeah, sure. Why?"

"You just seem...distracted, I guess," he had said. In truth, she had been skittish and uncharacteristically disheveled. Ollie had been startled to see her wearing baggy gray sweats under her coat. Nell didn't do gray. And she sure as hell didn't do baggy—at least, not that he'd ever seen. Her hair, normally shining with carefully styled waves, had been stuffed under a knitted hat. And then there was the scarf, again. That damn scarf, wrapped around her chin. Wrapped too high.

"Aren't you hot?" he had asked her. "It's like, eighty degrees in here." The café owners had compensated for the outside temperatures by cranking up the thermostat to uncomfortable heights.

"Hmm? No. I'm good," Nell had said. She twisted her body into a fusilli spiral, peering to look at passersby out the window, then pulled out her phone to check the time. "I can't stay long."

"Sure. That's fine."

"Hey, you mind if we switch seats?" she had suddenly asked.

"Now? Why?"

"I just... I like the view."

"Of Hanover Street?" Ollie had asked dubiously. What was there to see? Sure, the tourists loved it, but Nell was a local.

"C'mon, Ollie. Please? Humor me."

"Yeah, sure, okay." Hearing something desperate in her tone, he got up more quickly than he had intended. "Here."

"Thanks," she had smiled then, a real smile, and the sight of it came as a welcome relief.

They had stayed for another fifteen minutes. Nell did all the usual things. She played with her spoon, and talked, and laughed half-heartedly in the right places. But as he watched her, Ollie had gotten the eerie feeling that he wasn't actually talking to Nell, at all. She was more like hologram of the girl he knew. A nervous, frightened imposter. She checked her phone three more times while they sat.

Between sips, Ollie had asked her why she had stopped going to her cosmetology classes. She told him the classes had started to bore her, and he didn't argue. He asked her why she had stopped skating on Frog Pond with her friend Jocelyn. She said Jocelyn had started to bore her, too, and he didn't argue. He asked, finally, about the new bruises on her wrist. Nell had tugged down the cuff of her sleeve and told him a story about wrapping a dog leash too tightly around her hand.

Ollie knew what he was seeing. Of course, he did. He had seen it all before, in his own home. And still, somehow, he didn't argue.

The conversation had ended abruptly when Nell slurped her cup dry, jumped to her feet, and said she had to go. She had an appointment, she told him, over on Henchman Street. Even now, a week later, Ollie could clearly remember the odd expression he'd read

15

on her face: something between determination and fear. And then, she was gone, letting in a rush of cold air as she vanished out the café door. He doubted she had even heard his goodbye.

Ollie's knee bounced in agitation as the memory dissolved. Somewhere inside the walls, the archaic heating system's pipes rattled to life, blowing weak streams of hot air through the vents. Someone had spilled coffee creamer on the floor a few weeks ago and never cleaned it up; now, each time the heat kicked on, the blowing air spread the lingering, sour stench throughout the room. Ollie stayed in his chair, motionless save the knee, washed in waves of heat and odor.

A group in the hallway shared a sudden laugh; the sound echoed off the walls. He wiped his mouth with the back of his hand, staring at the open doorway. Pretending he was in on the joke. He did that a lot. Pretended. Mostly, he pretended that he wasn't so alone. It wasn't too much to ask, was it? He didn't want anything glamorous or royal. Just what other people had. Regular, happy people. The couples he saw on the subway, nuzzling necks and sharing conspiratorial whispers. The dad holding his little boy's hand in line at the grocer. The brides and grooms traipsing through the Public Garden in tuxedos and gowns, posing for goofy pictures in front of the Swan Boats. College pals roaming in drunken packs. The endless pairs of lovers on Instagram, faces pressed together and filling the entire frame.

We have each other, they all said, without saying anything at all.

That was all he wanted. Just...someone. Someone to be on his side. To make him feel normal, and listened to, and not so achingly solitary. But it wasn't to be. His size was like the Great Wall of Ollie: a barrier no one wanted to cross.

As it was, he only had one real-ish friend in the world, and he had let her down. Spectacularly. There had been no dog, of course. No leash on her wrist. No walking into door jambs, no tripping and falling. There was only someone leaving ugly marks on Nell's body, plain as day, and Ollie hadn't done a damn thing about it.

She had been sitting right there, five feet away, twice a week. He could have come right out and asked her: *What's really going on? How can I help?*

But he hadn't asked. And now she was gone.

Gone.

The word slumped him forward in his seat.

Where the hell *was* she?

Her roommates didn't know, and didn't seem too concerned, since she had more or less been staying with the new boyfriend anyway. The

16

last time he had spoken to her, Nell had mentioned an upcoming "weekend away" with The Guy. That would explain a few days' absence, but not a whole week. He supposed they could have extended their stay at the Vermont campground or Manhattan hotel or Provincetown scuba-diving expedition or wherever young lovers got off to nowadays. Anything was possible. But his gut was telling him that it just wasn't very likely.

She had also mentioned that unspecified "appointment" on Henchman Street.

Henchman was one of the North End's shorter roads. A nondescript cut-through, used mainly to jump over to the busier Commercial Street below. Ollie rarely ventured down there; he never had a reason to. As far as he knew, it held nothing but apartments. No office buildings, medical labs, or other kind of place where someone might have an appointment.

Which didn't make any sense at all, now that he thought about it. Where had Nell been going that day? And why had she never returned?

The heating vents had stopped blowing, though the foul odor remained. Traffic hummed noisily, relentlessly, out in the street.

Ollie had never thought of himself as the white-knight type. Hell, no one on earth had probably ever thought of him as the white-knight type. But if Nell really was in trouble, and if he was the one who happened to save her... Well, that opened up a whole world of possibilities, didn't it? It might even get him out of the Friend Zone if he played his cards right. And even if he didn't—a much more likely scenario—at least he could sleep at night knowing he hadn't been such a candy-ass, chickenshit loser. For once.

Ollie stared down at his sneakers, at the wide wooden floor boards, at the scattered bits of dust and dirt, knowing what he had to do. Or at least where he could start. Too little, perhaps, but hopefully not too late.

On the bright side, it looked like he finally had a "goal for the week ahead." Lorraine would have been so pleased.

Two

Twenty minutes later, Ollie stood at the corner of Charter and Henchman streets, wondering how soon was too soon to give up on his plan.

Henchman looked mostly deserted. Nearly identical rows of five-story apartment buildings lined both sides of the road, their fire escapes crawling in zig-zags down the brick walls. No trees, no balconies, no bike racks. Just a sidewalk, a single streetlamp, and a peekaboo view to Commercial Street down below. The lone signs of life: two boys throwing pebbles at a "no parking" sign while a bundled-up woman, probably their mother, stood by.

Ollie cracked the knuckles on both hands, feeling foolish. Then he pulled his coat zipper all the way up to his chin. A passing delivery truck sent a spray of dirty snow onto the sidewalk.

With a sigh, he began to walk down the small hill, peering at the mismatched doors, looking for an office. A salon. Something. Nothing stood out. Every step was a fight against the late-winter wind, which was whipping over the water and straight up the hill like an angry child.

He was almost to the bottom of the street when he saw it: A tiny sign, about the size of an envelope, affixed at eye-level near one of the sunken doorways. "Women's Resource Center," it read. "Open 24 Hours." The words were accompanied by a logo that weaved the acronym "WRC" into a shield-shaped design.

The building was brick, indistinguishable from all the others. In the windows above, he could see signs of apartment life: kitchen curtains, houseplants, protruding air conditioners. But the stairs to the Women's

Resource Center, whatever that was, went down to the basement level. Two cameras flanked the doorway. Both pointed directly at the spot where he was standing.

He stared at the camera on the left and it stared back, blinking its red light.

The morning's omelet began to gurgle in his intestines. What was this place? He felt like he was breaking some kind of a rule just by being here. It was a *Women's* Resource Center, after all, not a Nosy Young Men's Center.

Ollie was debating whether or not he should leave when he heard two short clicks, like latches being turned. A moment later, a woman peered out of the WRC door at the bottom of the dark staircase. She had dirty blonde hair and fair skin. Her smile reminded Ollie of a wild dog: bared teeth, with very little warmth.

"Hello," the woman said. "Can I help you?" Her tone indicated that she could not, in fact, help him at all. Or, more precisely, that she didn't want to.

"Hi," Ollie said. Taking a few hesitant steps forward, he reached the top stair. "I'm wondering... I was just..." He stopped.

The woman lifted her eyebrows but stayed silent.

Ollie pressed his hands together, cleared his throat, and started again. "Sorry. I'm looking for my friend. She's been missing. For a few days now. I think she came here, recently. She told me she had an appointment on this street, and I don't see anywhere else..." His sentence faded as he jerked his thumb to indicate the residential block behind him.

The blonde woman continued to stare.

"Her name is Antonella. Nell. I was wondering... Have you seen her? Can you help me?" He hunched, trying to shrink his tall and rotund body into the most innocuous form possible. He often tried this. It never worked.

"Your friend is missing?" the woman asked. Politely. Carefully.

He nodded. "Brown hair, kind of this long? I'm trying to find her. I mean, I don't know if she's *missing*, exactly, but I haven't seen her. I was getting worried. You know, just starting to wonder."

"Uh huh," the young woman nodded.

Ollie removed his baseball hat and held it in front of his chest like he was about to say the Pledge of Allegiance. "If you don't mind my asking, what is this place?"

"This is the Women's Resource Center."

"Yes, but...what do you do?"

She flashed a businesslike smile and launched into what sounded like a rehearsed speech: "The Women's Resource Center is a nonprofit organization that provides the women of Boston with information and access to important resources in the city, including health care, housing, childcare, nutritional services, and transportation."

Ollie nodded. "Can you check to see if my friend was here? And what resources she was looking for?"

"I'm afraid I can't. All WRC client services are confidential."

"Sure, sure. I get that. But if I could find out why she came here, then I might be able to find her. I think... I think something might be wrong. I think she might even be in danger."

"What makes you say that?"

The question came from inside the doorway.

The blonde turned, then stepped out of the way to make room for a petite brunette with a snugly fitting, button-down shirt. Though she couldn't have been more than five-foot-two, the woman radiated an air of firm command. Her arms were folded. If she was intimidated by his size, or affected by the frigid temperature, she didn't show it.

"Hi," he said, taking a few steps down and holding out his hand. "I'm Ollie Delgato. I live around the corner."

"Hello, Ollie Delgato," the woman said, shaking his hand and offering no name in return. He had never seen anyone blink so slowly, as though each bump of her lids was the result of a conscious, carefully considered decision. "What makes you think your friend is in danger?"

He swallowed. "I... I don't know, exactly. Just a feeling, I guess." Ollie didn't like the wary way she was looking at him, like he was a tranquilized lion on the verge of waking up. "She's gone. Not answering calls, that sort of thing. And she came here, I think... and I..." The sentence fell between them, unfinished.

The short woman nodded. Then she said, "You seem like a good friend, Mr. Delgato. I'm sorry we can't be of more help. But we have a strict confidentiality policy here at the WRC that prevents us from sharing any information about our clients." Like her colleague, she, too, sounded like she was reading from a script. Her smile was polite, but firm. Case closed.

Ollie opened his mouth to protest, then closed it again. He could see it was no use. He could ask all day, in a hundred different ways. She wasn't going to tell him a damn thing.

"Have a great day, Mr. Delgato."

Force of polite habit made him mutter, "Thanks." What was he thanking her for, exactly? Not kicking him in the nuts on the way out?

"I wish you the best of luck in finding your friend," the brunette added. Moments later, the impenetrable door closed, and he was once again alone on the sidewalk.

The cameras whirred and spun, tracking Ollie's movements as he turned, dejectedly, to leave. He fought the urge to flip two middle fingers: one for each camera. Instead, he trudged in defeat to the top of the small hill. A cracked and peeling historic sign hung above his head, mounted to the side of one of the buildings. The words were barely legible: *Henchman Street*. Such a strange name. It made him think of thugs, and dimwits, and mindless, mechanical cruelty. Ollie looked over his shoulder, then back up at the sign. His eyes narrowed into a squint.

Was it his imagination, or were the letters...moving? They seemed to be shifting, somehow. Fading in and out. There were no waving tree branches to cast shadows on the wall; not that high up. No scattered clouds, no flashing police lights. Nothing at all to alter the sign's appearance. And yet, the letters did seem to be changing, all on their own. Disappearing, and reappearing. Almost... shimmering.

Ollie slammed his eyes shut. It was a trick of the light, he told himself. A hundred-year-old sign that needed new paint. Nothing more.

Still, when the shiver ran up his back, he knew it had nothing whatsoever to do with the cold.

Feeling alternately imbecilic and pissed off, Ollie checked the fitness tracker on his wrist: not even 2,000 steps in yet, and the day was almost half over.

Shit. That meant he was also late for work.

He hustled his way along the sidewalk, doing his best not to make eye contact. In a neighborhood like this, Ollie didn't have to go far to run into old-timers—most of whom wanted to chat. Just a few blocks down, he heard his name.

"Afternoon, Ollie!"

He looked up to find an old woman peering at him through wire-rimmed glasses. She was sweeping slush from the entryway of a hair salon. "Hey, Mrs. Andolini."

"You coming to bingo?"

"Probably, yeah." A few months back, the neighborhood biddies had insisted that Ollie take his mother's old spot at the table. He pretended to mind but didn't really.

Ollie waved to Mrs. Andolini and kept moving, stepping around the ubiquitous valet-parking signs that cluttered the sidewalk. He barely registered the familiar sights: Framed photos of Sophia Loren and John F. Kennedy staring out from the shop window, surrounded by a haphazard assortment of Chapstick tubes, aspirin bottles, and various European soccer jerseys. Green-white-and-red flags waving next to displays of model trains, nativity sets, and fussy gilded teacups. The grocer's teetering pile of oranges, lending much-needed color to the winter gloom.

The North End, as usual, was showing its age. Everything wobbled, from the cobblestones in the street to the wrought-iron balconies hanging above his head. Sometimes Ollie could swear he felt the ghosts of the English Puritans who first settled the place in the 1630s, followed by successive waves of Irish and Jewish arrivals. Finally, around the turn of the last century, immigrants from Naples, Sicily, Genoa, and Milan had clumped together in protective tribes and elbowed the other groups out. By the early 1900s, the district was, essentially, all Italian. The language and culture still permeated everything within the half-circle haven of Commercial Street.

"Oll-ay!"

"Hey, Mr. Costa."

"Cold one today!"

"Yep. Sure is."

Passing vehicles created a constant, low rumble in Ollie's ears as he continued on. At his feet, a line of red bricks marked the path of the Freedom Trail, which guided history buffs to famous local sites like the Paul Revere House and the Old North Church. Ollie often found himself walking on the narrow brick trail like a gymnast on a balance beam, placing one foot in front of the other. He was doing exactly that when a voice called out from a nearby step.

"*Ciao,* Ollie."

He pulled his bare hand from his pocket for a quick wave. "Hi, Mrs. Toscano."

Back in the day, Mrs. Toscano would have said something like, "Tell your mom I have her chafing dish," or "Tell your mom it's seven tomorrow, not eight." Now, though, she just gave Ollie that same, sad smile. Every time.

He swallowed hard as St. Leonard's came into view. For so many years, it had been just a church. Sunday mass, shuffling feet, hours of little-boy boredom. A familiar place for a familiar routine. Then, quite suddenly, it had become something else: the site of his mother's funeral. Ollie had helped to carry the coffin down the aisle, hung his head in the front pew, and said goodbye. That was more than a year ago. And he hadn't been back since.

Francie Delgato had died of breast cancer. By the time they found the tumors, it was too late. Shortly before her death, Ollie had overheard her telling Mrs. Andolini that the cancer was "her penance," though he couldn't imagine what she meant. His mother had been a saint, right up there with ol' Leonard himself. Warm, patient, empathetic, funny, smart—hell, the woman practically had butterflies landing on her fingertips when she walked down the street. If moms were bingo games, he had won the whole pot: Across, down, and diagonal.

At the funeral, Mr. Mazza had squeezed Ollie's shoulder and suggested, in a roundabout way, that his mother had died not of cancer, but of a broken heart. When Ollie realized the daft old man was talking about his father—or, more accurately, his lack of a father—he had stifled an incredulous laugh. Ollie had only vague memories of the man, but they were enough. Matteo Delgato had been, by all accounts, a terrible father and husband. His disappearance was the proverbial "go out to the store for cigarettes and never come back," though in Matteo's case the "store" was a Saturday-night booze-cruise and the "cigarettes" were open taps of Michelob Ultra. To this day, no one was quite sure if Matteo had fallen off the deck into the frigid waters of the harbor, or if he'd just decided he'd had enough of family life and took off for sunnier cruises on the Florida shore. Either way, Ollie and his mom had never heard from the guy again, and they were better off for it.

His mother had been enough. More than enough.

But now Francie was gone. The money was gone, too, poured into expensive treatments and hospital bills that had done nothing but delay the inevitable. Ollie had just turned 18 when she died, making him not an orphan, exactly, but something that felt awfully close.

He turned the corner, grateful to leave St. Leonard's behind. He passed a tempting gelato display window and did the mental calculation: *large pistachio, 12 credits. Plus a cone, three credits. Jimmies, maybe one or two.* If he shrunk it to a small, that would be six credits, plus the cone, plus the jimmies, so...10 credits total. That wasn't so bad, was it? His feet slowed. On the Lighter Tomorrows plan, he was allotted 36 credits per day. He'd already had a ham-and-cheese omelet for breakfast, so that was, what? Seven credits? Lunch would be twice that.

Ollie scrunched his brow and picked up his pace. No. No gelato. He had to stay on the program. Lose the weight. Get a friggin' *life*, already. If not now, when? He had a scholarship to start Bunker Hill Community College in the fall—a full-ride scholarship, including tuition and fees. It was the break he'd been waiting for. That meant he had less than seven months to shrink himself down to a manageable size, merge seamlessly into the student body, and become the kind of person that guys wanted to hang out with and girls wanted to date. Seven months to achieve normalcy. Surely even he could manage that.

Ollie was winded by the time he reached the sloping asphalt entrance to Bonfiglio's Caffe and pushed open the heavy door.

The smells hit him in a wonderful wave: freshly ground beans; buttery dough; almond paste; cinnamon and sugar. Pastry display cases and a counter stood on the right, while a cluster of tiny round tables filled the space to the left. The silver, curlicued chairs called to mind an old-fashioned malt shop. Black-and-white tiles lined the floor. And on the back wall, shelves of antique coffee contraptions adorned with levers, pipes, gauges, and knobs had the look of a mad scientist's lab.

The job was mundane—serving coffee and cake, mopping floors, wiping tables—but came with one major perk: a tiny but low-rent apartment located above the shop. Ollie could never have afforded a North End apartment, even a studio, at regular rates. He had gotten both the job and the apartment courtesy of a lifelong friendship between his mom and Mr. Bonfiglio. And no small amount of pity, he was sure.

"Hey, Mr. B," Ollie said sheepishly. "Sorry I'm late."

Mr. Bonfiglio popped his head up from behind the pastry counter. "Ollie!" He waved a short, thick arm and tossed an apron. "No worries, kid. Beautiful day, isn't it?"

Ollie smiled. Mr. Bonfiglio thought every day was a beautiful day. What sort of day, Ollie sometimes wondered, would make him complain? A terrorist attack, maybe? A blizzard? Another Great Molasses Flood? He got a sudden flash of Mr. B at the window, watching waves of brown goo sweep away people and cars as it poured down the street. "Beautiful day, except for all that darn molasses," he would say, biting ruefully into his eclair.

"Where do you want me?" Ollie asked him, tying the black apron around his waist.

The older man rubbed his chin. "You get the tables," he said. "I'll get the register." His disheveled eyebrows, which staked an unnaturally large claim to his forehead, matched an equally disheveled demeanor.

"Will do," Ollie said.

Not long after, a crowd of college students pushed their way in, followed by a few families, tourists, and some of the elderly locals. Armpit sweat began to soak Ollie's shirt as he hurried to concoct dozens of lattes, macchiatos, and espressos. He scooped gelato from the freezer case, packaged up boxes of biscotti, and carried slices of ricotta pie and Limoncello cake to the tables. By the time his coworker Cara arrived for her shift, the place was a mess of uncleared plates and spilled cream.

"I got this," Cara told him, taking the order pads from his hand.

"Thanks," Ollie said, relieved. He took stock of the disarray with a grimace. Then he grabbed a clean rag and began making his way through the tangled cluster of chairs, wiping down the tabletops and stacking dirty dishes into a gray tub.

As he worked, his big stomach bumped against the chair backs. The too-tight apron dug into his chest. A boy with a cookie stared up at him with wide eyes, too young to hide his fascination. Among the dainty chairs and low ceiling of the café, Ollie imagined he must have looked like a curly-blond Godzilla tearing through a tiny Japanese village.

I am the fattest person in the room, he thought to himself, feeling the usual shot of anguish. *The very fattest.*

The boy was still staring. Ollie tried to ignore it, failed, and finally stuck out his tongue, making the boy laugh. By the time the mother looked up from her phone, Ollie had already turned his attention to the napkin dispensers.

He filled them absentmindedly, crumpling the delicate folds in his large hands. He wasn't thinking about the boy, or the napkins. He was thinking about Nell.

What now?

His visit to the Women's Resource Center had been an epic fail. He couldn't go to the cops: Nell was a legal adult, and he was nothing more than tier-2 friend with a hunch. Besides, he'd seen enough police procedurals to know that if—God forbid—something actually had happened to her, they'd probably consider *him* a suspect, just for getting involved. And he could only imagine Nell's reaction, upon coming home safe and sound, to learn that he had stuck his nose far enough into her business to file some kind of report.

Maybe the trouble was all in his imagination. After all, what did he have to say otherwise? Gut instinct? As anyone could see, his gut was too big and too focused on filling itself to offer much in the way of wisdom.

Ollie sighed, making his way to the back room. When he emerged with a new carton of napkins, he stopped short, confused.

A folded piece of white paper sat propped up on a napkin dispenser on one of the empty tables. Two words had been scrawled across the front in black ink: *Ollie Delgato.*

Ollie's brow furrowed. That hadn't been there just a minute before—he was sure of it. He dropped the box onto a chair and reached forward to pick up the note. He handled it cautiously, like it might prick his finger.

His gaze swiveled to inspect the café crowd again. The same singles, old men, and kids were sitting right where they had been moments before, still absorbed in conversations and hot drinks. The boy crunched the same cookie with purposeful bites, his interest in the giant waiter forgotten.

Ollie looked down at his name. Then he unfolded the paper to read the message inside: *Still looking for your friend? I know where she is, and how you can help her. Meet me at the west stairs of Quincy Market at six.*

His heart began to thud.

Six o'clock...tonight?

I know where she is, and how you can help her.

In that moment, Ollie knew two things for sure. One, he was going to have a toasted blueberry bagel with extra cream cheese (10 credits) for dinner. And two, he was going to have to eat it on the way.

*T*hree

Ollie's mother had loved Quincy Market: the people, the food, and most of all, the history. According to her many spiels on the subject, the long, narrow building had been constructed in the early 1800s as a sort of grocery store for nineteenth-century families. Back then, shoppers bought raw ingredients—fish, produce, bread, cheese, meat—from butchers and vendors on either side of the walkway. In modern times, the food stalls had transformed into tiny takeout restaurants, each offering quick-serve meals, snacks, and desserts of every conceivable variety.

Ollie entered at the east end and found himself immediately assaulted by the familiar cacophony of sounds and smells. The heat from dozens of grills and stoves was, initially, a welcome change from the chill outside, though it soon became stifling. He unzipped his coat and inhaled, savoring the spice and smoke in the air as he wound his way through the hungry crowds.

Enchiladas. Fried rice. Lamb kebabs. If the North End was Italy, then Quincy Market was the whole damn world. Visitors could sample Chana masala, corn dogs, beef teriyaki, and Spanakopita, then top it all off with saucer-sized cookies and gourmet cupcakes. And of course, there was the seafood: Lobster rolls and clam chowder were the stars of the show, but locals knew to also seek out supporting players like spicy tuna, oysters, and crabmeat salad on the ever-rotating menus.

If this had been a normal sort of visit, Ollie would have ordered a fried-clam roll and lingered under the high rotunda of the central seating area. Maybe listened for a while to the violinist playing for change in the corner. Instead, he hurried through the entire longer-than-a-football-field span of the market and pushed open the glass doors on the other end. The west end, as instructed.

Ollie checked the time; he was ten minutes early. Then he rezipped his coat, shivered, and settled nervously on the top step. Waiting.

The stairs faced the historic Faneuil Hall building and City Hall Plaza across the street. Ollie's eyes scanned his surroundings, searching for anything out of the ordinary. To his right, a pushcart sold hoodies emblazoned with the names of all the local colleges and universities. Another cart offered "Wicked Pissah" t-shirts, Boston Baked Beans candy, and various other tchotchkes. And directly in front of him, at the bottom of the granite staircase, an acrobatic street performer was trying to entice passersby from the top of an oversized unicycle.

Two huddled women were pointing—at him? No, just at the building. A lone man in a business suit approached the stairs, started climbing...and then passed through the market doors and disappeared. Ollie squirmed nervously. Was he in the right place? A group of twenty-something workers in paint-splattered clothes passed close to his legs, but didn't stop. A tall woman nearby seemed to be staring at her phone. Or was she? The acrobat finished a complex juggling routine and bowed to the gathered crowd.

Smattering of applause. Ones and fives tossed into a black hat on the pavement.

Ollie looked at his phone: five past six. Should he stand up? Walk around, maybe?

"You like show?"

Startled, Ollie glanced up to see the acrobat standing on the stairs. "Hmm?"

"Show? You like?" the man repeated, a wide smile on his sweating face. He seemed bigger, up close. His ink-black hair was just long and wavy enough to seem unruly. On his feet, he wore what looked like a pair of gray ballet slippers.

"It was...good." Ollie was confused, then realized that the man was holding his black felt hat in his hand. He wanted a tip. "Oh, sorry. Yeah. Here you go." Ollie reached into his front pocket, fished around, and dropped a dollar into the hat. He had to get rid of this guy, fast.

"I thank you," the Lycra-suited man said in a thick Slavic accent.

"Sure," said Ollie, bewildered. In all his years of coming here, he had never been directly approached by a street performer.

"My name is Laszlo," said the acrobat. "Laszlo Kravchenko."

28

And I care, why? Ollie thought. His agitation rose. This idiot was going to screw up everything.

"You are wondering, Kravchenko, like the famous Kravchenko Brothers of Ukraine?" the man asked. Then he flashed a proud, sheepish smile. "Yes, is true. They are my uncles."

The man's defined musculature was accentuated by the tight, metallic blue suit, which left nothing, unfortunately, to Ollie's imagination. Who was this jackass? "Listen, dude, I—"

"And you are Ollie Delgato," the man interrupted pleasantly. "Of the North End Delgatos. You are waiting for me, no?"

Ollie went still.

"You received my note?"

The cement stairs felt unsteady, suddenly. He nodded but didn't speak.

"You are looking for your friend. Antonella-Nell?"

"It's..." Ollie cleared his throat. "It's just...Nell. Like, a nickname. Who are you?"

"I told you. I am Las—"

"No, I mean, who *are* you? What is this? How do you know Nell?"

"I don't," the man shrugged. His face was hard and angled, punctuated by a narrow nose and somewhat beady eyes. "Not exactly. I only meet her one time."

Ollie's eye narrowed. Granted, he didn't know everything about Nell's life. But if she had been hanging out with a blue-suited, unicycle riding street performer, he felt pretty certain that it would have come up in conversation. "Where did you meet her?" he asked.

"At WRC. I work there."

"Uh huh." This guy was full of shit. What possible job could this burly man's man have at a Women's Resource Center?

"I saw you there, too. Yesterday? When you leave, I follow you."

"Well, that's..." Ollie sputtered. "Why?"

Laszlo studied him for a moment. "The Center. Is not what name says, if you understand. Is something else." When Ollie didn't respond, he continued. "You have heard of, how do you say, house violence? In house? When man hits wife?" He pantomimed a punch.

"Domestic violence?" Ollie supplied.

"Yes, yes. This. When this happens, there are places to go. For help. Centers." Laszlo emphasized the last word.

"That's what the WRC is?"

"Yes. But is secret. So you cannot tell." He lowered his voice and pressed a finger to his lips. "They need to get away from husband. Or

29

not always husband. Sometimes is father, or brother. Sometimes is boyfriend. Sometimes even other woman. Old and young. All kinds. You understand?"

Ollie nodded. Yes, he understood, too well. *Goddammit.* He had been right all along. About Nell's situation, about The Guy. Why had he not spoken up?

Maybe because it never worked. Not for him, anyway. All those years of bloody lips and ripped clothing on the playground...liquid soap from the dispenser in the boys' room, forced down his throat. He had tried telling his teachers. And what had it ever gotten him? Nothing. No, worse than nothing—it had gotten him a nastier beating the next day, after the kids learned he had ratted them out.

He had tried protecting his mother, too. He really had. Once, he had thrown his body between her face and his fists. He thought he could make it stop, but all he did was make Matteo Delgato even more enraged. And Francie had paid the price.

Ollie's mouth had gone as dry as toast. His tongue felt too thick, too heavy. Finally, he managed to ask, "How do you know all this?"

"Like I say, I work there," Laszlo said with a shrug. "Sometimes bad men come looking. They are not happy. So WRC hires me to be there. For protection."

"And that happens...a lot?"

"Enough, sure. They want to be big, powerful man again. Knock around little girls. And instead they find me." He laughed with unselfconscious delight. "Not good for them."

Suddenly, it all became clear to Ollie: That's why those women at the center wouldn't even let him through the door. Why they had been so wary and suspicious. They thought he was one of *those* men. They actually thought that he might be the one who had been hurting Nell.

"I could go back." Ollie said, floundering. "I could explain."

Laszlo shook his head. His arms and shoulders looked like blue peapods, bulging out at intervals. "They will not believe you."

"But you will? Why?"

"Because you are not that man."

"What?"

"You are not *her* man. I have seen that man, with her, and you are not him." Laszlo spread his arms. "I have been doing this long time, my friend. I see all kinds of bad things. Bad people. I see what they do not want me to see. But you..." he paused and chuckled. "You make it easier than most."

"What's that supposed to mean?" Ollie asked, feeling strangely insulted.

"It is good thing, Ollie Delgato. You show your insides on your outsides. You cannot help it. You are clear, like vodka. And I see right away, when I see you yesterday, that you are afraid for your friend. And if I am honest with you, I am feeling worried for her, too."

"Why?"

Laszlo gave him a long look, then said, "When the women come, they must choose. It is never easy, no? Sometimes, they want to go somewhere else. Secret places, to be safe. But to do this, you understand, they must stay gone. They must leave everything behind." He shook his head. "Never easy. But for some, it is only choice. I take them where they need to go, or I take them to someone else, who takes them to next person, and so on. Like, what do you call it...Under the Ground Railroad?" He paused. "This is one choice. But there are others."

"And Nell...she had to go away?"

Laszlo was watching his face. He seemed to be considering something. Then he asked, "How well do you know your friend?"

Ollie bristled at the question. "Well enough."

The acrobat nodded. "As I say, there are other choices. Your Nell did not want to leave. So she chose something else. Something more...temporary. I cannot explain more. But when they make this other choice, I take care of that, too. So, I bring her, and I tell her what to do. And then she was supposed to come back."

"What do you mean, *supposed* to?"

"I did not realize she had not come back," Laszlo continued. "Not until you came, looking for her. And then I did counting of days, and I realized..." He stopped, running a finger along a seam in his shiny suit.

"What?" Ollie said, leaning forward. "Realized what?"

"I realized that she should have been back already. There is time limit, you see. Time must be respected."

"Or what?"

"They must return in time, or they cannot return. At all."

"So, go get her!" Ollie almost shouted. He didn't understand most of what this strange man was saying, but he understood enough to know that something was wrong. Something bad.

"I cannot," the acrobat answered, shaking his head. "It is not allowed. I bring them, I tell them when to return. And then I hope that they do." He gave a small shrug. "It is up to them what happens next."

"What are you talking about? What the hell kind of a place is this?"

31

Laszlo sighed. "It is kind of place that...that I cannot explain. Some things you must see for yourself, yes? I can only say there is more to your world than you know, Ollie Delgato. More, even, than you could imagine."

"So what *can* you tell me?" Ollie asked, his eye beginning to twitch. "Is it too late?"

"No, I do not think so. There is still some time. But she might need help. Getting back, I mean."

"Then I'll go help her." The words came out of Ollie's mouth before he could stop them.

"You say that, of course. But I must tell you that it is not something easy to do," Laszlo said. "Where she is...it is not a kind of place that you've ever been before."

"I don't care," he told the acrobat. True, he hadn't traveled much, but how hard could it be? Hop on a plane or a bus or whatever. Find a hotel. He would make it work. His knee began to bounce—up and down, up and down, up and down—countering his bravado. Ollie lowered his voice and asked, "What do I need? Do I need a gun or something?" He had no idea how to use a gun or where to buy one, but it somehow seemed like a logical question.

Laszlo chuckled. "No. No guns in this place. You need only your brains, to be clever and smart. But you have those things, no?"

Ollie's lips curled with worry. "Not really," he admitted. His scholarship was for community college, not Harvard.

Laszlo waved a hand. "Yes, you do. I can see it in you. You have smarts behind eyes." He tapped his own lid for emphasis. "If you want to do this, I can tell you where she is, and I can tell you how to get there. But the rest you do alone."

"That's fine," Ollie nodded, screwing up his courage. *Fake it 'till you make it,* his mother had always said.

"And time limit is for you, as well," Laszlo said. "You must come back in time. Less than three weeks. You understand? If you have not found her by then, you must return anyway. Yes?"

Three weeks? Ollie was taken aback. "So long, you think?"

"Perhaps," the acrobat said, holding up his palms. "Perhaps much less. Hard to say, exactly. How long it will take."

"Oh." Ollie's mind began to spin. Now that he stopped to think about it, he'd tried the *fake it 'till you make it* routine lots of times and never seemed to advance beyond the first step. He chewed his bottom lip. Maybe this wasn't such a good idea. Maybe he should—

"All right, then." Laszlo interrupted his thought, slapping a hand against his metallic thigh. "I am cold. Freezing in this suit. Meet me tonight, at Visitor Center on Common. You know where this is?"

Ollie nodded.

"Good. They close at nine, and we must be there just before. Say, eight-thirty. You can do that?"

"I—" Ollie was getting confused. "Yes, I can be there. But why?"

Laszlo shot him an impatient look. "You must leave tonight."

"Tonight?"

"Yes! Tonight! What do you think? I just tell you, the time is ticking," he said, snapping his fingers three times. "Ticking! You want to help your friend, or not?"

"Of course I do. But *tonight?*" It was happening too fast. Ollie was having trouble breathing.

Laszlo got to his feet. "I understand," he said, brushing off his Lycra. "Is not easy decision. Now you know how those women feel, yes? Big decision, and not much time to decide." He flashed an apologetic smile. "You think about it. I will be there tonight. If you decide to come, I will see you there, and I will help you find your friend."

"And if I don't?"

"If you don't, you don't."

"But what will happen to Nell?"

The man regarded him thoughtfully, like a scientist studying a particularly odd specimen. "Sometimes, we can only do what we can do. This is sad but truth." He held out his hand again. "Whatever you decide, it was good to meet you, Ollie Delgato of the North End Delgatos."

They shook.

Laszlo's grip threatened to crush several bones in Ollie's hand. In a haze, he watched the acrobat walk down the steps, gather up his gear and a duffle bag, and disappear down the cobblestone street. The meeting was over, and yet, somehow, he was even more confused than before it had begun.

Four

Ollie made his way back home in a daze, sidestepping pedestrians on the Greenway. This was insane. He couldn't do this. He couldn't even think about doing this.

He couldn't just pack up and leave based on the word of some acrobat panhandler in Faneuil Hall. He had no idea who this Laszlo Kravchenko was, or even if that was his real name. He had no reason to trust the man. Ollie didn't even know where he was supposed to be going, or how he was going to get there. Or what he was supposed to do once he arrived.

He stopped at the carousel, letting his vision blur as the animals spun past. Kids squealed from the backs of lobsters, squirrels, turtles, and other whimsical creatures, most bobbing up and down in a smooth, mesmerizing rhythm as they revolved. The combination of music, motion, and mirrors made him sway unsteadily.

The whole idea was ludicrous. Of course, it was.

And yet.

Something else was pulling him, as well: Another, less rational thought, competing for his attention. It waved its little hands from the dark, lumpy recesses of his mind, jumping up and down with frantic enthusiasm.

What if this was it? His frozen-river moment?

That's what his mother had called it, anyway. According to Francie Delgato, everyone has a frozen-river moment at least once in their lifetime. In Francie's scenario, the metaphorical "you" is walking along, minding your own business, when suddenly you see a child flailing in a

34

frigid, running river. The child is moving quickly past, speeding with the current. You have no rope or life jacket. You are completely unprepared for the situation.

What do you do?

After setting the scene, his mom used to tick the options off on her fingers. If you jump in, you might drown, too. If that happens, two people will be lost. You might jump in and try to save the child but fail. Or you might jump in and save the child, but find that he emerges with permanent brain damage.

In the best scenario, you jump in, save the child, and both of you crawl out onto the other shore, healthy and alive. A happy ending for everyone.

Lastly, you could do nothing. No one would blame you. The current is fast, the water is icy cold. The child is far from shore. And you are afraid. So, you just watch him float by and hope for the best. When it's all over, his fate was his fate: You didn't alter it in any way, for better or for worse. It was just as if you had never been there at all.

Francie would drill through the various options and then ask Ollie: What would you do? Usually this happened when they were sitting around a campfire in New Hampshire or trapped in the apartment during a winter storm. He would always respond, of course, by saying he would jump in. No hesitation. Save the child! His mom never smiled or agreed. Instead, she would say, "Know who you are, before it happens. There might not be one right answer. But there will be a right answer for you."

Once, Ollie had asked his mother what she would do her in her frozen-river moment.

"It's not what I would do, *Bambino*," she had answered. "It's what I did." Then she got a faraway look in her eye, glassy and regretful, and he was sorry he had asked.

Ollie chewed the inside of his cheek. If Laszlo was telling the truth—a big if—then Nell had been seeking a "fix" for her situation, and had planned to leave for only a short time. What could she possibly have been doing? And since she was supposed to be back home already, but wasn't, something must have gone wrong.

A few terrifying possibilities wormed their way into Ollie's consciousness: a sad-faced newscaster on TV, sharing grim news of a discovery in the woods. Trial coverage sprinkled with phrases like "history of abuse" and "restraining order." Nell's smiling face peering out from the front page of the *Boston Globe*. "The victim in happier times," the caption might say.

Ollie sighed. He had never liked his mother's frozen-river scenario. When you looked at the math, jumping into the water was, by far, the worst choice. It came with so many more probable negative outcomes: one death, two deaths, brain damage, failure, and ridicule, just to name a few. Standing on the sidelines was a much simpler calculation. Do nothing, and the child would either live or die. Fifty-fifty odds. And you would live, regardless. A gambler would know instinctively which one to choose.

Now, though, Ollie wasn't seeing an anonymous, floating child in the river. He was seeing Nell. Her arms, flailing. Her bruised face, crusted with ice. Bloated and pained. Her hand, reaching out for his.

The carousel was slowing. A seal glided by, then a gargantuan grasshopper, and, finally, a peregrine falcon. As it came to a stop, the falcon's gaze seemed to rest on Ollie, its wings spread in frozen preparation for a flight that would never come.

Ollie stared into the bird's shining, dark pupils, mesmerized. And as he watched, the sharp beak lifted. The head, impossibly, turned.

It must be you.

The words echoed inside Ollie's skull. Startled, he stumbled backwards. The falcon's exposed belly lifted and dropped with each breath. Its talons twitched. The gray-and-white feathers shook with an invisible rushing wind. And then, just as suddenly, its head twisted back to its original position, facing forward. Its body went still. The knowing eyes returned to their original blank state, staring across the Greenway at nothing.

Shaking, Ollie looked left and right. Who else had seen it? But the parents and kids seemed oblivious to the changes. And when he looked back at the carousel, the falcon's body was as hard and lifeless as ever.

I'm losing it, Ollie told himself.

He'd had plenty of bad ideas in his life, but this had to be one of the worst. The sheer number of possible disastrous outcomes were as plentiful as jellybeans in a jar: He might say the wrong thing. Do the wrong thing. Take a wrong turn. Make an ass of himself. Lose one of his only friends by interfering, uninvited, in her business.

He could also make a bad situation even more volatile by jumping into the middle of it. He already knew from experience what that looked like, and how it usually ended up. He could do something stupid, even criminal, and wind up losing his job—or worse, losing his scholarship and all of his fragile future plans. He could stumble, and falter, and fail in any number of creative ways. In other words, just be the usual Ollie.

There were a hundred reasons not to do this. And yet he knew, as sure as he suddenly knew the sound of the falcon's sharp, high cry in his head, that he was going to do it anyway.

His mother had flailed in that river once. More than once. And he had been too young, too small, and too scared to do anything about it. But he wasn't small anymore. Oddly enough, he wasn't even that scared. His vision felt uncommonly sharp. His mind, clear.

This was his chance—maybe his only chance. And goddammit, he was going to take it.

He would do for Nell what he was never able to do for his mom. He was going to save her.

The voice came again, quieter this time: *Yessss. It must be you.*

A new crop of children hoisted themselves onto the animals' backs. No one chose the falcon. Alone, it soared into the cold wind as the next ride began. Ollie stayed rooted to the pavement as the music played, the creatures rose and fell, and the carousel spun around and around in an endless, extraordinary loop.

The sun was halfway through setting when Ollie appeared, backpack on his shoulder, at the Boston Common Visitor Center. The building looked like a life-sized gingerbread cottage, complete with cross-hatched windows, green moldings, cornices, and a multicolored roof. He blew a few hot breaths into his hands, looking up and down busy Tremont Street and then turning to peer at the bare trees of the Common behind him. Laszlo was nowhere in sight.

In the end, it had almost been too easy. Mr. Bonfiglio had been unsurprisingly accommodating about the last-minute request for time off. Next, Ollie had texted Lorraine to let her know he'd miss a few meetings. Then he stuffed a backpack with random clothing items, a toothbrush, and granola bars and made his way to the Common.

Now he was standing alone outside the small Visitor Center cottage, patting his pockets. Cash. Credit card. Cell phone. He didn't have a passport, so he hoped he wouldn't need one. He had never traveled out of the country. Hell, he had never traveled much farther than New England.

"You come!" said a booming voice behind him. Ollie turned to see Laszlo Kravchenko, arms outstretched. He had ditched the Lycra bodysuit for a pair of tight jeans and a black parka. His long hair seemed slightly frozen, as though he had left the house while it was still wet from a shower.

Ollie smiled warily. What was with the opened arms? Were they supposed to hug, like old pals? After a moment's hesitation, he moved forward to embrace the big man, resting his hands lightly on Laszlo's shoulders and then backing away.

"You come, you come!" Laszlo said again, clearly delighted. "I am so glad. You will help your friend."

"I have more questions."

"Yes." Laszlo clapped his gloved hands together. "Of course. I understand. But here we do first things, okay? They will be closing soon." He jutted a thumb toward the small building.

"The Visitor Center?" Ollie asked, confused.

"Yes. We go in there."

"Why?" His brow furrowed. That didn't make any sense at all. He thought they were *leaving* Boston.

"It is start. The first thing."

"But—"

"We have only few minutes. We must go in now. Then your questions. I promise."

Ollie sighed. "Fine."

"Good," Laszlo said. "So, first things. We go inside. You say nothing. Just do shopping, yes? Maybe buy something. I will do talking. Okay? You are understanding?"

Ollie nodded again. "Go in, buy something. Say nothing."

"Yes. Good." The large man seemed satisfied. "Okay. Now we go."

They walked around to the entrance, which faced the busy street. Laszlo pulled on the glass doors and walked confidently inside. Ollie trailed behind, toting his backpack.

Though he had spent all his life in the city, he had never stepped inside this building. He'd never had a reason to. He wasn't surprised to find that it was set up like a touristy gift shop. When they walked in, he saw two female employees and a handful of visitors.

"Can I help you?" asked the clerk, a fifty-something woman wearing a quarter-zip green fleece and an insincere smile.

"Yes, hello!" Laszlo said. "How are you? Beautiful day."

Ollie plucked a keychain off the rack and examined it. It was shaped like a Boston terrier and emblazoned with the words, "Bahk, bahk, bahk."

"I'm looking for Johannes Miller guidebook," Laszlo continued. "*Historian's Guide to Freedom Trail*. First edition."

Ollie returned the dog keychain to its hook and moved on to a small display of postcards. As he walked, he glanced up at the counter to see both employees looking from Laszlo, to him, and then back again to Laszlo. Their expressions were unreadable. He reached out to choose a postcard, pretending to be fascinated by a generic image of the city skyline.

Laszlo added, casually, "Elizabeth recommended I get it here."

As soon as he said it, Ollie felt a change in the room. He didn't even have to turn around to know that both women were now staring at him. He could feel their suspicion boring a hole through the back of his neck. Wishing he had a sip of water, he swallowed dryly and reached out to run his finger across the engraved glass of a Sam Adams beer mug.

"We might have one copy."

Ollie moved his eyes without turning his head. He watched her reach under the counter and pull out a thin, paperback guidebook.

"Oh, that is wonderful, thank you!" Laszlo said. "Exactly what I wanted."

He reached out, but the woman seemed hesitant to hand it to him. They stood like that, locked in a silent power struggle, for what seemed like several minutes. Finally, she stretched her arm far enough to place it in his hand.

Ollie had stopped at a display of blinking-light key chains, arranged alphabetically. He spun the rack. M, N, O...until he found his name. The keychain flashed on and off, on and off. *Oliver. Oliver. Oliver.* He grabbed it off the hook

"That'll be seven ninety-nine," the cashier said.

"Of course. My friend, here—" Laszlo turned to beckon Ollie. "My friend here has the money."

Ollie looked up, surprised. "Oh, right," he said. He carried the keychain to the counter. "I'll take this, too."

The woman stared down at the blinking name, then at Ollie's face. She looked as if she were memorizing his features. Then she took his money and asked, "Would you like a bag?"

"I'm good, thanks," Ollie answered, dropping the keychain into the front pocket of his jeans.

Laszlo flashed a high-wattage smile. "Thank you for book," he said. "I will start reading tonight, right away."

At this strange comment, the younger woman stepped forward and gave Laszlo a nod.

"Thirty-two, nineteen, twelve," she said softly.

Laszlo nodded back, then started moving toward the door. "Thank you, ladies!" he said. "You have wonderful night!"

But the clerk had already turned her attention toward another customer. Ollie stood there, rooted in confusion, until Laszlo led him out the front door into the cold.

"What the hell was all that about?" Ollie asked.

Laszlo waved a hand in the direction of the Visitor Center, as though dismissing everything that had just happened inside. "That was nothing," he said. "Just the way things are done."

"What things?"

"Things, things. You know. Nothing for you to worry about. We have now what we need," he said, lifting the meager paperback and giving it a wiggle in the air.

"A book?"

"Not just a book," Laszlo said. "A key." He looked around, spotted a bench nearby, and said, "Here. Come, come. Sit."

Ollie followed him to the bench. As he sat down, the cold seeped through his jeans and chilled his skin. He shoved his hands into his coat pockets and stared down at the book's cover: *Historian's Guide to the Freedom Trail*, by Johannes Miller.

Ollie didn't remember the women handing Laszlo a key. Maybe they had done it when he wasn't looking. Or maybe they had hidden it inside the book? He looked at the guide, which was flimsy and slight. Hardly big enough to hide anything in, even a key.

"Do you remember numbers she gave us?"

Ollie looked up at him in a panic. "No. Was I supposed to?"

Laszlo laughed. "No worries, my friend. I remember them. But you will need to start paying better attention. From here..." he paused. "From here, you will need to rely on yourself. Yes?"

"Yes," Ollie said, his heart starting to pound.

"The first number was thirty-two," Laszlo said, flipping the book's pages. About a third of the way in, he stopped and pointed at a page number.

"Page thirty-two," Ollie said.

"Yes. And the second number was..." Laszlo began to count the lines of text running down the page, first in his head, then out loud. "Seventeen, eighteen, and...there. Nineteen."

"So, the first number is the page, the second number is the line, and the third number is..." Ollie stared at the black-and-white text. "The word in the line?"

"That is right," Laszlo said, sounding pleased. "See? You are fast study. Smart behind the eyes. I knew it." He grinned. Then he slid his finger along the line, counting the words out loud.

When he landed on the twelfth word, he tapped his finger on it and looked up.

"Tombs," said Ollie.

"Tombs," Laszlo repeated. "That is it."

"I don't understand."

Laszlo reached for his arm and pulled him up from the bench. "The word is your key. Is all you need to get inside. And that," he said, pointing at the row of red bricks that started just outside the entrance of the Visitor Center, "is your door."

Ollie looked down at the bricks blankly. "That's the Freedom Trail."

"Yes. And no," Laszlo answered.

Ollie blinked. It was starting to dawn on him: This guy was bonkers. Genuinely ready for a rubber room. "It's not the Freedom Trail?"

"Yes, of course, but is also something else. Something...older. Much older. And bigger."

"Ah," Ollie said. He took a tiny step backward, then asked, "So, we're not going to go to the airport?"

Laszlo looked up at him, puzzled. "Airport? No. Who said anything about airport?"

"Or a bus?"

"No bus," Laszlo answered, shaking his head. "You need to listen to me. Are you listening? This is very important things. Do you want to find your friend, or not?"

"Yes," Ollie said, trying to keep his voice steady. What was he doing? What had he been thinking?

"Trail is marked with medallions, you see here?" Laszlo was still talking in a normal and reasonable tone, as though what he was saying made any sense at all. "Each one marks historical spot. Church, statue, whatever. And people stop, they take the pictures..." He paused, pantomiming a person snapping a photo. "One of these spots, these medallions, is the one you are looking for. But I am afraid, in this case, I cannot tell you which one." At this, he looked genuinely troubled.

"Why not?"

"It changes every day, you see. Location. Normally, they would tell me. People at center. But this one is a little..." He dragged out the last word with exaggerated flair: *leeeetle*. "It is off books, you could call it. Right? Because they do not know I help you. They do not know I bring

41

you here, to find her. And they can never find out. No one can. You understand what I mean? Big trouble for me. Big trouble."

"Right," Ollie said.

"So you must try key at every door. It will work at one. But it might take a while."

Ollie rubbed his jaw.

"So, what I am saying is, you must get going," Laszlo continued, pointing at the line of bricks.

"What, right now?"

"Yes. No time like now, am I right?" Laszlo said with a shrug. "Is getting dark. Best to do it before then. Here," he added, pressing a folded wad of colored paper into Ollie's palm.

"What's this?"

"Money."

Ollie opened his hand and looked at the paper. It was cut into squares and covered in unrecognizable symbols. Most of the pieces were either yellow or red.

"Look, Laszlo, I..." He didn't know how to finish his sentence.

Behind them, the employees of the Visitor Center were emerging through the large front doors. "Shit. I must go," Laszlo said, glancing at the women over his shoulder.

"Wait, what?" Ollie said, leaning closer and lowering his voice. "Where are you going?"

"You will be fine," the big man said. "You will find your friend, and you will bring her back home, and all will be good. And then you will come find me, and we will have party. Big party, to celebrate. Yes? You see it?"

Ollie didn't answer.

One of the women was jingling a noisy loop of keys, looking for the right one. When she found it, she inserted it into the lock and closed up the Visitor Center for the night.

"You take that," Laszlo whispered, closing his hands around the wadded-up paper in Ollie's palm. "When you get to docks, you give it to driver. All of it. And you tell him to take you to Herrick's End. You will remember that? Herrick's End. You pay him with that money. Is more than enough. Even if he..." he paused. "If he says no, you just show him how much money. And then he will say yes."

"Herrick's End," Ollie repeated.

"Yes. That's where your Nell will be. I am sure of it." Laszlo looked over his shoulder. "Ollie, this place..." his voice faltered. "As I say, is not an ordinary kind of place. You must trust this—" he tapped on Ollie's forehead. "And this—" he tapped on Ollie's chest. "Only those. Forget your eyes. Your eyes do not know as much as those. Yes? All right?"

Ollie gave a bewildered shrug. His eyes, at the moment, were seeing a man who might very well have just escaped from an asylum. What on God's green earth was this lunatic talking about?

The wiry man turned again, watching the two women hoist their bags and say their goodbyes. "I must go," he said. "You start the walking, and you try key at every place. Each one. Just say word. You remember word?"

"I...yes."

"Just say word. You will know right place when you find it. Then you enter key, and that is it. That is all you need to do. Yes? You will remember?"

"Yes. I mean, no. No! Wait. Just wait a second. Listen, this is crazy. I don't... I can't—"

"You can," Laszlo insisted. "You can do this, Ollie Delgato of the North End Delgatos. You can make your mother proud."

At the mention of his mother, an icy jolt ran through Ollie's limbs.

Laszlo Kravchenko of the Famous Ukraine Kravchenkos gave a jaunty, two-fingered salute over his eyebrow. Then he took a few backward steps, ducked behind the gingerbread cottage, and disappeared into the dusk.

Five

For several minutes, Ollie didn't move. The crumpled, colored paper stayed in his hand; the backpack rested against his leg.

Directly in front of him, the bricks formed a right-angled path: Straight, then left. Their deep russet color sat in defiant contrast to the dull pavement all around. You couldn't miss them. And yet, somehow, everyone did.

Commuters hurried in a herd toward the Park Street T station, ignoring the brick trail, and the Visitors Center, and the three statues—Religion, Industry, Learning—mounted nearby. They also ignored the befuddled, toweringly large young man standing like a statue himself, staring at the sidewalk in confusion.

Laszlo's words echoed in his ears.

A key. A door. The docks. A driver.

In the street, traffic lurched forward as the light turned green. Crowds began to gather near the curb, waiting for a chance to cross. City life hummed along in its usual dance of ordered chaos.

Ollie pressed his lips together as two emotions—determination and trepidation—battled for dominance. Finally, he abandoned them both and forced his mind into something closer to emptiness. He remembered the rush of clarity he had felt at the carousel. The relief of making a decision. Of taking action—taking *heroic* action, no less. He felt the notion wash through his body, steeling his nerves and straightening his back. Only then did he begin to walk.

The bricks led the way: forward, left. In less than a minute, he spotted the first medallion at his feet. Laszlo had told him that he should "try the key" at each marker until he found the right one.

What did that even mean?

Ollie peered down at the circle of bronze embedded into the pavement. He had never bothered to look at the medallions closely before. This one had a leaf design around its rim. Three words—"The Freedom Trail"—curved along the top edge, echoed in a reverse curve by the word "Boston" below. A carved, arrow-shaped object, like the spinning rod on a weathervane, sat in the dead center.

It was fairly small; maybe about 20 inches in diameter. And quite a nice piece of art, now that he really stopped to look at it. Probably too nice to be trampled by boots all day on grimy city sidewalks.

He hesitated. What had Laszlo told him? "Say the word." Ollie was supposed to stop at each medallion, say the word, and he would know when he'd found the right one.

Just say the word.

Ollie looked left and right. Men, women, boys, and girls swarmed around him. Someone would hear him. He would look like a lunatic. But these were city people. They were used to lunatics. Surely one more would hardly be noticed.

"Tombs," he said. It was more of a whisper, spoken through tight lips. Too soft. Ollie cleared his throat and tried again, louder.

"Tombs."

Nothing happened. No one looked at him, and the clouds didn't part in the sky. A car and driver didn't magically appear. Ollie snorted. Of course, nothing had happened. What did he expect?

Feeling a bit lighter, he continued to follow the path. He passed a sausage cart, then the three-tiered Brewer Fountain adorned with mythological figures. The city would turn the water back on in the spring; for now, someone had draped a blue scarf around Neptune's neck. The brick trail took him in a straight line all the way up to the State House, where the gold dome was muted by a wintery gray sky.

He found the next medallion implanted in the ground near the State House gate. It looked much the same as the first, although he noticed that the carved arrow in the middle pointed in a different direction.

There were almost no pedestrians nearby, leaving Ollie feeling less bashful as the word escaped his lips: "Tombs." Again, nothing happened.

The trail was long, he knew. At least a couple of miles, extending all the way through the North End, across the bridge, and into Charlestown. Was he expected to walk the whole thing, muttering about mausoleums and looking like a loon? The idea was looking less appealing by the second. Squirrels skittered past his feet as he plodded along, following the bricks down the stairs and through the far edge of the Common. Benches sat empty along the path. Gloom crept in from all sides as nighttime began to fall.

The Park Street Church was the next stop, on the corner. He paused momentarily at the circle on the ground, said the word, and moved on.

Ollie encountered a larger crowd of people at the next marked site. Even in the off-season, the Granary Burying Ground attracted all sorts, from tourists and students to those with an interest in the occult. The tiny but famous cemetery housed the remains of Paul Revere, John Hancock, Samuel Adams, and even the victims of the Boston Massacre. Thin, dark gravestones sprung from the ground at odd angles, padded by a layer of unraked leaves. Most of the stones seemed to be in danger of toppling.

A medallion sat in the sidewalk at the entrance of the cemetery's spiny, wrought-iron gate. Ollie waited for a gathered group to take their pictures. Then he approached the bronze circle and stood above it, noticing that the weathervane arrow pointed directly at the gate. That's when he understood why the arrow looked different on each medallion: At every stop, it pointed in the direction of the historic site itself.

"Tombs," he said.

When nothing happened, again, he had to fight to prevent a burst of hysterical laughter from bubbling up in his throat. This whole escapade was truly ridiculous. The loneliness, clearly, was messing with his head. He needed to meet some people. Join a dating site, maybe. Yes, that's exactly what he would do. He would follow the Freedom Trail as far as Bonfiglio's, then head upstairs to his apartment and create a profile. Angle his picture just right to hide his double chin. Forget about playing the white knight. Rejoin reality.

Crossing the streets and dodging pedestrians, Ollie hurried along from one site to the next: King's Chapel; the Ben Franklin statue; the Old South Meeting House; the Old Corner Bookstore. At each stop, he found the medallion and said the word. And at each stop, of course, absolutely nothing happened.

By the time he got to the Old State House and Boston Massacre site, the novelty had worn thin. Ollie was getting annoyed. And hungry.

The medallion here was bathed in shadow, smack in the middle of a wide alley. Buildings towered all around.

Ollie stood in front of the circular bronze marker and peered down. It looked like all the others. The tip of the center engraving pointed at the entry door for the Old State House. The usual four words—"The Freedom Trail" and "Boston"—curved along its edges.

"Tombs," he said.

The blueberry bagel had not been enough for dinner. He was debating the possibilities for dinner number two—or better yet, dessert—when he saw it.

A shadow. A new shadow, on the bronze.

Feeling foolish, he bent closer to the ground. His eyes narrowed. It seemed as though... No, that couldn't be. Ollie squeezed his eyes shut, then opened them again. Yes. It was there. The center of the marker, the part shaped like a weathervane arrow, had somehow raised itself off the rest of the medallion, creating a three-dimensional, almost mechanical-looking sculpture. Like an oversized watch face with only one hand.

Ollie stood back up. Tentatively, he tapped the arrow with the tip of his sneaker. It moved. He kicked it a little harder, watching as it spun around in a circle.

Holy shit.

Did he break it? Was this something he could get into trouble for? These things were probably worth a lot of money. They were city treasures, for God's sake.

He took off his baseball hat and rubbed his forehead, trying to remember the acrobat's strange, rushed instructions. *Enter the key.* What key? Laszlo had called the word the key. Did that mean, enter the word? How was he supposed to do that?

Ollie glared down at the small circle, trying to look stern. "Tombs," he said again. Then, louder: "Tombs!"

A nearby woman gave him a quick, nervous glance as she passed, clutching her purse to her side.

Ollie flushed. Then he pressed his closed fist against his mouth.

A word. The medallion was ringed with words. *The Freedom Trail. Boston.* Letters.

He dropped to his knees on the granite paving stones and removed the glove from his right hand. The bronzed weathervane arrow felt heavy and cold against his fingers. Ollie spun it gently at first, then more forcefully, until the tip of the arrow lined up with the letter T in the word "Trail."

47

He turned the arrow again, and again, rotating from one letter to another.

T.

O.

M.

B.

And finally, the last letter, found in the word "Boston:"

S.

As soon as the arrow stopped, he heard a click. Not a gentle, soothing click; more like the snap of a gun being cocked. He held his breath and stared.

One side of the medallion had popped open. It was only an inch or so, but definitely a gap. Big enough to grab. He reached his hand into the cavity and tugged. Slowly, the circular marker opened upwards, like a ship's porthole window.

Still on his knees, Ollie peered down into the hole and saw...nothing. Darkness. He looked up, wanting instinctively to share his finding with someone nearby. *Hey, check this out! It opened!* But when he looked at the other people in the alleyway, he noticed something odd about them.

They weren't moving.

He squinted. No, they *were* moving. Just very, very slowly.

A man in track pants was mid-stride in his run, one leg bent and one straight. A woman behind him was halfway through zipping her coat. Two guys by the wall were stuck in a stalled conversation; one had his head bent back in an unfinished laugh. And a pigeon dangled languidly above them all like a toy hanging from a crib mobile.

Everywhere he looked, the speed was wrong.

Ollie jumped to his feet. Out in the street, he saw cars crawling like drunkards. Even the sounds around him were slowed, almost muted, as they traveled to his ears.

His eyes darted with alarm back to the new hole in the ground. *Nope. No way. No goddamn way.* He was out of there. Whatever this was, he wanted nothing to do with it. This was a bad dream. Or at the very least, a bad idea. He was done. Time to wake up.

Ollie took a slow step backward, keeping his eye on the hole. Right foot, left foot. Slow and steady.

He had taken four steps, but the hole wasn't getting any further away. Feeling the hysteria rise in his chest, he tried again. *One step, two, three, four, five.* His body was moving, he was sure of it. But the hole wasn't. He was still standing right on top of it.

Finally, frantically, he spun around and ran.

Ollie didn't see the wall until he smashed into it, face-first. Even after that, he didn't see it: The wall didn't exist. There was nothing there. And yet it surrounded him on all sides, clearer than glass, taller than he could reach. He was trapped. Like a crazed mime, Ollie smashed the hard, invisible surface, banging and yelling in a guttural frenzy. No one outside noticed. No one moved.

His panic-stricken thought about breathable air was suddenly replaced by a panic-stricken thought about the hole at his feet.

It was growing.

No, not just growing. With wide-eyed terror, he noticed that it was deepening *and* growing. The middle was dropping faster than the edges, forming a funnel. He scrambled backwards, his shoulders slamming against the clear wall. As he stared, helpless and stunned, the funnel grew with steady, relentless precision, inching closer and closer to his size 14 shoes. A black hole, opening up below him.

Finally, the slant was too steep, and the pull of gravity was too strong: He groped and reached and whimpered, but there was nothing to hold on to. Ollie's feet slipped out from under him, and he fell.

Six

Ollie landed with a thwack. On dirt, it felt like, or maybe gravel. In the process, one particularly pointed rock managed to wedge itself between his right ass-cheek and the top of his thigh—no small feat, considering the bulbous amount of flesh that encompassed each of those separate areas. But cram itself it did, causing a groan of pain to erupt from Ollie's lips.

Cautiously, he opened his eyes. Other than the ignominiously wedged rock, he didn't seem to be hurt. He was lying on firm, packed earth in what looked like a tunnel. The uniformly beige-brown walls were visible by the light of five flickering torches, all poking out of tiny holes in the ground nearby. A handwritten sign stood behind them, leaning against the stone wall: "Please take only one," it said.

As Ollie read the sign, the first question that jumped to his mind was, *Why would I take more than one?* The second question, perhaps too slow in coming, was, *Where the hell am I?*

Ollie yanked out the stone and tossed it onto the ground. With a grunt, he struggled to get to his feet. Then he stood there, motionless, awash in a dizzying mix of relief, confusion and butt pain.

His backpack was gone. How it had escaped the life-sucking funnel, he didn't know. But wherever it had ended up, it wasn't here with him. He patted his pockets. His wallet was gone, too. And his phone. And his baseball hat, and his fitness tracker. He had only traveled a few feet, only fallen for a few seconds. How had he gotten here? Where *was* here? And where was all his stuff?

Ollie began to tremble. Hesitantly, he walked toward the torches. He reached out, wrapped a hand around the closest stick, and pulled it from its hole. *Please take only one.*

The next decision—which way to walk—was easier. He had landed at the beginning of the tunnel, and there was only one way to go.

For the first time, Ollie looked up. He saw nothing but hard, solid rock. No hole, no funnel. No sewer grate, or subway, or city streets. Just...rock. He swallowed. He was willing to ignore the impossibility of arriving here, if only it didn't make him think of the more terrifying impossibility of trying to get out.

Just keep moving, he told himself. He recognized the tone of his inner voice: firm and indifferent. It was the same voice he heard in his head when he noticed the whispers and stares. When Nico Venti and Roy Toscano had followed him, shoved him, and cracked his skull against the pavement hard enough to leave a concussion. When he finally realized that his dad was never going to send a birthday card, ever. When his mom was diagnosed. When he spent the first Christmas Eve without her, sitting at a table for one in Chinatown, fat tears dripping into his pork fried rice.

Just keep moving.

Past the torches, he saw a row of what looked like...were those wheelbarrows? Yes, wheelbarrows, lined up against the wall. They were each a bit dinged and dented, but otherwise appeared to be fully functional. Coils of rope and dozens of rolls of duct tape sat in messy stacks nearby. Ollie eyed the scene warily. What the hell had he stumbled into? Some kind of ultra-gardening competition? A serial killer's underground lair?

Ollie walked past the odd assemblage and moved further down the tunnel. His big feet landed like flippers on the dirt. Each step made a drawn-out crunching sound that echoed in the otherwise silent passageway. *Cruuunch, cruuunch, cruuunch.*

How far would he have to go? The torch, at least, seemed up to the challenge. It was thick and sturdy, with a tennis ball-sized knob ablaze with angry energy. And it stunk. Soaked in kerosene, he guessed. The flames' shadows made the walls skitter and roll around him. But they didn't reveal any secrets much beyond the immediate ten feet or so ahead. After that, it was only darkness.

Cruuunch, cruuunch, cruuunch.

Ollie tried to keep his breathing steady. His stomach, he knew, would start to growl soon. He thought about the box of granola bars he'd stashed inside his pack. Three flavors: peanut butter, cinnamon, and chocolate chip. He'd brought them in case of emergency, and he had to assume that a near-death drop into a torch-lit, food-free tunnel had to qualify. Not that it mattered now. The backpack, and the granola bars, were apparently long gone.

Ollie guessed he had walked the distance of one or two city blocks when he saw, finally, a doorway ahead. Light from somewhere beyond poured out into the hall. He hurried forward and peered around the corner, not sure what he was expecting to see. Another dreary tunnel, perhaps. A glowing exit sign. Or maybe, God willing, a deli counter.

Instead, he saw a short walkway. It led to a platform, where a man was waiting.

Ollie gasped. A person! He rushed forward, intent on running, when he realized: He was on a bridge. A narrow, stone bridge, open on the left side to...nothing at all. Vast, unchanging walls stretched high above his head and down into a seemingly endless expanse. The silence was total, as though even the echoes had nowhere to land. He was standing on the rim of an underground Grand Canyon. One wrong step, one wrong inch, and he would topple into the darkness. Fall for hours.

Ollie let out a long, tremulous breath and forced himself to concentrate on his destination.

The man. The platform. *Just keep moving.*

Legs shaking, he stepped gingerly. The bridge ended at a metal-grate platform, which supported a small, rectangular structure with a door and a window. It reminded Ollie of a toll-taker's booth on the highway. The door had been left open, revealing the seated figure of a thin man in a baggy, cobalt-blue jumpsuit. He was staring down at a clipboard in his lap, chewing the end of a pen. If he had noticed Ollie's appearance on the bridge, he didn't show it.

"Hi!" Ollie called out. His voice disappeared into the yawning space around him.

The man didn't reply.

"Hi!" Ollie said again, louder. "Hello?" The attendant couldn't be more than ten feet away; surely, he had heard him. "Hi, there! I'm, uh, I was hoping you could help me."

The man in the blue jumpsuit took one last chomp on the tip of the pen before removing it from his mouth. "How many?" he asked, sounding bored. He still hadn't looked up.

Ollie took two more steps, then three, on the grated platform. It was the only thing standing between him and unmistakable doom. *Don't look down,* he told himself. *Jesus, don't look down.* His legs were jittery, again. "How many...what?"

52

Two blue eyes finally lifted from the clipboard, looking at Ollie with impatience. "How many for transport?"

"Transport to where?"

The man wore a headlamp, like a miner. He gave a long, slow blink, then tapped his pen against the clipboard, three times. *Tap, tap, tap.* When he spoke again, he left an excruciatingly pregnant pause between each word: "How. Many. For. Transport?"

Ollie lifted a hand to shield his eyes from the headlamp's glare. He had hoped to ask the man about his missing backpack, and the closest exit, and maybe about the location of the nearest diner. But he was getting the distinct feeling that this might not be the right time, or the right fellow, for his questions. Instead, he looked over his shoulder, as though there might suddenly be more members in his party. "I, uh... It's just me."

"How many in number?"

Ollie opened his mouth, then closed it again. Finally, he said, "One."

It was, apparently, the magic word. As soon as Ollie uttered it, the man's demeanor changed. He seemed lighter, and happier, and filled with sudden purpose. "One," he repeated, checking a box on his clipboard with a flourish. Then he rose from his chair, lithe and strong, and began pressing buttons on a switchboard in front of him. "Leave your wheelbarrow over there. You'll get another when you arrive."

Ollie looked to his right, where another row of wheelbarrows sat along the wall in a tidy line. He considered pointing out his lack of a wheelbarrow, and therefore his lack of a need to leave one, then decided against it. "Listen," he said instead. "I was hoping you could tell me—"

The man held up a hand, silencing him.

Ollie pursed his lips in frustration. He stepped from one foot to the other, watching the operator concentrate on his knobs and switches. He heard clicks, clacks, and snaps, then another noise: the wheeze of a large gear above the booth as it began to turn, propelling a series of heavy cables into motion.

With that, something began to appear out of the gloom, attached to the overhead cables. Hanging. He squinted, watching as the shape got closer. His chin jutted back in surprise. It was a chairlift seat.

When the seat reached the platform, the man hit another series of buttons. The gear, the cables, and the seat all came to a sudden stop. The operator brushed the front of his jumpsuit, as if readying himself. Then he flipped up the safety bar with businesslike precision and stood there, looking proud.

"Transport for one," he said.

"For...?" Ollie looked at the hanging chair and then back at the man. "I'm not getting in that thing."

The attendant's eyes narrowed. "Transport for *one*," he repeated, putting an almost dangerous emphasis on the last word.

"No." Ollie shook his head vehemently. "Uh uh." He had never even been on a regular chairlift, the kind that went *up*, onto sunny, scenic mountaintops. There was no way he was strapping himself into one that went down, into...what? A prehistoric pit? The caverns of Hell? His feet stayed rooted on the bridge.

"It's fine," the man said with a sigh. He yanked on the chair, pulling down the cable as if to demonstrate its strength. "I ride them all the time. You'll be fine."

The attendant misunderstood. Ollie wasn't scared of the chair. He was scared of where it was going.

"Wh...what's down there?"

"Down there is not here," said the man in the blue jumpsuit.

Ollie took a step back. "No. Thanks. I'm going back." He jerked his thumb over his shoulder.

"Back where?" the operator said, sounding amused. Ollie turned to see that the doorway he had entered through was gone. Vanished into smooth, stone wall. All that remained was the bridge, the platform, and the chairlift. He was on a one-way trip.

Ollie swallowed. His fingers had gone cold and tingly, like all the blood had rushed elsewhere and left his digits to fend for themselves. "Fine," he muttered, as though the word gave him some kind of power. As though he had a choice, and was making it. Reluctantly, he took a few more steps on the metal grate, gasping a little as the platform swayed under his feet. Then he skittered over to the chair, spun around, and slid his large body onto the seat. It swung precipitously.

"What's the weight limit?" he asked. He didn't even try to control the alarm in his voice.

"You're fine," the man said, lowering the safety bar into place.

"But I'm heavy." He looked up at the single connection between the chair and the cable, trying to gauge its strength. "Really heavy." He could have provided his weight if asked, down to a fraction of a pound. He was weighed twice a week at every Lighter Tomorrows meeting. But the man didn't ask.

"Yep. You'll be fine. Usually, we have two on there. Sometimes three."

"Oh." That should have made him feel better. It didn't.

The man stepped back into his booth and grabbed a small black box. He brought it up to his face, pressed a button, and said, "One for transport!" in a loud bark.

Ollie heard a crackle, followed by a muffled reply: "Roger. Cleared for approach."

More clicks and clacks. The sound of metal scraping. And then, suddenly, he was thrust forward. The chair was in motion. With mounting hysteria, Ollie craned his neck to look behind him. The man in the blue jumpsuit was growing smaller. He was hoping for a reassuring wave, or maybe, God forbid, a smile. But all he got was a grim, satisfied stare.

Ollie spun back around. He clutched the safety bar with one hand and the torch in the other, overcome by a sudden torrent of terrified musings.

My hands are shaking so bad I'm going to drop this torch.

If I drop this torch, I won't be able to see. Not that there was much to see, besides a seemingly endless expanse of brownish, craggy wall and, he imagined, the black tar pits of Hades below. Still, as bad as this was, he knew that total darkness would be much, much worse.

If I drop this torch, I will light myself on fire and die screaming.

If I light myself on fire and die screaming, Mr. Chairlift Operator will not attempt to save me. That was for sure.

Why is this thing moving so fast?

Why am I doing this?

Where the hell am I going?

I've changed my mind. I've changed my mind. I've changed my mind.

The chair seemed to pick up speed as it traveled, whizzing past the jagged walls with frightening recklessness. Every few minutes, it would reach some kind of mounted post, where it would make a clunking sound, slow down, and then speed away again. It swung wildly each time it rounded a corner, causing a petrified whimper to escape from Ollie's otherwise tightened lips. He was alone, plunging deeper and deeper into the gaping darkness.

His heart was hammering louder than the wind that whipped past his ears. He slammed his eyes shut. When would this end? What was he thinking? He should never have followed that stupid Freedom Trail. He should never have listened to that crazy acrobat. He should never have asked about Nell.

Nell.

Was she really here? Was that even possible?

55

He heard his mother's voice: *Be brave, Bambino.*

I'm trying, Mama, he thought. *It's not going so well.*

Finally, the chairlift seemed to slow. Opening one eye, then the other, he saw that he was approaching some kind of terminal. The building's flat, yellow roof burst into the darkness like a Frisbee flying through the gloom.

For a sickening moment, Ollie thought he was going crash directly into it. Then the chair dipped, swung, and whooshed under the yellow roof. Ollie let out a loud "oof" as he came to a sudden stop. The safety bar jammed against his big belly. That was when he looked down and saw it: Beautiful, solid ground. Stone. He pushed up the safety bar and jumped out, hopping away from the chair like it was electrified.

Ollie dropped the torch onto the flat rock and fell to his hands and knees. Wonderful, dependable ground. He wanted to lick it. If he lived to be a hundred, he was certain he would never see anything more incredible.

Then he stood, turned around, and discovered he was wrong.

Seven

Ollie swayed on his feet. His vision blurred, then sharpened, then blurred again. His last meal was making its way back up his esophagus in a sour echo of cream cheese and bile. He was shaking. He was relieved to be alive. And he was more than a little stunned.

Despite all this, he understood.

With just one sweep of his eyes, it all became clear. He had thought he knew what his cosmos was made of. Weight and substance, order and logic, day and night, sky and ground. And he had been wrong. About all of it.

Some things you must see for yourself, yes? Laszlo had said. *There is more to your world than you know, Ollie Delgato. More, even, than you could imagine.*

He seemed to have landed in a cavern. Or at least, that was closest word his mind could find to describe the vast, anomalous expanse stretched out before him. It was...enormous. Existentially impossible to grasp. On and on it went, above and around, vanishing into foggy tunnels and wide horizons. Dipping in and out of sight with no discernible end. Ollie stood motionless, almost paralyzed by the immensity, as echoes fell down around him like whale song. Murmurs. Clangs. Splashes. The reverberations tickled his ears, not unpleasantly, and proved to his subconscious brain that the space was, somehow, enclosed. Finite.

He was standing on a rock. Shale, perhaps, or slate. Whatever it was, it had a uniformly gray-blue color and a mostly flat surface. It was also massive. In his haze, it occurred to Ollie that he could walk for a very long time on that rock without ever having to step on another. The stone formed a platform of sorts, like a landing pad, for the chairlift. Chairdrop? Ollie mulled this over for just a moment before leaving the thought to make room for the hundreds of others that were suddenly competing for his attention.

Beyond the rock platform, he saw water. This, too, was gargantuan, as though an entire Great Lake had been relocated underground. It seemed, at this distance, to be scattered with dozens of islands of varying sizes. Above the lake was a ceiling. It was a great distance above, perhaps as high as three Statues of Liberty stacked end-to-end. The ceiling also appeared to be made of rock, though it somehow let off a blue phosphorescent glow that infused the entire cavern in an eerie, pale light.

Below that domed ceiling, scattered in and around the lake, were people. Lots of people. Out on the water, in boats. Scuttling atop the surface of the islands. They were too far away for him to get any kind of a clear look.

Well, most of them were too far. One of them, as it turned out, was standing not five feet away.

Like the chairlift operator, this man wore a cobalt jumpsuit with a miner's hat and headlamp. But he was also...different, somehow. Something was off. His eyes were too large. Too round. His nose was too flat, and his nostrils too wide. His skin was so pale it was almost translucent.

"May I take your coat, Sir?" the man asked, his arm outstretched.

Upon hearing the words, Ollie noticed that he was hot. Uncomfortably hot. The winter of just an hour ago had disappeared, replaced by steamy, humid air. He found himself nodding. Yes. Yes, that would be good. Suddenly, he had no greater desire than to hand over his coat to this strange, expectant person.

Ollie pulled his arms from the sleeves, watching his own body move as though seeing through someone else's eyes. Three words—*Where am I?*—threatened to jump from his tongue. But he caught them just in time. If he was supposed to be there, if he had been invited, then he would know where he was. Asking the question would expose him as an interloper. No, better to remain silent, hide his shaking hands, and play along. He had to follow Laszlo's instructions. Meanwhile, another three words—*In too deep!*—screamed and kicked in his mind.

The blue-suited man took the parka without comment and walked to a nearby wall, where he lifted it onto a hook. It hung next to another coat, which hung next to another, and another, and another. Black, olive, tan, gray, red. Short and long. Hundreds of them, stretched out into the darkness. Ollie stared at the interminable line and wondered: How long had they all been hanging there? Who had left them? And, most importantly, why had no one returned for them? He flashed on a few possible answers, none of which were particularly reassuring.

The man fluffed and smoothed Ollie's coat, then pressed his foot against a pedal on the ground. With a grinding whirr, the hanging coats swung into motion, each moving a bit further away. The rotation reminded Ollie of a dry cleaner's spinning rack. Then, as suddenly as it had begun, the propulsion stopped. Ollie's coat had shifted one spot to the right. And in its place, a new, empty hook had appeared in the rock wall, waiting for the next arrival.

How incredibly odd. The thought had scarcely surfaced when he noticed something else: A distinctive hunter-green coat, hanging ten or twelve hooks down from his own. *Hunter green.* Ollie darted past the protesting attendant and reached out to touch it. Thick, thrift-store wool. Golden buttons. Kind of scratchy.

Nell's coat! It had to be! He wasn't crazy. *This* wasn't crazy! She was here!

He felt a firm tug on his arm.

"Sir, I really must insist..." the man said, looking perturbed as he lead Ollie away from the coats and back to his original spot on the platform. Then he asked, "Will you be requiring a wheelbarrow today?"

His mind still spinning, Ollie looked in the direction of the man's outstretched arm and saw yet another line of half-rusted wheelbarrows. Of all the strange sights he had seen since falling through that hole in the sidewalk, the ubiquitous one-wheeled wagons were perhaps the most disturbing. What the hell was the deal with these wheelbarrows? And the rope, and the tape? And why did the sight of them send a shiver of revulsion up his spine?

"Uh, no. I don't think so," Ollie said.

"Very good, Sir." The attendant folded his hands together and maintained a blankly pleasant expression.

"Okay, well...thanks," Ollie said. He glanced again at Nell's coat, as though it might impart some green-woolish wisdom. Some clues. Then he looked at his own. How would he get it back? With no tag or number, how would he prove which one was his?

The attendant's tight smile didn't invite further questions or conversation. His vacant stare gave only one, unspoken directive: *Time to move along.*

Ollie lifted a hand in a half-hearted wave and began to walk. As before, it was a one-way journey. With the chairlift platform and solid walls behind him, he headed toward the lake.

Each step was a potential hazard. Aside from the pale blue glow emanating from the tall ceiling, Ollie could see no natural light at all. The air was steamy and damp, with a smell like a musty, overcrowded barn. Moving beams—more headlamps, maybe—bobbed on the nearby islands. The boats in the water, similarly, had navigational rays that cut through the murk.

Ollie's eyes began to adjust to the darkness as he approached a cluster of people and a row of boats bobbing in the greenish water. The vessels' motors were enormous, far bigger than any motor he had ever seen. He peered at one of them as he got closer, then stopped, startled. It wasn't a motor at all. It was, unmistakably, a bird.

Swan boats?

The other version, the regular version, was a Boston institution, ferrying tourists around the Public Garden pond every spring, summer, and fall. Each had an oversized white swan statue perched in the stern to provide a seat for the pedaling driver, while the passengers rode up front on rows of bench seats. These boats were similar—bird in the back, people in the front—but strange. For one thing, they were much smaller than normal swan boats, with only three rows of benches instead of six. And for another, these swans were black.

Each craft was tied to a post and accompanied by a loitering driver. The drivers looked bored; some talked amongst themselves, while others stared off across the lake or smoked on makeshift benches.

A dock! Ollie's heart began to pound. Laszlo had told him to find the dock. To pay the driver. Well, here he was. He had found it! And soon, he would find Nell and get the hell out of there. He'd be the hero, she'd be grateful, and all of this aberration would be nothing but a distant memory. Bam. Smooth as Jordan almonds.

Almost done, he told himself. *You can do this.*

Taking a deep breath, Ollie headed toward the closest driver—a weaselly man wearing thick glasses. This man's jumpsuit was beige and dirty instead of blue and clean. A toolbelt of sorts hung around his waist, strewn with a variety of unidentifiable objects and gadgets.

As Ollie approached, the man regarded him with a curious stare.

"Hi," Ollie said, lifting a hand. "I'm looking for a driver. A captain, I guess. For a boat."

"Uh huh," the man replied. He didn't seem especially eager to provide his services.

"I'm going to..." Ollie paused. *What was the name of the place again? Herra-something... Like bend, or end...* "Herrick's End," he blurted. "I need to go to Herrick's End."

The man raised one eyebrow. "You all by yourself, son?"

"Yes, just me. One. One for transport," Ollie said, parroting the chairlift operator's preferred terminology. "Can you take me there? I can pay."

"Ticket?" the man asked.

"What?"

"Where's your ticket?"

"I...don't know." Ticket? Laszlo hadn't mentioned a ticket. "I can pay," Ollie repeated.

The man held up a hand with a scowl. "No ticket, no ride. Not to there, anyway."

"Okay, so where can I get a ticket?"

The grizzled driver snorted in disdain. Then he said again, "No ticket, no ride."

Ollie straightened, simmering somewhere between confusion and embarrassment. No matter. There were other drivers. Six or seven more, all looking like they needed something to do. Surely someone would take him.

He approached the next stall, where a similarly dressed woman was leaning against a coiled rope railing. Her weight made the rope sag. She had the same bizarre facial features he had seen on the man who collected his coat. Her nostrils were unusually broad, as were her eyes.

He opened his mouth to speak, but she beat him to it.

"Ticket?" the woman asked.

Again, with the ticket. "Look, I have money. Plenty of money. I can pay you."

"No can do, honey."

"But, please! I can pay! Whatever it costs. Please. I just need a ride."

"To Herrick's?"

"Herrick's End, yes."

"Need a ticket to get there, honey."

Ollie asked the next driver, then the next, moving down the line with equally bad luck at every stop. The chorus was the same from each driver: No ticket, no ride. Anger and frustration began to simmer in his belly. Laszlo never mentioned any tickets! Why not?

Ollie rocked back and forth on his heels. What the hell was he supposed to do now? Was there another dock? Another way? Could he swim? Could he walk? Walk where? All he saw were islands, and boats, and a vast expanse of puke-green water that seemed to spread in twenty different directions. Should he give up? Go home? Even if he wanted to, he didn't know how. Somehow he doubted that Mr. Stick-In-His-Ass chairlift operator would let him board the ride for a return trip.

One of the drivers, he suddenly realized, was watching him. Last in the row. She was sitting, hunched, on a plank of wood. Her off-white jumpsuit was well-worn; he could see patches of other, darker materials sewn over various rips and holes. She was young. Younger than the others, at least. Maybe even younger than him. Her hair was dyed purplish-silver, shaved on the sides and swooped into a wave on the top of her head. Her skin was the color of sunbaked clay. She was smoking something that might have been a cigarette, though Ollie doubted it. When she exhaled, a long plume of sugary pink smoke emerged from her lips.

She stared through the smoke. Stared at him.

Ollie felt a surge of something odd: dread and hope swirling together like the two halves of a chocolate-and-vanilla soft serve. Before he could lose his nerve, he skipped the next driver in the row altogether and followed the pink smoke.

As he approached, the girl took another drag on her strange, hollow stick. She was studying his face, not even trying to conceal her fascination.

"Not from around here, are you?" the driver said. A small smile curled at the edges of her lips.

He shook his head. Was she mocking him? Ollie could swear she was mocking him, and he would know. This girl's features looked more regular. More like his. Her eyes were brown. No giant nostrils or translucent skin. Just...normal.

She tilted her head. "What brings you to the Neath?"

Ollie tried not to cough as another plume of fuchsia smoke surrounded his face. *The Neath?* Had Laszlo mentioned that name? His mind raced. "I'm looking for someone," he answered. "And I need a ride."

"So I gathered," she said, tossing her stick into the water. "To Herrick's End, was it?"

Again, he bristled at her tone. It wasn't anything overt. Just a slightly amused inflection, as though they were sharing a joke he didn't understand.

"I have money," Ollie said. He reached into his pocket and pulled out the colored bills. "Plenty, see? You can have it all. Will you take me?"

The girl folded her arms. A curl of purple hair flopped onto her forehead. "You've been to Herrick's before?" she asked.

For a moment, he considered lying, then thought better of it. "No." Her eyes narrowed. "Why do you want to go there?"

"I'm looking for someone, like I said. A friend. She's missing. Someone told me I could find her there."

The girl cocked her partially shaved head and stared at Ollie for a long moment. She seemed to be studying him. Again. "I'm not supposed to take you without a ticket."

He nodded. He knew.

The driver bit her lower lip, looking indecisive. Like the others, she wore a toolbelt around her waist that was festooned with various odds and ends. Ollie thought he recognized an umbrella. And an old-fashioned telescope of some kind. He was trying to puzzle out a third item when she held out an opened hand. "Lucky for you, I need the money."

For a moment, he didn't move. Then Ollie jumped forward to shove the wad of square bills into her palm. "Thank you!" he said, his voice rising in surge of relief.

"Shut up, would you? Krite." The last word sounded like a curse. She grabbed his arm and pulled him close. "Be cool, all right? Nice and quiet. Just get in."

Ollie hustled into the hull before she could change her mind. He stood awkwardly beside the three rows of bench seats, not quite feeling comfortable enough to sit down.

The girl made no eye contact with the other drivers, who watched her curiously. Instead, she untied the rope that bound the boat to the dock, hopped on board, and gave the rock's edge a hard kick. Seconds later, the vessel floated out and away.

The driver flashed him an uncertain look. A miner's light hung around her neck; she slid it onto the top of her head, squashing the wave of hair, and turned it on. Then she walked back to her post behind the plastic black swan.

Ollie was afraid to speak. Afraid even to move, as though he'd lured a squirrel with a peanut and didn't want to scare it away. *Fake it 'till you make it.* For once, he might actually be advancing to the second half of the equation. *I'm doing it, mom,* he wanted to tell her, feeling almost giddy. *I told you I would.*

A sudden flapping movement jolted him from his reverie.

He stumbled backwards, smashing his spine against the metal railing. A giant, dark shape had risen up beside him. Two shapes. Wings.

Ollie's gasp stuck in his throat.

Alive. The statue was *alive.*

The driver seemed not to notice his terrified reaction. Calmly, she climbed onto the bird's back and grabbed a set of reins. "Here we go, girl," she murmured.

In response, the bird unfolded its head and let out a shriek: *Caw! Caw! Caw!*

It was a crow. Not a black swan—a giant, horrifyingly cranky crow. Everything about it was huge, and dark: the beak, the feathers, the apple-sized beady eyes. Like the dead-but-alive falcon on the carousel, but bigger. Badder. This bird was as tall as Ollie, if not taller. And the driver, as far as he could tell, was riding it.

"Atta girl," she said. "Here we go."

Her voice had a calming effect. After the initial kerfuffle, the crow settled into a slow, beating rhythm, using its immense wings to propel the small boat through the water.

Ollie slammed his eyes shut and concentrated on his breathing. *In, and out. In, and out.* When he was able to speak, he peeled open one eye, then the other, and said, "That's, uh, that's a big bird."

"This here's Mrs. Paget," the girl said, sounding proud. "She'll get you where you need to go."

Ollie nodded, unable to take his eyes off the wings. They had a spread of at least twenty feet. Their movement created eddies in the calm water below and hit Ollie's face with repetitive gusts of wind.

This will all be over soon, he told himself, rubbing his palms against his thighs. *Very soon.* Giant birds, plummeting chairlifts, never-ending coat racks—maybe it was all some kind of dream, or hallucination. Maybe he'd been drugged. Maybe it was a test, or a penance: Pass the test, prove your mettle, avenge your poor, departed mother. Live happily ever after. Was he passing? God only knew.

The giant crow, apparently named Mrs. Paget, was looking at him. Like a predator sizing up its prey.

Thinking about prey made Ollie think, perversely, about his lost granola bars. Golden brown oats. Crunchy pecans. Touch of honey melting on the tongue. Two bars per packet, with a little pile of crumbs left at the bottom. Usually, when both bars were gone, he would tip the packet upside down and—

Ollie swallowed. He got to his feet. "I don't suppose...is there any food? Where we're going?"

She raised one eyebrow. "Food?"

"Yeah. A restaurant, or a market, or something?"

The girl stared at him. Then she said, "No."

"Nothing at all?" He tried to hide his disappointment and failed.

"You do know where you're going, right?" she asked, concern in her voice.

"Well, yeah. Yes. I mean, sort of."

The driver looked doubtful. Then she pulled on the reins, which caused the crow to dip one wing and raise the other. The boat shifted direction. "How much do you know, exactly?"

"Some. I mean, not a lot, but..." He sighed and gave up. "Nothing. I know nothing. I only know that's where she is. She's there, and I have to find her and bring her home. That's all I need to know. It's like, a rescue mission." Ollie folded his arms and stared out over the water. The murk was thick, as though he could reach out and scoop it up with his hands. The water, too, looked darker now that he was over it, less like pea soup and more like minestrone. Deep, brown, steaming broth.

Damn, he was hungry.

Looking down, he noticed black streaks on the white floor of the boat. They were rubbery and patterned, like tire marks.

"What's with all the wheelbarrows, anyway?" Ollie asked.

She kept her eyes on the water. "What about them?"

"I mean, what are they for? I keep seeing them everywhere."

Clearing her throat, the driver said, "The women and the girls use them, mostly. For transport."

"Transport of what?"

She gave him a long look. "Heavy things."

In the distance, Ollie could hear vague clanging sounds and something that might have been voices. He assumed these came from the islands he had seen earlier, though now he couldn't see anything except the steamy fog. And there, in the boat, he heard only the soft swish of the crow's wings and the lapping sound of the water as it washed against the bow.

The driver was still watching him from the corner of her eye. Her expression was inscrutable.

"What?" he asked.

"Hmm? Nothing."

"*What?*" he asked again. Clearly, this girl had something she wanted to say. And if he was about to become regurgitated meat for

65

giant crow babies in some massive freakish nest, he figured he had a right to know.

The driver sighed. "Look, it's none of my business. But...it's not too late, you know. You can change your mind. You can go back."

"Why would I go back?" Ollie heard an unflattering squeal in his voice. He didn't want to admit, even to himself, that he liked her suggestion. "I'm almost there! I'm almost done, for Christ's sake."

"Weellll..." She dragged out the syllable skeptically.

"You told me you were taking me there. To Herrick's End."

"I am."

"So, what's the problem?"

The girl avoided his eyes. "It's a bad place, that's all," she said.

"Bad, how?"

"Bad, bad. As in, not good. As in, you might want to rethink this little plan of yours."

"That's not very specific."

She sighed. "Look, this place is...different. Different than the place you come from."

"You don't say," Ollie replied, eying the eight-foot-tall bird. Then he looked back at the driver. "Wait, how do you know where I'm from?"

She gave a quiet laugh and stared straight ahead, into the darkness. "Where you're from, there are restaurants. And holidays. And rock-and-roll, and sunshine, and special little parks made just for children to play." She nodded at her avian friend. "And you have boats with white swans instead of black crows. Does that sound about right?"

Ollie shifted.

"You have seasons that change," she continued. "Flowers, and bees. And tiny little round cakes. Sweet cakes. In different colors." Her eyes moved to his face. "You can go back to all that, you know. It's not too late."

He saw a sharp sadness in her features that made him want to reassure her. "I know," he said. "I will. I mean, I can. But first I have to find my friend. Then I'll go."

She smiled, looking rueful. "Almost there," she said. "Last chance. I can still turn around, if you want. You don't have to do this."

Ollie looked up at her, feeling raw. He did have to do this. There was no way to make her understand: Nell was out there, somewhere. She was in trouble, and probably scared as hell. And he knew exactly what she was feeling. Ollie knew what it was like to be despondent, and powerless, and completely, utterly, alone.

He could have helped her before, and he didn't. This was his last chance to make it right. To make so many things right. He saw a flash of grisly images—his mother, huddled behind the couch, hands raised like shields. Bright lights of an emergency room. Swollen lips. Splinted fingers. *No.* Ollie shook his head to dispel the pictures. As much as he would rather be anywhere else, he had to do this. He had no choice.

"She needs me," he said.

"Why?" the young woman asked. She seemed to genuinely want to know.

Ollie sighed. If he were smart, he would just keep his mouth shut. But there was something about this girl. She was just so...so something. He felt like he could trust her. Which was ridiculous—he had just met her.

Finally, he gave in. "Because someone is hurting her," Ollie sighed. "At least, I think someone is hurting her. I met a guy, who told me she was down here, and she should have been back already. She came here to escape, I think. Or get help, at this Herrick's End place. Then the guy told me how to get here, and..." He didn't bother finishing. She already knew the next part of the story.

The driver stared at him. He wished he knew what she was thinking. At the very least, she didn't seem to be wearing an expression of disgust, or pity. She seemed to be listening. Considering. Appraising him like a bubble-wrapped vase on Antiques Roadshow.

Finally, she nodded. "You're sure?

"I'm sure."

"You're a stubborn one, aren't you." It was more of a statement than a question.

"I guess so."

"All right," she said with a shrug. "Then listen to me carefully. You stay low, all right? And quiet. Don't let them see you."

"Who?"

"Anybody. You need to be absolutely invisible. Got it?"

Ollie nodded stiffly. She could see him, right? She knew he was six-foot-six and weighed ten kabillion pounds? In a list of tasks he was pretty much guaranteed to fail at, "staying low" and "being invisible" were right at the top. "And if they do see me?"

"If they do see you, then it's too late," the girl said, sounding grim. "And if anyone asks how you got here..."

He held up a hand, understanding. "I never met you."

She gave a quick, short nod. "That's right."

Ollie scanned the horizon. He still saw nothing. "So, what is Herrick's End, anyway?"

The driver didn't answer right away. Then she said, "You have to think in opposites, down here. Everything is pretty much the opposite of what you're used to. White bird, black bird. Aboveground, underground. Cold, hot. You see what I mean?"

He nodded.

"So you have to ask yourself, how did you get here?"

Ollie screwed up his face. "Well, I met a guy, and we had to buy a guidebook, then there was a weird hole-funnel thing in the ground, and—"

"No," she interrupted. "I mean, how did you find us? How specifically?"

"I...I followed the Freedom Trail."

The driver nodded, looking solemn. "And what's the opposite of freedom?"

He caught sight of it then. The fog parted, the dim light illuminated the gloom, and the facade rose up in front of him like a soaring, breathing nightmare. And the moment he saw it, Ollie knew he had made a terrible, terrible mistake.

Eight

Run.

That was the only thought in Ollie's head as the towering monstrosity emerged from the mist. It wasn't a building, exactly—that was much too ordinary a word. A Post Office was a building. A school was a building. This was...an architectural phantom. A lichen-covered, decrepit, fifty-story dungeon, leaning precipitously forward as though it might topple at any moment. Rough-edged windows scattered the surface like scars. It was impossible to tell where one floor ended and another began. Steam vents protruded at odd angles, spitting puffs of foul-smelling, orange gas. The roof, if there was one, disappeared into the rising haze. Menace oozed from every crack, every crooked ledge, every gaping hole. This monolith, this *building,* seemed to be staring at him. Half-alive, but mostly dead.

The stench from the belching vents wafted across the water, and Ollie held his breath. His arms and legs went numb. *Run, run, run.*

This couldn't be right. Nell was in *that* place? Why would Laszlo send her there? None of this made sense. It must be some kind of horrible misunderstanding. Maybe Laszlo had confused Nell with someone else. Maybe Ollie had gotten the name wrong. Ollie got a lot of things wrong, all the time.

He looked up at the crumbling fortress and shuddered.

"Get your head down," the driver snapped.

Ollie ducked, peering through the gap in the railing to see a dock straight ahead. It was patrolled by three or four men wearing angry red jumpsuits. Instead of heading toward them, the driver steered the boat to the left, toward a dark, abandoned outcropping of rock. Moments later, she bumped the boat against the edge, climbed off the crow's back, and jumped from the hull to the dry land with a rope in her hand.

The perturbed bird lifted its head, apparently ready to caw. "Uh, uh," she said, silencing it with a pointed finger. Then she turned to Ollie. "This is your stop."

It was happening too fast. He wasn't ready.

The girl tugged off the headlamp, letting it dangle around her neck. "You wanted Herrick's End, this is it." He waited for her to say, "I told you so," but she didn't. Instead, she gave him a sympathetic smile. "You'll be fine. You're a big guy. You can protect yourself, right?"

He wanted to laugh. If she only knew.

"Just do what I told you," the driver said, gathering the rope in her hands. "Stay down. Stay low. Don't let anybody see you. Find your friend and stay in the shadows. She'll know the way out of here."

Ollie gave her a questioning look.

"If they sent her down here, then they told her the way out," she said. "That's the way it works. Don't waste time, don't make friends, don't get seen. You don't exactly blend in down here. Got it?"

He gave a nervous nod. But still, he didn't move. His breath came in shallow pants.

The girl didn't move, either. A troubled expression crossed her face. Then she reached into her pocket, extracted the wad of cash he had given her, and stared down at it.

"What?" he asked.

"Nothing. I..." She shoved the money back into the pocket. "Listen, when you run into trouble—" She stopped, corrected herself. "*If* you run into trouble, come find me. Okay? You need to be careful who you talk to down here. Don't just...tell people stuff. If you need something, come find me."

He raised his eyebrows. "But I don't even know your name."

She waited a moment before answering, looking torn. Finally she said, "It's Tera."

"I'm Ollie," he said, reaching out a hand. "Ollie Delgato."

When they shook, her hand slipped inside of his like a guitar nesting in its case. He had expected her grip to be strong. He had not expected it to linger quite as long as it did, or for the press of her palm to send a sudden, electric surge through his body.

They stood like that, hands intertwined, until the crow's sudden, short *caw* broke the long silence.

70

Tera released her hand and took a step back. "I can't stick around here," she said, sounding apologetic. "So what's it gonna be? You staying or leaving?"

Leaving, he thought. *Leaving, leaving, leaving. With you.* Then he shook his head, as if trying to break a trance. "Staying," he said, though the word was hardly audible.

"You're sure?" she asked.

He nodded without enthusiasm.

"Okay, then..." Tera swept her arm in the direction of the rocky ledge.

Finally, hesitantly, his feet began to shuffle. One after another, they moved through the hull of the boat and onto solid ground. What was he doing? Ollie's heart pounded like a thunderous storm. With each thump came a refrain: *No, no, no, no, no.* His feet ignored it. Somehow, they kept moving until it was too late.

Tera reboarded her boat and climbed onto the crow's back. Then all three of them—the big kid, the purple-haired girl, and the enormous bird—watched each other as though something was about to happen. Nothing did.

"Head that way," she said, pointing over Ollie's right shoulder. "The line is over there. That's probably where she is."

"What line?"

She got a look on her face that was part sympathy, part incredulity. "Just go that way."

"What if I don't find it?"

"You will."

He wanted more information, while simultaneously wanting to know as little as possible. He wanted to ask her to go with him. Instead, Ollie only cracked his knuckles. One after the other, *pop, pop, pop.* Tiny, repetitive explosions of anxiety.

"Good luck," Tera said. She didn't add, *You'll need it.* She didn't have to.

"Thanks."

"Remember, keep your head down. Don't let anybody see you. And if anyone asks—"

"I know, I know," Ollie interrupted. "I never saw you."

She gave a nod. Then she snapped the reins and said, "Atta girl. Let's go."

The crow lifted its wings and swept them through the murky air. The boat turned and began to move away from the ledge.

Before she left, the driver gave Ollie one last look over her shoulder, accompanied by a sad smile. "See you around," she said.

He doubted it. And she looked like she doubted it, too.

Long after the boat left, Ollie remained. He stood on the shore and gazed into the fog, hoping some solution might suddenly appear there. But all he saw was more fog.

When he finally found the resolve to turn around and study his surroundings, Ollie discovered that he was standing on the edge of a strange, short little forest, made up mostly of stalactites. Or stalagmites? One kind hung from the tops of caves, he knew, while the other kind grew up from the bottom. He thought back to Mr. Eichenbaum's middle-school science class... What was the handy-dandy mnemonic they had learned for remembering the difference between the two? Stalac*tites* hold *tight* to the ceiling; you *might* bump into stalag*mites* while you're walking. Or something like that. These, then, were probably stalagmites. Whatever they were called, they were shaped like lumpy, solid Christmas trees, pointy at the top and coppery-colored throughout. Ollie couldn't tell if the hue was natural or if they had been stained by the orange smog spewing out of the nearby vents. Either way, they were painfully ugly.

More importantly for Ollie, they were plentiful. And hefty. Many of the formations were taller than he was, which meant that he had cover.

Stay down, Tera had said. *Stay out of sight.*

Wherever he was going, and however long it might take to get there, Ollie knew he was pathetically unprepared for the journey. He had no flashlight, no map, no tools, no food. He was wearing a pair of slip-on sneakers—ideal for walking the city streets, but not so ideal for traversing lumpy stretches of calcium-carbonated ground. He was hungry. So, so hungry. And possibly lost: Five minutes into the trek, he was already wondering if he had veered off in the wrong direction. He didn't have to wonder for long.

Just ahead, he could see a break in the stalagmite formations. A clearing. A road?

Ollie ducked down and crept to the edge of the lumpy thicket. He peered out and saw a wide expanse of smooth rock. Beyond that, he saw the monstrous building again; from this angle, he had a good view of its formidable entrance, which was blocked by an equally formidable iron gate. And in front of that gate, he saw people waiting in a line.

People and wheelbarrows.

Ollie squinted. There was a pattern to it. Every other person was standing, and the remaining people seemed to be sitting inside the carts.

No...wait. His eyes widened. The people in the wheelbarrows weren't just sitting: They were immobile. Tied up. Strips of duct tape and fabric covered their mouths and, in some cases, their eyes. Some even wore bags over their heads.

They were captives.

Most of the people standing in the line were women, but not all. There were a few kids and some men, too, hovering behind their hostages. All had grim looks on their faces. From the collected weary postures, Ollie guessed that they had been waiting for a very long time. The line disappeared around a corner, leaving him to wonder how long, exactly, it was.

His eyes swiveled back to the entrance gate, where a hefty man in a red jumpsuit was sitting behind a large stone desk. A woman stood in front of the desk, answering questions. Her arm was in a cast. Next to her, an extremely unhappy fellow wearing a business suit and brown loafers had been hauled out of his wheelbarrow by a guard. The well-dressed man struggled fruitlessly, his mouth taped shut, as the questioning went on.

Finally, the check-in process ended. The clerk behind the desk raised his arm, and the iron gate rose with a grinding squeal. Up, up, up. The guards pushed the businessman through the opening while he kicked, twisted, and hollered into the tape. The woman watched him disappear into the dark tunnel. Then she turned and walked briskly toward the nearby docks, giving Ollie a clear view of her battered, tear-soaked face.

She was leaving. The well-dressed man, it seemed, was staying.

The guard behind the desk gestured for the next person in line to move forward, and the process started all over again.

Ollie shrank back. What the hell was going on here? What kind of a place was this? His eyes scanned the line again, jumping from face to face, looking for some kind of answer or explanation.

Instead, he saw Nell.

Every muscle in his body seemed to contract at once. She was standing with the rest, far to the left, just before the line curved around the building. It was her. Dark hair. Ivory skin. Even at this distance, he could see the hot-pink glint of her fingernails. She was leaning against the wall, looking off into the distance.

Nell. Holy shit, she was right there. He had done it. He had found her!

He peeled his eyes away from her face and noticed, for the first time, that her hand was resting on the handles of a wheelbarrow, which seemed to contain a restrained, curled-up human being.

Clenching his fists in determination, Ollie crept along the edge of the clearing, staying hidden behind a row of stalagmites. Finally, he was directly across from her. Nell was wearing a black tank top, jeans, and socks. A sweatshirt and a pair of winter boots sat next to her in a pile on the ground. She looked sweaty and weary, but otherwise fine.

A guard paced beside the line; when he moved toward the front, near the entrance gate, Ollie took a deep breath. This was his chance. He pounced from his hiding place and sprinted across the clearing.

Murmurs began to spread through the line as a few heads turned in his direction. One of those heads was Nell's. She looked initially curious, then confused, then startled. She straightened as he approached, lifting her back from the wall.

"Ollie?"

He ducked into line behind her, trying in vain to hide his massive body.

A scrawny woman behind them clucked her tongue and hissed, "No cutting!"

"Ollie?" Nell said again, staring at him in disbelief. "What are you doing here?"

"I came to get you," he answered, out of breath. A proud smile began to spread across his face. This might be the stupidest, and bravest, thing he had ever done, but he had done it. She needed him, and he had come to her rescue. It was pretty impressive, really. He waited for her to gasp, or burst into tears, or embrace him. Wait, what if she fainted? He readied himself to catch her, just in case.

But Nell did none of those things. Instead, she just continued to stare. He watched her head tilt to the side, hazel eyes blinking, and he worried, suddenly, that she was in shock.

"Why?" she asked.

It was not a question he was expecting. He reached out to grasp her forearm. "Because...you were missing. And I found you. But everything's going to be all right now. I promise. I'm going to get you out of here."

Nell looked down at his hand on her arm. With a gentle motion, she pulled it away. "Ollie, what are you talking about? I'm fine. I'm not going anywhere."

He blinked. "But...but you have to."

"I have to?" she repeated, in the tone of a preschool teacher trying to calm a confused toddler. "You see how long this line is, dude? I've been standing here for days. There's no way I'm losing my place now."

In front of her, the man in the wheelbarrow was straining against the ropes that bound his arms and legs. He twisted his head to give Ollie a desperate look, yelling something unintelligible into the duct tape on his mouth.

"Who is that?"

She sighed. "You know who that is."

And of course, he did. "Nell, what's going on? What is this place? What's going to happen to him?"

"Him?" Nell responded, her voice hard. "He's going to get exactly what he deserves. Finally. And I'm going to make sure he doesn't ever do it to anyone else." Then she asked again: "Seriously, how did you find me? What are you doing here?"

"I...thought you needed help."

A generous smile made two dimples appear in her cheeks. "Oh, Ollie. I appreciate it. I really do. You're one of the good ones, you know that?" She patted his arm. Then she pointed to the struggling young man in the wheelbarrow. "But do I look like I need help?"

A chill began a slow crawl through his extremities. "But I thought...I mean, you looked like you had..." he faltered, looking down at The Guy. "What is this? Will he...?"

Nell lifted one eyebrow and pointed to the purpled bruise on her chin. "Is he really the one you want to be worried about, here?"

"No! Of course not. I just—"

"I'm not the first one he did this to, you know," she interrupted. "I found out his last girlfriend ended up in the hospital. And the one before that..." She dropped her voice. "She went missing. *Missing!*" A visible shiver shook Nell's torso. Then she pursed her lips. "That won't be me. No fucking way. This ends now."

"But I... I don't understand," he said. "When will you come back?"

Her voice took on an urgent note. "Look, I really do appreciate you coming down here, Oll. I do. You're a nice guy, and a good friend. But I've got this. And we don't have time to debate. You need to get the hell out of here, now, before somebody sees you."

"You're not coming?" he whispered. Confusion made him sway.

"Just go, please," she said. "Get out of here while you still can. I'm fine, I swear. I'll see you back at home."

Despite the oppressive heat and steam, he felt cold all over. What was happening? This was not at all how this was supposed to go. He opened his mouth to respond, to protest, but found that he had no words.

In the end, it was the small woman behind him, the tongue-clucker, who spoke. "Listen, kid," the woman said, leaning forward. Ollie could see pity on her face. "You see that guard? He'll make his way back here soon. Trust me, you don't want to be here when he does."

Nell nodded in agreement. "Seriously, Ollie. Please. You have to get out of here. *Now.*"

But he couldn't go. Could he? He hadn't thought beyond finding her. He hadn't thought about being alone, about leaving alone. He didn't even know the way. Panic ran through his limbs like forked spikes of lightning.

"Go!" Nell hissed.

Ollie turned, and he ran. In the distance, he saw the forest of bulbous lumps. He tried to focus. He tried to remember what he was supposed to be doing—*stay down, be invisible.*

He was almost at the other side when he heard it: "Got one over here!"

One more step. He stumbled and reached for the coppery mound of minerals. His hand brushed the surface, and then it was yanked away.

"Nice try," said a gruff voice. It belonged to a man in a red jumpsuit. Moments later, there were more men, more jumpsuits. He heard Nell's voice, her scream, somewhere in the distance: "Olllllllieeee!" He felt a brutal blow on his head, then another, and another. When it was over, his face hung low, dripping with blood.

Ollie didn't struggle as they dragged him. He didn't do anything at all. In a brief flash of consciousness, he felt the sudden, desperate need to say goodbye—to someone, or maybe something. He wasn't sure which. But by the time they tossed his body into the dark maw beyond the iron gate, the urge had disappeared entirely.

Nine

He was dreaming of chicken piccata. The cutlets had been pounded thin, battered, and browned to a golden crisp. Olive oil dripped from the fork as he lifted each warm, tender bite. Hints of lemon and capers. Slight snap of black pepper. A mountain of mashed potatoes hovered nearby, bathed in garlic butter and sprinkled with chives. He chewed slowly, savoring each mouthful. Groaning.

It was the groan that woke him.

One of his eyes opened; the other stayed shut, courtesy of a swollen lid and a thick crust of blood and mucus. Was it his own groan he had heard, or someone else's? At this point, Ollie could barely tell the difference. He had been locked in the shadowy room for hours with six other men and two women. They were not allowed to talk to each other. They were not allowed to talk to the guards. A plastic bucket in the corner collected all bodily excretions, and the stench of sweat, vomit, diarrhea, and urine choked him to the point of unconsciousness. He welcomed the blackouts. He prayed for them.

Ollie had awakened this time to find he was still curled up on the floor, his cheek crushed against the cold, gritty stone. With his one good eye, he stared at the removable slider at the bottom of the cell door. This was how the prisoners' "meals" arrived. The most recent offering was still sitting there, untouched by anyone. It appeared to be a large bowl full of leather belts, soaking in a beige broth, though Ollie knew that couldn't possibly be true. The water, if it was water, tasted as though it had been poured from an exhaust pipe into a rusty pitcher.

He was starving. He was shivering. He was surely about to die. And it was all, he knew, for nothing.

He had failed.

Ollie had been kidding himself, thinking he could play the hero. Believing his own white-knight, bullshit story. Why would someone like Nell ever need someone like him? Who was he, anyway? The fat kid. The freak. The easy mark. Fatherless, and now motherless. Useless as an abandoned penguin egg on the tundra, left alone to tumble in the harsh, unforgiving winds.

Nell had screamed his name when the guards caught him. At least there was that. Had she rushed out to try to save him? Did she even care? Or had she been too worried about losing her place in line? He'd probably never know.

The goons had patted him down before they tossed him into this hole, but had somehow missed the gift-shop keychain still tucked away in the front pocket of his jeans. He pulled it out, there in the darkness, and pressed the tiny button on the edge. *Oliver*, it flashed, over and over again. The shocking light seared into his eyeballs. *Oliver. Oliver. Oliver.*

He moaned. The pain was almost bad enough to drown out his torturous ruminations. Almost. Ollie stared at the stone floor, breathing in the stench, and he thought about his mother. Did heaven have a view to this place? He hoped not. He didn't want her to see him here. He had faced his own version of Francie's frozen-river analogy, and he had failed. He should have stayed on the riverbank when the splashing victim went by. He should have never gotten involved. Now, the victim had crossed safely, easily, to the other side, and Ollie was the one who was going to drown.

He had been a fool. A naïve, fractured fool. Did he actually think that Nell would throw herself into his arms? That she was helpless without him? What kind of a ridiculous fantasy had he been living in? Ollie wanted to snort at the absurdity of it. He almost did. Then a clacking sound came from the cell door.

"Get up," the guard barked. "Time to go."

They forced him to his feet.

Weak and disoriented, Ollie and his eight cellmates staggered through the door and into a narrow hallway, following each other in a slow, shuffling line. The man behind him whimpered. The woman in front of him muttered obscenities under her breath. Ollie stayed quiet.

When they came to a spiral staircase, one of the guards stepped aside and jerked his head. "Up here. Let's go."

The first prisoner in line obeyed, and the two behind that followed suit. Ollie, fourth in line, stopped to gape up at the stairs. They seemed to have been carved directly out of the stone wall, spinning in a tight loop up into the abyss. Impossibly high.

"Move!"

Ollie grunted as a hard object collided with his ribs. He dropped his eyes, lurched forward, and started to climb.

The first few steps were relatively easy. Each stair was short, which meant that Ollie didn't have to lift his leg much to get from one to the next. Soon, though, even that small effort became difficult. Then, intolerable.

The frayed group passed floor after floor, doorway after doorway, bypassing them all. His thigh muscles screamed in protest. His breath came in ragged gasps. Dizziness set in as he followed the stairs in endless, spinning spirals; when he glanced down to measure his progress, the ground seemed inconceivably far away. And still, they climbed.

One of the other men had already given up, slumping in sobbing protest. In response, the guards zapped him with something loud. The man screamed, rose onto his hands and knees, and began to crawl up the stairs.

Ollie's body shook all over. One wrong step, and he would go tumbling down the massive staircase. He shuddered. Then he realized that a grisly, 30-story fall might actually be better than whatever was waiting for him at the top.

He was lost in exhausted delirium when he heard a voice above him. "In here. Let's go."

Ollie's head snapped up. *Thank you, God.* They were stopping.

He slumped against the railing, blissful in the moment's rest. It didn't last long. The guards ushered the group up the last few steps and through an open doorway, which led to a surprisingly clean, white room with tall ceilings. Ollie had to shield his eyes from the sudden, unexpected brightness.

"Over there," one of the guards said. "Let's go."

The group shuffled to the room's far end. There were no chairs waiting for them; one of the women and several of the men collapsed onto the ground, panting. Ollie wanted nothing more than to join them, but something told him to stay on his feet. Jittery with fear and fatigue, he took in his surroundings. One wall was blank and white. Another was

79

full of large holes, each about the size of a sewer grate. Every hole had been assigned a number.

For several minutes, nothing happened. One of the men on the ground seemed to have passed out; Ollie nudged him with his foot.

"Wake up," Ollie whispered, then cast his eye toward the guards, who hadn't yet noticed.

The man nodded and struggled to sit up. As he did, a second door opened to their left. The guards stood at attention.

A woman swept through the doorway. To call her "old" was to call the galaxy "big"—she was, more accurately, ancient. The lines in her face had long ago transformed into deep grooves, less like skin than folded origami paper. Her oversized eyes spread all the way into her forehead, while her nose was little more than two semi-protruding holes. The woman's thick, yellowed dreadlocks defied gravity, ascending skyward into a sharp point. Her hair reminded Ollie of the stalagmites outside.

"Ma'am," the guards said in unison, bobbing their heads as she passed.

The woman barely acknowledged the greeting. Instead, she turned to take stock of the mangy group of prisoners.

"Stand up," she said. Her voice was soft yet sharp, the voice of a much younger woman, and it carried a heavy weight of warning across the room. The prisoners on the ground scrambled to their feet. The man beside Ollie started whimpering, again.

"I am the Reader," she said. "I will see all that you have done. And you will pay for your crimes. Only what you owe."

At this, the guards repeated the phrase in unison: "Only what you owe."

For one brief, deranged moment, Ollie felt like he was back in a Lighter Tomorrows meeting, listening to the members chant the LT motto. *Here today, lighter tomorrow.* He was teetering on the edge of hysteria.

"Only what you owe," the woman said again. Then she turned and walked to the center of the room, where a platform held two chairs. She settled into one of them, adjusted her robe, and folded her hands in her lap.

"I am ready," she said to no one in particular.

One of the guards jumped to attention. He walked across the room and grabbed the first prisoner in line, dragging the haggard man by his collar and depositing him into the chair next to the Reader.

"Raise your hand," she told him.

His eyes darting in confusion, the prisoner raised his right hand like a witness swearing on a Bible.

"Like this," the woman said. She held out her hand, palm first, and faced him.

The prisoner dropped his right arm and raised his left. He held out his palm. Even from a distance, Ollie could see that it was shaking. His own hands were already doing the same.

The woman pressed her wrinkled palm against his. She closed her eyes. Then she raised her other arm, stretched it out, and pointed her free hand at the nearby empty wall. She seemed to be concentrating.

Ollie held his breath. As he watched, a picture began to flicker on the wall.

No, not a picture. A movie. Her hand was projecting a moving scene. One of the people coming to life on the wall was...the man. The same prisoner who was sitting in the chair next to her. He was here, and he was also there. Ollie's heart began to pound.

The room went dead quiet as everyone watched the scene unfolding on the wall. The man was talking to a young boy. He was grabbing the boy. Slapping him across the face. The boy cowered.

Ollie turned his head away. He couldn't watch. He heard the young boy crying, begging the man to stop. Heard blows landing, heard the boy whimpering in pain. It was...sickening. Ollie felt vomit roil up from his stomach.

That episode was followed by another, and another. Ollie kept his eyes on the floor. Each time an attack came, he heard the same vicious words spewing from the man's mouth, the same cries from the boy. When would this end? Finally, Ollie looked up at the platform to see the prisoner sitting, stricken, watching himself on the wall. Watching himself hurt the little boy, time and time again.

The old woman, meanwhile, seemed unaffected.

"End," she said abruptly, and the movie disappeared from the wall. The screams and angry curses died out. The man sitting beside her had turned white. And to Ollie's left and right, his fellow prisoners had flattened themselves against the wall, terrified.

The Reader pulled her hand away. The man gathered his own to his chest in a uselessly protective gesture.

Two red-suited guards appeared at her side.

"Thirty-four," she said.

The guards nodded, grabbed up the shaking man, and led him to the wall filled with holes. His mouth was slack with dread.

"You will give what you owe," she told the prisoner. "Do you understand?"

"I'm sorry!" he said, fighting to free his arms. "Please! No! God, no! I'm sorry!"

The ancient woman gave the barest of nods to the guards. At that, they lifted the man and shoved him head-first into the hole marked "34." The man's scream echoed, then faded into the distance as he fell.

Ollie and the remaining eight prisoners cowered. One by one, each of the inmates in front of him marched to the platform, touched their palms to hers, and watched their misdeeds unfold on the white wall. After the skinny man came the middle-aged woman—a nursing-home attendant, apparently, whose "reading" highlighted her abuse of several elderly victims in her care. In scene after scene, she was shown pinching, hitting, withholding food, withholding pain medication, and even refusing access to the bathroom. The revolting examples went on and on.

"End," said the Reader, then, "Forty-one."

Down the 41st tube the abuser went, screeching like a hawk.

Next came the man who had passed out next to Ollie: a pot-bellied, grizzled sixty-something wearing a black sweatshirt. When he touched the reader's hand, the white wall lit up with video of him smacking around his small brunette wife. "Why do you make me do this?" the man was shouting. "Why?" Sobbing and helpless, his wife shook her head as the man grabbed a lamp from the table, lifted it high in the air above her, and brought it down with a mighty crash.

By the time Mr. Beer Belly went down his tube—number 17—Ollie was close to dry heaves.

"Next."

The guards grabbed Ollie and led him to the platform. Up close, the woman seemed even more otherworldly, as though she was only partially human. He was having trouble breathing. He wanted, more than anything, not to touch his palm against hers. But of course, he had no choice. Ollie lifted his arm, felt her bony hand against his, and waited with a stuttering heart.

The old woman pointed her other palm to the wall. She closed her eyes. Nothing happened.

She opened them again, looking at Ollie with suspicion. "Press harder," she said.

Ollie obliged. Still, nothing appeared on the wall. His legs jellied with relief. And then...a flicker. A movie began. Ollie, sitting across from Nell in a coffee shop. Though the film was black-and-white, her bruise was in color: violet and navy. It stained her cheek with an almost fluorescent glow. Ollie watched in horror, seeing himself look at the bruise, then look away. Sip his cappuccino. That scene morphed into another, in which Ollie asked about her wrist, got the answer about the dog leash, and asked no further questions. The next scene showed the two of them on the street. Nell telling Ollie how The Guy didn't want her hanging out with her friends anymore. How he kept track of her money and read her texts. Her eyes were darting, nervous. She looked pale. And Ollie, again, said nothing.

Breathless, Ollie slammed his eyes shut.

"End," the Reader said. She pulled her hand away as the room fell into momentary silence. Then she said, "Five."

"Wait, what?" Ollie yelped, opening his eyes. "No, you can't—"

The guards lifted him from the chair.

"Please, wait! I'm not that guy! Look at it again—the guy who was hurting her, that was her boyfriend. Not me! I'm not supposed to be here! This is all a big mistake! *Please!*"

The burly men ignored him. The wall and the holes got closer.

Ollie kept shouting: "You don't understand! I didn't do anything, I swear!"

The woman regarded him with an almost amused expression. "That is exactly right," she said. "You did nothing." She stood, stepped down from her platform, and glided across the floor in his direction. When she stopped, she was so close he could smell the mildewed crust of her skin.

"You don't understand! I'm not—"

"Evil cannot exist on its own," she interrupted calmly. "It requires a power source. In many cases, the power source is simply...nothing. Doing nothing. Saying nothing. Enabling. Implicitly agreeing by lack of action. All of these feed the abuse, empower it, embolden it. They make it monstrous, where it might have been meager. They make it live, and breathe, and thrive, and build in strength like a raincloud. And then, when the storm finally reaches you, you are confused. You ask: Why should I be tossed into the tempest? I am not to blame. I did nothing."

The Reader leaned closer. Her acrid breath fell hot on his cheek as she continued in a low, dangerous voice: "And you are correct. You did nothing. You were nothing. And so, that is how you shall remain, within these walls, until the end of your days. As nothing."

Hundreds of protests choked Ollie's throat as he stared at her, wild-eyed in terror.

"Only what you owe," the old woman said.

The guards repeated it in unison: "Only what you owe."

$\mathcal{T}$en

The Reader's words reverberated inside the tube as the guards pushed Ollie, face-first, into the hole marked with a number five. So, so small. He wouldn't fit. The claustrophobia came in a flood. But it was too late. He was already moving, speeding through the tiny tunnel in the endless dark, waiting for his oversized body to turn him into a human clog. And by the time he saw light ahead, he was already tumbling out. Landing, hard.

With a loud "oof," Ollie climbed to his knees. More stone floor. More scattered dirt.

Behind him, a panel slid across the hole, sealing it shut.

Ollie looked up to find himself in another cell, much smaller than the last. It had one small, barred window, a pit toilet, and a barrel filled with water. It also had beds. Sort of. They were more like burlap sacks stuffed with something lumpy and left on the floor, but Ollie wasn't feeling particularly choosy.

One of the beds was empty. The other was occupied by a lanky young man, who flashed Ollie a smile dotted with missing teeth.

"Howdy, Roomie," the man said. "Welcome to the fifth floor."

Ollie blinked at him, dazed. Then he stumbled to the closest stuffed sack, collapsed, and closed his eyes. *Sweet Jesus.*

"'Scuse the mess," his new cellmate drawled. "If I knew you was coming, I would've cleaned the place up." Then he chuckled at his own joke.

Curled into a fetal position, Ollie didn't reply. His elbows and knees had been battered by the bruising journey through the tube. He felt

85

cold, and clammy, and dizzy. If this had been a TV show, an EMT would be hovering over him, saying, "Get a blanket! He's in shock!" Whatever that meant. And in the next scene, he'd be huddled with a cup of hot chocolate in the back of an ambulance, sharing his harrowing tale. Cut to commercial.

This isn't happening. This isn't happening. This isn't happening.

"Might as well tell me your name," the man said.

Ollie said nothing; only squeezed his fists. Maybe, if he stayed that way long enough, all of this would disappear.

"Suit yourself. They call me Dozer, by the way. In case you was wondering." The man paused, then added: "No? Alrightee. Guess you won't be wanting none of this, then, neither."

Ollie cracked open an eye. The man was holding something that looked like beef jerky.

"Is that...?"

"They call it loosemeat. Don't know why." He shrugged. "Probably best not to know, that's my motto. Less questions you ask down here, the better. That's lesson numero uno for you. You're welcome." He chuckled again.

"Can I...?" Ollie seemed unable to finish a sentence.

"Have at it," Dozer said.

Like a pouncing cat, Ollie jumped up and grabbed the string of meat from the man's hand. He tore off a piece with his teeth, not caring what it tasted like. Not caring what kind of a creature it had come from. He swallowed and chomped again.

"Not bad, right?" the man asked.

Ollie nodded. It actually wasn't.

He studied his cellmate. The guy was ropy and firm, with the physique of a wrestler. He wore a brown jumpsuit draped with an odd collection of rags, most of which looked and smelled as though they had never been washed. He had dark skin, a dark beard, and dark eyes—well, one dark eye, at least. The other was covered with a piece of leather held in place with twine.

The man folded his arms and leaned back against the wall. "Whatever the old lady saw, it couldn't have been so bad if you ended up here. You got lucky, kid."

Ollie paused mid-chew, looking at his cellmate, and his cell, incredulously. "*Lucky?* I'm not even supposed to be here!"

"Me neither, friend. Me neither." The young man gave a shake of his head. "That there's the story of Floor Five."

"What do you mean?" Ollie asked.

86

"If the Reader don't see nothing too bad, she don't know what to do with us. So she sends us here."

Ollie coughed, choking on a chunk of meat. Once it had cleared his throat, he asked, "Where is...here?"

"Fifth floor is the Labor Force. In this shithole, that's like goddamn paradise." Dozer flashed more tooth gaps. His southern accent seemed to be getting thicker by the second. "Lots of folks wishing they could get down here."

Ollie gave another quick glance around the cell. *Wishing* to get here? Why would anyone possibly do that? "How long have you been here?"

"I was twenty-seven when I got grabbed up. But that was a long time ago."

Ollie's face betrayed his confusion. The man didn't look older than 24 or 25.

Dozer waved a hand. "Time moves different down here. Slower. You'll see. Something about the air, or the oxygen...it messes with you. Changes you. I mean, permanently changes you. Your body has to adapt. Lungs have to find a new way of working, or some such shit. And once it does—" He snapped his fingers. "That's it. No going back to the Brickside, for us. We're just fucked."

Ollie lowered the stick of meat. "The Brickside?"

"Yeah. You know, up there. Up above. The place you came from."

Ollie pictured, suddenly, the long line of red bricks that had led him here. The Freedom Trail. He tasted bile in the back of his throat.

"How long?" he asked quietly.

"How long, what?"

"How long until this place changes you?"

Dozer shrugged. "Few weeks? Not long. That's what they say, anyway. I wouldn't know. I've been stuck down here a hell of a lot longer than that." He pointed in Ollie's direction. "Won't matter much for you, neither. You're here, now. And once you're here, there ain't no leaving." At the sight of Ollie's stricken face, he added, "Hey, look on the bright side, mister guy-with-no-name. You'll keep those youthful looks of yours for a good, long time."

"Ollie."

The man raised an eyebrow.

"My name's Ollie."

Dozer grunted. "No, that won't work down here. You're gonna want something different. Something a little less...friendly."

Ollie slumped again on the sack.

Three weeks. Laszlo had told him that he had to get out, with or without Nell, in three weeks' time. And now Ollie knew why. If he stayed too long, his body would adapt to the strange atmosphere in this squalid, underground world—what had the purple-haired driver called it? The Neath?—and then he'd be stuck here. Permanently changed, permanently trapped. Forever.

"I'm in hell," he whispered, mostly to himself.

"Hell?" Dozer waved a hand and guffawed. "Uh, uh. Trust me, friend, this ain't hell." He rose to his feet. "Now *that,* on the other hand—" he pointed to the round window on the wall. "*That* is hell."

Finishing the last of the loosemeat, Ollie wiped his mouth with the back of his hand and stood. He walked to the small window and peered through the bars. He saw an empty courtyard, round, encircled by curved walls and irregularly shaped windows—hundreds of them, all overlooking the barren space. He craned his neck, then leaned closer, poking his face between the metal bars. Trying, and failing, to see the upper limits.

The courtyard, he figured, must be the center of the tower. And every window overlooking it probably led to a dank cell. Just like this one. No sunlight. No fresh air. Nothing but stone, and decay, and rank pestilence. And anger. Lots and lots of anger. He could feel it radiating like heat.

"Who's...out there?"

"Depends where you look," Dozer said, striding over to stand next to him. He pointed to the windows a few floors above. "Floors nine through thirty, those are your standard wife beaters. We got lots of those." He leaned forward and peered higher. "The pedophiles are above that. Then you've got your traffickers, child abusers, old-people abusers, rapists, hate crimes... Up and up and up. You get the idea. Something for everyone."

"So it's, like, some kind of underground prison?"

Dozer smiled ruefully. "If only. This ain't just about doing time. The whole point of this place is to stretch out the time. And to make the punishment real specific. *Real* specific. Eye-for-an-eye kind of shit, you know what I mean? The old lady, the Reader... She knows exactly what you did. *Exactly.* And that's exactly what you get back."

"I don't understand."

Dozer leaned a hand against one of the bars. "Let's say you liked to spend your days on the Brickside putting out cigarettes on your kid's arm. Guess what you get up on thirty-five?"

"Cigarette burns?"

"Think more along the lines of a blow torch, but yeah. You get the idea. Day, after day, after day."

"Only what you owe," Ollie muttered.

"Oh yeah. That there's their favorite line. Makes 'em feel good, I guess, about what they do. Makes 'em feel like God." He glowered, then straightened. "Anyhow, Floor Five ain't like that. Down here, it's just the Labor Force. No torture. So it's like I said, man. You got lucky."

Quite the ringing endorsement. Ollie could picture the ad: *Spacious room, furnished. View of courtyard. No torture.* He jammed his hands into his front pockets and set his mouth into a firm line. This place was no picnic, obviously. Still: Crumbling walls? Old ladies in robes? Sliding tubes straight out of a McDonald's playland? It wasn't exactly Alcatraz, either. There had to be a way out. There just had to be. And if there was, he would find it.

"What about you?" Ollie asked.

"What about me?"

"How did you end up in here?"

Dozer's face darkened. "Mistaken identity. Trumped-up. Whatever you want to call it."

"Framed?" Ollie asked.

"Where I'm from, they don't even bother with all that." He sighed and shook his head. "Some poor white girl got attacked. It was real bad. In my neck of the woods, that means it's time to play 'blame the black guy.' They found their man soon enough. I was pumping gas in the next town over. So I guess that was good enough for them."

"You got arrested? What about the evidence?"

The young man snorted. "Never even got that far. The girl's sisters knew about this place. As soon as I was a 'person of interest," they grabbed me up. Drugged me, too. Some big guy helped 'em drag me to some weird...hole thing, and...well, I guess you know the rest."

"They brought you all the way up to Boston?" Ollie asked, his brow furrowed.

"Nah, man. They got holes everywhere. All lead to the same damn place."

Ollie didn't know what to say.

"Don't get me wrong," Dozer added. "I was no angel up on the Brickside. None of us was, I suppose. But I didn't hurt that girl. I would never do something like that. The Reader knew it, too. She didn't see nothing too bad on that wall of hers, so I landed on Five." Dozer jerked his head to the right. "It's all the same kind of shit, up and down the hallway. Small mistakes. White collar, hand-slap kind of stuff. Stealing a pack of gum. Pyramid schemes. Wishing harm on your mother-in-law." He chuckled. "But nothing like them ones upstairs."

Ollie tugged absently on one of his dirty-blond curls. "And what if the Reader doesn't see anything at all? Does she let people go free?"

"Well, that there's the rub, ain't it?" Dozer said. "Everyone's got something to see. Even the best of us." He ran a tongue over his remaining teeth, making a sucking sound. "Don't worry none about all that. Keep your head down and you'll do just fine. And like I said, best not to be too curious. Just mind your business and count your blessings. Trust me, kid, it could have been a lot worse."

Count his blessings? Was this guy for real? Ollie turned to stare out into the empty courtyard. At the moment, his single blessing seemed to be the fact that he was not, apparently, sharing a cell with a serial killer. So at least there was that. *One,* he counted. *One blessing.* His chest constricted. His fingers trembled. And the bars on the window shimmered into a teary blur as he tried not to count all the unappreciated blessings he had so recklessly, so foolishly, left behind.

After his duties on the Herrick's End "Labor Force" became clear, Ollie wondered if torture might have been preferable.

He and twenty or so other laborers spent their days in brown jumpsuits, cleaning up after prisoners. Repulsive, filthy, seething prisoners. In the mornings, he emptied shit buckets into a chute. By midday, he was cleaning floors and walls. Until now, he'd had no idea the human body could create so many disgusting substances. He'd also had no idea that a person could spew those substances around a room in so many creative ways.

By afternoon, the group made it to the mossy-walled kitchen, where mountains of pots and pans awaited scraping. Then came the laundry. There were no set hours, or breaks: It took as long as it took. He and his fellow laborers ate whatever was handed to them, whenever it was offered. Which wasn't often. Most of the food was mysterious and bland; as long as it didn't smell rotten, Ollie ate it—though once it did smell rotten, and he ate it anyway.

Everywhere he went, every room he entered, Ollie had only two main objectives: survive; and search for an escape. He peered under doors, around corners, and at ceilings. He looked for knives, sticks, or anything that might be used as a weapon. He tried to analyze and memorize the convoluted layout of the cells and stairs and floors, but found the effort onerous. Traveling through the prison was like stepping inside of an Escher print: colorless, directionless, and totally devoid of logic.

The first two days passed in a robotic fog. His throat ached from the near-constant effort of trying to suppress his gag reflex. He kept his mind as blank as possible. Any thought, about anything, was too awful to bear. Instead, he learned to turn his actions into words, and repeat those words incessantly. He whispered "scrub, scrub, scrub" while scouring the floor, or "stack, stack, stack" while piling wooden trays. He counted his steps as he walked down the mildewed hallways. He counted torches as he passed them. He avoided everyone's eyes. He talked to no one, save Dozer, and even that was limited to a strange kind of grunted exhaustion.

It wasn't until the second night that Ollie learned about the fights. He was drifting off to sleep when he heard a roar; the sound made him jerk awake in a startled panic.

"Easy, there," Dozer said. "It's just the Knockdowns."

The roar he heard was cheering, Ollie realized. Cheering, in hell. Reluctantly, he rose from his burlap sack and walked to the small window. For the first time since he had arrived, the inner courtyard had a few people in it.

"The Knockdowns?"

"Just what it sounds like," said Dozer. "One by one by one." He lifted an index finger in the air, then let it topple.

Throughout the tower, prisoners had begun to poke their arms and faces out of the cell windows that overlooked the courtyard. Some were shouting. Some were banging mugs and bowls against the metal bars. Hundreds of eager, impatient spectators, all combining into a blur of mounting hysteria.

Ollie looked down again at the ragtag group on the ground. "Who are they?"

"The fighters? Just prisoners. Volunteers."

"But...why?"

Dozer shrugged. "Something to see. It keeps the yardbirds happy. And if you win..." His voice trailed off. "There's benefits."

"Like what?"

"Privileges. Extra food. Torture breaks. Even the possibility of parole, if you win enough times. Or at least that's what the Warden promises. Never seen him make good on it yet." As he spoke, Dozer's expression stayed curiously blank.

Ollie gave his cellmate a sideways glance, putting the pieces together. The eye patch. The missing teeth. "You did it? The fighting?" he asked.

Dozer shrugged. "While back, sure. I was fool enough to believe it might make things better for me in here."

"But it didn't?"

"No, sir, it did not," he said. "And as my momma always told me, there ain't no education in the second kick from a mule. So I cut my losses and got out while I still could. Some guys ain't been so lucky."

Ollie didn't even want to know what he meant by that.

They watched the evening's entertainment together, staring through the bars as the men and women down below pounded each other with merciless, frantic brutality. The winner of each matchup faced off against the other winners, bracket-style, until the group had been whittled down to one final survivor. Then, just when Ollie thought it was all over, another roar erupted. A large wooden door opened to reveal a hulking beast of a man; he had to be seven feet tall, and nearly as wide as the door he had walked through. He wore only cut-off pants and flat, tied-up sandals. His bulging, golden-brown chest was pockmarked with scars.

"Who is *that?*" Ollie asked.

Dozer leaned closer. "They call him The Mallet."

The Knockdown champion's reward for winning was, it seemed, another fight, this time with the giant. The two men battled with predictable results, leaving the smaller one to be dragged away—only partially alive, from the looks of it—to the sound of jeers. Then The Mallet lifted his arms, took in the admiration of the crowd, and made his triumphant exit.

When it was over, Ollie looked down at the mess the fighters had left behind: pools of blood; scattered clothing; and a hunk of something that looked like skin and muscle. He knew he'd probably be summoned to clean it all in the morning. If not tonight. *Please, God, not tonight.* Wearily, Ollie stumbled back to his burlap sack, curled onto his side, and fell into a restless, troubled sleep.

On the morning of his third day, Ollie and a few others were assigned to refresh the torchlights on one of the main thoroughfares. He'd been slowly getting to know some of his Floor Five labormates, as he'd come to think of them. Edouard, Alfred, and Martel traveled just ahead of him in the hallway—those three lived in the same cell and always seemed to be together outside of it, too. Along the opposite wall, Dozer walked behind Collins, a dude who had stood to inherit half of a crime-family fortune until his brother had conveniently shoved him underground and out of the picture, and Milowka, a white-haired car thief whose talents had landed her in hot water with the wrong sort of people. A lanky guy named Jumar meandered closer to the center of the hallway. Ollie didn't know much about him, yet, other than his propensity for inventing creative curse words.

The Labor Force's interactions were always supervised, which made chatting difficult. But Ollie was getting the feeling that the fifth-floor crew managed to look out for each other, nonetheless. The day before, he had seen Jumar help Milowka stack dishes on a tall shelf. The Edouard-Alfred-Martel trio had given Ollie welcoming nods; Martel had even slapped his back companionably when they passed each other in the kitchen. And just that morning, Collins had winked and slipped him a chewy, round disk that looked like cat food and tasted like a mint leaf. Ollie had no idea what he'd done to deserve that, but he was damn grateful.

Though none of them had been "angels" up on the Brickside, as Dozer had put it, their crimes had been minor. Hardly deserving of a lifetime of filthy servitude and torment. Ollie caught Milowka's gaze in the hallway and smiled; she stared back at him, her silver hair standing on its ends as though protesting its position on her scalp. Her eyes, on the other hand, looked dead.

Ollie sighed and continued on his way. With shuffling feet, he toted a can of kerosene and counted his steps as he followed the guard. *Sixty-six, sixty-seven, sixty-eight...* He had been wearing the same clothes since he arrived: jeans and a t-shirt, topped with the requisite brown jumpsuit. His underwear had developed a crunch that chafed his testicles, making him walk with a kind of crooked limp. The pain was pretty much constant, now. Pain, and gnawing hunger, and loneliness, and despair.

And it was only day three.

As always, his eyes scanned his surroundings for any potential weakness. Unlocked doors. Unguarded hallways. Ceiling vents. And as always, nothing presented itself. He was dipping the first torch into the fuel can when a shout pierced the hallway's silence.

"Move aside! Warden coming through!"

Startled, Ollie straightened. A nearby guard reached out an arm to slam him against the wall. Ollie froze in place. Across the hall, Dozer was also standing at attention.

The sound of skittering footsteps echoed in the tunneled-out hallway; quiet at first, then disconcertingly louder.

Another guard appeared. "Move aside! Warden coming through!"

The skittering sound amplified. Something about it made Ollie's skin crawl. Then the source of the noise appeared, and he knew why. It was children. A dozen of them, maybe. They formed a circle around a balding, smarmy-looking man, gangly as a scarecrow. He wore a well-cut suit in cool, slate gray. His face was clean-shaven. He looked untouched by the grime of his surroundings. Indeed, he looked untouched by anything at all.

Ollie recognized him immediately. Not him, personally, but his type. Ollie used to see guys like that at Bonfiglio's Caffe every day. They wandered over from the Financial District in packs, glancing impatiently at Ferragamo watches while hollering into their cell phones and snapping their fingers at the waitstaff. This Warden, Ollie could see, was just another smart, narcissistic overachiever. Probably cruel, too. Nothing special, or unexpected. No, it wasn't the man that made Ollie shiver.

It was the children.

They moved like a school of fish, adjusting their own strides to maintain an unbroken circle around him as he traveled. The kids varied in ethnicity and gender, though most seemed to be about seven or eight years old. Their eyeballs were so clouded that Ollie wondered how they could possibly see, yet they all seemed to maneuver quite well. Almost too well. They mirrored the Warden's movements without touching him, or the walls, or any obstacles in their way.

As they got closer, Ollie could hear them making clicking sounds with their mouths. Like bats in a cave. Weirder still, he could swear that the children seemed to be emitting a yellowish, murky glow. The fog surrounded each of them, ultimately encasing the Warden in an un-broken ring of...what exactly? And what was wrong with their eyes? Why did they look like they had cataracts? Were they protecting him? Was this grown man using children as his bodyguards?

Ollie's fellow laborers struggled to reposition themselves and make room for the ring of children to pass. But Jumar, who had been closer to the center of the hallway, couldn't move quickly enough. The yellow fog floated over his arm as the odd little group glided by, leaving him to scream and fall to the ground. It wasn't until the Warden and children had walked past that Ollie saw what had happened: Jumar's arm was gone, reduced to red jelly on the ground.

Ollie gasped and stepped forward to help him. Then he caught his cellmate's eye: Dozer was staring at him and shaking his head warningly. Ollie paused, confused. The nearby guard yanked his shirt.

"Back to it," the guard said, shoving Ollie in the direction of the kerosene.

With a trembling hand, he reached for a torch, and the fuel. He squeezed his eyes shut, then, with difficulty, forced them back open and started counting anything he could see: the pebbles on the ground; the lines on his knuckles; the number of times the torchlight flickered. *Thirty-one, thirty-two, thirty-three...* Ollie willed his body to keep moving, to keep functioning. He tried to forget the Warden and the blind mutant children. He tried to forget the Knockdown contests, the long sleepless nights, and the stench of his own, filthy body. Most of all, he tried to ignore Jumar's wails of agony as the guards picked him up, tossed him into a wheelbarrow, and carted him away.

I'm going to die in this place.

He hadn't believed it until that moment. And when the truth landed, it hit with a sudden, thundering wallop: Ollie had been clinging to a mirage. He had been crawling around on his hands and knees, stinking of puke and kerosene, gagging on mystery meat and sawdust, thinking it would all end soon. He had been hanging his hopes on some fool notion of "fairness:" He would find a way out, because he deserved to find a way out. Or, barring that, the Reader would reappear, recognize his innocence, and set him free. Or maybe Ollie would somehow work his way into freedom. Parole. Justice. Whatever.

It wasn't until he watched a gaseous fog sever an innocent man's arm for no particular reason that Ollie realized: There was no fairness here. There was no justice. Those were quaint, forgotten notions. Brickside notions. And he wasn't on the Brickside anymore.

He would die here, surrounded on all sides by evil and feculence and gloom. And when he did, they'd toss his body into the green lake and let his bones sink to the bottom. He'd never be buried beside his mother. Mr. Bonfiglio and the neighborhood old-timers and his LT friends would wonder, but never know, what had happened to him.

What have I done? Even unspoken, it pierced like a wail. *Dear God, what have I done?*

Ollie had watched his last sunrise, patted his last puppy. He'd never use his scholarship. He'd never play another video game, or fall in love, or make a snowball, or watch the pigeons strut through the Prado. He'd never eat biscotti again. Not even the shitty kind, with cranberries and white chocolate.

Instead, he was scurrying through dark hallways like a sewer rat, choking on fumes and cleaning fluids. Aching in constant pain. Cursed.

Ollie balled his fists and shook his head, hard. He needed to stop thinking. Thinking only made things worse. He needed to focus on the task at hand. Tears ran in rivers down his cheeks as the mantras spun in endless, delusional loops: *Dip, dip, dip. Light, light, light.* After the torches came the mopping. *Splat, splat, splat.* Then the dishes, then the laundry. Thousands of steps through dim, oppressive tunnels. *Two hundred and ninety-two, two hundred and ninety-three, two hundred and ninety-four.*

Ollie thought about his old fitness tracker, now long gone, and grimaced at the irony. How about that: After so many years of trying, he'd finally stumbled across the most effective weight-loss program in the world. Well, in this world, anyway. Before long, he'd have washboard abs, rock-hard pecs, rickets, and probably an intestinal parasite or two. No meetings necessary. No app.

Be careful what you wish for, he thought. Ollie could already feel his sanity oozing, dripping, like a half-browned marshmallow in a s'more. He would lose weight, and then he would lose his mind. Or maybe vice versa. And absolutely no one would care.

Eleven

The next morning, Ollie woke to a kick in the ribs.

"Up, both of you," a female guard growled. "Clean-up needed in the office."

Ollie rolled over, confused and groggy, in his burlap sack. The guard was already gone.

"Shee-it," Dozer drawled from across the room.

"What's she talking about?" Ollie asked, rubbing his eyes. "What office?"

"*The* office," Dozer said with a groan. "There's only one."

"What does that mean?"

"It means, put on your best duds, bud. We're going to see the Warden."

Ollie felt a chill run up his back, remembering the oily man, the circle of children, the deadly yellow fog. The Warden was clearly a man best avoided. Marching straight into his office, wherever that was, seemed like a colossally bad idea.

"Does it have to be us?" Ollie asked.

Dozer flashed him an incredulous look and didn't bother to answer.

The two men slipped on their jumpsuits and headed into the hallway, where a different grouchy guard was waiting with a mountain of cleaning supplies for the unspecified task ahead. Ollie and Dozer gathered up the various brushes, mops, and liquids and began to follow him through the maze of hallways.

Four days, Ollie thought to himself. Four on the Labor Force, plus one in the holding cell on his first day. If Laszlo had been right, that meant he was five days down on a three-week deadline. *Sixteen days left.*

The guard was twenty or thirty steps ahead. Out of earshot. Ollie leaned to his left, lowered his voice, and asked: "So what's the deal with the Warden?"

Dozer's eyes darted to the guard's back. "What do you mean?"

"He runs the place, right? How'd that happen?"

His cellmate answered quietly, "All's I know is, they say he was a prisoner once. There was some kind of a risin' up. Riots, and stuff. Like a..." He paused, searching for the word.

"A mutiny?" Ollie supplied.

"Yeah. He started a mutiny, like on a ship, and he killed the guy in charge. Then he became the guy in charge. End of story."

"A long time ago?"

Dozer shrugged. "Before my time."

Ollie digested this information as they turned left. The red-suited guard remained well in the distance. "And what's with the kids? In the circle?"

Dozer glanced over his shoulder before answering. "Hollowskin juice, they call it."

Ollie's eyes widened.

"He keeps the kids hopped up on the stuff." Dozer's voice was so low Ollie had to strain to hear it. "It turns them into weapons. To protect him. Word is, he thinks someone else is gonna do the same thing that he did. Try to take over, I mean. So, he keeps them around him all the time. Anybody comes close, and it's—" He sliced his neck with a finger.

"But...whose kids are they?"

Dozer shrugged. "Don't know. His, maybe."

Ollie shuddered. He thought of several possibilities, none of them good. He had seen female inmates at Herrick's End, of course. Maybe—

"Let's go," the guard barked from up ahead. "Move it."

Ollie was glad for the interruption. He didn't want to think about the children anymore. He didn't want to imagine where they had come from, or what their futures held.

Ahead of them, the carved-out path widened and branched into a fork. As they followed to the left, he twisted his neck and peered down to the right. The road not taken. That hallway was unusually dark, with no torches whatsoever. After twenty feet or so, it vanished into pure blackness. A heavy, wrought-iron gate blocked the entrance, reminding Ollie of the menacing fence at the Granary Burying Ground, back in what he now thought of as the Brickside. He felt, suddenly, like he was walking along a demented, backwards version of the Freedom Trail, gawking at the sites like tourist.

"What's down there?" he whispered, pointing into the dark space beyond the gate.

Dozer gave it a quick glance. "Off-limits."

That much, Ollie could see. "Why?"

"That's Solitary. Nowhere you want to be, trust me. *Top-level inmates*," he added, giving the last words an ominous emphasis.

Ollie stared at him. The answer struck him as absurd. "What do you mean, top-level? This whole damn place is top-level!"

"You'd be surprised," Dozer said, hoisting the bag onto his shoulder. "In this place, there's one crime worse than all the rest."

"Oh yeah? What's that?"

Dozer stopped walking and turned to face him. "Pissing off the Warden," he said. "Remember that, kid. Once you get on that man's bad side, it don't matter none if you're a murderer or just a pickpocket." He shook his head. "If you get lucky, he just kills you. But if you really dill his pickle..." Dozer's gaze traveled back to the dark, nameless corridor. "Well, let's just say I ain't fixin' to find out, and neither should you. Got it?"

"Got it."

"Good. Now keep your head down and your mouth shut."

"Right," Ollie said. It was the same advice the purple-haired girl, Tera, had given him, back in the boat. Suddenly, he pictured them clearly: The girl with the toolbelt. The giant crow with the ridiculous name. The two of them were probably boating around the lake that very second, sharing a good laugh at his expense.

"You come up with a new name yet?" Dozer asked.

"What?"

"A new name. I told you, that one ain't gonna fly in here."

"Oh, right. No, I...didn't."

Dozer grunted. "I'll come up with something," he said.

I won't be here long enough to need a new name, Ollie wanted to say, but found the words stuck in his throat.

They stayed quiet after that, struggling with the armfuls of supplies as they traveled. The walk seemed endless: up and down stairs, around corners, through narrow and broad passageways. At one point during the journey, they stepped aside to let a group of five pass: two red-suited guards in the front, two in the back, and, in the middle, an enormous man that Ollie recognized as The Mallet. The Knockdown fighter was walking with a shuffled gait, his wrists and ankles shackled.

"Move aside!" one of the guards shouted unnecessarily, as Ollie and Dozer were already flattened against the wall.

The guards were leading The Mallet into a nearby room; it was well-lit and over-stuffed with boxes, paper bags, and rolls of something that looked like thick, colored tape.

"That there's medical," Dozer murmured.

Ollie nodded, trying to not to stare. It was so rare for him to come across someone taller and bigger than he was. So strange. But this man was truly a giant. He wore strapped sandals, short-shorts, and a stretched white tank, none of which even began to cover his girth. The hard, muscled flesh bulged and popped, as though his entire body had been created by a balloon-twisting clown. His skin had the tawny glow of a Pacific Islander.

For one fleeting, brave second, Ollie caught The Mallet's eye. The two men stared at each other in the dark, crowded hallway. And then, just as abruptly, the connection was severed. The Mallet's guards led him into the medical room, and Ollie and Dozer's guard led them back into the tunnels.

As he left, Ollie turned for one last look. He watched the giant man hunch and struggle to fit through the tiny doorway, and then, moments later, disappear.

The Infirmary. *Another stop on the Unfreedom Trail,* Ollie thought. *Please don't forget to tip your driver.* He furrowed his brow. His brief encounter with The Mallet had left him feeling heavier, somehow, as though he had arrived empty-handed and left with the weight of something he didn't understand.

Finally, they rounded a bend and Ollie knew, without question, that this had to be the place. It was a dead end: A smallish cavern complete with its own island and, if he wasn't mistaken, an actual moat. The island supported an octagonal-shaped building with no windows and a low roof.

As they got closer, Ollie could see that the water in the moat flowed in a strong, circular current. There was no way across. And on the island, standing like statues at perfectly measured intervals, he saw the children. They stared straight ahead, unseeing, all connected by a thread of lethal, golden fog.

Hollowskin juice, Ollie thought, and then felt himself shiver.

Ollie's guard shared a hand signal with another on the island. A long plank began to rise out of the moat and Ollie realized, after a startled moment, that it was a bridge. The guard stepped onto the plank and began the crossing.

Ollie looked at Dozer questioningly. The lanky man adjusted his eyepatch and motioned with his arm: *Go!* So, Ollie scurried onto the thick plank of wet wood, toting the mop and bucket and bottles, trying not to fall into the churning water that lapped at his feet.

Thirty seconds later, all three of them were across.

"This way," muttered the guard. Though he was using his usual gruff tone, Ollie could swear he heard a note of something else in the man's voice. Was it fear?

Two of the zombified children blocked the door. At a quiet word from the on-site guards, the boy and girl slid to the side, bringing their gaseous entrails with them. The door opened, and Ollie's guard shoved a nearby wheelbarrow at them and pointed at the doorway. He, apparently, wasn't going in.

All rightee, then. Ollie threw his tools inside the wheelbarrow, cast an apprehensive glance at Dozer, and stepped inside.

He didn't know what he was expecting. Bubbling cauldrons, maybe? A howling pit of hideous beasts? What he saw, though, was...an office. A perfectly ordinary, executive-style office, complete with a wide desk, several chairs, a bookshelf, and even a small wastebasket. The furniture was rudimentary, but symmetrical. Clean lines. Wood and hammered metal.

IKEA for Dungeons, Ollie thought.

He also noticed the smell of cologne in the air, and the claustrophobically low ceiling. Primarily, though, he noticed the body. It lay in a crumpled pile on the floor, mangled and bloody and very, very dead.

The Warden, on the other hand, didn't seem to notice the body at all. Or the cleaning crew's entrance. He had his feet propped up on his desk, smiling evenly at a short, plump man who sat facing him. The visitor was trembling. A river of blood from the body had traveled across the wood floor, almost reaching the terrified man's feet.

For a moment, Ollie didn't move. Couldn't move. Then Dozer tugged on his sleeve. Silently, the two of them moved toward the body and began unloading their supplies.

The Warden ignored them. "Axel, was it?" he asked his visitor.

The plump man nodded. It was more of an involuntary tremor than an agreement.

"Welcome, Axel." The Warden's smile was ingratiating. "Tell me, do you also have some concerns about the comfort of your stay here at Herrick's End?"

The man shook his head, hard. He seemed unable to speak.

"Are you quite sure?" the Warden asked, looking puzzled. "I was told you've been voicing some very strong opinions on the subject. Like your friend Rocco, here." He nodded casually at the twisted body on the floor.

"N-n-no, sir," the man managed. "No concerns."

"Ah, well, that is very good to hear," the Warden replied, leaning backwards in his chair and pressing his fingers together. He wore a bespoke gray suit and a red silk tie. "Very good. We want all of our guests to have a satisfactory experience. Don't we, Rocco?" He looked down at the body, still smiling.

Ollie had been watching the chilling interaction from the corner of his eye. But when the Warden glanced in his direction, he turned his full attention back to the task at hand: lifting the feet—Rocco's feet—while Dozer lifted the shoulders. Together, they placed the body in the wheelbarrow, folding it in half to make it fit. Then Ollie fell back onto his knees and began sopping up the puddle left behind.

"Can I trust, Axel, that you will continue to have no concerns?"

Axel nodded again; a rapid, insistent bob. His curly hair bounced with the motion.

"Because I would hate to learn, sometime in the future, that you have been expressing displeasure about any aspect of our fine establishment."

"No, sir."

"If that happens, we will have to have this conversation again. And I don't want to have this conversation again. Do you, Axel?"

"N-no, sir."

"Hmm. Rocco said the exact same thing, as I recall. And yet here we are." The Warden heaved a deep, regretful sigh. "I'll tell you what. I'm going to give you a unique opportunity to show me that you're serious about your promise."

Ollie lifted a blood-soaked towel and threw it into the wheelbarrow on top of the body. Dozer opened the liquid cleaner and poured it onto the still-stained wood floor. Together, they scrubbed in silence.

"When you sign this contract, you will demonstrate your commitment to me," the Warden said, waving a piece of paper in the air. "The contract states that you are willing and happy to volunteer in our noble Knockdown competition. It's quite an honor to be asked, Axel. Quite an honor. Are you up for the challenge?"

The pudgy man's trembling grew stronger, like a chihuahua in a pet-store cage. "I-I'm not much of a fighter, Sir."

"Ah, come now, my friend," the Warden said, tapping a folder on the desk. "Your file says otherwise."

"But that was... that's..."

"True, you only fought people who were smaller and weaker than yourself," the Warden interrupted. "Children, was it?" He opened the folder and pretended to read. "Ah, yes, children. And I suppose you weren't fighting them so much as..." His voice trailed away as he tossed the folder back onto the desk. "No matter. You're here now, and you have a choice to make. So what will it be, my friend?"

The Warden grinned as he waited. He was slick, clean, and trim—almost beautiful. His skin was flawless in the torchlight. His teeth were large and bright. He had the kind of face that got the girl, and the promotion, and pretty much whatever else he wanted. Back in Ollie's world, he might have been a sleazy politician. Or an ambulance-chasing lawyer. Or a model, grinning down from a billboard along I-93, selling watches or donuts or car insurance. The specifics didn't really matter. The suits changed, but the vermin underneath stayed the same.

Axel signed the paper.

"Wonderful," the Warden purred. "I think we shall call you...The Axe Man."

Ollie and Dozer had finished their clean-up. Ollie stood, reached for the handles of the wheelbarrow, and pushed it toward the door. The body was heavy, but Ollie, of course, was heavier. The Warden had not acknowledged their coming or their going; they were invisible to him. Ghosts in the background. The Help.

Ollie could smell the victim's congealing blood, metallic and sweet. He ignored the stench and kept his head down. He didn't have a choice. No one had choices here: not Ollie, not Axel the Axe Man, and certainly not the poor guy folded inside the wheelbarrow like a pie crust. No one, that is, except the Warden. The one wearing the smirk. The one with all the authority and control, deserved or not, earned or not, making everyone else dance to his demented tune.

Ollie knew that song. He had danced that dance. And as he stole one last look at the smug and satisfied man behind the desk, he wondered: Why did power always seem to find the ones who deserved it the least? In that way, he knew, this mystifying, magical, upside-down world was not so different from the one above it.

———————⌒⌒⌒———————

Once they disposed of the body—unceremoniously, down a dusty chute—Ollie and Dozer moved on to their other thankless tasks of the day. First kitchen, then laundry, then cell maintenance on floors nine-through-thirty.

These were known in-house as the "wife-beater floors." If Ollie was lucky, the inmates were out for daily exercise, torture sessions, or mealtime when he arrived. If not, he had to sidestep temperamentally challenged men and women of varying sizes while trying to clean their detritus and empty their piss buckets. In the previous days, he had only gotten as far as Floor Twelve. Today, they started him at Seventeen. By the time he got to Twenty, Ollie felt like a beaten-down gorilla, hunched and dragging his knuckles on the ground.

Cell 20C: Three men, all angry.

Cell 20D: Two men, one sleeping. The other stared out the barred window, singing in a language that might have been Chinese.

Cell 20E: Blessedly empty.

Cell 20F: Two women, hissing. One spitting.

The next cell, 20G, held only one man, sitting on the floor with his back against the wall.

Ollie stood in the doorway and did his usual risk-analysis scan before entering. Nothing hanging from the ceiling. No one hiding in a corner with a maniacal grin, coiled up and ready to pounce. No sharp objects aimed in his direction. Check, check, and check. It was just the one guy on the ground. Sitting perfectly still.

Too still?

Ollie's gaze fell again on the seated prisoner. Goosebumps tickled his arms. Even in a place like this, where everything felt wrong, all of the time, something here felt...even more wrong than usual. What was it about that man? That inert, unfamiliar but somehow familiar man? Why did just the sight of him make Ollie feel like he was about to swallow a scream? He tilted his head to the side, taking a few more steps into the cell. Then his chest tightened suddenly, inexplicably, as a flood of memories crackled his mind with kaleidoscopic confusion.

Spaghetti, splattered against the wall.

Crowded subway car on the Green Line, holding a big hand. Looking up at a crush of adults.

Acqua di Gio. Cigars. Stale beer.

The wash bucket slipped from his hands, hit the ground, and toppled. Sudsy, brown water pooled around the soles of Ollie's shoes. He stepped forward, then forward again, leaving wet footprints as he walked. His breath returned to him in short, pained gasps.

More memories flashed.

Electric guitar and drums, thumping the stereo. Making the ice jump in his glass.

His mother, leading him inside a closet. Pressing a finger to her lips. Closing the door.

Muffled thumps.

Sobbing, shouting. More thumps. Afraid to leave the closet. Afraid to stay.

Ollie fell to his knees, staring into the prisoner's face.

The man had a prominent nose, bent from injury. A cauliflower ear on one side. Squinty, blank eyes. Pale skin pockmarked with imperfections. His lips, though limp, seemed curled into a perpetual scowl. Drool dribbled from his mouth.

Ollie stared and stared until his eyeballs felt dry from the effort. His fingers had gone cold. The man was stooped and frail. He was older. Almost unrecognizable.

Almost.

When Ollie finally spoke the word, it came out in an incredulous whisper: "Papa?"

His father did not respond.

Ollie lay his hands flat on the floor as the room spun around him. This wasn't possible. It just wasn't possible.

"Papa?" he said again, his voice rising. "Wake up!"

He shook his father's shoulders. The man's head bobbled like a doll. His hands were curled into fists, knuckled by arthritis. If he heard Ollie, or recognized him, he gave no sign.

"It's me! It's Ollie!"

But he could see already—it was no use. His father's eyes, faded and pale blue, had turned in his direction, but saw nothing. Alzheimer's? Delirium? Mental break?

Ollie shook him. Slapped him. "Wake up, you son of a bitch! Wake up!"

"Hey!" barked a voice from the doorway.

Ollie looked up, startled. He was holding his father's jumpsuit by the collar.

"Step back from the prisoner," the guard ordered.

"But he's...he's my..." Ollie stammered. Turmoil clouded his vision.

"Step back," the guard repeated. This time, it sounded more like a threat. Another red-suited man appeared, then another.

Shaking, he dropped his father's collar and stumbled backward. He peered deep into the old man's eyes, searching for any sign of life, of recognition, of...anything. All he saw was cold, clear blue.

"Get him down to Five," the guard growled, and Ollie felt a rough yank on his arms. There was no time for goodbyes, or good riddances, as they dragged him from the room.

Ollie half-walked, half-stumbled down 15 flights of winding stairs. With each turn, he could feel his confusion transforming into sickening clarity. And by the time he reached his own cell, shoved inside by two sets of meaty hands, Ollie's newfound comprehension had already morphed into something else. Something that felt an awful lot like white-hot, boiling rage.

Twelve

Ollie's anger was a faceless glob, spreading in every conceivable direction. It came as an almost welcome jolt, like biting into a cinnamon Atomic Fireball and feeling the heat all the way down to your toes.

Every moment he had tried to suppress, every ounce of fury he had tried to deny—all of it rained down in a sudden, thundering hailstorm. The indignities. The fear. The fists. The insults. The cowering. His mother had shielded him, protected him, used her own body like a crash-test dummy. And then, when even that was not enough, she had taken matters into her own hands.

Francie had sent his father here, to Herrick's End, to keep them safe. And to make him pay what he owed.

Ollie saw the truth, finally, and every damn thing about it sucked. On the one hand, his mom had lied to him. She had made him believe that his father had abandoned them. On the other hand, what choice did she have? Francie could have run, he supposed. But she would never have left Ollie behind. And even if they had both left, it would have done no good. His father would have found them. And the only thing more dangerous than making Matteo Delgato mad was making him look like a fool.

Ollie paced the cell, trying to remember that day. The day his father had "disappeared." There was, supposedly, a booze-cruise. An accident of some kind, dutifully reported to the police. Ollie vaguely recalled being sent to stay with a neighbor, though he hadn't been told why. He had stayed there for days while his mother was gone. He had assumed, in his little-boy way, that she was off taking care of grown-up things. Money things, maybe.

But now he knew what she had really been doing. Visiting the WRC. Getting help from someone like Laszlo. The Freedom Trail. The wheelbarrow. The rope. The speeding chairlift. Standing in line. Escaping the Neath and leaving his father behind. It was the big regret he had overheard her talking about. The reason she had said she needed to "do penance," and why she had thought she deserved her cancer.

Whatever I did, I did for you, his mother had told him. She had wanted to protect her son. She had made the only decision she thought she could, and then lived with the consequences. Though not for very long.

Maybe the guilt really *had* given her cancer. And since she had done it for Ollie, maybe that meant the cancer was his fault, too.

Ollie marched across the cell and clung to the metal bars in the window, squeezing until his knuckles turned white. "FUUUCK!" he screamed.

Fuck his father, and these bars, and the fucking cancer, and this fucking cell, and the filth, and the hunger, and the exhaustion, and the stupid fucking decisions that had landed him here in the first place. Fuck whoever had built this fortress of revenge. And fuck everyone who had ever done anything bad enough to deserve a spot inside.

He fell to his knees as the sobs choked him.

Somewhere up above, other inmates heard his wail and reacted, shouting their own obscenities and jeers into the stale courtyard air.

Ollie looked down at his fingers, already calloused and chafed. Was it really just a week ago that these same fingers had been tying strings into bows on bakery boxes? And swirling hearts into the foam on Mrs. Giovanni's morning latte? His stomach clenched. God almighty, he missed ravioli. He missed violets in clay pots. And Freddie Maggione's wheezy pug, Betty Boop, waddling down the sidewalk, sniffing every pole. Ollie even missed the sailboat-shaped water stain on his apartment ceiling, and the weird groaning noise the pipes made during the winter. Fleece blankets. Fresh-squeezed lemons. Autumn leaves.

The homesickness and grief buckled him like a burst appendix, sudden and agonizing.

Whimpering, Ollie curled into a fetal position, resting his cheek on the grainy dirt floor. He stayed like that, paralyzed, for what must have been several hours. Then, finally, he heard the cell door open.

"There you are," Dozer said, sounding relieved as the door slammed shut behind him. "Where'd you—"

Ollie jumped to his feet, interrupting. "I have to get out of here."

"What?"

"I have to. There has to be a way out."

Dozer shook his head. "Kid, I told you. Ain't no way. If there was, don't you think I would've done it by now?"

But there had to be. Furious desperation had filled his entire chest cavity and was threatening to blow. This couldn't be the end. He would not wind up like his father, wasted and alone. There was so much more he had to do. He was only nineteen, for Christ's sake! Nineteen, with a job, and a studio apartment, and good luck at Bingo, and a full scholarship—all just waiting for him to return. He was on the cusp of a better life, an awesome life. He'd get a career, a *real* career, and someone to love him. They'd take couples' vacations together. Beach vacations. No, mountain vacations. And they'd get a car. He'd always wanted a Mustang. Black. No, silver. A silver Mustang with leather seats and a cup holder big enough to hold a 32-ounce Slurpee.

Impatience and frustration mingled together in Ollie's gut, leaving him feeling like he might retch. There was no question in his mind: He *would* get out. He had to. But the question was, could he do it in time?

"This...lung thing," he said, hearing the desperation in his voice. "The breathing thing. You're sure it's three weeks? After that, you can't go back to the Brickside?"

Dozer collapsed onto his burlap sack bed. "Sure? No. I ain't sure of nothing. All I know is what I hear. But yeah, that's what they say. About three weeks. Longer for some people, shorter for others. I've heard of some people lasting months, but that's..." His sentence trailed off as his expression turned serious. "Look, kid, it don't matter about how many days. The truth is, your clock ran down the minute you got in here, understand? I know it ain't what you want to hear. But the sooner you accept it, the better off you'll be."

"But—"

"No buts," Dozer interrupted, sounding like every stern schoolteacher Ollie had ever known. "Boy, I swear, sometimes your porch light ain't on all the way. I'm trying to tell you something, here. You need to forget all that. In this place, the wrong kind of hope will only get you killed. You feelin' me?"

Ollie nodded, dazed.

Dozer flashed him a sympathetic look. "Knockdown's starting soon," he said, pointing toward the round window. "How's about we watch?"

"Nah," Ollie replied. He never had the stomach to watch the inmates pummel each other, but tonight the thought seemed particularly revolting. He stood up, trudged to his own sleeping sack, and lay back down in pretty much the same position he'd been curled up in all afternoon. Staring at the wall.

"Hey, Dozer," he said.

"Yeah?"

"Thanks."

Silence followed.

Then Dozer said, gruffly, "Ain't nothing. Get some sleep."

But it was something, of course. Dozer's friendship, such as it was, was pretty much all Ollie had. Maybe for the rest of his life.

He closed his eyes and thought of his dad's hollow, blank face: Seeing nothing, hearing nothing, knowing nothing. Maybe, in the end, there really was only one escape from this place. And his father had already found it.

Ollie fell asleep to the sound of cheers and screams in the Courtyard. The chaos followed him into his dreams. By the time the squeal of the cell door woke him the next morning, he felt almost paralyzed with hopelessness.

Day six, he thought. Nearly one week, lost. And he was no closer to finding a way out.

The hours passed in their usual, dismal way. Dirty dishes. Dirty clothes. Dirty surfaces, everywhere. And it was all made worse, somehow, by the knowledge that his own father was sitting, drooling, somewhere nearby. Ollie kept his head down, repeated his mantras, and, as always, searched for anything that might lead to an escape.

Finally, the time came to fill the water buckets. Though Ollie didn't like the chore, exactly, he might describe it as his least loathed part of the day. The job involved carrying empty buckets outside to the water trough, filling them, and then lugging them back upstairs to the various floors. It was hard, heavy work, but it was significantly less gross than most of his other duties. And it at least allowed him a few blissful moments outside the prison walls.

Ollie pushed open the wooden exit door and paused for a moment, breathing in the air. No one would call it fresh. Rusty pipes still belched orange smog, and an unpleasant sharpness permeated his eyes and lungs. Still, it didn't smell like sweat or human excrement, and that alone made it sweeter than syrup.

Outside. This was the closest he'd get to freedom. Ollie looked to his left, where a red-suited guard leaned against the brick wall. Just one guard. But the guy was beefy, with one of those zapper things hanging from his belt, and he was watching Ollie with a stare that said, *Just try it, kid.* With a sigh, Ollie kept moving.

He approached the trough, which was long and low and filled to the brim with relatively clear water. He had to fight the urge to jump in; the idea of submerging himself, of washing his rancid, crusty skin, was almost more than he could resist.

Instead, he dunked one of the buckets deeper than was necessary, letting his hand linger for a moment in the cool liquid. The pain relief was so startling, so blissful, that he didn't immediately react to the noise coming from the ground near his feet. A "psssst" sound.

Ollie looked down. He saw...a girl. A teenage girl, with a swooping purple mohawk. She was holding a finger in front of her lips. Telling him to stay quiet.

His eyes widened. It was the boat captain, he realized with a start. The same girl who had dropped him off six days before.

Tera.

"What are you—"

She shushed him again. Then she said, "Get down here."

"What?"

"Get down here!"

Ollie looked left and right. Then, perplexed, he dropped to the ground, joining her behind the trough.

"Put this on," the girl whispered. She was holding out a red jumpsuit. A guard's jumpsuit.

For a moment, Ollie didn't move.

"Do you want to get out of here or not?"

He nodded. Of course, he did. He had never wanted anything more.

"Then put this on. Just pull it over the brown one. Hurry up."

Ollie squirmed on the ground, shoving his legs and arms into the openings. The suit was, amazingly, large enough to accommodate his body as well as the brown jumpsuit he was already wearing, plus the jeans and t-shirt below that. Finally, he zipped it up to his chin.

Tera glanced at him, seemed satisfied, and climbed up into a squat. "Okay. You ready? We're going to have to move fast. Just stay with me."

"Wait, what? But—"

"But what?"

"My...cellmate," Ollie said. "He's still in there."

She held up her palms.

"I have to get him out, too."

"Sorry, dude. The arrangement was only for you."

What arrangement? he wanted to ask.

"We've got to move. Now."

Ollie looked up at the looming, dilapidated tower.

"Well?" she asked. "What's it gonna be?"

Stupefied, he rose onto his knees and held onto the side of the trough; everything was spinning.

"All right, then. Ready?" She rose in slow motion, craning her neck up and around. "Now! Move!"

Tera jumped up, and Ollie followed. Was this really happening? Was he really getting out? Before he had time to process it, they had rounded the corner and walked smack into the waiting guard. Ollie's stomach dropped. It was all over. He waited for the guard to zap them both. To call for backup.

But the guard did neither of those things. Instead, he held out a palm. Tera, for her part, did not seem surprised to see him. She reached into her pocket and pulled out a thick stack of colored paper. It looked more or less like the same wad of "money" that Ollie had paid her a few days before. She dropped the entire stack into the guard's hand. He grunted, closing his fingers around the cash. Then he waved them along.

She pulled Ollie into the shadows, and they ran.

Thirteen

"Keep your head down."

Ollie and Tera crouched in a shadowy clump of stalagmites. To their left, two guards sauntered along the shoreline. They didn't appear to be looking for a prisoner, or even aware that one was missing. When they disappeared around the bend, she jumped up.

"Now. Let's go."

He followed her, again. He would have followed her anywhere, this compact, mysterious, rescuing angel. He wondered, not the first time, if she was real. Was he back in his cell, dreaming? Had he fallen into the water trough and hit his head?

"Over here."

Tera climbed down a small ledge that was bathed in darkness. Ollie tried to do the same, but couldn't see the ground well enough to master his footing. He stumbled, scratched his hands and arms on the calcified surfaces, and then climbed back to his feet. When he stood, he saw a boat tied onto a stake on the shore. A familiar giant crow sat in the back, watching their approach with wary, onyx eyes. Mrs. Paget.

"Quiet," Tera warned. Ollie thought she was talking to him, then realized that she was pointing a finger at the bird, which had begun to open its beak and lift its wings. "Shut up. I mean it. I don't want to hear it."

The wings dropped; the beak snapped shut. Ollie had not thought it was possible for an animal to look quite so...resentful. He also had not thought it was possible that he would someday feel the need to apologize to an eight-foot, pissed-off crow.

"C'mon, get in," she said, unwrapping the rope from the stake. That time, she was talking to him. Ollie needed no prodding; he jumped from shore to boat without hesitation. Tera followed. She climbed onto the back of the crow and whispered something in its ear. The bird puffed its feathers before lifting two huge, black wings into the murky air. With a mighty flap, they were off.

Ollie felt the wind on his face and gasped at the suddenness of it, at the freedom. Had they done it? Had they really done it? He dared to turn and look at the tower, now retreating into the pumpkin-colored fog. It looked much the same as it had the first time he saw it: still tilted precipitously, still emanating an almost audible hum of evil. As the boat sped away, Herrick's End grew smaller by the minute. Soon, it would be gone. But not for Ollie. He knew already: It was too late. Like a parasite crawling into a fresh wound and settling under the skin, the place had infested him. He shivered.

As if echoing Ollie's thoughts, the crow opened its beak in a sudden, defiant cry: *Caw! Caw! Caw!*

"That's enough," Tera said. Her petite frame—five-one or five-two, he'd have guessed—made her seem childlike, but her stern, hardened gaze gave the opposite effect. At the moment, that gaze was focused squarely on Ollie. "And *you*," she said accusingly. "What happened to staying low? Staying invisible?"

He stammered, trying to formulate an answer.

"What did I say when I dropped you off?"

"You, uh..." Ollie cleared his throat. "You said to stay out of sight."

"That's right. I said don't let them see you. Don't let anybody see you. And then what did you do?" She continued on, not pausing to let him reply. "You jumped right out into the damn clearing. Right under the lights! Krite almighty. What were you thinking?"

Ollie stared at her. "You saw that?"

"Yeah, I saw that. I knew it. I knew I shouldn't have brought you there." Her tone was softening. "I tried to stop you. I told you not to go. But you wouldn't listen."

He nodded.

"I knew you weren't...one of them."

He nodded again and said, "Thank you."

She let out a short, frustrated puff of air.

"No, really, *thank* you. That was crazy! You saved my life!"

"Yeah, well..." Tera turned her attention to the reins in her hand. She was wearing the same getup he'd seen her in before: an off-white jumpsuit studded with holes and patches; a headlamp; and that strange toolbelt full of arbitrary items that didn't look anything like tools.

"But...why?" he asked.

"Why what?"

"Why did you come back for me?"

She didn't look at him. For several seconds, all he heard was the sound of water lapping against the sides of the boat and the whistle of air in his ears. Then she said, "What does it matter? I came. It's done."

"You said there was...an arrangement? What did you mean?"

Tera dropped her eyes to meet his. "You ever heard that expression about not looking a gift horse in the mouth?" she asked.

"Well, yeah, of course. But—"

"You know where that comes from?"

"You mean, the expression?" Now Ollie was tipping from mere confusion into complete befuddlement.

Tera tightened her grip on the reins. She seemed to be studying him. "Back in the day, if you wanted to buy a horse, you would inspect its teeth," she said. "Make sure it was healthy and whatnot. Make sure you were getting your money's worth. But if someone *gives* you a horse, for free, you don't look at the teeth. You take what you get, and you say thank you."

"Right. But—"

"Do you want the damn horse or not?"

"Yes!"

"Then quit looking at the teeth. The teeth are fine. Got it?"

"Yes. Got it," he said. Suddenly, his three layers of clothing became unbearably oppressive; sweating and squirming, he pushed up the brown and red sleeves. It didn't help.

Mrs. Paget pushed the boat through the darkness, led by a single, dim headlight at the bow. Gradually, the nothingness gave way to hazy, distant sights. Ollie squinted into the gloom, making out shapes, colors, and what looked like human figures. The boat began to slow as they passed small outcroppings of land, possibly islands, dotted with ramshackle structures and a blur of movement. People, mostly women, hustled this way and that. As far as he could tell, no one seemed to be paying any particular attention to Tera's passage. Or her passenger.

He felt a wave of elation followed by a brutal slam of regret: He had left Dozer behind. The one guy who'd had his back in that hellhole. Not to mention all those other Floor Five captives, who hadn't done anything to deserve that kind of monstrous, interminable existence—

No. Stop. Ollie scrunched his face and shook his head. He couldn't think about that now. For all he knew, this was some weird trick. He had to keep his wits about him.

"Where are we going?" Ollie asked.

"We have to get you somewhere safe," she answered. "Just stay down. We're almost there."

Stay down? How exactly was he supposed to do that? After slouching and twisting in various useless ways, he finally lay flat on the bench seat, limiting his view to the phosphorescent glow of the ceiling high above his head. The longer he stared upward, the more he could swear that the roof of the cavern was...moving. Undulating. Before long, he found himself mesmerized by the radiating pulse of its light—like a vast, blue, beating heart, bursting out of the rock itself.

Ollie tried to keep still. He tried to keep quiet. But he didn't like the way the crow was eyeing him, as though it was thinking about dinner. Specifically, about dinner in the form of the fat, juicy, helpless human lying on the seat nearby. Ollie could imagine the bird taking a few steps, leaning forward, and casually pecking his eyes out with its machete-sized beak.

A loud clunk and a jerk knocked him out of his musings. The boat had hit something.

"All right, we're here," Tera said.

They had stopped at a dock. Beyond that, Ollie could see faint outlines of yet another stalagmite thicket.

Mrs. Paget stretched both wings, looking unconcerned.

"Let's go." Tera hopped out of the boat and looked over her shoulder.

Ollie got to his feet, steadied his balance, then stepped aside when it became clear that Mrs. Paget intended to exit the boat next. The bird's feathers brushed against his face as it passed. He rubbed his nose and stifled a sneeze.

Tera held out a hand to the crow, which ambled toward her and allowed itself to be hooked up to a lead. Together, they stepped off the dock and onto a sandy shore. It was a surprisingly pleasant spot, like a moonlit beach where teens might gather to drink and screw around.

"Coming?" she asked, turning to look back at Ollie.

Hell, yes, he was coming. What else was he going to do? His heart pounding, Ollie scrambled to keep up.

The three of them walked in silence along a well-worn path. At first, he saw nothing else: just the path, the stalagmite forest, and the water. Then the bumpy calcifications gave way to a more barren landscape dotted with strange tufts sticking out of the ground in neat rows, like crops. Beyond that, they passed a scattering of small sheds, or possibly houses, constructed mostly out of tin sheeting, cobbled wood planks, and textiles that might have been bed sheets. The structures were surrounded by haphazard assortments of wheeled carts, bottles, buckets, and clotheslines strung with earth-toned jumpsuits and socks.

This must be the company town, he realized. Or, in this case, the prison town, full of people who kept Herrick's End running and well-supplied.

"Most people are inside now, eating," Tera said in a low voice. "We just need to keep moving."

At the mention of eating, Ollie's stomach gave a piteous growl. Tera stopped in her tracks to look at him.

"Was that you?"

His face flushed red. "Sorry. I haven't eaten in a while. I mean, they gave me food, but..."

She held up a hand in a "say no more" gesture. "I'll get you something soon. First, we just have to drop off Mrs. Paget." Tera pointed to her left, where Ollie saw a building that looked like a stable. Most of the stalls were already filled with other freakishly large black crows, but one stall was empty; Tera walked the bird inside and closed the waist-high gate.

"Good girl," she said, patting the black feathers.

Caw! the bird responded.

"Yeah, yeah, I know," said Tera. Then she dug around in a small storage area and emerged with a bucket full of seed, pinkish chunks, and some sort of scaly, six-legged creature that Ollie could swear was still alive. She dropped the bucket into the stall, where Mrs. Paget descended on it ravenously. Ollie winced as the bird tore the small wiggling animal in half and tossed it down its gullet.

"That should do it," Tera said, sounding pleased. She wiped her hands on her pants and looked at Ollie. "You ready?"

It was such a simple question, really.

Yes, he was ready. He was ready to collapse. He was ready to cry. He was ready to start therapy to try to unpack his disaster of a childhood. He was ready to go back in time by a week and restart the day when he had made the most horrible, half-witted, moronic decision of his life. And just a few hours ago, he had been ready to die.

But that wasn't, of course, what she was asking.

"Yes," he said, straightening. "I'm ready."

They left the stable and returned to the dirt path, passing only a few more structures before stopping in front of one that seemed particularly dilapidated. The front "door" was no more than a curtain. The walls were made of random collections of materials—metal, wood, stone chunks—that seemed precariously balanced on each other, rather than firmly connected. There were no windows. The roof, such as it was, looked almost like a quilt, sewn together with patches of plastic, fabric squares, and possibly animal skins.

Ugly as it was, the house also gave Ollie an unexpected feeling of comfort, like a home-baked cake that looked terrible but probably tasted terrific.

"Home sweet home," Tera said.

"You live here?"

She nodded.

"Oh! It's...nice."

"It's a dump."

"No! It's—"

"It's a dump," she said again, this time with a happy shrug. "But it's my dump. And I'm afraid it's all we've got. Unless you want to sleep in the stable with the crows."

He shook his head, hard.

"Yeah, that's what I thought." Tera sighed. "So, here's the thing. This isn't just my house. I live with a bunch of other people. Women. And they might not..." Her voice trailed off.

Ollie tilted his head.

She shifted and continued. "They might not be so...*open* to the idea of you staying the night. They're going to be a little skittish, you know what I mean?"

Ollie thought about the men he had encountered at Herrick's End. Yes, he definitely knew what she meant. "Maybe we should just forget it," he said. "I don't want to get you in any kind of trouble."

Tera waved away the suggestion. "Nothing like that," she said. "It's just... Well, they might say no."

Ollie swallowed. Of course, they would say no. This was a house full of women, living a hop, skip, and boat ride away from a prison full of violent offenders. And here he was, a hulking giant of a man, dressed in a prison-guard uniform, appearing at their door to ask for shelter. Pinkie-swearing to behave himself. "So, what should we do?" he asked.

Tera opened her mouth to answer but was interrupted by a voice beside them. "Maybe you should just ask."

A woman had appeared in the doorway. She wore a long, dark braid and a wrap of ivory-colored fabric that looked vaguely like a sari. Her arms were folded.

Tera jumped at the sound. "Ajanta! Hi. I was just..."

"You know we can hear you, right?" the woman said. She spoke in a soft, Indian accent. Ollie guessed she must have been about 40 years old.

"Right, of course." Tera looked sheepish. "This is, uh, Ollie."

Ajanta looked him up and down. "Not really a guard, I take it?" Tera shook her head.

The three of them stood in awkward, tense silence. Then the older woman pursed her lips and looked around. "Well, I suppose you'd better get inside."

She disappeared behind the curtain. Ollie and Tera looked at each other in surprise, then scrambled to follow.

The house was larger than it had appeared from the outside. Ollie stepped through the doorway to find one big room filled with a hodgepodge of bunks, washbasins, stools, and rickety shelving units. In the center of the room, a fire pit simmered while the smoke rose through a hole in the fabric ceiling. Two more young women sat in front of the fire, both staring up at Ollie with wide, mistrusting eyes. He looked down at his shoes.

"This, apparently, is Ollie," Ajanta said. "Ollie, this is Derrin and Kuyu." She pointed to each as she said the name.

The two women, whose arms were intertwined, were a study in opposites: Kuyu was petite and pudgy, with dark curls. She seemed to be of Asian descent, with a broad, heart-shaped face, full lips, and lopsided eyebrows. Almost everything about her was round and rosy. The tall, angular Derrin, on the other hand, had stringy blonde hair and eerily pale skin. She reminded Ollie of the blue-suited men he had first encountered in the Neath. Her eyes were too large. Her nose was too small. She looked more like a child's drawing of a woman than an actual woman.

"Hi," he mumbled.

For a moment, no one spoke. Then Kuyu asked, "What is he doing here?" And not in a friendly kind of way.

Tera took a deep breath. "Ollie is from the Brickside."

"Yeah, no shit."

Tera shot her a glare and continued. "He's not one of them, okay? He came here looking to help a friend, but..." She faltered, her gaze traveling to his face. "But it didn't work out. They grabbed him up over there, and I got him out. Today. A few hours ago. As soon as things die down, I'm going to get him to the exit hatch. But he needs somewhere to stay tonight."

"Just tonight?" Kuyu asked.

Tera nodded.

Ollie slumped as best he could, trying to look humble and grateful and innocent all at the same time. Mostly, though, he was staring at the fire. Just above the flames, a pan rested on a metal grate, simmering with small strips of white meat that crackled as they cooked. The smell was smoky and torturous; saliva flooded his mouth.

When Derrin finally spoke, her voice was graveled. "What do you know about this guy, Tera? This is crazy."

Kuyu, who seemed to be about 21 or 22 years old, nodded in enthusiastic agreement. Two lumps on her shoulders looked like a football player's pads: one white, one black. As she shifted, the shoulder pads shifted, too: revealing themselves to be not pads at all, but living, breathing little creatures. Each had smooth fur and a protruding ivory-colored bill, giving them the look of fuzzy cannonballs with platypus mouths.

"I told you, he's not one of them," Tera said.

"How do you know?"

"I just do, okay? Do you trust me or not?"

Ollie watched silently, half-expecting Tera to break out another parable about horses and rotten teeth. She didn't.

"Of course, we trust you," said Kuyu. "It's him we don't trust."

Ajanta stepped forward. "There's only one way to know for sure."

A long silence followed. Then, Tera's eyes widened in recognition. "No," she said. "We're not doing that."

"You know it's the only way."

"No!"

"What?" Ollie interrupted. "Doing what?"

"Nothing," Tera said. "We're not doing anything."

Ajanta stepped closer. "Ollie, we have a...substance that can tell us quite a lot about a person. It can show us a person's intentions, and character. It can tell us if we need to be afraid of him, or if we will be perfectly safe in his company." She smiled sweetly.

Ollie found himself nodding. "Great! Great, let's do that." He looked at Tera.

"No," she said again, her mouth set in a firm line.

"Why not?" he asked.

"Because she's not telling you the whole story," Tera answered, glaring at Ajanta. "It's too dangerous."

"Those who have nothing to hide have nothing to fear," said Kuyu, who sounded like she was reading from a fortune cookie.

"I have nothing to hide!" Ollie turned out his palms to Ajanta. "Really! Nothing. How does it work?"

The older woman cleared her throat. "It's called Dark Heart. A reactive powder. The darker the heart, the more it reacts."

"Reacts...how?"

Tera touched his arm. "I'm telling you, Ollie, it's some bad shit. Seriously bad. If it does react, it hardens your body. Your skin. Some people even get paralyzed. Like, permanently."

"But I don't have a dark heart," he said. If anything, his heart was too light. And too fragile, and too trusting, and too incredibly stupid. Obviously. He swallowed and turned back to the group. "So, it will be fine. I'll take it."

"You understand the risks?" Ajanta asked, one eyebrow raised.

"Yes."

"All right, then." She looked at the others. "We're all in agreement, then? If there is no reaction, he can stay the night."

Derrin and Kuyu nodded. Tera gaped at them and refolded her arms. "No! I am not *in agreement*."

"Sorry, Tera. It looks like you're outvoted," Ajanta said. She walked to other side of the small room and began rummaging through a shelving unit.

"Don't do this," Tera said to Ollie. "We'll figure something else out."

"Like what?" he asked.

She stared at him but didn't answer.

Ajanta was walking toward him with a cup of liquid and a small vial of powder. She poured the powder into the cup, stirred it with a tiny stick, and then placed it in his hand.

No one spoke. The smell of the fire-grilled meat wafted past his nose, driving Ollie to the brink of something savage. He stared down at the foamy liquid. In contrast to the meat, the cup smelled like...nothing. Which was a shame, considering that it might be the last drink he would ever have.

"*Salute,*" Ollie said, lifting the cup. The Italian toast made him think of his mother, which made him want to cry. Then he raised the liquid to his lips, said a silent prayer to whatever god supervised the proper function of magical reactive potions, and poured it down his throat.

All four residents of the little house watched him intently. Tera held a hand over her mouth. Ajanta took a few steps backward. Derrin and Kuyu seemed not to move at all.

Within seconds, Ollie felt a tingle rush through his limbs. His fingers and toes got a zap of simultaneous static electricity; his vision became impaired with squiggles of white and pink light. Then, the squiggles became...images. He saw a flash of himself at age eight, stealing a pack of AA batteries from Mario's Mercato. He saw himself lying to his mother. Passing along a nasty rumor about a boy even less popular than he was. Cheating on Mrs. Newsome's civics quiz in ninth grade by writing all the answers on his sweaty palm.

Venial sins, Father Thomas would have called them. *Say two Hail Marys and two Our Fathers, and all will be forgiven.*

The minor infractions continued to blink, flooding Ollie with low-grade embarrassment and shame. And then, they just...stopped.

Ollie looked down at his hands. He tried to ball them into fists, wondering if his muscles would obey the command from his brain. They did. And then he wondered, too late, if a dark heart was inheritable. Could his father have passed it down through the bloodline like an overbite? Was Matteo about to screw him over again?

"How long does it usually take?" he asked.

"Not long," Ajanta answered.

They waited. Ollie shifted from one foot to the other. Then he asked, "Can I sit? My feet are really killing me."

Kuyu looked at Derrin, then shifted to leave room on the log.

Ollie settled down beside them. Next to his head, the platypus-cannonball creature on Kuyu's left shoulder stretched out its head, sniffing him. Ollie stiffened but didn't move.

A few more minutes ticked by. The women shot each other telling glances over Ollie's head while he pretended not to notice.

Finally, Ajanta heaved a deep breath. "Well, it seems as though we have our answer."

"Or, that shit doesn't work," Kuyu muttered.

"We agreed to the terms, and Ollie complied. One night," Ajanta added, moving her stern gaze to Ollie. "That's it. After that, you're on your own."

He nodded. "Thank you. Really. Thank you so much."

No one answered.

Tera rubbed her hands together and sauntered over to the fire. "How about some dinner?" she asked him.

Kuyu's head snapped up. "Hey, we never agreed to—"

"Krite, Kuyu, he's starving. What the hell is the matter with you?"

The brunette thrust out her lower lip. "He'd better not eat all of it."

"I won't," Ollie said, eyeing the crackling pan with desperation.

Tera reached for a spatula and scooped some of the white meat into a wooden bowl. "Looks like blindfish tonight," she said, handing the bowl to Ollie. "Made with Ajanta's secret blend?"

Ajanta gave a modest shrug.

Ollie took the bowl. When no one handed him a fork, he began eating with his fingers. Blindfish, it turned out, tasted a whole lot like cod. It was tender and oily, flaking at his touch. He couldn't identify the seasoning and didn't care. Whatever it was, it was spectacular. Salty and simmery and piquant. *Wicked good*, as they said back home.

Conversation resumed around him. Ollie's belly began to warm. His muscles began to relax. He saw Tera watching him; they shared the briefest of smiles. She was so pretty. Not in a conventional, scrawny model kind of way—more like a badass beauty. She'd be right at home in one of his video games, leading a team of soldiers into battle. Piloting a fighter jet. Ice-climbing up a sheer cliff to retrieve a hidden treasure.

He remembered, suddenly, the first time they had met and introduced themselves. How her hand had slipped so naturally inside of his. How it had lingered there for a moment or two longer than was strictly necessary.

And here she was again, smiling at him—at him!—across a smoldering fire. This crazy-cool, gorgeous girl, who had just single-handedly saved his life. He felt a wash of gratitude. And suddenly, he felt something else, too. Like the fish seasoning, he couldn't quite put a name to it. But he knew that he liked it. A lot.

Fourteen

Ollie woke on the floor the next morning, close to Tera's bunk, with his head resting on a wadded-up coat. He was stiff, chilly, and coated in his own drool. He had, miraculously, slept through the entire night without waking once.

Lifting his arm to his face, Ollie breathed in the clean, soapy smell of his skin. The housemates had allowed him a bath in the outdoor tub after dinner, complete with warm water and a handful of fizzy, cleansing salts. He was still speechless this morning. Flabbergasted at his luck.

He rolled over to survey the room. Only Kuyu was up, tiptoeing around the fire circle with her two round, fuzzy companions. She was making breakfast, from the looks of it. As Ollie watched, she settled onto one of the logs and started peeling oblong objects that looked like aquamarine potatoes. As the peels landed on the floor, the strange little animals sucked them up into their bills.

Kuyu worked quietly, chopping and tossing the pieces into a pan. Then she started the fire. Before long, the smell of crisping food roused the others from their sleep.

He tried not to stare as Tera sat up and stretched. Her bronze skin emerged from the sleeveless nightshirt in many more ways than he might have imagined. Well, that wasn't entirely true. He had imagined it. He probably shouldn't have, but he did.

She looked down at him. "How'd you sleep?"

"Good, thanks. Great."

She nodded, then threw back her blanket and walked behind a changing curtain in the far corner. Ollie didn't move. A few minutes later, she emerged wearing the off-white jumpsuit of the day before.

There was little conversation in the one-room house as the group gathered for breakfast. Kuyu's potatoes, if that's what they were, retained their aqua color after cooking, though they tasted much like any other potato he had ever eaten. Unlike Ajanta, Kuyu seemed to have little interest in food prep; this meal was more utilitarian than delicious. Ollie barely noticed. He had woken with a painfully empty stomach and was grateful to be offered anything at all that didn't involve belly-up toads floating in a prison-cell bucket.

One of the furry creatures sniffed around his feet as he ate.

"What are they?" he whispered to Tera.

She chewed, swallowed, and then answered. "Trogs."

"They're kind of cute."

"Yeah. In a weird sort of way." She tilted her head. "They're built for the water. See that fur? It's like otter fur. Super thick. And the big bill helps them scoop stuff up."

"What do they eat?"

"Almost anything. Insects, little fish, scraps. That sort of thing."

"Can I...?" Ollie held up a tiny piece of potato.

Tera shrugged. "Sure."

Ollie placed the small chunk into his palm, then held out his hand. The trog scuttled closer, sniffed, and slurped the offering into its bill. Ollie laughed.

The women looked at him, startled.

"Sorry," he muttered. Then he turned back to his plate.

"So, Tera, what's the plan for today?" Ajanta asked pointedly.

Ollie knew what she meant—*What's the plan for getting this guy out of our house?*

"Going to the Tea Party first," Tera said. "He needs something to wear."

All eyes turned to Ollie, who had removed both of his Herrick's End jumpsuits and was back down to his base layer of jeans and a t-shirt. No doubt, if he wanted to fit in, he was going to have to change his clothes. But why would she bring him to a tea party for that? Ollie furrowed his brow and kept silent. As Tera had explained it the night before, they needed to lay low, just for a day or two. And then she would bring him to something called the "hatch," where he would make his way back home. And Ollie had nodded, hiding his unease. What other options did he have? He couldn't go back to get Dozer. There was no way he'd make it out of Herrick's End—not again. He needed to bide his time, keep his mouth shut, and do whatever Tera asked him to. It was his best and probably only chance at survival.

He had no choice. Right? There was nothing he could do.

You did nothing. The Reader's words echoed in his memory, making him squirm. *Evil cannot exist on its own.*

Derrin's voice broke through the quiet. "Better make it soon," she said, peering through the front-door curtain. "Looks like we've got Reds out there."

"What?" Tera jumped to her feet. "Why? What are they doing here?"

"Oh, I don't know, Tera. Maybe looking for an *escaped prisoner?*" scowled Kuyu. She spoke with her mouth full. "Thank you very much for that."

"No way," Tera said, shaking her head. "I paid McNulty. He was going to take care of it."

"Oh, right. Because McNulty is always so reliable."

"All right," Ajanta interrupted. "That's enough." She took a turn peeking through the curtain, then pivoted back to her housemates. "You two, get going," she said, pointing to Tera and Ollie. "The rest of us will get rid of them. If they stop here."

Ollie scrambled to his feet.

"Stick to the bridges," Ajanta continued. "Leave Mrs. Paget in the barn."

When Tera opened her mouth to argue, Ajanta shushed her with a raised hand. "Leave her. We'll burn the suit."

All eyes fell on the bright red guard's jumpsuit, lying like a crumpled body in the corner of the room.

Ollie looked from one to the other, panic mounting in his chest.

"It'll be fine," Tera said to him. She was already clipping the tool belt around her waist. "Let's go."

They were out the door before he'd had a chance to finish the chunk of potato in his mouth, jogging down a dirt path behind the house. His left sneaker was only partially on; Ollie hopped on one foot to fix it before scurrying to catch up with her.

"The Tea Party?" he asked, already feeling out of breath.

Tera nodded. "It's like a market. Busy. Good place to disappear for a while. Plus, we need stuff."

"But...I'm going home soon, right?"

"Yes. Of course." She combed a finger through her purple-silver hair. As he watched her from the corner of his eye, he noticed she wasn't wearing the headlamp. "We just have to be careful, that's all."

The fog of the previous days had lifted; the blue light from the cavern's ceiling was startlingly bright. It lit up the landscape like a turquoise sun. Ollie straightened, struggling to get his bearings. It was, he realized, the first semi-clear view of the Neath he'd had since he arrived.

The islands he had previously glimpsed through the haze now looked less ominous and more ordinary, spread out along the lake's surface. People bustled. Boats floated. Smoke rose from tiny houses. A pervasive mat of groundcover carpeted the hills with tiny, multicolored flowers in gold, white, pink, and coral. Each flower gave off a small sparkle; combined, they glistened across the landscape. The scenery was surprisingly appealing. He might even call it...cheery. If not for the monstrous crows, green water, and pervasive blue radiation, he could have been forgiven for thinking, for just a moment, that he was back home.

"This way," Tera said, leading him down a small hill. In the distance, Ollie saw a long, rickety bridge. It appeared to be constructed of popsicle sticks.

"It's, uh, brighter out today," he said.

"Hmm?" She glanced up. "Yeah. It goes in cycles. This will last a few days, now."

Ollie didn't reply. He was too busy staring at the bridge, which was getting concerningly closer. They weren't going over that thing, were they? It looked like it would be lucky to support the weight of a starving hamster. The bridge was narrow, crooked, and nonhorizontal to the waterline, dipping up and down in strange little bumps and jags. Thin "support" beams, maybe four inches at their widest spots, jutted out from the base at inconsistent angles before disappearing into the water below.

"Over here," she said, heading directly, of course, to the bridge.

He watched her confident stride and tried to imitate it. Damn, he liked to watch her walk. Not that he should be thinking about such things now. His life was on the line, for God's sake. He'd just narrowly avoided a permanent career as a dungeon janitor, and he wasn't out of the woods yet—for all he knew, he was about to become bait for the blindfish in some gruesomely unexpected way. *That's* what he should have been focusing on. Not to mention, once he left this place, he'd never see this girl again. But damn, he did like to watch her walk.

At the base of the bridge, Tera climbed the three stairs and turned to look back at him. Ollie hadn't moved.

"You coming, or what?" she asked.

He shook his head. "It's not going to hold me."

"It will."

"I'm telling you, it won't." He was awash, suddenly, in memories of a lifetime of humiliating avoidance. The tire swing hung with light rope. The see-saw. The roller-coaster seat with the unforgiving lap bar.

"And I'm telling *you*, it will."

Ollie clenched his jaw. He climbed the stairs and made a tentative step onto the bridge. His belly rubbed against both sides of the narrow railing; the plywood base dipped with his weight. He looked up: It was a long way across. If the bridge broke in the middle, or if he fell, he'd have to swim back to shore. It was too far. Even under the best, non-shark-infested conditions, he'd never make it. And from what he'd seen of this place so far, a shark would probably be preferable to whatever was swimming under the surface of all that green soup.

Tera held out a hand. "I've gotten you this far, haven't I?"

He nodded.

"Well, then?"

Ollie blew out a gust of air. He reached for her. There it was, again: A strange, wonderful jolt as their palms pressed together, like a shot of dopamine on a fast track to his brain. And just like that, he felt light enough to float. Light enough, even, to cross a toothpick bridge.

Up, down, around. After that swaying, tipping bridge came two more just like it, each connecting one island to the next. They held his weight, somehow, though Ollie would swear they had to defy the laws of physics to do it.

At the fourth island, the foot traffic started to pick up. Tera and Ollie's solitude was broken by the irregular arrival of other residents, all of whom seemed to be hurrying and gossiping and carrying all manner of bundles and boxes. Before long, the group became a crowd, the noise level grew to a rowdy buzz, and Ollie's attire attracted more than a few curious stares. When the path crested at a small hill, he caught sight of the scene below and stopped short.

The Tea Party. It had to be. Like Quincy Market back home, it had narrow walkways with numerous individual stalls on either side. But this market was entirely...afloat. Wooden docks connected shoppers to bobbing platforms, each of which supported an open-air hut packed with merchandise. People also seemed to be selling sundries out of nearby rowboats, paddling with one hand and waving products in the air with the other.

It was a good-natured cacophony; merchants hollered over each other in an effort to attract customers, while visitors pushed and haggled. All of them somehow made their way along the teetering docks without falling over the sides. Laughs and greetings mingled with the bartering. Colorful bits of fabric had been strung together like banners from hut to hut. Varying strains of music competed with each other from different areas of the market. Trogs were there, too—lots of them, resting on people's shoulders and waddling around at their feet, scooping up whatever food scraps had fallen to the ground.

A bizarre bazaar, Ollie thought. He felt lightheaded.

Tera tugged on his sleeve. "We've got to keep moving."

He nodded and turned to follow her, joining the group of pedestrians on the dirt path down the hill. The people around him all wore off-whitish jumpsuits in various stages of disrepair. He saw a variety of skin tones and hair colors and sizes, though he was, of course, the tallest and heaviest person in sight. Some of them looked like "regular" people, and some of them looked more like Derrin and the coat-check attendant—translucent and overly wide-eyed. He was peering surreptitiously at a passerby when something made him startle: A long, blue tube, falling in front of his face and landing on the ground with a splat.

Ollie jumped back and stared. The tube, as long as a ruler, was glistening. And...wiggling. He looked at Tera with alarm, but she just kept walking. The others kept walking, too, stepping around the glowing, squirming tube with casual disinterest.

Finally, Tera noticed his absence. She backtracked against the flow of the crowd. When she reached his side, she asked, "What's wrong?"

"It just fell!" Ollie said, pointing to the ground. "Right in front of me! It came out of nowhere."

Tera nodded, nonplussed. "Yeah. It's a wormwalker. They do that."

As he watched, the thing curled and uncurled its tubular body, revealing two long rows of tiny, suction-like feet. They writhed and waved, reaching out into the air, grasping at nothing. A shiver of repulsion shot up his spine. "But...where did it come from?"

Tera said nothing; she only pointed. Up.

He tipped his head back. The ceiling. The glowing, living, undulating ceiling. His throat went dry. "That's what's up there?" he asked, swallowing a retch.

"Yep."

"Worms?"

"Wormwalkers," she corrected.

He heard his mother's voice in his head: *Madonna mia.* The lightheaded feeling from earlier escalated into a near faint. "And they just...fall?"

"All day long," Tera said with a shrug. "They're all wiggling around up there, and sometimes one of them just loses its grip, or whatever. I mean, there has to be thousands of them. Maybe millions. So yeah, they fall. A lot."

As she spoke, a trog scampered past her feet and made a beeline for the floundering, slimy invertebrate. In one swift move, the animal gobbled it up, leaving a long, damp spot on the ground.

Ollie looked at the glutinous stain. He looked at this girl, this mysterious, fiery girl, who was risking so much to help him for reasons he couldn't understand. He looked down the hill at the teeming market below. The creatures. The noise. The distant view of a towering, beastly prison. The goddamn ceiling made of phosphorescent worms.

It was all too much. His knees gave out, and he landed on the ground with a dusty wallop. The pedestrians behind him barely noticed; they simply flowed around his motionless body in a ceaseless, steady stream.

"Am I ever going home?" he asked. The question came out in a whisper.

"Yes," Tera said, leaning forward. Her voice was insistent. "I promise. It's just going to take a little doing, that's all."

The trog approached Ollie's foot and sniffed. Then it scampered up his legs and shirt, resting, finally, on his shoulder. Ollie stayed where he was, too exhausted to react.

"Looks like you made a friend," Tera commented, folding her arms.

Ollie turned his head to come face-to-face with the creature, now only inches from his nose. Small, dark eyes peered at him through a thick coat of fur. Knowing eyes. Its claws pierced the skin on his shoulder. The emanating musk reminded Ollie of low tide at the North End wharves: an unsavory mix of fish and kelp and salt.

The animal blinked. A small bit of the half-consumed wormwalker still dangled from the corner of its beak; with a noisy slurp, it sucked the last of the wriggling blue tube into his mouth. Then it settled onto

Ollie's shoulder, closed its eyes, and let out a grunt of satisfaction that sounded suspiciously like a sigh.

"All right, let's keep moving," Tera said, starting to turn.

"Wait!" Ollie called out. "What about...this?" He pointed to the creature on his shoulder.

"Just leave him," she answered with a casual wave. "He'll be fine."

And that was how, a few minutes later, Ollie found himself walking under the archway entrance of the Tea Party with a sleeping trog on his shoulder and a knot in his stomach. He hunched as best he could, trying to blend in with the crowd, as he followed Tera's darting movements through the barrage.

"Two for ten! Won't get any better!"

"Nix your mettle! Nix 'em up over here! One at a time!"

"Trog feed! Ten pounds for six!"

A woman pulled on his sleeve as he passed, pleading, "Gimme a loller, will ya?" He shook his arm free and kept moving.

The food stalls had a few things he recognized: blindfish fillets, lettuce-like leaves, and blue chunks of something that had to be wormwalker meat. The rest, piled in baskets and scattered around tables, he couldn't identify. And most of it didn't even seem like food. Shiny black rings. Jars full of white, lumpy goo. Yellowy blocks. Brown slabs. Tufts of something that might, or might not, have been human hair.

Mainly, though, he saw potatoes. Mounds and mounds and mounds of potatoes. They came in every size and shade. The place was a veritable rainbow of tubers, piled into neat pyramids, toppling onto the ground, and poking out of every bag and pocket.

Despite the underwhelming appeal of the offerings, Ollie's stomach began to growl. Some of the venders had cooked up ready-made samples, and the spicy scents wafted in the air like an invitation. He was ready to accept, no questions asked. But Tera had other ideas. She dragged him forward, tugging at his sleeve.

The merchandise huts were less colorful, if no less noisy. Most of the items for sale seemed to be rudimentary tool-like objects or basic articles of clothing. Shoes, hats, toolbelts, miner's hats. Chisels. Pots and pans. Torches. Hammers. Anchors. Strangely curved spoons.

The sellers tried their best to get him to stop. They shouted, grabbed at his arms, and waved random objects in the air like trophies. Ollie ignored them all, watching Tera's back. Watching his feet. The docks swayed with the uneven weight of pedestrians, tipping precariously. There were no railings.

Finally, Tera came to a stop; it was so sudden he bumped into her back. She was standing in front of a hut that looked much like all the others. A wooden sign dangled from the top: "Nikki and Floyd's," it read, with a smaller line below: "Brickside Curiosities."

Tera looked up at him. "You need to let me do the talking in here, okay?"

He nodded.

There was no chaos and mess at this shop. No shouting. Instead, Ollie saw only shelves of neatly arranged and labeled objects. He stepped forward, drawn by curiosity. The floating floor swayed beneath his feet.

Christmas lights, circa 2006, read one label, posted next to a string of colored bulbs. Below that came a description: *Hung on indoor trees. Primarily used to illuminate gift-giving ceremonies.*

The next object was a fabric strip, dotted with a pawprint design. An accompanying sign read: *Dog collar and tags, circa 1979. Used to shackle and identify non-humans.*

Ollie eyes swept the space with sick fascination. Cassette tape, circa 1984. Ski goggles, circa 2012. Hub cap, circa 1955. A pair of Doc Martens, circa 1991. There had to be nearly a hundred items, all displayed like treasures. No prices were listed.

A man and a woman watched him from behind a makeshift counter. They were, he assumed, the Nikki and Floyd from the sign. The woman was the taller of the two, with black skin, bright white teeth, and a white fur shawl. The man was scrawny, pale, and overwhelmingly brown: brown hair, brown hat, and a dowdy brown vest slung over his jumpsuit.

"Ah, Miss Tera!" the woman said. "Just the one we wanted to see!"

"Hey, Nikki." Tera hopped from the dock to the platform. The water swished around it as she landed.

"Any idea what this one is?" Nikki asked, holding up a small silver appliance.

"That depends," Tera answered.

"On what?"

"On whether or not you can help me."

Ollie stepped further inside, still studying the array of objects. A Bic pen. A pair of contact lenses in a plastic case. An ice tray. As he neared the display closest to the counter, he saw something small and made of leather.

Man's wallet, folding type. Portable collection unit for paper money and plastic cards. Three letters formed a monogram in the center: O, D, and P.

"Hey!" Ollie yelped, pointing. "That's mine!"

No one immediately replied.

"That's mine!" he said again. "Oliver Paul Delgato. Me. Where did you get that?"

The scrawny man looked at Tera. "Who's this?" he asked her.

She waved a hand and flashed Ollie a warning look. "Nobody you need to concern yourself with. Listen, Floyd, I need some stuff."

"What kind of stuff?" Nikki asked.

"Not this kind," Tera answered, tilting her head in the direction of the shop's shelves.

Floyd tapped his fingers on the wood counter. "All right," he said. "You help us make an I.D., and then we'll talk more about your *stuff*."

Tera paused, then nodded and pointed. "That," she said, "is a waffle iron. You pour the batter into there..." She paused to flip the lid open. "And then you close it, and it bakes."

"Like a cake?" Nikki asked, her brow furrowed.

"Sort of. It's like...a breakfast cake."

"What's with all the little squares?" Floyd asked.

Tera shrugged.

Ollie knew the answer. He had used plenty of waffle irons, and pizzelle presses, and even waffle-cone makers for ice cream. The scored, deep lines on the iron gave the batter room to expand and allowed it to cook more evenly, while also providing a greater surface area for crispy, perfect edges. Plus, the square pits made ideal receptacles for maple syrup. Obviously. But he kept his mouth shut. About that, and about the damn wallet. Tera had told him to let her do the talking, and he was in no position to contravene.

"Let's step into my office," Floyd said.

Nikki stayed at her post, watching as Tera, Floyd and Ollie passed through an opening in the curtain behind the counter and exited through the back of the shop. The trog shifted on Ollie's shoulder and made a series of snorting sounds.

Tera cut to the chase as soon as they were alone. "I need a resident jumpsuit. For him."

Floyd looked Ollie up and down. "That's a big suit," he said. "So?"

"So, it's gonna take a while. Few days."

"I don't have a few days."

133

The bony man rubbed the rim of his hat. "I don't know. That's gonna be tough."

"C'mon, Floyd, who do you think you're talking to? I know you can get it."

"Maybe. What else?"

She waited a beat before answering. "An exit pass."

"Ha! Now I know you've lost it, my friend. Are you crazy?"

"I know you can find one. Just one. That's all we need."

"Oh, just one exit pass. Is that all?" He laughed out loud. "Even if I could get it, it's not going to be cheap."

"I figured," she said. "So, what do you want?"

"What do you have?"

Tera squirmed. "Right this second? Not a lot. But I'm good for it. You know I am."

Floyd shook his head. "Whoever this guy is to you, Tera, he's not worth it."

"If I want a therapy session, *Floyd*, I'll go back in there and talk to your wife," she snapped. "Will you do it or not?"

For a moment, neither of them spoke. As the standoff continued, Ollie couldn't help but notice the man casting curious glances at his Levi's.

"You like my jeans?" Ollie asked, perking up.

"That what those are?"

"Yes!" Ollie answered. He held out his leg. "Denim! Super durable. Useful down here, I'll bet."

Floyd grunted.

"I'll give them to you. If you can get us the pass." He looked at Tera, whose mouth was curling into a surprised smile. His heart leapt stupidly at the thought that he might have impressed her.

Floyd rubbed his chin. "Okay," he finally said. "I'll do it. For those."

"Great," Tera said.

After an awkward silence, Floyd motioned with his hands. "Go ahead, then. Hand them over."

"What, *now?*" Ollie asked. "Right here?"

"Yeah, right here," Floyd said, looking confused. "Where else?"

Tera held up her palms.

Perspiration began to seep from his pores. They had to be kidding. This was like every fat guy's waking nightmare. He wasn't going to take his clothes off. Not in the back alley of some barely floating flophouse of stolen shit.

Not in front of her.

"But, isn't there some kind of...changing room, or something?" he asked.

Floyd folded his arms. "Kid, do we have a deal or not?"

"Yes! We have a deal. It's just...I mean, what am I supposed to wear?"

"I'll get you something." Floyd waved vaguely toward the shop.

Good God. He was actually going to have to do this. Ten seconds later he was standing, fully humiliated, in a pair of sweat-stained tightywhities, clutching the keychain in his right hand. The trog had barely budged.

Ollie held out his Levi's. Floyd took them, disappeared through the curtain, and reemerged a minute later with a pair of what might have been pajama bottoms. Brown, of course. Avoiding Tera's eyes, Ollie slid his legs through the holes. They were too small. The seams strained from the pressure.

I'm usually clean, he wanted to tell her, his cheeks flaming. *I'm going to look better soon. I'm on a plan. I'm losing weight.*

"So, we have a deal?" Tera asked Floyd.

The man nodded. "Give me a few hours."

They shook hands, and Floyd disappeared once more behind the curtain.

"Well then. It looks like we have some time to kill," Tera said, looking pleased. "Feel like a snack?"

Asking if Ollie wanted a snack was like asking if the Queen wanted a corgi. "Sure," he answered. "I could eat."

"Nice negotiating, by the way," Tera said. Then she added, with a wink, "And nice Fruit of the Looms."

Fifteen

The ubiquitous potatoes, as it turned out, were not potatoes at all. They were a Neath crop known as rhizers, which grew readily and heartily in the cavern's soil in an almost infinite variety of colors and shapes. Ollie's portion, served directly into his hand from a Tea Party stall, looked like roasted fingerlings, Kelly-green, with a visible sprinkle of salt. The oil dripped through his fingers and landed on the dock below.

Ollie tasted one of the long chunks and let out a rapturous groan. The smell of food had awakened the trog on his shoulder; it snuffled and turned, tickling Ollie's neck with its fur as they left the docks for land. Minutes later, they arrived at a cobbled-together archway enveloped in emerald moss, with intermittent sprigs of tiny silver flowers. A sign at the top of the arch read, "Blackstone Park."

The name had not taxed anyone's imagination. As promised, the park was a roundish spit of land completely covered with black stones. Copious benches and odd tufts of long-leafed, tree-sized ferns dotted the landscape. Near the center, a statue sat atop a small hill. It looked like a person. A king on a throne, maybe. Something historical.

Ollie stared, feeling an unexpected pang. Benches. Broad leaves. Monuments. Mothers and children, scampering. Couples strolling along the water's edge. If he squinted, blurring out the details, he could almost imagine he was looking at a Boston scene. He envisioned, suddenly, the zany animal carousel on the Greenway near his apartment. That carousel would fit right in here, he realized: a spinning, mechanical fantasyland where grasshoppers and whales were the same size and jangly music played on a loop. Around and around and around.

Tera headed for a bench near the shore. Ollie held out his dripping hand as he walked, trying not to twist an ankle on the shifting bed of stones. Finally, they were seated, and he lifted another buttery chunk to his mouth. *Goddamn*, he thought, his mind blank to anything else. It was warm and soft on the inside, with an earthy, salt-and-peppery peel. Just the right amount of chew.

"Good?" Tera asked, looking at him with amusement.

"Mm hmhf," Ollie responded sheepishly with his mouth full. He mashed a bit in his fingers and held it out for the trog.

Tera popped a rhizer into her own mouth, chewed, and swallowed. "Yeah, Ruth makes the best. You've gotta find her, when you're in there. The others are okay, but Ruth..."

She didn't finish, but Ollie nodded. He understood. After a few more bites, he asked, "So, I take it you haven't been down here long?"

She raised an eyebrow. "What makes you think that?"

"Oh, come on," he said. "The waffle iron? Fruit of the Looms?"

Tera regarded him thoughtfully. Then she said, "I've been here for about six years."

"Six?" Ollie was surprised.

"Yep." She looked down, pushing the chunks around in her hand. More softly, she clarified: "I was thirteen."

"Oh," Ollie said. "Wow, that's... Wow. Can I ask...why?"

Tera leaned back against the bench. She stared out at the greenish water and the dark cavern beyond. "I'm here for the same reason everyone else is here. I made a choice."

He chewed his lip, not understanding.

"My mother was...well, let's just say she was not a good person. And my father wasn't much better. Things got bad for me, at home. There was..." She stopped, cleared her throat, and continued. "There was abuse. Someone told me about a place, in the North End—"

"The Women's Resource Center," Ollie interrupted.

"Yes. They helped me. They gave me options. There are other centers like that, all over the place, and they could have moved me. Hid me somewhere up there. But I would've been a foster kid, God knows where, with God knows who." Her voice trailed off. After a moment, she went on: "Or, I could have brought her there." She jutted her chin out, gesturing at Herrick's End in the distance. "I would have been safe. I would have gone back home, and she would have stayed there. In the tower. She would have deserved it." Tera's face darkened. "Sometimes I think I should have done it."

"Why didn't you?"

Tera sighed. "I don't know. In the end, I just couldn't. You've seen what goes on in there." She looked at him, and he nodded. "They told me exactly what it was. Exactly what would happen to her. And I thought about it, believe me. But...I don't know. I guess I just couldn't do that to anybody. Not even her. So, I took the third option." She spread her arms wide. "Welcome to Option Three."

"Wait," Ollie said. "Are you saying you sent *yourself* down here? Instead of her?"

"Yep. We all did."

"Who's we?"

"All of us," Tera said, pointing at the crowded market. "Everyone here."

"Everyone? Every single person in the Neath is a vict—"

"Uh, uh, uh," Tera interrupted. "We don't use the v-word down here. That's not what we are. We're here because we made a choice to take back control. That's what the Neath is. It's a sanctuary. A place to start over."

"But why do some of the people look so...different?" he asked, encircling his face with a finger.

"Oh," she nodded. "That's just adaptations. Some people are third generation, or tenth generation. They were raised here because their parents were, and their parents before that."

"So those people didn't make a choice to be here," he pointed out.

"Yeah, true enough. But the same could be said of any immigrant's kids. Anyhow, it's not like we can go anywhere. Once you're here, you're here."

"Because of the lung thing? The change?"

She gave him a sad smile. "Yes. And that's exactly why we have to get you out of here, fast."

"Would you escape? If you could?"

"I told you, this *is* the escape. We chose to be here. Why would we want to leave?"

Ollie bit his tongue as his eyes swept the space around him.

"I know what you're thinking," Tera said. "But it's not so bad. The people are nice. Well, except for Kuyu, some days." She laughed. "We support each other. And everyone knows what's up on the Brickside. Abusers, bullies, power-hungry pricks. All doing whatever they want, while everyone else pays the price. Nothing changes. You know what I'm talking about."

Ollie swallowed. He did know—better than she realized. He even knew some of them by name. His own father, for one. The Guy. Ashlee

Barnes over on Salem Street, who engineered a telemarketing scam to bilk seniors out of their life savings. She got away with it, and eventually started another one. Nathan Cannevale and Matt Endrizzi, Ollie's childhood tormentors extraordinaire, now all grown up and revered as hometown heroes at Engine 8/Ladder 1.

He had sort-of known the woman on his block—Maggie something, nice lady—who called the cops on her husband and wound up strangled five days later. In the end, the husband had been sentenced to fourteen years for manslaughter. "A joke," Ollie's mother had called it. She and her friends used to whisper about the details when they thought Ollie wasn't listening. Fourteen short years in a minimum-security prison. No, not a prison—a "correctional and rehabilitation facility." Three squares a day. Mattress, pillow, and time in the yard. He even had the option to take classes while he was there: "Expository Writing" was one offering, along with "Culinary Arts." Then he'd probably get released early, to put all that learning to good use. Hell, killing his wife might end up being the best thing that ever happened to him.

"You see the news," Tera continued. "Restraining orders don't work. Restraining orders get you dead. And all of these women's centers, with their safehouses and underground escape routes... They mean well, but what kind of a system is that? It's like bullshit witness protection. The victim has to give up everything, go into hiding, give up a whole *life,* and what does the abuser have to give up? Nothing. Not one damn thing. Where's the justice in that?" She curled her lip. "And trust me, abusers are clever. Very clever. It's all about control. Nobody understands that. Everybody asks, 'Why don't you just leave?' Right?"

Ollie gave an answer that was half shrug, half nod. He was remembering, suddenly, the time when one of the neighbors had pulled his mom aside in Bella Donna's Hair Salon and asked that very question in a thick whisper: *Francie, for God's sake, why don't you just leave?*

"I'll tell you why," Tera pressed on. "Because up there, there's nowhere to go. That's the reality. If they want you, they'll get you, no matter where you go. Especially nowadays, with social media, tracking software, driver's licenses, cell phones..." She paused, appraising her surroundings. "Down here, it's different. You don't have to be afraid. No one's going to find you. You're free to be whatever you want to be. To follow your dreams."

They sat quietly, watching the water lap the rocky shoreline. Then Ollie asked, "So, what's your dream?"

Tera pursed her lips, hesitating. Finally, she straightened and said, "I'm an artist. A painter. Portraits, mostly. How about you?"

"Me?"

"Yeah, you. What's your plan?"

Ollie blinked. In his head, he suddenly heard Lorraine's voice: *What are your plans for the week ahead?* He almost blurted out something about caloric restriction and stair climbing. But Tera, of course, was asking about his grand plan. His aspirations for the future. That old chestnut.

"I have a scholarship," he said. "For a local college."

"Nice!" she said. "What are you going to study?"

"Medical imaging. Ultrasound, X-ray, all that. They have a pretty good program there."

"Oh!" Tera said, sounding surprised. "Well, that's...that sounds interesting. And what about the girl?"

"What girl?"

She gave him a look of bemusement. "*The* girl. The one that got you into this disaster. Tank top? Pushing a wheelbarrow? Ringing any bells?"

He held up a hand, wincing. "Her name is Nell. She's a friend from back home. She went missing. Or at least, I thought she was missing. I thought she needed help, but..."

"But she didn't," Tera finished for him.

He nodded.

"Well, I think that was pretty damn good of you, anyway. Trying, I mean. Coming down here. Not many people would have done something like that."

"Yeah, well, I didn't exactly have the full picture of what I was getting into." Which was, he realized, the actual, award-winning Understatement of the Year.

"Mmm," she agreed. "But I bet you still would have done it. Even if you had known."

He laughed. "I think you're giving me too much credit."

"Oh, I don't think so," Tera said, leaning over to share one of her rhizers with the trog on his shoulder. "Maybe you're not giving yourself enough."

"But you just met me."

She shrugged. "I'm a pretty good judge of character. You have to be, down here. And up there, too, I guess." Her head tilted as she studied him. "You don't even know, do you?"

"Know what?"

"How great you are." Tera said it matter-of-factly, as though she were describing a weather pattern. Then she grinned, slurped the last

140

of her rhizers, and patted his leg. Her hand left a greasy palmprint on the borrowed pants. "In a world full of dandelions, Ollie Delgato, you are a sunflower."

"A...sunflower?"

"Yes. Big, and bright, and always looking for the light." Her gaze turned affectionately stern. "Even when there's no light to find."

He had to resist the urge to turn and peek over his shoulder, as though she might be talking to someone else.

"Did you know the sunflower is the only flower in the world with the word 'flower' right there in its name?" she asked.

Ollie shook his head, mute.

"It's true. So nice, they named it twice."

She mesmerized him, this girl. This tiny, smart, crackle of a human being. Where did she come from? How had he landed here, next to her? And why did her proximity, her mere presence, make him suddenly feel like he had forgotten how to use the English language?

A light rain began to fall; without speaking, Tera removed the umbrella from her tool belt and popped it open. She gestured for Ollie to move closer and join her. He did, looking questioningly into her large brown eyes as he slid along the seat of the bench and ducked his head. The rain made a pattering sound on the plastic, surrounding them in a hypnotic, steady rhythm. Their faces were inches apart. Ollie could feel the heat from her arm; he could smell her breath. He had never leaned in for a kiss before, but he imagined that this was exactly the kind of moment when someone might do just that. She was beautiful. Prickly but beautiful, like a desert cactus in bloom. Ollie was so engrossed in his metaphor that it took him a moment to consider the fact that it was raining.

In a cave.

"Wait a sec," he said, pulling back. "Where is the rain coming from? We're underground."

"It's not rain," Tera answered.

"Then what is it?"

"It's the wormwalkers."

Ollie peered out from beneath the umbrella, looking up at the glowing blue ceiling. Drops of cool liquid hit his face. "But...they're still up there."

"Yeah, it's not *them* falling. It's..." Tera gave an apologetic grin.

Ollie looked at her blankly. When understanding finally dawned, his mouth stretched in revulsion. "Is this... Are you saying... They're peeing on us? Is this worm pee?"

141

"Worm*walkers*," she corrected.

Ollie wiped his face desperately with his sleeve. "It's all over me!"

"Relax," Tera smiled, waving a hand. "It won't hurt you. Happens once a day around here. It's great for the soil, actually. We'll have to get you an umbrella."

"Sure. Umbrella, chemical bath, whatever." He shuddered and huddled closer to her, trying to move the entirety of his big body out of the line of fire.

The trog crawled down Ollie's arm and began licking his fingers with a long, darting tongue. Tera laughed and rumpled the creature's fur. Then she threw an arm over Ollie's shoulder as the three of them waited, together, for the urine storm to pass.

The last drops were still sporadically falling when Tera got to her feet. It was time, she told him, to check back in with Nikki and Floyd.

Ollie clung to the umbrella, not quite ready to leave its shelter behind. On the way out of the park, he peered up at the small hill and pointed. "What's the statue?"

"Hmm?" She turned her head. "Oh, that's not a statue. That's George."

"Wait. What?" Ollie's feet slowed. "That's a living person up there?" Though he was still at a distance, he looked to Ollie to be made of stone. And perfectly, completely still.

"Yeah," Tera said, turning again. She looked impatient. "He's been here forever. Hundreds of years. This place was his idea. George Herrick."

Now Ollie's feet stopped altogether. "George Herrick, as in, Herrick's End?"

"Yep. C'mon. Keep moving."

"What's he doing up there?" Ollie asked, staring in fascination. The motionless man's eyes were open. His arms lay on the arms of the chair in a formal seated pose.

"Waiting, I guess. That's what they say."

"Waiting for what?"

She shrugged. "I have no idea. But listen, Ollie, we don't really have time for—"

"Can I go up there? I mean, can anyone go up there?"

"Well, yeah. Of course. People go up there all the time."

"Can we go? Just for a second?" This, he had to see. A living man, hundreds of years old? Sitting in a park? Something about it called to him, stirred him, in a way he didn't understand.

Tera sighed. "Fine. But just a second."

Ollie gave her back the umbrella and started to climb the hill, slipping on the loose rocks beneath his feet. Before long, he was forced to bend forward, using his hands to steady his ascent. The trog sunk its claws into Ollie's shoulder while Tera followed behind. Both of them grunted in complaint.

At the top, Ollie rose to his feet. The statue—Ollie shook his head and corrected himself—the *man* had gray skin, cracking and crumbling with almost incalculable age. Ollie imagined he could pick away at the man's face, chip it down to bone, using nothing more than a fingernail. His clothing was nondescript and covered in dust. If he was breathing, Ollie could see no evidence of it. The man didn't blink, or cough, or turn his head. He simply stared straight ahead, a disintegrating part of the scenery.

"This guy's not alive," he protested.

Panting from the climb, Tera pointed to a sign posted next to the man's chair.

Ollie approached the sign. In small hand-carved letters, it read: *Here sits George Herrick, Founder of the Neath, 1693. Friend to witches. Lifter of the downtrodden. Remorseful and repentant, until his end doth arrive.*

Ollie turned and gave her a quizzical look.

"It's a long story," she said.

He didn't move.

"We really don't have time for this right now. You do know there are people looking for you, right?"

"C'mon, Tera! This guy is 300 years old!"

"More than that," she grudgingly admitted.

"Just the Cliff's Notes. Please."

Tera rolled her eyes. "Fine. You're familiar with the Salem witch trials?"

Ollie held out his palms. Of course, he was familiar.

"George Herrick was the Salem town marshal for all that," she began. "Or the deputy, or some such thing. Whatever he was, he spent his days dragging innocent people out of their homes and tossing them into jail. People who were falsely accused of witchcraft. Some of them died in jail first, because the conditions were so horrific. One poor guy got pressed to death with stones. The rest hung at the gallows. George

Herrick was a henchman for all of that. One of these "just doing my job" types, like a Nazi guard or something."

Ollie's eyebrows shot up. "So, what's with all the 'friend to witches' stuff? Doesn't sound like much of a friend to me."

"Well, that's where things get tricky," she said. A purple wave of hair fell into her face; she pushed it away. "As it turns out, there *were* witches in Salem. There were witches everywhere. Still are, of course. They just weren't the people who got scooped up into Mr. Herrick's paddy wagon."

"Sooo...?" he asked.

"So, the real witches decided to teach ol' George here a lesson. Gave him a little taste of his own medicine. I'm not sure of the details, but suffice to say he came to see the error of his ways." She noticed a couple strolling nearby and paused to give them a nervous wave. Then she lowered her voice before continuing in a rush. "As the story goes, he became deeply sorry for the pain he had caused, and the deaths he had a hand in. So, he worked with the witches to create a safe space for them and others like them to live, free of persecution. Free from fear." She held out an arm. "He helped them create the Neath. The whole thing was his idea."

Ollie looked around, dazed, as if seeing the place for the first time.

"You have to understand," Tera continued, "back then there were no women's centers. No safe havens at all. Just religious zealots and a rigid patriarchy and a shitload of bonfires and nooses. The Neath was Herrick's solution to all that. And as a reward, the witches granted him long life."

"How long?"

She shrugged. "No one really knows. According to the legend, he's waiting here for something."

Waiting for something. Ollie considered this as the big leaves on a nearby fern-like tree waved in the breeze and sent shadows dancing across the ground. Which was strange, because there didn't seem to be a breeze to blow them.

"He created the prison, too?"

Tera shook her head. "No, no, no. That came after. At first, the Neath was supposed to be a kind of paradise. A heaven under the earth, I guess. But as the years went by, some of the people down here started getting a little antsy. They thought, why just escape? Why not get a little revenge, too, while we're at it? That's when they built Herrick's End." She paused, looking at the motionless man. The fern trees surrounded him like a protective, swaying squad. "George didn't like it. To him, that was the opposite of what he wanted this place to be. But by that time, he was already a little creaky, apparently, and...there wasn't much he could do. They created the prison, and they named it after him. And then he went still as a stone."

"But...why?"

"Why did he freeze like that, you mean? I don't know. Just part of being really old, I guess."

Ollie scratched the trog's fur absentmindedly. "And he never talks?"

"God, no. Sometimes he writes notes. People will find them on his lap, first thing in the morning, as though he wrote them in his sleep. They leave paper and pencils, and sometimes he writes."

"How does he write if he's frozen?"

"Got me. I guess he's just...mostly frozen?"

Ollie stared at her, and then at the man, fascinated. "What kinds of things does he write?"

She shifted from foot to foot. "Usually, it's just simple requests. A blanket, maybe. Or he'll ask someone in particular to do something. It's like he sees all of us, and knows who we are, even though he never leaves this spot." She shrugged again.

If George Herrick heard her, he made no sign.

"And what about the witches?"

"What about them?" Tera looked left and right. She waved again and smiled, this time at a woman walking alone.

"What happened to them? The ones who started this place, with George? Are they still here? Do they know what the Warden is doing over there?"

"I don't know. I guess they left."

"Left for where?"

"Krite, man, I don't know. That was a long time ago. What does it matter? Now, c'mon. Enough. We really have to go." She looked over her shoulder. More park visitors were wandering nearby.

It struck him as wobbly, this story. Why would George Herrick harden to stone as he aged? And if the witches had created The Neath to be a place of peace and sanctuary, why would they have allowed the later inclusion of a torturous prison? Maybe they simply got fed up with being victims, with hiding, and decided to use their powers to exact a little vengeance. Who could blame them? Thousands of men and women had died in witch hunts around the globe, long before the Salem trials. Maybe this place was the reason those hunts had finally ended.

Ollie took a step closer to the brittle man, then another, while the trog on his shoulder sniffed the air. Could he touch him? What would a 350-year-old man feel like?

He was about to find out. His hand hovered, inches from the cemented arm.

And then, George Herrick's head began to turn. Slowly, almost imperceptibly, at first. Then, faster. The man's neck pivoted to the left until his glassy, gray eyes were staring into Ollie's own.

Ollie froze.

Nearby, he heard Tera gasp.

George Herrick's mouth fell open, sudden and sharp, as if on a broken hinge. A sound came from his throat. A strangled, tortured gurgle.

Herrick's eyes searched Ollie's, desperate and urgent. And then, he spoke. The words erupted like croak, barely audible: "Tell Widow Hibbins zero. Lion's feet will dig. As I am, so he will be." The old man paused, wheezing, and then continued: "The rightful ones tarry in the place that is not a place. All will be mended. The waiting is done."

George Herrick's mouth snapped shut as quickly as it had opened. His groan, rattling and ancient, echoed across the surface of the rocky hill.

His head fell forward.

Tera gasped again.

Nearby, someone screamed.

Ollie stretched out his hand, ready to search for a pulse. But he knew already: It was no use. The man was gone.

"No!" Tera said, reaching out to stop him. "Let's go!"

Parkgoers started appearing from all sides. More screams. A few were pointing at Ollie. Covering their mouths.

"What did he say?" a nearby woman called out.

A man stepped closer to Ollie, almost touching him. "What did he tell you?"

"We have to go," Tera said grimly. "Now."

She yanked on his arm and they slid down the hill, the shiny black stones shifting like a thunderous sandstorm at their feet.

Sixteen

Tera didn't say another word as she hustled Ollie through the park, over the rickety bridges, and back to her house. He suspected she would have slammed the door, if the door wasn't a curtain. The roommates, luckily, were out.

Finally, she spoke: "What the hell was that?"

"I don't know!" he answered. "The guy just...came alive! I mean, I know he was already alive, but he came *really* alive. And then he just...uh..." Tera had told him to think in opposites down here. *What's the opposite of alive?* he wanted to say. But didn't.

"Who are you, really?"

"What do you mean, who am I? You know who I am!"

"I thought I did. Why did he talk to you? Herrick never talks to anybody, Ollie! Like, ever!"

He looked at her helplessly, running a hand through his short, dirty-blond curls.

"All this time, he was waiting for something. Was he waiting for you? Did you know that was going to happen?"

"No! Jesus, of course not! I'd never even heard of the guy before today." An hour ago, she'd called him a "sunflower." Now she was looking at him like he was poison ivy. "I swear to God, Tera. I don't know what that was. I didn't touch him. I didn't do *anything.*"

"Okay," she said, starting to pace. "Okay. Let's think this through. This is bad. People saw us there. They're going to think you killed him."

"But I didn't!"

"That won't matter!" She rubbed her lips. "Okay. We can manage this. It's fine. It's going to be fine. What did he say?"

"Nothing! Just nonsense. Random words."

"What words, specifically?"

Ollie paused. The directive came back to him, strangely clear: "He said, 'Tell Widow Higgins...' No, wait. 'Tell Widow *Hibbins* zero. Lion's feet will dig. As I am, so he will be.'"

"What the hell does that mean?"

Ollie shrugged helplessly. "Then he said something like, 'The rightful ones tarry in the place that is not a place.'"

"What rightful ones? What place?"

Ollie lifted his palms. "I don't even know what 'tarry' means."

"It means 'wait,'" she said. "What else? Anything?"

He chewed his lip, trying to remember. Then he recited the sentences like lines from a play: "The rightful ones tarry in the place that is not a place. All will be mended. The waiting is done."

"That doesn't make any sense."

Ollie shook his head.

She sighed. "It doesn't matter. Either way, you're screwed. If they weren't looking for you before, they sure as hell will be looking now." She rubbed the back of her neck, blowing out a puff of air. "This is going to delay things. You'll have to stay inside."

"Here?"

"Yes."

"What about the others? They only agreed to one night."

Concern flashed across her features. "I'll take care of it."

"Tera—"

"I'll take care of it," she said again. "They have to let you stay."

And they did, if not enthusiastically. For the next two days, Ollie tried to make himself invisible in the tiny house while Derrin, Kuyu, and Ajanta kept him in their suspicious sights. Nikki and Floyd managed to procure a jumpsuit for Ollie, but the exit pass, apparently, was proving more difficult. Each time Tera prodded, they told her "soon." As the hours ticked by, Ollie began crossing squares off an imaginary calendar and monitoring his breathing. Was he changing? Were his lungs already adapting? He didn't feel any different. Was that a good thing? Or bad? Either way, the window was closing. And a persistent claw of panic was starting to burrow a hole through his gut.

Ollie slept on the floor. He helped where he could, when he was allowed. He peeled. He chopped. He tidied. He mopped up puddles after the daily wormwalker urine storm leaked through holes in the roof. He sorted through the rhizers to find the sweet varieties, then made a Neath-ified version of his grandmother's potato-spice cake. Much to his surprise, the women loved it. They also seemed to enjoy his singing voice, which meant that Ollie soon found himself offering up hourly acapella renditions of pop songs they had never heard of. Singing for his supper, he supposed. And waiting, waiting, waiting.

The trog, meanwhile, had become a semi-permanent attachment to Ollie's body; usually on his shoulder, sometimes on his stomach or curled up next to him on the floor. At some point during the second day, Ollie decided to name him Meatball. Partly because the creature did, in fact, look like a furry sphere of ground beef, but mostly because the name reminded him of Hanover Street. And La Sicilia Trattoria. And his mother's blue-and-white Pfaltzgraff dishes resting on a lace tablecloth, ready for seconds of hot spaghetti.

When Tera was there, they spent all of their time together. She taught him to play Rat-a-Tat, a puzzle game involving narrow wooden pegs and not, thankfully, actual rats. Their meals consisted mainly of blindfish stew, rhizer stew, and the ever-popular blindfish-rhizer stew combo. Sometimes their knees would touch while they ate, huddled together by the firepit. For maybe the first time in his life, he barely noticed the food. The knees, he noticed. And when hers rested against his, she didn't move them away.

Sometimes she'd leave for hours to work a shift on the crow boat, check on the progress of the pass, or finagle whatever deals she was finagling down at the Tea Party. When she was gone, Ollie missed her smell: an oddly beguiling combination of handmade soap, leather, and bird-barn musk. He missed her sarcasm and her dubious sideways glances. He missed the deep trumpet of her laugh, always loud and sudden. During the quiet times, Ollie found himself plotting ways to make her laugh again, conjuring knock-knock jokes from memory like a six-year-old boy.

He began to hate Tera's shapeless jumpsuit, and to wonder about the compact, strong body that hid somewhere inside. He spent whole chunks of hours imagining what it might be like to touch her skin. To feel the curve of her stomach. To run his fingers through her hair: the rough, shaved sides morphing into a soft, silvery purple swirl.

Chores kept him busy and distracted. Unless, of course, Tera was there to help. On his second afternoon in the house, the two of them found themselves hanging laundry on the line out back. Every time Tera bent over to reach into the basket of wet clothes, her jumpsuit collar would hang forward, sometimes just enough to—

"So, why medical imaging?" she asked, startling him.

"Huh?"

"The scholarship. You're going to be an x-ray tech, right?"

"Oh, right. Yes." He cleared his throat.

"Why?"

Ollie pinned a ratty old facecloth on the clothesline and considered his answer. "I had to pick one of the majors, and that one sounded interesting," he said. "Well, kind of interesting. The pay is supposed to be good. And I hear the hours are good, too. Flexible." It seemed bizarre to be discussing such things now, in this place. Work hours. Paychecks. College majors. Even as he said the words, the concepts seemed as distant as lunar craters.

"Hmm," Tera replied, reaching into the basket again.

"Hmm, what?"

"Nothing. It's just, I guess I can't quite picture you doing that, is all."

This made him smile. "And what can you picture me doing?"

"Food, actually."

He stopped pinning and turned to look at her.

"Food?"

"Yeah. You're good at cooking. And you seem to love it. I see you all the time, talking with Ajanta. Looking over her shoulder while she makes things. Maybe you could be a chef."

He snorted and reached into his basket. "Oh right, that's just what I need. More food in my life."

She looked confused. "Why not?"

"Because...I'm fat?" The words popped out before he could stop them. He wanted to add a "duh," but wisely didn't.

"Who told you that?" Tera said, her eyes narrowing. He got the feeling, suddenly, that if he gave her some names she would kick her laundry basket aside and go hunt them down.

"C'mon. Nobody had to tell me," Ollie said. A beige sock dangled from the tips of his fingers. "I mean, don't get me wrong, plenty of people *have* told me. You remember school recess, don't you? Not exactly known for its subtle insults."

"Well, I think that's ridiculous," Tera said, folding her arms across her chest. "You like food. You're good with it. You should work with it if you want to."

"I'm not saying I don't want to." He'd actually thought it about it plenty of times. Culinary school. Maybe even his own restaurant, someday. Or a bakery. But he could imagine the jokes. The whispers. *Of course, the fat guy makes the best cupcakes!*

"Then I think you should do it," Tera said, reaching for the line. She moved one towel to make room for the next. "All I know is, I like mealtime a lot better since you've been here."

"Yeah?" he asked.

"Yeah." She turned back to face him. "In fact, I like a whole lot of things better since you've been here."

It was something about the way she said it. The way she was looking at him, as though she wanted him to know she was serious. It made an electric pulse skitter, unrestrained, across his chest.

Her brown eyes twinkled, daring him to look away.

He didn't.

A slow, sly grin spread across her face. The next thing he knew, a balled-up sock hit him in the shoulder. Ollie's mouth popped open in surprise as he stared at the wet spot it left behind. Then he stared at Tera, who looked quite pleased with herself.

"Oh, it's on," he said, dipping his hands down into the laundry basket.

Tera yelped and did the same. Moments later, they were both dodging a nor'easter of blizzarding clothes, laughing until it hurt.

On the third morning, Ollie was extracting a piece of something sharp from Meatball's webbed foot when Kuyu burst through the curtained door. "We've got Reds," she said breathlessly, her dark curls falling around her face. "Two houses down. They're making the rounds."

"Shit!" Ajanta said, dropping her hands onto her hips. Her glance swept over the cramped interior of the one-room house, as though she might suddenly find a new hiding spot. She tugged on her long braid. "All right. Let's not panic." Then she looked at Tera and added, "We'll keep them occupied. Take him to the studio. And don't come back until we get you."

Tera didn't argue. She jumped to her feet and grabbed Ollie's arm. "Let's go."

Startled, Ollie stood. He gathered Meatball in his arms and accepted the torch that was offered, feeling like someone had just yanked the floor out from under him. Ajanta was still gripping her braid. Derrin had her arms wrapped around Kuyu's torso. All of them wore an expression that he could only describe as piteous dread.

The room started spinning. What was happening, here? Should he say goodbye? Or thank you? Either one seemed like an admission he didn't want to make. In the end, he just nodded, then followed Tera out the door.

They ran for ten or fifteen minutes through a thick patch of stalagmites, ducking and weaving as needed to navigate. Though it was technically morning, the wormwalkers above had transitioned into a darker cycle, leaving Ollie and Tera dependent on the torches to light their way. At a clearing, Ollie spied a tiny building ahead.

"This is my studio," Tera explained. "We'll be okay here. Not too many people know about it."

Ollie gave her a sideways glance. "Oh! So, why didn't we come here in the first place?"

"Because there's no food here, or beds, or supplies. And because... it's private. I don't usually let anyone in here." Her words were gruff, but Ollie could hear a tinge of emotion behind them. Was she embarrassed?

Tera approached a door that was, he was surprised to see, an actual, solid door. She pushed it open, walked into the darkness, and began lighting torches on the walls.

Ollie stepped inside and stomped the limestone dust from his shoes. By the time he looked up, the contents of the studio had been illuminated. He stood and stared, struck dumb with sudden, unexpected awe.

The paintings were everywhere. They surrounded him on all sides, hanging on walls, propped up on the floor, and leaning against easels. Each one, it seemed, was a study in humanity. Ollie walked in slow amazement around the small space, looking at the faces, the bodies, the glinting eyes and waving hair. The colors were impossibly vibrant, making the portraits appear to glow from within. The faces glowed, too—with happiness, with life. He saw friends, shoulder to shoulder. Couples, holding hands. Proud smiles. Groups and pairs and singles. Laughing men, fierce women. Happiness and strength. Companionship.

Love.

He moved wordlessly, bending when he had to. Peering closely. Touching the frames. Finally, he rubbed his eyes, overcome with the wash of emotions that were so obviously embedded inside each stroke of paint. With a start, he realized what he was seeing: This was Tera's Neath. This was how she saw her world, and her friends, and her freedom. Smiling faces. Clasped hands, holding tight to one another.

The truth blazed to life before his eyes, as clear and as beautiful as a rising sun.

Tera wasn't hiding out. She wasn't escaping, or settling, or missing anything at all. She had found her family, and herself. These were the colors of her soul.

Slowly, Ollie turned to look at her, as if for the first time. He lifted Meatball off his shoulder and dropped the creature onto the floor.

Tera was squirming, tugging on the ends of her sleeves. "I just dabble," she said. "They're not very good, I know."

He took two steps and stood in front of her.

"I don't get much of a chance to practice," she added, almost to herself.

She didn't even see it, he realized.

Tera was still talking, saying something about the shortage of paint and the lack of light.

How could she possibly not see it?

Her apologies pained him. He couldn't hear any more; he had to make her stop. Ollie reached out to touch her cheeks in wonderment. And when he closed his eyes and kissed her, he tasted the colors, too— silvers and golds and aquamarines, shocking his tongue like Frangelico mousse. Lifting him off the ground. Carrying him away, finally, to something that felt like home.

They had only been in hiding for an hour when Tera announced that she wanted to paint his portrait.

Ollie didn't mind. It gave him an excuse to sit and stare at her. He watched, amused, as she lost herself in the process, squinting at the canvas, mixing the paints, dabbing the brush with tiny, delicate thrusts and then transitioning to aggressively sweeping strokes. Watching an artist, he thought, was like watching an animal instinct come to life. Inhibitions were gone. Restrictions were gone. And all that was left was desire.

They spent the rest of the day like that: painter and subject, in seclusion. Ollie turned to the left and turned to the right, following orders as they came and indulging Tera's demands. Mostly. Every few minutes, he would interrupt the proceedings to walk across the room and kiss her, again. He couldn't get enough. He wanted to crawl inside her jumpsuit and live there, kissing every inch, every day. For the moment, though, he would settle for her lips. He would sit as still as he could, resisting as long as he could, watching her work. Then he would fail the exquisite test, give up, and sweep her into his arms again.

"C'mon, let me see it," he teased, touching her face, her hair, her arms. He peered over her shoulder at the back of the canvas.

"No!" she said, covering his eyes with a grin. "Not yet. It's not done."

"You show me yours, I'll show you mine…"

"You don't have one," she pointed out.

"I hope we're still talking about paintings."

Tera's loud laugh was interrupted by a knock at the door. They pulled apart and shared a nervous glance.

"Who is it?" she called out.

"It's me," came a voice.

Tera opened the latch and swung the door open. Derrin was standing outside. "They're gone," she said.

"Like, gone, gone?"

Derrin nodded. "Well, for now, anyway. They asked us about a hundred questions. Said they were looking for an escaped prisoner, blah, blah, blah."

"What did you tell them?"

Derrin shot her an annoyed look. "We gave them a map to your studio. What the hell do you think? We lied." Then she jutted her chin toward Ollie. "We bought you a little time. But Ajanta says you'd better get him out of here, fast. They won't give up that easily."

Ollie's stomach dropped.

"All right, thanks," Tera said. "Tell her I'm going to check on the exit pass."

Derrin nodded, turned on her heel, and disappeared around a lump of stalagmite.

Ollie and Tera stood in awkward silence. Finally, she looked at the easel and said, "I guess we can finish that later."

"Right," he said, nodding.

"Nikki and Floyd will close up soon. We don't have much time."

"Right," he said again.

"Okay, then. You stay here. I'll be back soon."

"What?" His head snapped up. "No way. I'm coming."

"Uh, uh." She shook her head. "This whole place is looking for you."

"I don't care. You're not going out there alone. For me."

"Ollie, it's—"

"I'm coming," he interrupted, pulling himself to his full height.

Tera sighed, realizing she had lost the battle. "Fine. I guess it's just as well. That way, you can leave straight from there."

He blinked. "You mean...not come back here?"

"Well, no. Not if we get the pass. Once we have that, we can go right from the Tea Party to the exit hatch."

Ollie's hand went reflexively to the trog on his shoulder. He dug his fingers into Meatball's thick fur. "Oh. Right. Well, yeah, I guess that makes the most sense."

"We don't have much time," Tera said again. She was avoiding his eyes.

Ollie's throat had gone dry. "Right. Of course."

"Okay," she said, nodding. Rocking back and forth, heel to toe, heel to toe. Staring at the floor.

"Okay," he echoed. Or, at least he thought he had said it. He might have just thought it. Ollie looked around the small room, at the paintings. He had kissed her there, right in that spot. And over there, by the easel. And over there, in the chair. Just minutes ago, this space had seemed like a cocoon of warmth and euphoria. Now, suddenly, it just seemed dark. He could almost see his bliss evaporating into the dim, dusty air.

They took simultaneous, deep breaths. Something passed between them, then; something unsaid. Something that made a lump of sadness expand in his throat.

Nothing left but the leaving, as his mother used to say.

Without another word, they walked outside, closed the door behind them, and started down the path toward the first of the wobbly bridges. This time, Ollie hardly noticed their dilapidated condition. He hardly noticed the green water, or the nearby splash of a fallen wormwalker, or the various shacks and shapes in the landscape. He only noticed her, and the tightness in his chest that was making it increasingly hard for him to breathe. Was this the adaptation everyone kept talking about? Or something else?

At the Tea Party, most of the vendors were closing up shop for the day, packing up boats and tying fabric flaps. Ollie found himself hoping, irrationally, that Nikki and Floyd were already gone. But when he and Tera arrived at the shop's floating platform, the namesake owners were still there.

"Be right back," Tera said, walking toward the counter. The three of them held a hushed conversation, which Ollie watched from the corner of his eye. Items were exchanged. Quiet promises were made.

He heard only snippets: "tomorrow..." and "make another on the..." and then, something that sounded like "Laszlo."

Ollie straightened. A sudden image of the acrobat popped into his mind: blue suit, strong accent, hooked nose. *You are smart behind the eyes, no?*

He must have misheard. He tried to think of other words that sounded like "Laszlo," and came up with nothing useful. Last row? Cat slow? Pass go?

Ollie ran his fingers absently through Meatball's fur as the trog snuffled closer against his neck. His brow was still furrowed when Tera reappeared at his side.

"All set," she muttered, slipping something into his palm.

He looked down at the card in his hand. It was completely blank. Just a lemony rectangle. "What's this?"

"That," she said, "is an exit pass."

"Are you sure?"

"Sure, I'm sure. Why?"

"No reason." Ollie eyed the generic card dubiously, his question about Laszlo momentarily forgotten.

"All right, let's get out of here," Tera said, pulling him along. "The fewer people we see, the better."

They wound their way through the dispersing crowds, finally reaching the spot where the docks met the land. The card felt cold and sharp against his palm. He stared down at it. The yellow seemed to glow.

This was it, then. His ticket out. The one thing he had prayed for, had not dared to hope for, was here, now, in his hand.

As if noticing she was suddenly alone, Tera turned. "Come *on!*" she whisper-shouted.

And then Ollie heard himself say the strangest, most implausible thing. "I...can't."

"Why the hell not?"

He tugged at the end of his sleeve. What was the matter with him? What was he doing? "My friend is still in there," he said. "Dozer. And lots of other innocent people, too. The whole fifth floor! How can we just leave them there?"

Tera gave him a long look. "Come over here," she said, pulling him aside. They ended up next to a small building, some kind of a storage shed, near the Tea Party's entry gate. "Ollie, I'm sorry about that. I really am. But there's nothing you can do for them. We only have one exit pass, and you're almost out of time. You need to go, now."

"But—"

"None of this is your fault. You did nothing wrong. Look at me!" she said, lifting his chin with her finger. "This is your only chance. And I'm not going to let you blow it."

He swallowed, trying to find some useful words. When none appeared, he grabbed her hands in his and squeezed.

"No," Tera said, pulling back. "Uh, uh. I won't be the reason you stay here. I can't."

"But—"

"No," she said again, more firmly. "You have a life somewhere else. A bright future—*above* the ground. With sunshine, and ocean waves, and cute little kittens, and like, I don't know, fried dough. You have people who miss you."

No one like you, he wanted to say. Instead, he asked, "Did you have a different name? Before, I mean. Up there."

Her forehead wrinkled. "Why?"

"Just wondering, I guess." He thought of Dozer's suggestion that he find a new name, and of all the unusual monikers he had heard since landing in the Neath. Reinvention seemed to be the default setting for new arrivals.

Tera's mouth tightened, then loosened as she bit her bottom lip. When she finally spoke, her voice was quiet. "Teresa," she said. "Teresa Martinez."

He smiled. "That's a nice name."

"Thank you, Oliver Delgato."

For a moment, neither spoke. Then he asked, again, the one question he knew he shouldn't. "Why did you rescue me that day? Why me?"

Tera folded her arms. "What does it matter? You're leaving now." As she said it, he saw a quick flash of pain in her expression.

She doesn't want me to go, he thought. The realization made his heart leap, and then fall. "Please, I have to know," he said. And he did. Screw horses and teeth. He couldn't leave this place, leave her, without at least knowing that.

Tera ran a hand through her lavender hair. "If I tell you, will you keep walking?"

He nodded.

"Fine, then. Here it is. I rescued you that day because someone told me to."

Ollie's head cocked to the side. This was not the answer he had been expecting. "Who?"

"I got a note," she answered.

Note. Why did that word send a tingle down his spine? Ollie's eyes widened. "Wait. Are you saying George Herrick wrote you a note? About me?"

"That's what I'm saying."

"But why?"

"I have no idea."

"What did it say?"

"What difference does it make? He told me to get you, and I got you. That's what you do around here when the 350-year-old creepy founder guy gives you a job to do. You do it. End of story. Can we go now?"

"What did it say?" He asked again, his voice quiet and firm.

Tera inhaled a deep, resigned breath and pushed it out. "It was addressed to me," she began, looking uncomfortable. "It said, 'Save the savior who is not a savior. Use the treasure that is not your treasure. Pay the man who is not a man."

Ollie stared at her, puzzled.

"I got it the day before I picked you up," she added.

"The day...before?" This just kept getting weirder. "So, what made you think it was about me?"

"I didn't. Obviously, I had no idea what it meant," she continued. "Then, after I saw you have all that...trouble, with the girl, I figured that maybe you were the, uh, savior that wasn't a savior."

Ollie felt his face redden.

Tera continued: "And the treasure that wasn't my treasure...I thought that probably meant the cash you gave me. So I used that money to bribe McNulty. A guard."

"The man who isn't a man?" Ollie asked, perplexed.

"Yeah, well, the general consensus is that McNulty's not much of a man, so I figured he fit the bill." She shrugged.

"But how could George Herrick know all that the day *before* I even got here?" he asked. Though they were back on dry land, he could swear he still felt the docks swaying beneath his feet.

"I don't know," Tera answered, "I honestly don't. But that's the way it goes down here, sometimes. You can't always explain it."

"Really?" he deadpanned. "I hadn't noticed."

She ignored his tone. "Anyway, it worked. Here we are. You got out, you've got your exit pass, and the clock is ticking. Can we go n—" Tera stopped. Her body tensed. She had seen something over his shoulder.

"What?" Ollie asked.

"Get behind the shed," Tera said, though her lips had hardly moved.

"The shed? Why?"

"Just do it, now," she hissed.

Robotically, he followed her instructions, hiding behind the small wooden structure. Then he peeked around the corner to see her standing there, alone.

"No matter what happens, you run," Tera said, just loud enough for him to hear. "Take that pass, go to the hatch, and get yourself home. Do you understand?"

"Tera, what's going—"

"Promise me you will go back home," she interrupted. When he didn't answer, she said it again, louder: "Promise me!"

"I promise," he said, still perplexed.

And then he saw them: Two red-suited men, approaching from the hill. Heading straight toward Tera. Closing in fast.

"Well, hello, boys," she said. "What seems to be the pr—"

Tera's last word morphed into a muffled grunt as the men grabbed her, wrestled her into submission, and tied a gag around her mouth. It happened blindingly fast.

"Just the pretty lady we've been looking for," the guard leered, yanking her arm and pulling her face close to his. "We hear you've been harboring fugitives. Naughty, naughty girl."

Ollie staggered out of his hiding place. "Hey! Let go of her!" he shouted.

One of the Reds kept a hold on Tera while the second lunged for Ollie. The man's big, meaty hands dug into his elbow, holding tight. No matter how he writhed, Ollie couldn't pull himself free.

An involuntary cry escaped his lips as dismay and sickening comprehension engulfed him. *No! No, no, no!*

The Red had another gag ready and leaned forward to shove it into Ollie's mouth. That was when it happened: a quick blur of fur and teeth and snarling rage. Meatball had leapt off of Ollie's shoulder like a jack from a box, flinging himself into the face of the sneering guard. The creature's bill opened wide—too wide, freakishly wide—and flashed row upon row of stacked, chiseled teeth. And as Ollie watched, stunned, his formerly cuddly companion sunk those teeth into the guard's cheek and ripped out a fat chunk of flesh in a single, grisly spurt.

The Red shrieked and grabbed his face, dropping Ollie's arm in the process. Blood poured onto the ground below. The first guard, now flustered, stepped closer, dragging Tera along.

She managed to get one arm free of his grip, pulled the gag from her mouth, and screamed: "Ruuuuun!"

The commotion had attracted others; in the distance, more red suits approached. Three, no four. Five. Coming fast.

"Ruuuuun!" Tera yelled again.

So many guards. An advancing sea of red.

Even in his panic, Ollie knew: There was nothing he could do for her now. The show of force was overwhelming, and bearing down fast. He needed to get help. He needed—

Meatball scrambled up his leg, claws jabbing. Everything spun around him in revolting, breakneck circles...the market, the water, the people, the red suits.

Promise me, she had said.

I promise, he had answered.

His face still wet with another man's blood, Ollie turned, and he ran.

Seventeen

Ollie's feet pounded the thin slats of the bridge planks, making the structures buckle and sway. One bridge, two bridges, three. Meatball didn't falter, digging in for stability. Finally, they reached Tera's island and made their way to the house. Gasping and heaving, he fell through the curtained door and stumbled inside. The women stared.

Ollie fell to his knees. "She's gone," he panted.

"What?" Alarmed, Ajanta hurried to his side. "Who?" But she knew, of course. They all knew.

"They took her! Reds. They just showed up and—" He paused, filling his lungs. "They dragged her away. They tried to take me, too, but Meatball just...attacked the guy. His face... With his teeth. She told me to run. And more were coming, so fast, so I... So I..." Ollie stopped talking and started crying. His head dropped.

The women gathered, staring down at him. A soft sensation tickled his hand. Meatball was nuzzling him. Ollie reached for him, clutched him to his chest.

Ajanta's voice cut through the hard silence. "Did she get the pass?"

Ollie looked up. His vision was blurred. "What?"

"The exit pass. Do you have it?"

"Ye... Yes," he answered, confused.

"Good," she said. "Take it and go. Get out of here."

He wiped his face with the back of his sleeve. What did she mean, go?

The women had already turned and begun talking amongst themselves. Harsh, insistent murmurs laced with anger and fear.

"What are we going to do?" he asked them, climbing to his feet.

Ajanta gave him a withering look over her shoulder. "Don't worry about it. Just go."

Don't worry about it? Was she kidding? "Please," he said. "What can I do?"

Derrin and Kuyu clung to each other; they turned as one. "Haven't you done enough?" Derrin asked.

"What can we do?" he asked them again, his voice a desperate whisper.

Kuyu's mouth curled into a sneer. "What can we do? Oh, I don't know, let's see... First, I thought we'd go knock on the front gate. Bring a dessert, maybe. 'Yoo hoo, boys!' Show a little leg? That might work."

No one laughed.

Ollie's body had gone stiff. Tears welled again, stinging his eyes, but he didn't move.

Kuyu lifted her palms. "And then, I don't know. Maybe they'll let her go, maybe they won't. Either way, it's fine, right? You got your precious exit pass. I'm sure they'll set her up with a nice little place in there. A penthouse, maybe. We all know Herrick's End is famous for its deluxe accommodations and fine customer service. Well, look who I'm talking to. You know better than anyone, don't you, Ollie? So, you tell us. What kind of a stay is she in for?"

As Kuyu spoke, the women's collective rage floated across the empty space, encircling him, choking him. Meatball seemed to feel it, too: The trog's feet curled ever tighter around his shoulder blade.

Ollie's legs wobbled. Despair blocked his throat. What could he say? What possible response did he have? Kuyu was right. Ollie had ruined Tera's life. He had shown up where he didn't belong, and he had destroyed everything.

The women turned away from him. They wanted him to go.

He tried to remove Meatball from his shoulder, but failed at that, too. With a deep, shaking sigh, he left one hand on the trog and used the other to pull back the curtain. And then Ollie did what he always did. The only thing he was good at: He walked away.

Ollie's body felt even heavier than usual as he dragged his feet along the dirt path. Hunger pangs raked through his stomach, and he welcomed them. He deserved them. Tera was suffering, and so should he. Maybe he'd spend the rest of his miserable life camping in stalagmite forests, wearing the same pair of crunchy underwear, plucking slimy blindfish out of the pea-soup lake. Sleeping with regret under a ceiling of worms.

When the studio appeared ahead, just the sight of it made him want to weep. Where was she now? What were they doing to her? Was she crying? Fighting? Worrying about Mrs. Paget? Regretting every decision she had made during the past two weeks?

Ollie balled his hands into fists and pressed them against his forehead. Thinking of her in that place, he wanted to vomit. He almost did. Leaning forward, he placed his hands on his knees and took several deep breaths.

Ajanta and the others would take care of it. They'd make a plan.

He wanted, more than anything, to believe it.

Ollie approached the studio and tried the handle. It was unlocked. Once inside, he paced. He cracked his knuckles. He found a couple of dried loosemeat sticks, ate one, and fed the other to Meatball. He found piles of Tera's papers on the small table and began rifling through them. Most seemed to be musings about color studies and composition, though one was a map. She had drawn it herself.

Ollie held it up to the beam of light. He saw all the various scattered islands and bridges, labeled with names. The Neath was bigger than he had realized. He saw Herrick's End, and the Tea Party, and Blackstone Park, and even the chairlift terminus and the dock where he had first met her. Tera had also mapped out all the crow boat routes with dotted black lines.

And there, on the far end of the drawing, he saw one, tiny word: "Hatch."

The way out. He had promised Tera he would go, and now he could. Nothing was stopping him. He had the exit pass. He had the map. All he had to do was drop the trog outside, set him loose, and go.

So simple, and yet so impossible. Because Ollie knew, as sure as he knew how far to stretch the perfect pizza crust, that none of it mattered. He could have a chauffeured limo waiting outside the door that very minute to whisk him straight back to his North End apartment, and he still wasn't going to leave her. Not there. Not now.

As Ollie lowered the map, something caught his eye. One easel among many, turned to face the wall.

Tera's unfinished portrait. Of him.

His stomach clenched. Then, like pressing a finger into a bruise, Ollie walked to the easel and turned it, slowly, until the beam of light from the doorway illuminated the colors on the canvas.

Ollie's breath slowed. He took a step closer.

The boy in the painting was fair-skinned and handsome, with warm brown eyes and light, floppy hair. He was smiling, at ease. His body was large, powerful, and capable. And he wasn't alone. He had his arm thrown over the shoulder of a much smaller girl. She had darker skin and partly shaved, purple hair, and was leaning into his side with a toothy grin. She looked happy and safe.

The tall kid was a gentle giant. Crinkles of amusement lined his eyes. His oversized form was inviting, almost reassuring. A brown fuzzy trog sat on his shoulder, looking up at him in open adoration. The artist's message was clear: This guy was somebody you'd want to know. Somebody you'd want to love.

As Ollie watched, his doppelganger's smile turned stern in the shadowy light.

Go get her, said a voice in his head.

Tera had risked everything to rescue him from the bowels of hell. She had known all the horrible, probable consequences, and she had hoisted up her jumpsuit, strapped on her toolbelt, and done it anyway.

Ollie knew he could never match Tera's courage. He almost certainly couldn't match her scheming, or her smarts, or her skills. But if he had any hope of becoming the person she thought he was, he knew he at least had to try.

He lifted Meatball off his shoulder and held the trog in front of his face, until they were eye to eye. "Change of plans, buddy," he said. "I need to see a guy about a thing. You in?"

Meatball's tongue darted out of his squat beak and licked Ollie's nose. He was in.

Eighteen

Ollie found a torch and a small can of kerosene—just enough to light Tera's drawing table. He cleared the surface of everything except her charcoal pencils, a few sheets from her sketch pad, and her map of the Neath. Then he got to work.

Meatball supervised the effort for a few minutes, then fell into a deep sleep punctuated by a symphony of grunts and wheezes. By the time the trog woke the next morning, Ollie was surrounded by scribbled notes and blueprints. His hair was sticking out sideways in the spot where he had been clutching it. His hands and face were streaked with pencil smears. He had worked through the night. He felt good. He felt ready. He lifted Meatball onto his shoulder and headed out.

When he got to the Tea Party, Ollie did his best to ignore the wonderful, rhizery smells wafting from the various floating stalls. He stepped over the skittering trogs and splats of fallen wormwalkers and muscled his way through the crowded docks until he found the sign he was looking for: "Nikki & Floyd's: Brickside Curiosities." Tossing the tent flap open, he stepped inside.

The couple was standing behind the counter, talking. Floyd was instantly recognizable in his rumpled brown garb. Nikki, likewise, was wearing her usual fur shawl, though that day's color was more chestnut than white. For the first time, Ollie wondered: Where did the fur come from? As the obvious answer dawned, he reached up to touch Meatball's thick coat and shuddered.

The pair's murmured conversation came to a sudden halt when they noticed him.

"Do you remember me?" Ollie asked.

They looked at each other. Then Floyd said, "Sure, kid. Of course, we do."

"They took Tera."

Two nodding heads. Two sad looks. "Yeah, we heard," Floyd said. "Damn shame, that."

"I need your help."

Nikki raised an eyebrow. "With what? Child, you're not thinking of going over there, are you? That's a fool's errand, nothing more."

"I need to find someone, and I think you know where he is."

"Oh, yeah?" Now Floyd looked amused. "Who?"

"Laszlo Kravchenko," Ollie said.

Nikki and Floyd stopped moving, stopped fidgeting. Ollie could see them actively trying not to look at each other. Trying not to react in any way.

"Never heard of him," said Floyd.

"Bullshit," Ollie replied.

The couple shared a sideways glance. Finally, Floyd leaned a hand on the counter. "I suppose we could ask around," he said, the words falling lazily. "Maybe. Depends on—"

"Let me guess," Ollie interrupted. "It depends on what's in it for you?"

Floyd shrugged, unapologetic.

Ollie reached into the pocket of his off-white jumpsuit. When he lifted his hand, a keychain dangled from his fingers. He pushed the small button on the side, and the flashing started: *Oliver. Oliver. Oliver.* The blinking word lit up the dark tent like streaks of lightning.

Their eyes widened.

"Whoa," breathed Nikki.

"How long will it do that?" Floyd asked. His expression was greedy.

"Forever," Ollie lied, not feeling the need to explain the particulars of lithium coin-cell battery life with the miscreant who had already stolen his wallet. "How do you know Laszlo?"

Nikki looked at her husband, then heaved her furred chest with a sigh. "Laszlo is a Runner," she said. "Like a go-between. He lives on the Brickside, but he comes down here sometimes. For the WRC. He ferries people, and stuff, whatever. Sometimes he brings us...items. For the shop."

"Can you contact him?" Ollie asked.

"I don't know. Maybe."

He dangled the keychain. "Yes or no?"

166

"Yes, probably," Nikki admitted. "If we need to."

"Good. Then do it. Today. Get him down here. I need to talk to him."

They paused, then nodded. Nikki reached for the keychain.

"Uh, uh, uh," Ollie said, snatching it back into his palm. "First, Laszlo."

Floyd folded his arms.

"And I need a little money," Ollie added. "For food."

After a long, hard stare, Floyd reached into some hidden crevice. He pulled out a small wad of colored bills and passed them across the counter.

Ollie took the cash without comment. Then he looked at Nikki. "You shouldn't wear fur," he said. "It's cruel." The money went into his pocket, and his mind went to his next stop.

A group of crows is called a murder.

Ollie had learned that odd fact sometime back in middle school, but it hadn't made any sense to him until now. As he approached the barn, a dozen giant, feathered heads emerged from the stalls, accosting him with a sudden, thunderous chorus of caws. Murderous caws, you might call them. Or at the very least, not the friendliest of welcomes. Even Meatball felt the hostility; he jumped at the sudden outburst and pressed himself against Ollie's neck.

The hammered-together, mostly tin structure didn't look much like a Brickside barn—it wasn't red or charming—but it did smell the same. No, he corrected himself: It smelled worse. He detected notes of dank earth, expired food, and decomposing bird poop, all mushed together and hovering like a toxic cloud.

Ollie paused and held an arm over his nose. How would he find her? Every one of these damn crows looked exactly the same: enormous, black, and beady-eyed.

In the end, he felt her more than saw her. She was watching him, neck tilted, feathers ruffled. She gave her head a shake.

"Hello, Mrs. Paget," Ollie said, approaching the stall warily. He peered over the edge; her food bucket was empty. He held up his hands in an "I come in peace" gesture, then reached over the door to grab the bucket's handle. Carrying it to the nearby alcove, Ollie copied Tera's motions from just a few days before: He held his breath, dipped a large scoop into a container full of seeds and writhing creatures, and filled the bucket.

He carried the nauseating stew of animate and inanimate foodstuffs back to Mrs. Paget's stall, past a complaining, jealous line of cawing birds. Ollie dropped the bucket in front of her, then jumped back as she attacked it ravenously. Lizard-like legs and the unmistakable glow of wormwalker segments flew in all directions. He might have seen one or two loose eyeballs before he shut his own eyes. When he opened them again, she was picking the last scattered bits off the ground.

Ollie took a step closer.

"All good?" he asked.

Mrs. Paget turned her attention back to him and blinked. Insofar as a crow can look mistrustful, she did.

"I've got some news," Ollie told her. "Bad news."

The giant bird moved closer. Her head poked out of the stall door, towering above his. She seemed to be listening intently.

"It's Tera. She needs help."

The crow's feathers gave an almost imperceptible shake, as though a breeze had passed through her stall.

"I was hoping we could come to some kind of understanding, you and I," he added.

Mrs. Paget went still. Then, as he watched, two huge, onyx wings rose behind her body. Her throat emitted a plaintive wail: *Caw! Caw! Caw!*

Ollie met the bird's eyes. "I know," he whispered. "Me, too."

At his next stop, Derrin was the first to spot him. She was digging some kind of trench beside the house, huffing and puffing and attacking the ground with a ferocity that belied her thin, fragile frame. When she saw Ollie approaching, her mouth popped open into a pink circle.

"What are you doing here?" she asked. Her voice, as always, sounded old and grainy. Her skin was so thin he could very nearly see the sinewy jaw muscles clenching underneath. Two trogs sat on her shoulders, one black, one white. Her stringy blonde hair wrapped around them like a blanket. Both appeared to be fast asleep, despite her strenuous efforts.

"Hi," Ollie said, approaching with cautious steps.

"You're supposed to be gone," Derrin said.

"Yeah, well, that didn't really work out."

Derrin shot a glance at the house. Her voice dropped. "You'd better leave. They won't be happy to see you."

"I know. But I have to talk to them." He gestured toward the door. "You mind if I...?"

She leaned on the shovel and shrugged. "Your funeral."

Ollie took two steps, then stopped when he heard her say, "Wait."

Derrin sighed theatrically, tossed the shovel onto the ground, and caught up to him. "It'll go better if I do it."

"Thanks."

"Wait there." Pulling aside the curtain, she disappeared inside. Ollie could hear raised voices through the walls. When she finally emerged, she waved him in. "Come on, then. Better be quick about it."

He nodded and stepped across the threshold, where he found, as expected, three glaring women. Two of them had their arms crossed.

"You have five minutes," Ajanta said.

"Two!" countered Kuyu. She tossed her head back in indignation, sending her curls bouncing. "What the hell do you want?"

"I know you don't want to see me," he began, shrinking as best he could. "It's my fault, what happened to her. And I want to make it right."

Kuyu snorted.

"Look, I get it," Ollie said. "But it doesn't matter how this happened. What matters is—"

"Oh, that's rich, coming from the guy who *made it happen,*" Kuyu said.

"Guys!" Derrin said. "Just let him talk."

Ollie shot her an appreciative look. He took a deep breath. "Please. We have to do something."

"What makes you think we're not?" Ajanta retorted, a defensive note in her voice.

"No, I mean...something big."

"We're working on a payoff," Derrin told him. The other two flashed her dirty looks, but she continued. "A bribe. We might be able to—"

Now it was Ollie's turn to interrupt. "No," he said again. "Something bigger. Even if you do get her out, they'll just come for you next. Where does it end? Besides, Tera's not the only innocent person in there."

"Not our problem," Kuyu said. "Look, kid, unlike Tera, we're not going to get all moony-eyed over you just because you walk in here with some cockamamie plan. I don't know why she did all this for you, but w—"

"That's the thing," Ollie interrupted. "She didn't."

"Oh, she did get all moony-eyed," Derrin said.

"No, I mean she didn't do this for me. Not at first. She did it..." He paused. "She did it because George Herrick asked her to."

The room went silent. On Ollie's shoulder, Meatball spun in a circle and resettled.

Finally, Ajanta spoke. "What are you talking about?"

"She said he sent her one of those notes," Ollie said with a sigh. "One of those stupid riddles that he wrote in his sleep, or whatever. He told her to rescue me, and he told her how to do it. But that's not even the weird part. The weird part is, he sent it to her the *day before* I got down here. George Herrick knew I was coming before I did. He knew I was going to screw it all up and get myself thrown into that prison. And if he knew all that was going to happen, he must have known this was going to happen too, right?"

"Why *you?*" Kuyu asked, looking dubious.

"I...I don't know."

They stared at him. Ajanta's face wore a troubled expression. "Look, Ollie, we appreciate your concern," she said. "But what you're asking is too dangerous. We can't risk it."

Ollie reached into his pocket and pulled out a folded piece of drawing paper. "Just look, please! I have a plan."

"I'm sure you do," she replied, with just a hint of condescension. "But I have a responsibility to these girls. And to myself. Tera made her choices, and now we have to make ours."

"This isn't just about Tera!" Ollie said, his voice cracking. "I mean, yes, it's about Tera. But it's about the others, too! My friend Dozer didn't do what they accused him of. Even the Reader saw it, and still, it doesn't matter. He's still trapped. The whole place is wrong. It's run by a goddamn lunatic! I've seen it! I *know* you know it!"

"So what *is* the answer, smart guy?" Kuyu asked. "Hugs and handshakes? You want us to close the whole place down and set all the psychos free? Maybe round up our abusers and serve them water-lily pie?"

Ollie gave her a weary look. He had never felt so tired. So afraid. "That's not what I'm saying," he told her. "I know you don't trust me. If I were you, I wouldn't trust me, either. But can you trust George Herrick?"

At that, three pairs of eyebrows raised.

"Herrick told me, 'All will be mended.' He even told me how."

"Told you how?" Kuyu asked. "Like, specifically?"

Ollie stuffed the paper back into his jumpsuit pocket, stalling. "Sort of, yeah."

"Sort of? What does that mean?"

"He gave me some...instructions."

Ajanta stepped closer, her expression betraying a mix of anticipation and fear. "What kind of instructions?"

"He said, 'Tell Widow Hibbins zero. Lion's feet will dig. As I am, so he will be.'"

All three of them stared at him, their faces blank. Kuyu and Derrin were leaning against each other, as always, like bookends with no books.

"What the hell does that mean?" Kuyu finally asked.

"I...don't exactly know," Ollie admitted.

"Oh, Ollie," Ajanta sighed. "Please, just go home. Take your pass and go back to the Brickside. This is not your fight."

"No. I won't leave her," he answered, spreading his feet apart. "I won't. I'm going to get her out. I have a plan. Please, will you help me?"

The women glanced at each other. Then Ajanta said, "You're a strange kid, you know that?"

Ollie noticed the softening of her tone and took it as a good sign. "What have you found out?" he asked. "Do you know where she is?"

Derrin looked at Ajanta. Kuyu shifted her weight. No one answered.

"Oh, c'mon," Ollie prodded. "I know you've been asking. So where have they taken her? What floor?"

Ajanta hesitated, then sighed. "As far as we can tell, they took her to the fighting pit."

Ollie blinked. "The what?"

"You know, for the Knockdowns. The fights."

His stomach dropped. "They're making her fight?"

"No! Jesus. They have prisoners in there, usually women, to take care of the fighters. Cleaning wounds, and cooking, and...other stuff."

At her last words, the room fell silent.

Ollie cleared his throat. "You're sure?"

"As sure as I can be, yes."

"All right," he said, trying to ignore the twitch that had started in his left eye. "All right. I can work with that." Ollie's mind raced. Then he looked up. "Tera told me you guys work in food service at Herrick's, right?"

"Yeah, us two," Kuyu nodded at Derrin. "So?"

"What does that involve, exactly?" he asked.

"We deliver food, bring it to the kitchens, that's it."

"Who's the food for?" Ollie asked. "The prisoners?"

"No, it's the good stuff. For the guards."

"Uh huh. Uh huh." Ollie thought about this and about the charcoal-penciled notes in his pocket.

"And Ajanta, you drive the crow boats?"

"Yes. Going on five years, now."

"You know Mrs. Paget? And she knows you?"

"Of course."

"That's good." He pressed his hands together. "That's very good. We can use all that." Then he asked, "What about the witches? What do you guys know about them?"

"The...witches?" At this question, Ajanta looked genuinely dumbfounded.

"Yeah," he nodded. "The ones that founded the Neath, with George Herrick. Tera told me they used to be here, but now they're not. Do you know where they are?"

"Krite, Ollie, they're long gone," Kuyu said.

"Yes, but where?"

"How the hell are we supposed to know? And what does it even matter?"

But it did matter, somehow. It was all connected. Ollie knew it. He *felt* it, like the light touch of a mosquito on his skin.

He had one last question, this one for Kuyu. "I'll bet you know a lot of people around here," he said to her.

"A few," Kuyu acknowledged.

"Do you know anyone who could smuggle something inside the prison?"

"I thought we wanted to smuggle someone *out*."

"We do, yes," he nodded. "But first, I have to get something in. A message."

Kuyu sucked in her cheeks. "Yeah, I know someone. But it won't be easy."

Ajanta was watching their exchange warily. "Kuyu," she said, a note of warning in her voice.

"What?" The girl gave an exaggerated, innocent stare.

"I hope you're not talking about who I think you're talking about."

"Why not?" Kuyu challenged. Then she looked up at Ollie. "I can take you to her right now."

172

"No, you absolutely will not," Ajanta said.

"You're not going anywhere near that rat hole," Derrin echoed.

Kuyu rested her hands on her hips. "Why not?"

"Because I said so, young lady," Ajanta said, mirroring the girl's defiant gesture. "And you know perfectly well that you'll never get past the bouncers."

"But I could," Derrin said, taking a step forward.

Ollie looked from one to the other. He didn't know who, or what, they were talking about, and he didn't care. He could tell from their postures: The tide had turned.

A slow, satisfied smile began to curl at his lips.

Ollie, Ollie, oxen free, he thought, catching sight of himself in the dusty wall mirror. *Come out, come out, wherever you are.* It was a face he barely recognized. Narrowed eyes. Sunken cheeks. Determined expression. A face that knew everything was about to change. And that the people who took her were about to wish they hadn't.

Nineteen

In the end, it was Derrin who went with him, and Ollie was glad. If he had to go wandering into the unknown depths of the Neath, Derrin was the housemate he wanted by his side. With her lanky frame, flat profile, and saucer-like eyes, she looked like she'd be right at home swimming among the blindfish at the bottom of the lake. She oozed bad-assery. No one would mess with him while she was around; of that, he was fairly sure.

The goodbyes, however, had worried him. Derrin and Kuyu had clung and kissed like Derrin was going off to war, which couldn't bode well for the outing. He didn't know anything about their destination other than its name—"Moseby's"—and the fact that someone there could get a message into the tower. That was all that mattered now.

They traveled by boat and on land for nearly an hour before finally arriving at the endpoint. At least, Ollie assumed it was the endpoint. Moseby's had no sign; only a crowd milling outside in a loosely formed line. They seemed to be waiting for entry through a glowing, open doorway.

Derrin bypassed the line altogether, walking directly toward the two men who guarded the entrance to the gaping hole. They were tall and lithe, like her, with noses that had been reduced mostly to tiny airholes in the center of their faces. Despite the lack of bulk, they looked threatening—but not, apparently, to Derrin. One of them nodded his head to acknowledge her, and she strolled through the entryway without so much as a comment.

The waiting mob erupted in protest at Derrin's easy admittance. The other bouncer put a freakishly long-fingered hand on Ollie's shoulder.

"He's with me," Derrin called over her shoulder.

The same man released his grip, his expression inscrutable, leaving Ollie free to scurry though the dark hole. He tried to ignore the outcry behind him, and the gnawing feeling of unease in his stomach.

The opening led to a tunnel, which led to a wider, enclosed space. Live music from unfamiliar instruments vibrated his feet. Torches glowed in a variety of colors, casting a rainbow of flickering light onto the walls and the people. Hundreds of people, or so it seemed. They danced and shouted and drank, groping each other and falling into delirious piles on the stone floor.

The smell was a choking fusion of sweat, fermentation, kerosene, and smoke. To his right, a group of musicians all seemed to be playing one long, shared instrument; it looked like a table-sized guitar with six or seven rows of thick strings. To his left, huge wooden barrels stood in formation, each filled with a different type of bubbling, colored liquid. Patrons lined up ten-deep in front of each barrel; when they got to the front, they handed their coins to the server and dipped their cups into the roiling grog. Or at least that seemed to be the intention. In reality, the process was a messy shoving match in which more of the precious liquid ended up on the floor than in anyone's mouth.

Derrin floated impassively through the boisterous crowds. Ollie followed, less impassively, ogling the shadowy, writhing bodies and smoke-choked corners. The seating areas were round, each filled to capacity and encircling a well. Just typical water wells, as far as he could see, complete with buckets and ropes. The circular arrangement of the seats reminded Ollie of a Lighter Tomorrows meeting, causing a series of faces to flash suddenly into his mind: Big Vince. Lorraine. Christine. Jose. And, of course, Nell. He clutched his stomach, feeling homesick to the point of nausea.

"Lovie, lovie, lovie," someone crooned in his ear.

Ollie spun, startled. A woman had reached out to clutch his arm, her voice buzzing like a chainsaw. She was upside down: hanging from her knees on some sort of trapeze bar that was suspended from the ceiling.

"Lovie, lovie! Want some lovies?" the woman asked.

Ollie snatched his arm out of her grasp.

He hurried to catch up with Derrin, but was stopped again by another trapeze swinger. This one was a wiry young man, sitting upright on the bar and wearing only a linen wrap around his waist. He managed to rake his fingers against Ollie's chest as he swooshed past.

Ollie pushed the man away. His eyes darted. Where did Derrin go? Did he lose her? When he caught sight of her stringy hair, he shoved his way through the press of drunkards until he was behind her again.

She had stopped in front of one of the wooden barrels, gazing silently at the woman who was sitting on a stool behind it.

The woman was tiny. Her body type made Ollie think of Mr. Bonfiglio—stocky and stiff—though this woman had none of Mr. B's warmth. Her eyes were like colorless beads. Four long, reddish braids dangled from her head; two on each side.

"Derrin!" the woman said, stroking one of her braids appreciatively. "My God, would you look at this. Has hell frozen over already?"

"Moseby," Derrin replied. Her face betrayed no emotion.

"Come for a pint, have you?" the small woman asked in a cockney accent.

Derrin shook her head, then tipped it in Ollie's direction.

Moseby looked from one to the other. "He's come for a pint, then?"

"He's come for your services," Derrin answered.

"Ah!" the woman said, giving Ollie a once-over. "Well, we've plenty of those. What's your pleasure?"

Ollie stepped forward. "I need to get a message to someone."

"What kind of someone?"

"Someone inside Herrick's End."

Moseby took a drag on the hollow stick in her fingers and blew out a puff of shamrock-green smoke. "That so?" she finally said. "That's a big ask, handsome."

"Yeah, well, it's important."

"How much is it worth to you, then?"

Ollie didn't know how to answer. It was worth everything. Anything. Tera's life depended on it.

"He can't pay," Derrin interjected. "But he can do one better. I hear you still haven't found a worthy adversary for your favorite game."

At this, Moseby perked up. "Not in a while, no." She looked Ollie up and down. "He is a big one, isn't he? What's your tolerance, son?"

"My...?" Ollie looked at Derrin in confusion.

"It's high," Derrin said, folding her arms. "Just look at him. He can hold his own."

Moseby stroked her braids again. "All right. Sure." Excitement had started to creep into her voice. "We can give it a try. But if he dies, you're responsible for getting him out of here."

"Wait, what?" Ollie asked.

Derrin looked unconcerned. "And if he wins, you deliver the message. Tonight."

"Tonight?" the woman objected.

"It's urgent," Derrin said.

Moseby thought about this for a moment, then lifted her chin. "Right, then."

Ollie watched them shake hands. "Wait a second!" he yelped. "What do you mean, *if he dies?*"

"Don't worry about it," Derrin said.

Moseby, meanwhile, reached for a round wooden disc and used it to cover the open top of the barrel. Then she stood on her stool and placed her plump hands on her hips. Even standing on furniture, she was shorter than Ollie. A grin of anticipation spread across her face.

"Ladies and gentlemen!" Moseby bellowed. "Tonight is a special night, indeed! Gather round and stack 'em up! We have a new contender for Aristotle's Bottles!"

A cheer erupted. The music sped up as the strings on the strange, giant instrument twanged in sudden double-time. The crowd began to gather and push, shoving Ollie's body closer to Derrin's.

"What the hell is Aristotle's Bottles?" he hissed.

"It's a drinking game," she said. "Moseby's favorite. But she hardly ever gets to play because...you know."

"No. I don't."

"Because no one ever wants to go up against her," she shrugged. "She's kind of a legend."

"What kind of a drinking game?" Ollie asked fearfully. Despite the name, there didn't seem to be any actual bottles involved at all. Instead, servers had started arriving with trays of squat, empty jars.

"The usual kind. Where you drink. A lot." Derrin paused and looked at him sideways. "You do drink, right?"

Ollie paused, debating his response. Back at home, he was still years away from legal drinking age. His mother had usually allowed him a small glass of red wine with Saturday supper, and he'd once had few shots with a plumber who'd been hired to snake the clogged drain at Bonfilgio's one rainy night.

But that answer would not get him any closer to finding Tera. So instead, he said, "Sure, I drink."

177

"Good," Derrin nodded. "A guy your size, you can probably knock 'em back, right?"

"Right."

Moseby was still standing on her stool, waving her arms and whipping the crowd into a frenzy. Even the trapeze swingers had paused their swaying, with many standing or sitting on their bars to watch the mounting action below. Someone brought a second stool for Ollie, who sat with a thud.

"You'll do fine," Derrin said, leaning over to shout in his ear. "Do it for Tera."

Ollie gripped his knees and watched as one of the bare-chested waiters began to flip the jars upright and fill each one with a bubbling brew. The liquid hissed and popped, sending up sparks in a dazzling array of purples, greens, and whites.

He looked across the makeshift table at the small woman, who grinned.

"All set, boss," the server said, backing away.

The crowd began to chant: *"Stack! Stack! Stack! Stack!"*

Moseby gave a sweeping bow. Then she dropped into a sitting position on her stool and started moving some of the jars around.

Ollie turned to look at Derrin, confused.

"Make a pyramid," she shouted above the crowd noise, pointing.

Tentatively, he followed Moseby's lead and began stacking the filled cups. Five on the bottom, four on the next row, three on the next, two on the next, then one on top. Fifteen cups for each of them. All filled to the rim.

The yelling and cheering had reached an almost deafening level. Moseby seemed to soak it in, placing her own cups slowly and theatrically. When her stack was finally complete, she pumped her fists at the gathered mob.

"What are the rules?" Ollie yelled across the table.

"What?"

"The rules!" he yelled again, even louder.

"Ah, the good gentleman wants to know the rules of Aristotle's Bottles," Moseby called out to the crowd, garnering a response of laughter. They quieted somewhat as she continued: "The rules, my friend, are simple. You start here"—she pointed to the lone jar at the top of his pyramid, then made a zig-zag motion with her finger to indicate all the following rows—"and you end here." At the last word, she jabbed the final jar on the left of the bottom row. "The first person to drink that one, and keep it down, wins."

Another cheer went up. Ollie swallowed.

"My dear Derrin, will you do us the honors?" Moseby asked.

The willowy woman walked behind the barrel. She placed one hand on Moseby's shoulder, and one hand on Ollie's.

"All ready?" Derrin asked them. When both nodded, she lifted her voice above the din and said: "No one would choose a friendless existence on condition of having all other things in the world. So says Aristotle, and so say I."

"Hear, hear!" the crowd said.

"Hear, hear!" Moseby repeated, reaching for the single glass jar on the top of her pyramid. "To new friends!"

Dazed, Ollie followed her example and lifted his own top jar.

They clinked the glasses together. Then Moseby held her cup up to the spectators and tossed the liquid—all the liquid—down her throat in one smooth gesture. Cheering surrounded them on all sides as she wiped her mouth with one of the thick braids.

Ollie looked down at his own glass. The curdled smell was worrying enough. But the mysterious, fizzing brew was also setting off sparks, most of which were landing with painful acuity on his cheeks.

For Tera, he thought. Then he closed his eyes, brought the glass to his lips, and took as hearty a swig as he could manage.

The burning was immediate, and agonizing. The liquid slid down his throat like a snake wrapped in tire spikes; every drop seemed to claw and scrape and fight its way from mouth to esophagus. It did not taste like wine. It did not taste like bourbon. It tasted, as far as he could tell, like rancid apple cider blended with jalapeno peppers and actual, boiling lava. It was truly, truly awful—the worst thing he had ever tasted, including the slop he'd been subjected to at Herrick's End. It was fire and brimstone, liquified. And he'd only had one gulp of one glass, with fourteen left to go.

When he managed to unsquint his eyes, Ollie saw that Moseby the Pint-Sized Drink Destroyer was already on jar number three.

He had to hurry. Bracing himself, Ollie took another swig, and another, then twisted his body into contortions. He couldn't breathe. And already, the effects were kicking in: Not a drunkenness so much as a throat-clogging, vision-blurring, panic-inducing haze of misery. Not even one jar finished, and already he was having trouble sitting upright on his stool.

What the hell was in this stuff?

Moseby chugged the fourth glass, and the fifth. She laughed heartily and did a little butt-wiggling jig on her stool, much to the roaring pleasure of the gathered crowd. Then she swallowed down her sixth.

Ollie gripped the edge of the barrel, steadying himself. His body was reacting to the horrid brew the way it would react to any poison: It was rejecting it. He covered his mouth with a hand as the retching started.

"Hurry up!" Derrin was shouting in his ear. "Drink, dammit!"

The jostling crowd echoed her sentiments: "Drink! Drink! Drink!"

Ollie staggered to his feet. He couldn't do it. There was no way he could catch up. He'd be dead by the fifth glass, let alone the fifteenth. He shook his head, trying to clear it. He thought back to the rules of the game. Moseby's zigzagging finger. Top to bottom. First to last. He dropped his jar onto the table.

"What are you doing?" Derrin yelled.

Ollie stared across the surface of the covered barrel, swaying left and right. He watched his opponent toss back her seventh drink. He listened to the jeers and the shouts. Then he shot his hand out, swept it from left to right, and knocked most of his precarious pyramid to the ground.

The glass and liquid landed with a shattering crash. Derrin stared at the shards, and at Ollie, with open-mouthed astonishment. The noise around them fell into sudden, almost complete silence.

Moseby jumped up to stand on her stool. "What the bloody hell?"

Ollie ignored them all. With a single extended finger, he tipped over the remaining jars on the bottom row. All but the last. That one, he picked up. Then he held his nose, choked down the sparking liquid, and slammed the empty jar onto the wood. The room spun in wild circles.

He coughed and clung to the barrel. Then he said, "I win."

"You w—?" Moseby gave a stunned stutter. "You didn't *win!*"

"Yes, I did. You said we start with the top and we end with this one." At that, he lifted the glass he had just emptied. "You said, 'the first person to drink that one wins.' And that's what I did."

"*And* you have to drink everything in between!" Moseby's voice rose to high squeak.

"You didn't shay...say that," Ollie said. His mouth seemed to have stopped working. He watched as the woman's small body morphed into two blurry bodies, then three.

"But I... But it's..." Moseby scanned the crowd, then looked up at Derrin. "That's bollocks!"

Derrin gave a small shrug. Her shocked expression had changed to one of hesitant pleasure.

"You tollme the rules," Ollie slurred. "I jush followed them."

For a moment, no one spoke. Moseby's face was turning a deep shade of purple-red. The gathered spectators began to murmur and chatter. Finally, they began to cheer.

"Winner!" someone shouted.

Moseby's crimson braids whipped from side to side as she took in the reaction of the crowd. She sputtered and protested, but the group was already dispersing in search of the next distraction.

"So?" Ollie said, leaning over the barrel. His head was spinning like a Tilt-A-Whirl and he was fairly certain he was twelve, maybe eleven, seconds away from projectile vomiting, but he had to get an answer. "You'll do it?"

Moseby fell butt-first onto her stool. "Fine," she said through gritted teeth. "I won't forget this, Derrin."

"I would expect nothing less," the lanky woman said, unconcerned. "The boy won fair and square. Now, you have to get his message to Tera."

"No," Ollie shook his heavy head. "Not Tera."

Derrin spun back to look at him. "The message isn't for Tera? Then who?"

Ollie pulled a rolled piece of paper out of his pocket. "Get thith to a prisoner named Dozer. Fiff...fifth floor, Labor Force. By tonight," he said. The contents of his stomach were creeping back up into his throat.

Moseby took the paper and looked at it dubiously. "What's so important?"

"Tonight," Ollie said again, ignoring the question.

"All right, all right. Krite."

"An Aristotle promise is an Aristotle promise," Derrin said. She leaned closer to Moseby and flashed a cold smile. "I believe it was the great philosopher himself who said, 'A wise man does not expose himself needlessly to danger.' If I find out you didn't keep your promise, I'll be back here tomorrow. And the next time you enjoy one of those delicious drinks of yours, you'll be swallowing the glass along with it."

"Yeah," Ollie said. Or tried to say. But his tongue was too thick, his lips, too heavy. He jabbed a finger in Moseby's general direction. Then he fell backwards, hoping that someone, somehow, would catch him.

No one did.

Twenty

The message came early the next morning—too early. His "package" had arrived. Despite an astounding hangover that chiseled at his temples like a coal miner, Ollie dragged himself out of Tera's bed, bid goodbye to the housemates, and somehow made his way to the Tea Party.

When Ollie staggered into Nikki and Floyd's shop, the eponymous couple sat side-by-side behind the counter. Nikki wasn't wearing the fur shawl this time; just a light-colored, cotton wrap. Floyd wore his usual brown garb and dour expression. The floating platform bobbed beneath them.

Ollie didn't bother with small talk. "You found him?" he asked.

Nikki gave him a raised eyebrow. "He's out on the docks. Waiting."

"What did you tell him?"

"I told him we had a job for him," Floyd said. "A big job. He's gonna be pissed when he finds out the truth."

"Don't worry about Laszlo," Ollie said, glancing over his shoulder. "I'll take care of it."

"Well, well, well." Nikki sounded amused. "Aren't you the big man all of a sudden."

Ollie gave her a cold stare and reached into his front pocket. "Here," he said, handing over the keychain. "As promised."

"It still blinks?" Floyd asked suspiciously.

"That little button, right there."

Floyd pressed it, and the three of them stared in momentary, spellbound stillness as the name flashed on and off, on and off.

Oliver. Oliver. Oliver.

Ollie felt a tug of something. He remembered standing in another shop, in what seemed like another lifetime, buying the keychain. Who was that guy? He could hardly recall.

Meatball shifted on Ollie's shoulder, breaking the trance. "We're good?" he asked.

Nikki looked down at her husband, who responded with a reluctant shrug. "We're good. He's out there, to the left."

Ollie gave them a curt nod and walked toward the exit, pushing aside the canvas flaps. There, through the crowd of milling shoppers, he saw him.

The acrobat.

Laszlo sat on an overturned crate, staring out over the water. He wasn't wearing the shiny blue suit, though his "regular" clothes were nearly as tight. His fingers tapped impatiently against his thighs, which looked like two planks of split firewood wrapped in black fabric. His silvery button-down shirt seemed out of place in the murk, shimmering and stretching. He looked like a man from another place and time. Ollie had looked the same way, just two short weeks ago. Now, he stared at Laszlo's profile with a mixture of fury and homesick pining.

The acrobat reached into a paper bag on his lap and tossed bits of rhizer to a pack of scurrying trogs at his feet. Ollie approached the empty crate next to him and sat.

Laszlo looked up and gave a bland, indirect smile of greeting. Then he did a doubletake. His small, dark eyes widened into discs.

Ollie's face remained impassive. "Well, if it isn't Laszlo Kravchenko, nephew of the famous Kravchenko Brothers of Ukraine," he said pleasantly. Coolly.

Laszlo continued to stare. Finally, he spoke. "It is...Ollie?"

"You got it," Ollie said, scratching the brown trog on his shoulder. "Ollie Delgato, of the North End Delgatos. You look confused. Oh, wait. Did you expect me to be over there?" Ollie pointed across the water to the Herrick's End tower in the distance. "Surprise! I got out."

Laszlo stammered something unintelligible.

"An umbrella would have been nice," Ollie continued, his voice smooth. "I think I'm the only one down here who doesn't have one. Maybe you could just make it a standard part of the Laszlo Kravchenko Deluxe Travel Package. Did you know those worms up there pee on us once a day?" He pointed one finger up at the ceiling, not moving his eyes. "What am I saying. Of course, you know that. You know all about this place, don't you?"

Meatball skittered down his arm and hopped onto the dock, joining the other trogs in the search for dropped rhizers.

"Ollie, my friend, I—"

"Your *friend?*" Ollie guffawed. "Oh, that's good. You knew I'd end up in that shithole. You knew exactly what would happen to me if you sent me down here. And you didn't care. How does it work? Does the Warden pay you to send unsuspecting morons down here to staff up his Labor Force?"

"No! I mean, yes, I do know Warden." Laszlo was sputtering, stunned. "He is asshole. Grade-A asshole, as you say. But no, I would not do that to you. I would never do that."

"So why, then?"

Laszlo seemed to be marveling. "You are free?" he asked. "You were in there, and you got out?"

"Yeah, that's right. No thanks to you."

A long-haired merchant rowed by in a boat filled with accordion fans and multi-colored fabrics. "Beautiful, beautiful!" she screeched in a distinctly unbeautiful voice as she passed. "Something nice for your girl?" The two men waved her away.

"Mr. Ollie, Oliver, I would not send you into harm's way. Never."

"Why, then? Why did you send me at all?"

"I was following instructions," Laszlo said. "Very...how do you say...specific instructions."

"Instructions from who?"

"You would not believe me if I say."

"Try me."

Laszlo rested his hands on his trunk-like legs, not answering.

"Instructions from *who?*" Ollie asked again.

The acrobat inhaled, then said, "From George Herrick."

Ollie leaned backward. "George Herrick is dead."

"Yes, I hear this. Very sad. But before he was dead, he used to leave notes. Usually small kinds of things. And one day, he left note to me. With my name."

"What did it say?"

"It said, 'When you find the lost boy looking for the lost girl, send him to me.'"

The two men stared at each other. All around them, conversation and laughter and clomping boots echoed in the thick cavern air.

"So, what?" Ollie said. "What made you think that was me? That could have been anyone." But even as he said it, he knew it wasn't true. The lost boy, looking for a lost girl. The savior who wasn't a savior. Of course it was him. Pathetically, obviously him. How was it possible that Herrick had written not one, but two messages about Ollie, before Ollie had ever stepped foot in the Neath? Another note, another peek into the future. The witches, it seemed, had blessed ol' George with more than just a long life.

"Why would I make up such thing? I would not!" Laszlo said. "I ignore this note. It make no sense to me. But then, you come to the Center. You ask your questions. You give your name. And I hear you talk, and I think: Lost girl! Confused boy! That must be the one. And so, I write note to *you*. To meet me, at stairs. I think that you will not come. But you do come! And you tell me your story, about your missing girl, and I think, Hey, this must be all right. He wants to go to Neath, and George Herrick wants him to go to Neath, so I must send him, yes? What else can I do?"

Ollie felt like he had opened the door to a closet full of nonsense words, and they had all come tumbling down onto his head at once. "Stop, stop," he said, holding up a hand. "Why would he want me down here? What does that even mean?"

"I do not know," Laszlo said, looking forlorn. "How am I to know? When George Herrick tells you to do something, you do it. That is all."

"Well, you did it, all right. You got me tossed into the pits of goddamn, fucking hell." Ollie dropped his head into his hands. "And now Tera's in there, too."

"Tera?" Laszlo straightened. His ruddy complexion began to pale, like milk pouring into tea.

"Yeah. You know her?"

For a moment, he seemed at a loss for words. His Roman nose cast a long shadow on his cheek as the seconds passed. Then, in a low voice, he said, "I know her."

Ollie stared at him. "You brought her down here, didn't you?"

The acrobat nodded. "Many years ago. She came to WRC, looking for help. Like so many." Laszlo's expression hardened as he stared out over the olive-hued water. "She could have chosen revenge. Me? I think probably that she should have. But she did not. She chose forgiving. And a new life, and a new name. That was...what? Five, six years ago? She was just child."

The two men regarded each other, sharing a long look of unspoken things.

"Yeah, well, she's all grown up now," Ollie finally said. "And she's in a world of shit. Thanks to you, and thanks to me."

"Tera is really there? In the prison?"

"Yes, she is. And you, my *friend*, are going to help me get her out."

"But I do not—"

"You misunderstand," Ollie interrupted, giving the acrobat a stern, unwavering stare. "I'm not asking."

They lined up next to each other like descending-height Russian dolls: Ollie and Laszlo on the end, followed by Ajanta, Derrin, and Kuyu. Meatball had been left back at the house.

Tall, conical stalagmites kept them hidden. They peered across the open clearing at another, much longer line, where people stood behind wheelbarrows as they waited. And waited, and waited. Some waited for vengeance, some waited for justice. But it was getting harder for Ollie to tell which was which.

It was the same spot, more or less, where he had hidden only two weeks before, after Tera and Mrs. Paget had first dropped him at the murky shore outside of Herrick's End. This time, though, felt nothing like the last. He wasn't scanning the line of people. He wasn't nervous, or confused, or unprepared. Ollie knew exactly what was coming next. He welcomed it. The tower rose up into the orange smog, beckoning him. Daring him to enter. He stared back, unblinking.

"There," Laszlo muttered, pointing at a red-suited guard in the distance. "That is my guy."

Ollie tore his gaze away from the crumbling walls. He nodded, then turned to his left. "Everybody remember the plan?" he asked in a loud whisper.

Four heads nodded. Beside them, a wheelbarrow stood at the ready, along with some rope and a small fabric bag.

Kuyu lifted the rope. "You sure this is necessary?" she asked dubiously.

"Yes," Ollie said. "If they recognize me, we're screwed. I have to look like a new prisoner." And who better to play the role of his angry little victim than Kuyu? She'd probably kick him a few times for good measure. Or for fun. But Ollie didn't say that last part out loud. "You guys are all set with the food?"

"Yes," said Derrin.

"Everyone remember the rendezvous points?" Ollie asked.

Again, four nods.

"Good. I can't guarantee the timing, but we'll get there." Eventually. Hopefully. Maybe. But again, he didn't say those last parts out loud. He clenched his jaw as the decrepit, tipping tower loomed over them, mocking their plans. "I was in there," Ollie murmured, staring up. "And she came for me. I'd still be there now if not for her." Then he drew himself to his full height and turned to face them. "She would have done the same for any one of you."

Ajanta tugged on her braid. Laszlo looked like he might be about to cry. Kuyu slipped her arm through Derrin's and clung.

"All right, then." Ollie raised his voice as loud as he dared. "Let's go get our girl."

Kuyu was the first to move. She reached for the fabric bag and held it aloft, facing Ollie. He ducked and allowed her to slide it over his head. The world went dark. Then he climbed blindly into the wheelbarrow and curled his body into a ball as the others tied his wrists and ankles.

"Good luck, my friend," he heard Laszlo say. "I will see you very soon."

"Be careful, Ollie." That was Derrin.

A silent squeeze. That had to be Ajanta.

Ollie heard muttering and crunching footsteps. Then he heard Kuyu's voice. "You ready, big guy?"

"Ready," he answered, sounding muffled.

"And you're sure you want to do this? It's not too late, you know."

He smiled reflexively at her words. They were the same words Tera had used when she first dropped Ollie here and tried to dissuade him from going after Nell. Wrong place, wrong time, wrong girl.

But that was then.

"I'm sure," he said.

Kuyu grunted, hoisting the handles. His body jostled inside the wheelbarrow as she pushed him through the edge of the stalagmite forest, out into the clearing beyond, and eventually took her place in the line. They had sliced a few holes in the bag to let in air and a little bit of light, but for the most part Ollie saw nothing.

He didn't know how long they waited. Hours, at least. Finally, they reached the admittance desk. Kuyu, to her credit, did an impressive job. She told them his name was Devin. She described unspeakable acts. She even shed some tears.

The guards untied him and hauled him out of the wheelbarrow, as he knew they would. They dragged him with violent, terrible force, as he knew they would. And as they raised the heavy iron gate and threw him into the dark hole beyond, Ollie closed his eyes. He imagined himself plunging into a cold river. Holding his breath. Rising to the surface. Lifting his arms with strong, even strokes.

She was there, somewhere in the current, and he would find her. Not rescue her—no. The thought was laughable. But he would find her. And when he did, one of two things would happen: They would swim, or they would drown. Together. There were no other options. Because once he had her hand in his, he was never letting go.

Twenty-One

The rest of the day passed like a prolonged, painful episode of déjà vu.

As before, Ollie found himself processed and tossed into a cell full of alternately terrified and angry prisoners: five men, this time, and one woman. Some were silent, some were sobbing, some were ranting. Blood pooled in his cheeks. Throbbing pains racked his head and upper body. A bowl of steaming sludge sat near the door, untouched, next to a stack of bowls and spoons.

Ollie ignored it all. He sat curled against the wall, stared at his knees, and waited. He kept his head hung low. The bag was gone, but he still did his best to hide his face and minimize his height. He could not get recognized as an escapee. His name was Devin now. Devin the Abuser.

When the cell door opened, Ollie jumped to his feet before the guard even gave the instructions. He knew what was coming. *Who* was coming. A few minutes later, they approached the winding staircase, and he began to climb. And climb, and climb. His leg muscles burned like the ovens at Queen's Pizzeria on Thacher Street, and still he climbed. Behind him, the others gasped and faltered. But Ollie did not cry out, or slow down. He gritted his teeth, and he climbed.

Finally, the group arrived at the door to the white room. It was just as clean and sparse as he remembered: One wall studded with holes and numbers, another wall blank. Two empty chairs sat on a platform in the center.

As the guards lined them up against the wall, a few of the prisoners collapsed onto the ground from exhaustion. Ollie stayed on his feet and moved to the head of the line. This time, he wanted to be first. He did not want to hear their wails for mercy, or see their grisly crimes projected onto the alabaster wall. He wanted only to see the Reader.

Ollie knew he could not end up back on the fifth floor or, God forbid, anywhere worse. He had one goal: to get to the Knockdown fighting floor. That's where Tera was, so that's where he had to go. And the yellow-haired Reader was the only one who could get him there fast. His job, now, was to talk her into it. He knew from his visit to the Warden's office that they wanted volunteers. So, he would volunteer. No problem. Easy-peasy. He cracked his knuckles as his throat went dry.

To his left, a door opened. The guards straightened. A ripple of fear traveled through the room.

She had arrived.

Ollie wasn't jarred by her appearance this time: the deep folds of skin, or the thick, gravity-defying pile of golden dreadlocks on her head. Her gray eyes were so large they took up most of the upper half of her ancient face. She floated past the line of prisoners without looking at them, then stepped up onto the platform and took a seat.

The woman blinked her big lids. Then she addressed the line of prisoners. "You are here for a reading," she said. "I will see all that you have done. And you will pay for your crimes. Only what you owe."

The guards echoed reverently: "Only what you owe."

It was the same speech she'd given the last time, and probably every time. Though Ollie was willing to bet he was the only prisoner who had ever heard it twice.

The woman's long, twisted fingers curled in her lap. "I am ready," she said.

A red-suited guard approached the line. Wordlessly, he grabbed Ollie by his collar and hauled him to the platform. Ollie took a step up and stumbled into the empty seat.

The Reader's face was as blank as the wall behind her. If she recognized him, she gave no sign.

"I want to be a fighter," Ollie blurted, before she could speak. "For the Knockdowns. I volunteer."

The old woman seemed not to have heard him. "Hold out your hand," she said.

"But I volunteer," he said again, quickly. "I'm ready."

She regarded him calmly, curiously, not unlike a cat watching a fish in a bowl. "Hold out your hand," she said again.

Ollie's heart hammered. Had she not heard him? "You don't understand. I have to get to the fighting floor. I'll be great. Look at me. I'm huge. I'm a great fighter." He swallowed, realizing too late that great fighters probably didn't say things like, "I'm a great fighter."

Annoyance flashed across the Reader's face. She gave a casual nod to one of her guards, who stepped closer and reached for Ollie's arms. They began to wrestle, Ollie holding his arm stiff while the guard expertly fought to lift it.

It's not working, he thought, hysteria beginning to rise. *Why isn't it working?* His eyes flitted around the room as his mind raced. He saw the line of prisoners, more approaching guards, and the ancient woman, now growing impatient in her chair. He saw the wall full of holes, each one numbered. All out of order. *Seventeen. Forty-two. Twenty-nine.*

A second guard held down his right arm while the other lifted his left.

Ollie's pulse jumped in growing panic. *Holes. Numbers.* One hole, he now noticed, looked different from the rest. That hole was bigger than the others, and higher. It had no number at all. He leaned forward, straining against the guards' strength. No, wait. He had it wrong. The hole didn't *need* a number because it *was* a number! Perfectly round. A zero.

Zero.

What had Ajanta called it? Not the fighting floor... the fighting *pit.* As in, down below. Lower than level one. Zero!

"Widow Hibbins!" he shouted.

At that, the Reader startled. She held up a finger; the guards dropped his arms.

"Is that...your name?" he asked.

She didn't answer. She didn't have to: The look of surprise on her face and the thin, pressed line of her mouth said enough.

"I have a message for you," Ollie said, talking fast. He pushed the guards' hands away. "From George Herrick. He told me to tell you, 'Zero.'"

Jesus, he hoped he was right. If he was wrong...if *this* was wrong...God only knew where he was going to end up. His legs began to tremble.

Finally, she spoke. Her voice rumbled like a coffee grinder. "Is that so?"

Ollie gave a rapid nod.

"Let me see," said the Reader.

"See...what?"

She held out her hand.

He hesitated. But what choice did he have? He had to make her understand.

Their palms touched. Ollie concentrated, remembering that day in Blackstone Park. For a moment, nothing happened. Then, something flickered on the wall. A grainy, black-and-white movie, pouring from her hand. He saw himself, standing in the park. Fern-like trees and brackish water materialized behind him. Tera stood to his left. And to his right, the impossibly old man. George Herrick. Former Deputy-Sheriff of Salem Village, 1692. Transporter and persecutor of witches.

Everyone in the white room watched as Herrick leaned forward, whispered something into Ollie's ear, and then slumped. Dead.

The woman lowered her hand, turning away from the wall to look at him.

"I didn't hurt him," Ollie whispered. "I swear. I didn't even touch him."

The mountain of dreadlocks lurched as her head tilted to the side. Then she asked, "What did he say?"

Ollie blinked, trying to remember the exact words. "He said, 'Tell Widow Hibbins zero. Lion's feet will dig. As I am, so he will be.'"

"What else?" she asked.

"Uh, after that, he said, 'The rightful ones tarry in the place that is not a place. All will be mended. The waiting is done.' And then...he just...died."

"I see." The yellow-haired woman looked down at her twisted hands. The silence lengthened, making him squirm. When she looked up again, she raised her index finger and pointed toward the wall pocked with holes. Her eyes still on Ollie, she called out, "Zero."

Two of the closest guards stepped forward. They grabbed Ollie's arms and dragged him out of the chair. A third guard appeared with a tall, rickety ladder that seemed to be made of twigs. The guard propped the ladder under the unnumbered hole and stepped aside.

"Climb," he said.

Ollie looked back at the woman, a.k.a. the Reader, a.k.a. Widow Hibbins. Then he faced the ladder, held his breath, and began to climb. By some miracle, the first rung held, then the next. He was genuinely surprised when he reached the top.

"You will give what you owe," she called up to him. "Only what you owe. Do you understand?"

He sighed. Of course, he understood. Ollie knew exactly what he owed. He looked down at the dispassionate guards and the trembling group of prisoners. He looked down, one last time, at Widow Hibbins. And then he dove head-first into the tube, eyes wide open to the darkness.

The terrifying tunnel was like a waterslide without the water. Or the fun. Ollie stretched his arms in front of him and clenched his teeth as he sped through twists, turns, and stomach-churning sudden drops, waiting for the inevitable moment when his thick belly would bring the ride to an abrupt stop. He would die there, trapped. The bodies would pile up behind him for years before anyone figured out the problem. What would they do then? Wait for decomp to turn the bodies into skeletons and then wash the whole mess out with a hose?

Ollie was imagining the wet pile of bones when he felt the tunnel give way to empty air. He landed, hard, and let out an "oof" of pain and shock.

Krite. What was with this place and all the hard landings? Would it kill them to throw down a pillow or two?

He struggled to his feet, holding a hand on his back like a 90-year-old man. He seemed to be in a hallway. A bespectacled attendant stood at a podium nearby, looking much like a host in a restaurant, though Ollie strongly suspected that he wasn't about to be led to a table for drinks and Buffalo wings. The man reminded Ollie of the chairlift operator he had met when he first entered the Neath: blue jumpsuit; clipboard; no eye contact, whatsoever.

With a slight limp, Ollie approached the podium.

"How many for entry?" the man asked, not lifting his eyes from the clipboard. He did not seem at all surprised that a giant, pale, disheveled prisoner had just fallen through a hole in the ceiling.

Ollie wanted to tell the man that he was, clearly, alone. A single person. *One* person. He wanted to scream and slap the guy's cheek and tear that goddamn blue-crayon of a jumpsuit off his body, leaving the smug asshole to stand there, naked and scrawny, surrounded by shreds of fabric on the dirt floor.

Instead, he exhaled and said, "One."

With a satisfied swish of his pen, the man made a mark on his clipboard. Then he adjusted his glasses and shouted over his shoulder: "One for entry!"

Two Reds appeared almost instantly, rounding the corner as though they had been waiting there. Each guard grabbed one of Ollie's arms and began dragging him.

"Easy, I'm coming! You don't have to—"

Before he could finish the sentence, the guard on his left reached out and punched Ollie's head. Just punched it, savage and fast, with the force of a coiled-up spring. The pain was an explosion of color. Ollie's vision swam. His legs gave out. And suddenly, they did have to drag him.

Time passed strangely after that, and Ollie couldn't say for sure how long they traveled in the hallway. But by the time they reached a vast open space, he could see well enough to figure out where he was, and the knowledge bent his lips into a smile.

The pit. It had to be.

The first things he noticed were the birdcages. Colossal, swaying birdcages in a wide variety of shapes. They hung at different levels; some high up near the ceiling, others closer to the ground. But these cages didn't hold birds—they held people. Fighters, if he had to guess, waiting their turn to fight.

He knew it as soon as he saw their faces: purpled and swollen, scrappy and wary. They all reminded him of Dozer, complete with an array of eyepatches, slack jaws, and missing teeth. Some huddled in the corners of their hanging cages, while other gripped the bars and stared down at him with grizzled curiosity. And hostility.

The smell of the place was surprisingly neutral; not nearly as throat-closingly nasty as every other Herrick's End floor he had stumbled across. It was the size, he assumed. The pit was big enough to dilute the stink, leaving only a vague odor of mildew and mud and, oddly enough, ginger. He definitely smelled ginger. Or that could have been the blow to the head.

The guards dropped his arms and approached another two guards, and the four of them commenced a garbled staff meeting. Ollie could only make out every third or fourth word, but he heard enough to understand that they were bickering about the available cage space, or lack thereof, for this newest prisoner. They also seemed pleased about his size, and pleased that the Warden would be pleased about his size. While they talked, Ollie's eyes flitted around the cavern in desperation: Where was Tera? He didn't see Dozer, either.

They were both supposed to be here. The plan depended on it.

He was squinting into the dusty haze, trying to see into the uppermost cages, when the meeting ended. The guards were sharing a joke. "Let's see how he does in there," one of them said, then grabbed Ollie's arm and pushed him to a set of stairs. The men guffawed in the mean way he recognized from his youth; bullies gathering force, feeding off each other. That sound usually meant bad things for Ollie.

The stairs led to one of several suspended walkways above the ground. Ollie couldn't tell if he was still dizzy from the head punch or if the platform itself was swaying; either way, he was having trouble keeping his balance. His feet clanked on the metal grates as he walked.

The guard stopped beside one of the hanging birdcages. "Running low on space, so you'll have to share," he said, grinning. "You two should get along just fine."

Slowly, painfully, Ollie turned his head. Inside the cage, sitting cross-legged on the floor, was the largest human being he had ever seen. He recognized him right away: The Mallet. The undisputed champion of the Knockdowns. Pounder of men. Breaker of bones. Peeler of skin.

Ollie's throat went dry. The Mallet stared at him through the bars, expressionless.

The guard inserted a key into the door and yanked it open. Ollie flinched. The Mallet didn't move.

"In," said the guard, and Ollie heard the note of cruel amusement in his voice. The door slammed shut behind him.

"Have a good night, boys!" Laughter reverberated around the cavern.

Ollie stayed rooted to his spot. The swinging motion was subtle, but enough to turn his stomach. A single thought echoed in his mind: *I will die in this cage.* Probably torn to pieces. Maybe crushed. He held on to the bars for balance as he looked up at the legendary brawler now standing only feet away. Ollie expected to see rage, or dumb brutality, or maybe a ferocious sneer that bared a set of filed-down, pointy teeth.

Instead, he saw something else entirely. The Mallet's expression wasn't menacing, or angry. It was only...sad. And then the mighty man opened his mouth to speak. "You'll get used to it," he said, his voice deep and thick. "After a while, you don't even notice it."

Ollie stared at him.

"The swinging, I mean," the big man continued. "They hang us for security. They think it makes it harder to escape."

"Does it?" Ollie asked, finding his voice.

"Eh," The Mallet shrugged. "Maybe."

"You're..."

"I'm Leonard."

"But I thought—"

195

"They give us names when we get here. Ridiculous names." He laughed softly. His hair was balding and caramel colored. "But you can call me Leonard."

Of all the names on the planet, that was perhaps the last one that Ollie would have guessed belonged to this terrifying hulk of a man. "That's...my church," he heard himself say.

"What?"

"My church, back home. It's St. Leonard's."

"Ah," the big man said. "Well, I can assure you, it was not named after me."

"Right. No." He cleared his throat. "I'm Ollie."

"Very nice to meet you, Ollie. Welcome to my cage."

Ollie loosened his grip on the bars. If this man intended to kill him, the attack did not seem imminent. If anything, the Leonard Formerly Known as Mallet gave off an air of...exhaustion. Resignation, maybe. Ollie could suddenly picture him sitting behind a massive desk, chewing on a massive pen cap and typing up a massive report for his boss. Ordering a massive cake for his coworker's birthday. At the very least, he seemed uninterested in immediate violence.

"You must be a volunteer," Leonard said. "One of the brave and stupid? Trying to improve your station?"

"Something like that," Ollie replied. "And you?"

The big man laughed again. "No, not me. I am not one of the brave. I am one of the duped."

Ollie wasn't sure how to respond. "You look brave," he offered.

Leonard smiled. Aside from his size, he was astonishingly ordinary looking. Bronze skin. Sturdy neck. No tattoos. "The Warden lured me with a job offer," Leonard said, staring out into the darkness of the pit. "A 'security position,' they called it. Temporary. Luxury accommodations. More money than I'd know what to do with. Plenty of money to send back home. Of course, when I got here, there was no job. I was not an employee; I was a prisoner. A prize pit bull in a fighting ring." Leonard's smile was bitter. His legs were still crossed; now, he rested his hands on his bended knees in a kind of meditative pose. "And I've been here ever since."

Ollie stepped closer, losing his grip on the bars. His voice dropped to a whisper. "But you're twice the size of these guys! Those guards? You could..." he faltered, his thoughts coming in a rush. "You could... I don't know, do something! You could get out of here anytime you wanted to!"

Leonard shook his head. "The Warden won't allow it."

"What do you mean, he won't al—"

"He has my family," Leonard interrupted, his green eyes turning hard. "Or at least, he knows where they are. And how to reach them. If I—" he stopped. The unfinished sentence hung in the air between them, its meaning clear. Leonard straightened. "Sorry," he said. "It's been a while since I've talked to anyone. Most of the time they keep me alone. I guess I'm..."

Ollie was shocked to see the man's eyes go glassy with tears. Whatever he had expected of the dreaded Mallet, this was not it.

"But why would the Warden make you come down here? I thought all the fighters were volunteers, looking for rewards. And the Knockdowns were just...stupid shit. Entertainment for the prisoners."

"Is that what you heard?" Leonard replied, looking amused. "I'm sure that's what he wants everyone to think. But no, the Knockdowns aren't for the prisoners. In this place, nothing is for the prisoners. Nothing good, at least. The Knockdowns are for the Warden. Just another one of his sick, twisted inventions. He enjoys watching people suffer." His voice had gone brittle.

Ollie remembered watching the slick-haired Warden pass him in the hallway, surrounded by cloudy-eyed, captive children. Remembered the yellow fog, the severed arm. The body of Rocco crumpled on the office floor. Solitary confinement for those who crossed him. The screams of prisoners, endless, agonized screams, behind closed doors. He shivered.

"I'm getting out of here," Ollie said, surprising himself. "You should come with me."

The big man let loose a surprised, quiet chuckle. "Good on you. It's important to have dreams."

"I'm serious," Ollie insisted. "I have a plan."

Leonard looked at him with an expression of pity. "Sure, kid. Don't we all."

Before Ollie could respond, another shout echoed through the cavern. "One for entry!"

Leonard's eyebrows lifted. "Two in one day? That's strange."

Moments later, two guards dragged in the newest Knockdown volunteer. Ollie ran to the edge of his cage and peered through the bars, straining to get a look at the man's face. The prisoner, likewise, was looking around, searching the cages. Their eyes met.

Dozer stared up at Ollie with an intense expression of confusion.

Ollie stared back, almost weak with relief. Against all odds, Dozer had received his message, and followed his instructions. He nodded down at his friend. *Trust me,* he tried to say, using only his body language and his eyes. *It's all going to work out fine.*

The guards conferred together, then walked up three stairways and tossed Dozer into a cage high above. Ollie watched him go with a thudding heart. He was here. Tera wasn't, yet, but Dozer was. The plan was clicking into motion. It was a start.

"Every finish needs a start, right?" he said out loud, maybe to Leonard, maybe to himself. But as he gripped the bars and looked around at the yawning pit, the hanging cages, and the helpless, battered faces, even he had to admit that this particular start wasn't looking terribly promising.

Twenty-Two

Sleep didn't come; Ollie settled for closed eyes and a middling doze. The swinging motion of the cage was surprisingly soothing, but not soothing enough to overcome the *squeak, squeak, squeak* that accompanied the sways.

The squeaking, and the pitiful moans of his fellow prisoners, had drilled a hole into Ollie's consciousness by morning. He wasn't even aware that the night had passed until people, mostly women, began streaming in from either side of the cavern, pushing carts. The carts' wheels also squeaked. He winced, holding his head. What fresh hell was this?

"Who are they?" Ollie groaned.

Leonard rolled over onto his side and glanced down at the ground. "Slop wenches," he answered groggily. "They bring the food and piss buckets."

Slop wenches. For the love of God. Ollie was trying to wrap his mind around the awful job title, and the promising prospect of breakfast, when he shot upright. *Slop wenches.*

He jumped to his feet, rushed to the bars, and scanned the hunched figures on the ground. All women. Some were pulling out trays or stacking buckets. Others were tearing hunks of bread and spooning a greyish soup into small bowls.

Down to the left, a woman was climbing the stairs. She stood straighter than the rest. A tuft of purple hair swept high off the crown of her head.

199

Ollie covered his mouth with a hand. A swell of joy threatened to lift him off the ground. She was there. *Right there,* right in front of him. He had found her!

Tera's ankles were shackled together, making her gait awkward. She was dressed in a ragged brown jumpsuit patched with rags, not unlike the one he had worn on the Labor Force. She was delivering bowls of soup to the various cages, and she looked tired. And beautiful. And somehow noble, despite the rottenness that surrounded her.

Ollie held his breath as he watched her.

"Something wrong there, friend?" Leonard asked.

"Hmm? No. Nothing." *Nothing at all.* Slowly, Tera got closer, taking care not to spill the bowls as she walked.

She stopped first at two other cages along the walkway. When she reached Leonard and Ollie's cage, she looked up, stifled a scream, and dropped a bowl of soup. It poured through the grates and landed on a guard below, who started shouting.

Ollie covered his lips with a finger. *Shhh.*

Tera didn't move. Her mouth was still open in shock.

The guard was already bounding up the stairs, furious, shaking the soup from his sleeve.

Ollie crouched down next to her. "Be ready," he whispered. "Soon."

She nodded dazedly, her eyes full of questions.

The guard was at her side minutes later, pointing at his wet red sleeve, spouting a furious stream of nonsensical insults. Tera dropped her head and offered apologies, using one of her rags to dry the sleeve while she and Ollie shot each other furtive glances. The altercation was interrupted by a noisy commotion near the side doors.

"Warden coming through!" someone yelled. "Move aside! Warden coming through!"

All sound and motion in the pit ceased. Guards stood at attention. Slop wenches froze their spoons in midair.

The Warden strode into the pit with his hands clasped behind his back, looking as pleased as a looter in a riot. The familiar ring of children surrounded him, still generating the cloud of deadly gas. The Reds and servants gave them a wide berth.

The angry, soup-stained guard forgot about his wet uniform and hustled down to greet the Warden. As soon as he left, Tera reached through the bars to squeeze Ollie's hand, then hurried away. Leonard watched the exchange with curiosity but didn't comment.

Down below, several guards and the Warden shared a conversation that Ollie couldn't hear, though it soon became clear that the Warden was making choices. He pointed to the various fighters, listened to the counsel of the guards, and then either nodded or shook his head.

"What are they doing?" Ollie asked.

"Making the roster," Leonard answered grimly. "For today's Knockdowns."

A Red walked into the center of the room and clanged a bell. "Lineup!" he bellowed. When the cavern fell mostly silent, he glanced down at the clipboard in his hand and said: "First up...Viper!" At this, the caged inmates broke out into stomps and shouts. Ollie couldn't tell if they were happy or upset. The guard waved his arm to quiet them. "Viper, choose your opponent."

Tense stillness followed. Ollie followed everyone's gaze to a brawny man standing with his hands on his hips in a nearby cage. The man seemed to be considering his options. Finally, Viper made his selection. "I choose The Roughneck!" he shouted. This caused another reactive explosion from the surrounding inmates.

The guard nodded and made a note on his clipboard. "Match two...Deathstalker!"

More cheers and stomps.

"Deathstalker, choose your opponent."

The prisoner hesitated only a moment before pointing to a woman in a nearby cage and shouting, "I choose Medusa!"

At the sound of her name, the woman pumped her fists and snarled at him.

The guard looked up and around. When his eyes rested on Dozer, he smirked. "And we see Dozer has made a return trip to join us here in the pit. Didn't get enough, the first time around?" the guard asked, generating a roar of laughter. He continued with a stern shout into the void: "Dozer, third match! Choose your opponent!"

Ollie held his breath. Dozer scanned the room, looking down at the birdcages below his. Then he pointed at Ollie. "I choose... The Butcher!" he shouted. It took a moment for Ollie to realize that Dozer was talking about him.

Cheers went up all around.

Ollie looked up at him and mouthed, *The Butcher?*

Dozer shrugged and grinned.

The selections continued until all the available slots were filled for nine fights.

When it was done, Ollie looked over at his cagemate. "They didn't call your name," he said.

Leonard gave a weary smile. "They never do. Everybody just knows. I'm...what's waiting. At the end."

"So, they save the best for last?" Ollie said, trying, and failing, to cheer Leonard up.

"Something like that, I suppose," Leonard answered, staring off into space.

Ollie sighed. It was all so disgustingly unfair. So crooked, and cruel, and small. But he couldn't worry about all that now. One thing at a time. Dozer had done his part, thank God. Now they just had to wait.

As the day passed, all the fighters were let out of their cages for training and calisthenics. Ollie hopped around, stretched his legs, and did his best to look like he knew how to throw a punch. His size alone would intimidate some of them; it would have to be enough. Throughout the day he tried, and failed, to get close to Dozer. He also looked for Tera. But much to his frustration, she didn't appear again.

When night fell, guards herded the selected fighters into two lines, standing next to their opponents. Dozer and Ollie finally stood shoulder to shoulder and shared a quick nod. Showtime.

The tower's prisoners let out a roar as the fighters entered the courtyard. Ollie craned his neck: The empty expanse loomed impossibly high above his head. Hundreds of faces peered out of the small round windows. Spitting. Hollering. Cheering. And down here, on ground level, the Warden supervised it all from a throne-like gilded chair, surrounded by his zombie-trance children and a gaggle of guards.

The Warden stood, and the noise died down. "Lower the board!" he decreed, lifting a hand. At his command, a cranking sound echoed in the courtyard as a counterweight stone began to rise off the ground. At the same time, a large, wooden-framed chalkboard inched downward from somewhere high above. The two objects passed each other in the space above the fighters' heads, moving in opposite directions, connected by a gargantuan chain. Each link was the size of a human head.

The scoreboard continued its slow, dramatic arrival—*clankety, clankety, clank*—until it came to rest on the ground near the Warden's chair. One of guards hoisted something that looked like an oversized piece of chalk onto his shoulder. At that, the Warden stood again, and shouted: "Scorers, ready?"

"Scorers ready!" The guard with the chalk answered.

"Fighters ready?" the Warden yelled.

Ollie's fellow prisoners gave a hearty response: "Fighters ready!"

The Warden returned to his seat, scooched his butt into a comfortable position, and lifted a hand. "Warden ready! And begin!" Cheers erupted. Cups banged against bars.

"Match One, Viper and The Roughneck!" announced the scorer, who also wrote each name on the giant chalkboard. The two selected men remained in the center of the courtyard, while the rest shuffled off to the side.

Ollie found himself leaning against a wall, next to Dozer. When the fight began and the noise levels rose, Dozer leaned closer and said, "I told you I'd think of a good name for you, Roomie."

Ollie resisted the urge to look at him, instead continuing to stare straight ahead. "Yeah, thanks for that," he muttered, though "The Butcher" was, admittedly, a hell of a lot better than most names he'd been called through the years. Then he added, quietly, "I see you got my message."

Neither man turned his eyes away from the action in front of them. Viper already had The Roughneck struggling in some kind of a choke hold. "Y'all better know what you're doing," Dozer answered, barely moving his lips. "I left the fifth floor for this shit."

"We do," Ollie said.

The first fight wrapped up quickly; Viper shot his arms into the air while his outmatched opponent lay in a heap on the ground. The crowd seemed pleased. Ollie looked on with worry—he needed more time to talk to Dozer, to explain things. This was moving too fast. After The Roughneck was dragged away, the guard with the huge stick of chalk entered the score onto the board and announced the second match-up: "Deathstalker and Medusa!"

The pudgy man and wiry-haired woman stepped forward. A bell sounded, and the scrapping began.

Ollie leaned to his left again. "Just make it look real," he said. "I'll let you win."

"Oh, you'll *let* me win, will you?" Dozer replied, finally turning to look at Ollie. His black skin was smeared with dust; his one good eye twinkled with amusement. "I swear, boy, you're nuttier than a squirrel turd. You ain't got much of a choice, now, do you?"

"Just make it look good!" Ollie whispered, his cheeks reddening.

Dozer grunted and pushed up his sleeves. Ollie cracked his knuckles. *Pop, pop, pop.* In front of them, Medusa had kicked the Deathstalker in the groin and then tried to strangle him. He, in turn, had wriggled free of her grasp and made contact with a right hook. Hair and blood and spit flew in all directions as the tussle continued. Finally, the man kicked his opponent to the ground, stepped on her torso, and lifted his arms.

"See that? That's what I get when you *let* me win," Dozer said, pointing. "I get to fight that psycho. And then, if that works, I get pounded by The Mallet. So, thanks for all that."

Ollie opened his mouth to respond, then felt a shove from behind.

"Dozer and The Butcher!" someone announced.

Another shove propelled him into the center of the courtyard. Dozer jogged in place next to him, raising his fists in a ready position. Ollie did the same. His heart was thudding in time with the cups pounding the bars above his head.

"You said you'd make this worth my while," Dozer said, struggling to be heard above the roar of the crowd. "How much we talkin'?"

Ollie switched his weight from one hip to the other. "It's, uh, not exactly all worked out yet."

A bell rang. The fight had started. Dozer looked at him suspiciously. "What do you mean, it ain't worked out yet?"

"I mean, I'll have it. Of course, I'll have it. I just don't have it...yet."

Dozer crunched his face up and swung. He popped Ollie in the shoulder, sending him reeling.

Ollie gasped and grabbed his shoulder. "What the hell was that? You're not supposed to really hit me!"

"Oh, no? I thought you said to make it look real?" Dozer landed another blow, this time in Ollie's gut. With a loud grunt, Ollie clutched his stomach and fell backwards onto the dirt.

"What are you doing?" he said, or tried to say, but he couldn't find enough breath to form the words. The crowd was chanting: "Get up! Get up! Get up!"

Dozer hopped from foot to foot, waiting. Seething. "I swear to God, boy, if you got me back down here for nothing, I'll kill you my damn self."

Ollie struggled to his feet and swung wildly. He missed, then swung again and hit something, though he couldn't be sure what it was. Wherever his punch had landed, he was certain that Dozer had allowed it to happen. When their heads were close enough, Ollie caught his eye. "We're going to get you out, Dozer," he said, as loud as he dared. Then he gasped for breath and said it again: "We're going to get you out of Herrick's End."

Dozer paused. The words had landed as hard as any jab.

"Soon," Ollie said. "Just trust me. And stay ready."

His former cellmate gave an almost infinitesimal nod.

"Now hit me. Hard."

An eyebrow shot up over his eye patch.

"You have to win, right? Make it look good."

Dozer hopped from foot to foot. "You're batshit crazy, you know that? I ain't seen no one like you down here before. Never."

"Is that good or bad?" Ollie asked.

"Hell if I know," Dozer said. Then he tilted his head from side to side and cracked his neck. It was the last thing Ollie remembered seeing before his face hit the ground.

"Thanks for going easy on him."

Ollie and Leonard were swinging in their cage, nursing their wounds. Or, more accurately, Ollie was nursing his wounds while Leonard looked on, wound-free.

Leonard shrugged. "Any friend of yours," he said.

Ollie had predicted that Dozer might make it to the end to face The Mallet, and had prepped Leonard to pull his punches. After a confused, whispered conversation mid-fight, the two men had managed to stage a fairly believable mock battle in which The Mallet, as expected, emerged victorious, and Dozer only appeared to be unconscious in the dirt.

In truth, Dozer was fine. And Ollie was fine, too. Or mostly fine.

Most importantly, Tera was fine, and currently standing in full view of Ollie's suspended cage. She was only a few hundred yards away, clumped in a group of shackled slop wenches and first-aid carts on the ground. She looked up and winked at him, and he smiled, his heart thumping. Then she turned back to her work.

Ollie cracked his knuckles. They were all here, and ready. Soon, the wenches would disappear through the doorway and Tera would be gone until tomorrow. Another opportunity, lost. Now was the time. He craned his neck, peering around the cavernous space, but saw nothing. *Now!* he wanted to shout. *Now, goddammit!* But all he could do was slump in a defeated heap, trapped in a birdcage, throbbing with pain. Waiting.

Weariness overcame him. Ollie was leaning his head against the bars, fighting to keep his lids open, when something flashed in his peripheral vision. A movement, high up to the right. He lifted his head and stared. It was...someone jumping. Hanging?

He saw a flash of sparkle. Something reflective. Fabric.

Ollie climbed to his feet as recognition dawned. A wide smile spread across his face. He was looking at an acrobat in a tight blue suit, swinging effortlessly from platform to platform. Graceful and strong. Silent.

Laszlo.

Ollie looked down at Tera; she hadn't yet noticed. No one had. Most of the prisoners were asleep or exhausted from the night's brutal events. The guards were talking amongst themselves or walking solo rounds. The slop wenches were gathering the first-aid supplies and carts, getting ready to leave for the night.

High above them all, Laszlo leapt like a lemur through the air, swinging from cage to cage. Hanging by his fingers beneath the metal-grate walkways. And as Ollie watched, astounded, the acrobat swung himself up, snuck behind a patrolling guard, and swiped a hanging key ring from a hook on the man's jumpsuit. Ollie held his breath, his knuckles turning white. But the guard did not see, or feel, or notice anything. The red suit just kept walking. And Laszlo disappeared once again into the darkness.

Ollie pressed himself against the bars, willing Laszlo to see him. He tried to catch Tera's eye without luck. Then he turned to face his cagemate.

"Whatever you do, just stay quiet," he said.

Leonard had been drifting off to sleep. Now, he looked at Ollie with a dazed expression. "What?"

Ollie pressed a finger to his lips just as the sparkling blue acrobat appeared out of the darkness and flung himself against the bars of their cage.

Leonard jumped to his feet. "What the—"

"Shhh!" Ollie said. "It's okay!" He spun around to Laszlo, who had tucked his gray-slippered feet onto the floor of the cage while clinging to the bars. He looked comfortable and relaxed. He did not look like a man who was hanging by his fingers in the open air, one wrong move from a disastrous plunge.

"You made it!" Ollie said.

"Of course, I make it," Laszlo replied, sounding mildly insulted. He looked at Leonard. "Who is your very big friend?"

Leonard was standing stock-still, staring. "I- I'm Leonard."

"Leonard," Laszlo nodded. "I am Laszlo Kravchenko of the famous Flying Kravchenko Brothers of Ukraine. But we are now worrying about more important things, yes?" He let go of the bars with one hand and held up a key.

Ollie looked over his shoulder. One guard was strolling along an upper walkway but hadn't noticed anything amiss. Two more guards were engrossed in conversation down below. Tera was still there, though she seemed to be packing up her cart. He willed her to look at him, and when she didn't, he tried to send a mental message: *Don't leave. Five more minutes. Please.*

Laszlo slid around the outside of the cage to reach the door. He inserted the large key in the lock and turned it; Ollie heard the quick click.

Laszlo looked up, pleased. "Now the rest?" he asked.

Ollie nodded. "Now the rest."

Leonard watched the two of them in mute confusion. Ollie held up a hand: *Just wait.*

Laszlo grinned and swung away into the blackness. Ollie tried to track his movements, but it was like watching a dragonfly dart from reed to reed. He hung, he leapt, he clung, always silently, moving among the swaying cages. Each time he landed, he put a finger over his lips to silence the surprised inhabitant, then turned the key in the lock. And since Ollie couldn't hear the whispered conversations that followed, he could only hope that Laszlo was following the plan as they had discussed it: telling each prisoner to stay quiet, wait for the signal, and then head for the main arched doorway once they were free.

Ollie began to sweat. Laszlo's stealth seemed to be working—so far, anyway. None of the guards had noticed his movements. None of the prisoners had given away the game. One by one, he unlocked each cage door, leaving behind a slew of astonished fighters to cling to the bars and watch as Laszlo finished his rounds.

Hurry, hurry, hurry, Ollie thought, cracking his knuckles again. *Almost there.*

Just then, a slop wench looked up from her cart. She spotted Laszlo—a giant, iridescent blur swinging somewhere above her head— and she screamed. The sound pieced the sleepy cavern like a jolt from a defibrillator paddle. The guards jumped to attention, looking up and around in all directions. Another wench screamed, then another.

In the confusion, Laszlo landed on top of one of the hanging cages. He reached up to grab the chain, pulled himself to full height, and stretched out his free arm.

"Now is time!" he bellowed. *"Now is time!"*

For a moment, all went still. Then, a primal cry erupted and echoed against every rocky surface in the carved-out chamber. Cages rattled. Doors swung open with ear-grating squeals. Slop wenches shrieked and crouched. The handful of remaining guards scurried in wild, helpless circles. And with one thunderous blast of whoops and leaps, dozens of the tower's mightiest and angriest inmates were suddenly, shockingly free.

Twenty-three

Leonard stood frozen, staring at Ollie with wide eyes.

"Go!" Ollie shouted.

When Leonard still didn't budge, he said it again: "Go! Hurry! We have to move!"

Leonard looked at the unlocked door and tentatively pushed it open.

"Jump!" Ollie said, pointing.

Leonard nodded. He hesitated for a fraction of a second before jumping and landing on the metal platform below with a ringing clang. Ollie followed behind, and together, they ran through the chaos. All around them, inmates were leaping, crashing, sprinting, and screaming with a ferocity that Ollie could only describe as a war cry. Laszlo, he saw, was swinging towards them. Down on the ground, Tera stood still as the mob shoved past.

Finally, he was next to her. "Are you okay?" he asked, touching her face.

"I'm fine. We have to get out of here."

"Right. But first you have to call the guards."

"What? Why?"

"Call more guards, and tell them all to go that way." Ollie pointed toward the archway, where the escaped fighters were heading. Where Laszlo had *told* them to go. They didn't know, of course, that he had also created a kind of funnel of capture for them there, and that the route was not an escape but a dead-end. Ollie felt a little bad about the subterfuge. But he couldn't very well set the prison's most violent group of prisoners loose in the Neath, could he? And he had needed the chaos as cover. While the guards were busy rounding up the Knockdown fighters and returning them to their cages, he and his friends would escape in the other direction.

Ollie, Laszlo, and Leonard hid behind a row of carts. Tera watched them go, then painted a look of fear and panic on her face.

"Heeeeelp!" she screamed, running toward the swinging doors. "Heeeeelp! Escape!"

Dozens of red-suited men appeared, brandishing zapper rods. She pointed them in the direction of the archway and they ran off with determined looks.

"Okay, they're gone," Tera said, poking her head over the carts. "Now what?"

Ollie stood. Derrin and Kuyu had told him to find the nearest kitchen. All the kitchens, apparently, had back staircases and dumbwaiter lifts, rarely used by anyone but the cooking staff and unlikely to be monitored during the pandemonium of their manufactured crisis. Based on his observations, Ollie assumed the fighting pit's kitchen was on the other side of the big double doors that the slop wenches had been using to come and go. "The kitchen's this way?" he asked Tera.

She nodded.

"How far?"

"Close," she answered.

Ollie pointed to the shackles on Tera's ankles. "Leonard, can you...?"

Leonard took a moment to survey his surroundings. Then he reached for a nearby toppled cart. He tore the axel from the bottom, lifted the metal bar, and smashed it against the chain connecting Tera's shackles. With a clang, they broke apart.

They all stared at the shattered bit of chain, and then at each other. And then, they ran: Tera led the way, followed by Ollie, Laszlo, and Dozer, with a lumbering Leonard bringing up the rear. But as they neared the double doors, they could see a group of red-suited men interrogating a whimpering clump of wenches inside.

"Shit," Ollie muttered. He held out his arm to stop the others. The doorway was blocked. He saw ten guards, maybe, and at least as many servants. He gritted his teeth. This was not part of the plan.

"Is there another way in?" he asked Tera.

She shook her head grimly.

Should they hide and wait? There was no time. Soon, the guards would head back this way with the captured prisoners and the pit would fill once again with people. They had two minutes, tops.

Sonofabitch. Ollie's head swiveled left and right. As far as he could tell, there were only three ways in or out of the pit: the arched doorway where the escaped prisoners and guards had fled (now blocked), the kitchen doors (now blocked), and the ramp that led out into the courtyard.

The courtyard it was.

"Out there, hurry!" he pointed and whispered.

They scampered like rats up the ramp and out into the now-empty heart of the tower, where Ollie and Dozer had been fighting only hours before.

"Now where?" Laszlo asked, craning his neck. For the first time, he was starting to look concerned.

"We have to go up," Ollie said. "Tera, is there an elevator?"

"Up?" objected Dozer. "Why the hell would we go—"

"There's one," Tera said. "But it's that way." She jerked her thumb to indicate the archway they had just passed through. "There are stairs around here somewhere," she added, spinning in an uncertain circle.

Stairs wouldn't work, Ollie knew. They'd never make it. They had only a minute or two before the guards found them out here. His head swiveled. He saw no other sets of swinging doors. No tunnels, no numbered holes in the walls.

All he saw was the boulder counterweight, resting on the ground. A spike and hook connected it to a thick chain, which extended up into the open reach above their heads.

Ollie stared at it, trying to remember what he had seen earlier at the start of the Knockdowns. *Lower the board!* the Warden had shouted, and then two things had happened simultaneously: The counterweight had risen, and the scoreboard had descended. Each had moved in direct opposition to the other. *Clankety, clankety, clank.*

They had to be connected by the same chain, with a crank or a winch at the top of the tower controlling the motion. Somewhere above, the massive chalkboard was hovering. Weight, counterweight. Disturb one, affect the other.

Two guards emerged into the courtyard with narrowed eyes and a matched set of sparking prods. They started marching toward Ollie and the group.

"Get on the chain!" Ollie shouted, pointing. "Climb! Hurry!"

His friends looked at him in confusion. Then they looked at the guards and started running. When they reached the counterweight, Tera went first, scrambling over the stone and climbing the chain like a macaque. Ten feet up, she slipped her arms and feet inside the massive links and held on.

Laszlo followed, leaping gracefully. Then Dozer made a less graceful but equally effective lunge. Ollie and Leonard brought up the rear. When Leonard started to climb, Ollie stopped him.

"Wait," he said. "I need slack. Can you...?" He pointed to the hook connecting the taut chain to the boulder. Leonard nodded. He understood.

"Hurry up!" Tera shouted from above their heads.

With a loud grunt, Leonard grabbed the chain and pulled. The Reds were approaching, fast.

"Just a little more," Ollie wheezed, struggling to spin the hook and release its grip. "Just...a...little..."

Leonard's face turned crimson, then purple.

"It's...coming..." Ollie said. "Just a little..."

The guards were only feet away. He wouldn't make it. The hook was moving, but there wasn't enough slack. He couldn't free it. One of the Reds reached him, tried to peel his hands from the metal. A foot shot out of the air—Dozer's?—and kicked the guard's head, knocking him back. The other Red stepped around the fallen body and lunged.

Ollie's fingers felt like they might break from the pressure. He gave the hook one last, agonizing yank and suddenly—it spun. The bonds holding the chain to the boulder were broken. Ollie was too stunned to move. Luckily, Leonard wasn't: The big man grabbed the chain with one hand and Ollie's wrist with the other. Somewhere high above, the giant scoreboard began to fall. And the chain, now holding all five of them, began to rise.

The jerk was sudden; Tera screamed. Ollie gasped as his feet left the ground and the chain started its fast climb into the heights of the tower. The only thing standing between him and a fatal plunge to the ground was Leonard's meaty hand, which gripped Ollie's wrist like a vise.

The scoreboard passed them on its way down. The wind whipped past his ears as they picked up speed. Up, up, up. He was faintly aware of hundreds of eyes watching them from the surrounding cells as they ascended. Shouts and whoops echoed. Ollie's hand was sweating, slipping. How long could Leonard possibly hold him? How long could the others hold themselves? What if the chain snapped?

Then, he heard a shout: "Jump!" It was Tera.

Ollie tried to look up, but all he saw was Leonard's hulking body above him.

"Jump!" she yelled again.

The ascent was slowing. Something had changed. The chain began to sway as his companions, he assumed, made the leap. By the time he saw the wooden ledge, it was almost too late. Tera, Dozer, and Laszlo were already standing on it. How would he reach it? There was no way—

Ollie's thought was interrupted when Leonard swung him, wildly, and then let go of his hand. For one long, sickening second, Ollie was airborne: Just him, the shapeless oxygen, and a view of the ground, fifty stories below. He floundered his limbs in terror, reaching for the ledge. His fingers brushed the wood but found nothing to grip.

Ollie gasped. This was it. He was going down.

A hand grasped his forearm. Then another hand. Grunting, shouting. They were telling him to hold on. They were pulling. Minutes later, somehow, Ollie found himself splayed belly-first on a wooden platform, heart pounding, wondering what the hell had just happened. When Leonard landed behind him, the whole platform shook.

"Move!" Dozer was shouting. "Get up!"

Still shaking, Ollie scrambled to his feet. All five of them ducked as the chain whipped past their faces, flinging itself around the cranking gears of the platform they were standing on. Down below, the scoreboard hit the ground at full speed and shattered into pieces. The impact sent a kind of sonic boom echoing throughout the courtyard.

From their windows, hundreds of inmates cheered the spectacle.

Ollie, Tera, Laszlo, Leonard, and Dozer looked at each other, shock splayed across their faces.

"What in the Sam Hill?" Dozer gasped.

Tera ran a trembling hand through her purple hair. Leonard was bent over, panting. Laszlo stepped forward to peer over the edge.

Ollie tried to catch his breath, to still his heart. They were stuck on a skinny platform that had not been built, clearly, to hold so much weight. It jutted out only a few feet from the wall, but it was big enough to traverse. Carefully.

"This way," he said, his voice shaking. A strange mixture of astonishment, optimism, and fear was bubbling through his veins. He had gotten them to the top. He had done his job. Now he could only hope that Ajanta, Derrin, and Kuyu had done theirs.

Ollie led the group off the platform and into a torchlit hallway, creeping along until he finally found a staircase that led up instead of down. Dark and unusually narrow, it would have been easy to miss.

"Well, that don't look right," Dozer said dubiously.

"This is very strange stairs," Laszlo added. "Stairs for skinny people only."

Ollie agreed with both of them but held his ground. "We have to get up to the roof," he said, trying to project a confidence he didn't feel. *Just keep moving. Stick to the plan.* In truth, he had no idea if the weird little stairwell would lead to the roof. But at the moment, it was their best—and only—option. "I'll go first."

He stepped through the opening and began to climb, winding up and around in almost complete darkness. Ollie could hear the others shuffling behind him. The further he got, the tighter it got; soon, he was ascending sideways. Something brushed against his face and he jumped. What was *that?* He couldn't see anything. His body was pressed on all sides; he began to hyperventilate. This was a mistake. A claustrophobic, panic-inducing dead-end.

He was about to call out, to tell them to turn around, when a sliver of light appeared ahead. Ollie pressed forward and popped out of the dark stairwell like a Heimlich Maneuvered chunk of food. The air, murky and orange-tinted, felt glorious. He sucked it in.

Dozer landed next to him, blinking and squinting.

Then came Tera, and Laszlo.

No Leonard.

They waited, looking at each other nervously. No one, it seemed, wanted to ask the obvious question: Had he gotten stuck? Ollie stared at the narrow opening, willing the big man to appear. Finally he saw something pushing its way through the breach. A hand. A foot. And then an entire, gargantuan body, turned sideways. With an "oof," Leonard squeezed himself through the crevice and collapsed.

"Jesus," he coughed. "Where are we?"

"We," Ollie said proudly, "are on the roof."

Teracotta shingles lined the surface. Steaming pipes surrounded them, belching smoke into the thick air. They were still inside the cavern, but damn high up. So high that the wormwalkers above their heads looked less like one solid, writhing mass and more like individual, writhing tubes.

"Stand up," Ollie told Leonard. "Take a look!"

Herrick's End

The fighter grunted and rose to his feet, joining the others at the edge of the roof. When he saw the view below he gripped Ollie's arm. In another world, it might have been a picture on a postcard. *Wish you were here in the Neath!* The rusted smog immediately surrounding the Herrick's End tower gave way to a crystalline, sweeping scene: Teal-green water wrapped like a hug around the islands. Life teemed in the boats, on the land, and over the narrow, white bridges. People, crows, and other creatures he didn't recognize played their parts as tiny chess pieces on a massive board. Distended fern fronds swayed in unseen wind. And even at this distance, the tiny, multicolored flowers sparkled in the light of the blue ceiling, creating a kind of sequin effect across the entire cavern.

Ollie struggled for words. "It's..."

"Beautiful," Tera finished for him with a satisfied smile. "It's beautiful."

"Yeah, it kind of is," Dozer said, sounding surprised. "But what are we doing here? I hope you ain't expecting me to jump."

Ollie swallowed. *Not technically,* he wanted to say. Instead, he pasted on a bright, false smile and said, "Now we just have to be patient. Just a few minutes. It's fine. It's all planned out."

The five of them looked at each other uneasily. Finally, Tera said, "If Ollie says it will be fine, then it will be fine. He's gotten us this far, hasn't he?"

The others nodded. Ollie flashed her a grateful look, then let his gaze travel to the ground far below. *C'mon, c'mon, c'mon,* he thought.

As the minutes passed, each of them seemed to lapse into their own musings. Leonard continued to ogle the expansive view. Dozer lay on his back, shut his eyes, and threw an arm over his face. Laszlo jogged in impatient circles, then began wandering the roof.

Tera sat cross-legged on the tiles and started tugging on her shackles. Though Leonard had broken the chain that connected them, the two metal clasps still encircled her skin like ugly, oversized anklets. Ollie sat down next to her.

"Are you okay?" he asked.

"I'm fine."

"Did they... What did they make you do?"

"I'm fine," she said again, using her free hand to pat his arm. "Really. It wasn't so—well, yeah, it was bad. But now it's over."

His brow furrowed. "For the moment, anyway."

"Thanks for coming to get me," Tera said.

Ollie flushed. "I was only returning the favor."

215

"I guess that makes us even, then."

The red of his cheeks deepened.

"Your friends seem nice," she said.

Her words struck him. *Friends*. She was right, he realized. This odd assortment of peculiar people *were* his friends. And that meant that he had made more friends in two weeks in this godforsaken, underground hellscape than he had made in a lifetime on the Brickside. How was that for irony?

Ollie laughed. Softly, at first, then louder. And then it took over: A belly-rocking, all-consuming laugh that left him doubled over and crying.

Tera looked on, starting to giggle herself. "What's so funny?" she asked.

"It's just...it's just..." He couldn't speak. He didn't want to. The laughter felt so good, like a cleansing flush for his entire body. He wanted to sit like that forever, holding her hand, laughing at nothing.

He was so lost in the mirth that he didn't, at first, notice the constriction. It came slow and steady: an increasing pressure that seemed to crush the air out of his lungs. Suddenly, Ollie couldn't breathe. He gripped his chest.

"Ollie? What's wrong?"

The compression tightened. He tried to inhale but failed.

"Ollie?"

He bent over, gasping. Dozer and Leonard approached, looking concerned. He couldn't speak, couldn't move. He thought, for the second time that day, that he was probably about to die. And then, just as quickly as it had started, the pressure disappeared. He gulped the air, resting his hands on the shingles.

"Is that the first time that's happened?" Tera asked him softly.

Ollie nodded. He looked up to find them watching him with knowing, sad expressions.

"It's the change," Tera said. Her face looked somber.

"What, the lung thing?"

She nodded.

He searched their eyes, feeling the panic start to well. "So, what, that's it? I'm done?"

"No, no," Tera assured him, reaching again for his hand. "Not yet."

"It takes a bit," Dozer said. "A few more times like that. If that was just your first, you've got a little while, yet."

"How long?"

At first, no one answered. Then Leonard said, "It's nothing to worry about. You've got time." He flashed a smile that Ollie recognized as forced.

The awkward silence that followed was interrupted by Laszlo's voice, booming and sharp. "Ollie, my friend! I think I find who you are waiting for!" he called out, swinging in from some higher point on the roof.

They looked up in time to see a sweeping flash of feathers and flight.

Tera's eyes lit up: "Mrs. Paget!"

The giant crow swooped around the tower and came in for a landing, scattering the roof tiles with her feet. Tera ran to her and wrapped her arms around the bird's neck.

Caw! Mrs. Paget replied.

It took all of them a moment to notice Ajanta, holding the reins on the crow's back.

"Nice to see you, too," Ajanta said, smirking.

Tera looked up, gasped, and held out her arms. The two women embraced wordlessly.

"You found us," Ollie said, his voice heavy with relief.

"Yeah, well, it wasn't easy," Ajanta replied, glancing down at the scene below. "The Reds are all out. High alert. I take it you managed to make a bit of a ruckus down there?"

He nodded.

"You certainly got their attention," she said. "I think they might have spotted me on my way in."

Ollie's stomach knotted. "We'd better hurry, then," he said. "Tera, hop on."

Ajanta gathered the reins and scooted forward to make some room.

"What?" Tera looked from one to the other.

"Hop on," Ollie said again, gesturing toward the empty spot on the crow's back. "We have to hurry."

"Are you crazy?" Tera asked. "We can't all fit on there. We'll kill her."

"Of course not," Ollie said. "We have to go one at a time. You go first. Then they'll come back for each of us. That's the plan."

"That's your plan?" Leonard said, eyes wide. "She's supposed to make a gazillion return trips up here?"

"Look, gimme a break, okay?" Ollie retorted. "I didn't have a lot to work with!"

A thwacking sound startled them; Ollie turned to see a rod of pointed wood on the roof near his feet.

"What the hell is th—"

"Shit," Ajanta said. "They followed me. They know we're up here."

"What are those?" Dozer asked, pointing at the stick.

"Poison darts," she answered. As the words left her mouth, another dart whizzed by Leonard's ear. He ducked.

"But...from where?" Ollie asked.

The answer came with sickening speed. From the corner of his eye, he saw them: A flock of crows, flown by red-suited guards, gliding on the horizon. More darts landed on the roof like wooden spikes of rain.

"Go!" Ollie shouted, pushing Tera towards the bird. "Hurry!"

"What? No!"

"Tera, I'm serious! You need to get out of here, now!"

"No! I'm not leaving you all here alone!"

He was going to say that Ajanta would come back for each of them, as planned. He was going to tell her that everything would be fine. But as the poisoned spikes fell from the sky and the flock of flying guards flew ever closer, he knew it wasn't true. This was it. The scheme was shot. Mrs. Paget wouldn't make it back for anyone else. She'd be lucky to get one of them out of there.

The rest of them must have known it, too. Laszlo and Dozer had already hidden behind a nearby steam vent; Leonard was shielding Tera with his body.

"Please, Tera!" Ollie said. "Please! You have to go now!"

"I'm not leaving you behind," she said, her mouth set into a firm line.

Their standoff was interrupted by Dozer's voice behind them.

"Well, hell, if she ain't gonna go, can I?"

"What?" Ollie spun around.

"Yes," Tera said, pulling Dozer forward. "Go. Get on."

"What? No way!" Ollie sputtered.

"Ollie, I'm not going. Someone might as well use it. Otherwise, Ajanta came all the way up here for nothing."

A new barrage of darts fell.

"Krite!" Ajanta shouted, ducking her head in a near-miss. "Whoever's coming better come fast!"

"He's going," Tera said, shoving Dozer toward the crow.

"You did say you owed me one," Dozer said, flashing Ollie a gap-toothed grin.

"Fine!" Ollie threw up his arms in surrender. "Go on. Get out of here."

Ajanta held out her hand; Dozer grabbed it and leapt up onto Mrs. Paget's back.

Caw! Caw! The bird screeched in protest.

"For heaven's sake, I'll be fine," Tera told her. "I'll see you back at the barn." She smoothed the crow's feathers, then looked at Ajanta. "Take care of her," she said.

Ajanta nodded. Her long braid slipped over her shoulder as she leaned toward Ollie. "So, I guess it's Plan B, then?" she asked.

He lifted his palms helplessly.

"I'll tell the others," Ajanta said with a firm nod. Then she reached into her pocket and pulled out a small, burlap package. "Here, take this. You might need it."

Ollie took the package without comment, his eyes growing wide with dismay.

She snapped the reins. "See you at the bottom." She and Dozer gave the group one last, long look. Then the great black wings swooshed up and out, and they were gone.

Ollie stood there, dumbfounded, watching them disappear. He turned to Tera. "Why did you do that? I was trying to get you out! That was the whole damn point of coming back here!"

"The point is to get us *all* out," she corrected him.

"And how are we supposed to do that now?"

"Uh, guys? I think we'd better move," Leonard interrupted.

Ollie looked back out across the hazy expanse. The airborne attackers were so close he could see the guards lifting the long, tubular blowguns to their mouths and puffing up their cheeks, ready to blow.

"What's Plan B?" Tera shouted, breaking out into a run.

He didn't have time for the long answer, so he gave her the short one. "I think it starts with getting the hell off this roof!"

Twenty-Four

And then there were four.

Together, they ran. Darts rained down around them, mostly missing their targets. All except one.

Ollie heard the cry when he was almost to the wall. He turned to see Laszlo, yowling, holding his leg.

"He's hit!" Leonard shouted.

Together, they struggled to help the limping acrobat out of the line of fire.

"It...burns," Laszlo gasped through gritted teeth.

Tera, Leonard, and Ollie shared a grim look between them.

"The poison is spreading," Tera said. "We've got to get it out."

Ollie glanced over his shoulder. The flying crow army had almost reached the roof. More blowguns had already been hoisted, readied.

When he turned back around, Tera's hand was on the protruding dart. She gave him a questioning look, and he nodded.

Tera gripped the wooden stick, took a deep breath, and pulled. The dart made a sucking sound as the tip ripped again through the flesh.

Blood spurted all over the shiny blue Lycra. Laszlo threw his head back and howled.

"C'mon! We have to go!" Tera shouted.

They half-pushed, half-carried Laszlo toward the doorway that was little more than a slit in the wall.

"No, no, no..." he moaned. "Not in there. Not again. I do not fit."

"Sorry, buddy," Leonard said. "It's the only way down." Then, without warning, he shoved Laszlo through the tiny opening, pushing until the blue suit disappeared into the darkness. Leonard squeezed in behind him. Ollie did the same and reached for Tera's hand, but she waved him off.

"One sec," she said. She looked around, found a loose pipe, and yanked it from its post. Then she entered the narrow doorway and wedged the pipe in behind her, sealing the passage—at least temporarily—against pursuers.

The stairway, as before, was impossibly tight. Leonard pushed Laszlo, and Ollie pushed Leonard, until they reached the section that began to widen. Finally, the group picked up speed.

Laszlo limped and groaned; the others tried their best to carry him. When they reached the hallway and the landing that led to the tower's main staircase, they started to descend. Five steps in, Ollie held up a hand to stop them.

"What is wrong?" Laszlo asked.

Ollie pressed a finger against his lips. He pointed down into the darkness.

The others paused and listened. Distant voices echoed off the stone. Feet on stairs. The sounds were getting closer.

"They know we're up here," Tera whispered.

The four companions backtracked stealthily. Ollie looked left and right, feeling his heart pound. One direction would lead them back to the rickety platform over the open courtyard; the other would lead them back to the roof stairwell. Either choice would lead to certain doom. And right in the middle, he saw a single, closed door.

He swallowed and pointed. The others nodded.

Ollie turned the knob. It wasn't locked. He pushed it open a crack and peeked through the opening. When he saw what was inside, he stopped, blinked, and then swung the door wide. The others peered around him.

They were looking at a dining room. The table in the center was extraordinarily long, covered with a tablecloth and dozens of serving platters filled with food. Twenty or thirty chairs surrounded it. And every single chair was occupied by the slumped over, motionless body of a Herrick's End guard.

"It's the mess hall," Ollie said. He knew this, or at least suspected, because Derrin and Kuyu had told him about it as the group had crafted their loosey-goosey jailbreak blueprint. The guards had their own dining area at the top of the tower, far away from the riffraff. Cooks prepared the meals each day with food brought in by specially selected Neath providers—two of whom happened to be Tera's roommates.

Leonard stepped inside the barren, rectangular room, which echoed the shape of the central table. He approached one of the slumped guards, picked up a limp arm, and let it fall. "Are they...?"

"No," Ollie said. "Not dead. Just sleeping." When Tera looked at him in confusion, he explained, "It was Derrin and Kuyu. They laced the food with...something. They never told me what."

Her eyes grew large.

"How long to be asleep?" Laszlo asked, limping over to poke at one of the men's faces.

"I don't know," Ollie admitted. "They said it would buy us time, but they didn't seem to know how much."

"That's why there were no guards to stop us when we went to the roof," Tera said, the sudden realization spreading across her face. "They were already asleep."

Ollie nodded.

"That's my girls," she grinned.

"These guys might be asleep, but the others aren't," Leonard pointed out, eyeing the hallway. "We're about to have company. We need to shore up this door."

Unanimously, their eyes roamed the room and fell on the largest object within it. Moments later, Tera, Ollie, and Leonard pushed the table the ten feet or so required to block the doorway while the unconscious guards flopped to the floor around them.

Panting, Ollie leaned forward to rest his hands on his knees, then looked over at Laszlo in growing concern. The acrobat was moaning and leaning against a wall. Had they removed the dart in time? Was the poison still making its way through his bloodstream? As if he could hear Ollie's thoughts, Laszlo gave him a reassuring wink. "Is very good," he said, pointing at the table.

"Oh yeah, it's great," Tera said, tearing a strip of fabric from the tablecloth and wrapping it around the wound on Laszlo's leg. "We've just sealed ourselves into a room with no possibility of escape." As soon as she tugged the knot tight, voices rumbled in the hallway outside. More guards.

Ollie glanced around the mess hall uselessly. Two colorful tapestries hung from hooks, each displaying a scene of underwater battle between human warriors and giant, swimming serpents. Two round windows overlooked the courtyard.

Tera jogged across the room to a small metal flap on the wall. She pulled it open and looked inside. "It's a dumbwaiter," she reported. "We could ride it down."

Leonard approached the tiny opening. It was about the size of a dorm fridge. "What, one body part at a time?" he asked.

"I could fit, if I scrunched up," Tera said. Then she sighed. "But yeah, you're right. It's no good for all of us."

Ollie straightened. "So, you go, then! You can fit. Get the hell out of here."

She shot him an incredulous look. "You really don't listen, do you?"

"Jesus, Tera, please! Just go! The three of us...we'll figure it out. Right, guys?"

Leonard and Laszlo nodded, though neither looked convinced.

"See? We'll figure it out. Go. Please, just go." He held open the dumbwaiter flap.

A jiggling sound came from the door; someone was messing with the knob.

"What are they even doing up here?" Ollie asked, his voice laced with desperation. "They're supposed to be downstairs, dealing with the fighters. That was the plan! Upstairs guards, asleep. Downstairs guards, down the fucking stairs!"

"I guess they didn't get the memo," Leonard answered wryly.

Blood rushed to Ollie's ears. They were out of time, and out of options. He hadn't saved her. He had failed, and now they would all pay the price. What happened to the prisoners who attempted escape? Where did they end up? Not on the cushy fifth floor Labor Force—of that, he was nauseatingly sure. He had led them all into disaster.

His eyes flitted around the room in a wild canvas. Left, right, up, down.

The tapestries. They were huge, splayed end-to-end with cautionary depictions of underwater monsters and the men who foolishly tried to vanquish them. The woven cloths were identical in size; ten-by-twenty, if he'd had to guess. Big enough to be used as parachutes? Two tapestries, four people. Each person grabs two corners, they jump through the round windows, and *voila*: The four of them float gracefully to the bottom of the courtyard and land with a silent, gentle swoosh.

Except, of course, that they weren't exactly a silent, gentle group. Also, Ollie was pretty sure that a parachute had to be made of plastic, or maybe nylon, to work. And that the fall, while terrifyingly high to him, might not be high enough for the wind resistance to kick in and slow their descent.

His friends were talking rapidly, debating; at the door, someone was starting to shove and fight against the blockage.

Ollie tuned them all out. He turned toward the enormous table. It looked like something he might have found in a North End antique store, with an old-world, European style and massive claw-foot legs.

He went still.

Claw-foot legs.

What had George Herrick told him? *Tell Widow Hibbins zero. Lion's feet will dig. As I am, so he will be.*

Ollie's head tilted to the side as he stared.

Lion's feet will dig.

The table legs did, in fact, look like actual animal paws. Lion's feet, perhaps, with pointed claws.

"The legs," he murmured.

The others stopped talking and looked at him.

Ollie lifted himself to his full height. "We can't go down the stairs, right? They're all over the place out there. We can't make a parachute. We can't use the scoreboard to go down because, well, we already smashed that into a million pieces. Mrs. Paget is gone, and she can't come back. And we can't go down in the dumbwaiter because we don't fit. Obviously."

"Is this your idea of a pep talk?" Tera asked, raising one eyebrow.

"What I'm saying is, we can't jump fifty stories all at once," Ollie continued, his voice getting louder. "But we can jump them one at a time."

A look of real concern passed over Laszlo's face. "I think I am not understanding the English," he said. "What are you saying we do?"

"I'm saying we make a hole, in the floor," Ollie said. "Right there. And then another, and then another, until we're all the way down."

"Now I think *I'm* not understanding the English," Tera interrupted, hands on her hips. "Are you nuts? We'd need a jackhammer for that."

Ollie smiled. "Or a mallet." He turned to look up at Leonard, then crouched to touch the floor. The dirt crumbled in his hand. "Look at this stuff. It's like dried-out Play-Doh. It's a wonder this place is still standing. You can get through that, right, Leonard?"

"Using what?" the big man asked.

"One of those." Ollie pointed to the claw-foot legs.

More shouts from the hallway; more shoving at the door.

Seconds later, Leonard, Tera, and Ollie were struggling under the weight of the table, trying to lift a corner off the ground. Once they did, Leonard stood on one foot and kicked out with the other, smashing into the leg until, finally, the screws came loose, and it clattered to the ground. Leonard pulled it out of the way, and Ollie and Tera let the table drop with a thundering crash.

Puzzled, Leonard stared down at it. "Now what?" he asked.

"We're going to break through that floor. Well, mostly you're going to break through the floor. But we'll help."

"That will only get us one floor down," Leonard pointed out.

"Yes, but they're not expecting us to be one floor down," Ollie said. "They're expecting us to be in *here*."

Laszlo lifted his hands. Sweat was dripping off his forehead. "But, my friend, when they get in here, they will see hole, and they will know where we went, yes? They will just follow." He looked sad to be sharing this news.

Ollie had no response. For a moment, no one spoke. Then Tera's finger shot into the air. "No, they won't," she said.

"What?"

"You guys go down, and I'll cover up the hole after you leave. With the tablecloth. And I'll put a few chairs in the way, and maybe a few of these guys—" she pointed at the sleeping guards—"so no one falls in. It will just look like a mess. Like there was a struggle. They won't even notice the hole. Then I'll go down in the dumbwaiter, and I'll meet you at the bottom."

Ollie tried to argue. The last thing he wanted to do was leave Tera behind. But even he had to admit, it was their best chance. Maybe their only chance. "Fine," he said. "We'll work on the hole. But you need to make sure that dumbwaiter works before we leave."

Tera nodded and ran to the wall. Leonard and Ollie took turns using the thick claw-foot leg to pound a spot on the floor near the center of the room as Laszlo looked on, clutching his wound.

The lion's foot was, in fact, digging. The floor was thin and brittle, as Ollie suspected it would be. And then, faster than he would have dreamed possible, the solid floor gave way to a startling, gaping hole.

Ollie looked over his shoulder at the door. Any minute, the guards would be through. Then he noticed that Tera had returned from tinkering with the dumbwaiter. "It works?" he asked.

She gave him a thumbs-up. "Ready to go."

He removed the tablecloth and handed it over. "So, you'll cover it? And—"

"Go," she interrupted. "I've got this. I'll see you at the bottom."

Ollie nodded, feeling a sharp pain in the pit of his stomach. "You'd better," he said. He reached out to touch her cheeks. And then he kissed her, hard and desperate, trying to remember her lips, her taste, her smell, even before they were gone.

By the time he turned around, Laszlo had already disappeared down the hole.

"Land on the good leg!" Leonard called after him, then looked at Ollie. "You coming, Mr. Butcher?" he asked, winking, before following Laszlo with a leap.

Ollie gritted his teeth. He didn't bother to look down before he jumped. What would be the point? He didn't care what was waiting for him. He only cared what he was leaving behind.

Twenty-Five

He fell as if in a dream, farther and faster than he had expected. Along the way, Ollie saw flashes of home: disposable coffee cups; pink buds on spring trees; the steep climb on Snow Hill Street; his black PS4 controller, sitting snugly between both hands.

The landing was hard—that, he did expect. His head hit something solid, probably ground, hurting for only a moment before the blackness settled in. It felt strangely enticing, the dark. Like a hammock of insignificance. He wanted to swing there, lazily, until even that was gone.

It was settled, then. He would sleep. Ollie was feeling quite pleased with his decision, quite content, until he saw his mother's face. Francie Delgato broke through the murk with the force of a north Atlantic winter wind. She was wearing the burgundy button-down blouse, the one with the white collar. The one she saved for Christmas morning and occasional Sundays. She led him up the marble steps, worn in the middle from a hundred years' worth of footfalls, into her tiny Fleet Street apartment. She took him to the galley-style kitchen. Asked him, as always, to reach the colander in the high cabinet.

Rigatoni today, she told him, smiling. *And eggplant.* Her cheeks were plump. Her eyes, brown and glossy as tempered chocolate. He kissed the top of her head and inhaled, taking in the familiar scents of her lavender shampoo and baby-powder deodorant. Then, suddenly, they were at the Museum of Science. She centered him under the T-Rex, giggling like a child as she snapped the picture. She fixed the chain on his bicycle, hands greasy. She sat with him at the dining room table:

Once more, she said. *Four times five is twenty. Four times six is twenty-four.* The numbers danced.

I can't do it, he insisted.

You can, she said. *You can do anything.*

His mother took his hand, again. Together, they carried Ollie's dying gerbil to the statue of St. Francis, patron saint of animals, in the Old North Church yard. The statue had a bird perched on its shoulder. *Pray for this small soul,* his mother implored. St. Francis didn't respond.

Can he save him? Ollie asked, clinging to the gerbil's carrier.

He knew the answer, even before his mother shook her head sadly.

Why? Ollie didn't understand, would never understand. He cried deep, hollowing sobs.

The gerbil died later that afternoon, under a pile of wood shavings. At first, Ollie pushed his mother away when she tried to console him. She had failed. She had prayed to St. Francis, and she had failed. What good was his mother if she couldn't even save his best friend? But then, gradually, he ate her offerings of parmesan toast, and he melted like whipped butter into her outstretched arms. She was softness and warmth and fingers running through his hair. She was everything. She was all he had. Until she, too, was gone.

"Mama." The word escaped his lips in an undulating ribbon of pain.

St. Francis, pray for this small soul.

Ollie squeezed his eyes shut. *Mama, I can't do it.*

You can. You can do anything.

I can't. It's too hard.

She was holding the gerbil, he noticed. Patting its small brown head. *Forgive me, Bambino,* she said.

There is nothing to forgive, he answered.

Forgive him.

He knew who she meant. The anger swelled in him like an inflammation. *Never.*

Forgive him, Francie said again. *That is your key.*

"Ollie?"

He heard his name, and he moaned.

"Ollie!"

He cracked open one eye.

"You all right there, buddy?" Leonard was peering down at him, looking worried. "I think you landed on your head."

Ollie propped himself up on the palms of his hands and took in his surroundings. His vision blurred, then focused. They had fallen through the floor—or the ceiling, depending on how you looked at it—and landed in a high-walled, windowless room. A storage room, from the looks of it, stacked with jars and bulging bags. Rubble from the excavation lay scattered all around them.

"Yeah, I'm good," Ollie grunted, climbing to his feet. The fleeting images of home, and of his mother, were already disappearing into the dust cloud around him. Then he pointed to Laszlo's wound. "How are you?"

"Is spreading, I think. The poison. I am feeling a *leeetle...*" Laszlo didn't, or couldn't, finish the sentence. His skin was growing paler.

"We have to get him out of here," Leonard said. "We have to keep going." He picked up the claw-footed leg from the floor, pursed his lips in concentration, and swung. Hard.

As Leonard pounded the brittle ground, Ollie glanced up at the hole in the ceiling, relieved to see that Tera had managed to cover it with the tablecloth after he jumped. Had she made it into the dumbwaiter before the guards crashed through the mess-hall door? Had she managed to squeeze her body into the tiny cart and shut the panel door behind her? How did she lower it? *Did* she lower it? Was she still hiding in there now, just seconds away from capture?

Tremors shook his body. *Stop,* he told himself. *Focus. Tera is more than capable of taking care of herself.*

Leonard was already making progress on their next hole.

Wham, wham, wham.

How long could they continue? Surely the pounding noise would attract attention, even with some of the Reds still unconscious upstairs. How many floors did they have to penetrate? Forty? Fifty? How much damage could the table leg take before it started to splinter? More importantly, how much jumping damage could he, Laszlo, and Leonard take before something cracked beyond repair?

"Uh, guys?" Laszlo said. He was standing behind them.

They had to hurry. They had to get Laszlo out of here. Ajanta would know how to help him. She must have a pill or a potion to counteract the poison. But how would they get to her in time?

"Guys!" Laszlo said again.

"What?" Ollie and Leonard said in unison. They spun around to find the acrobat pointing.

At an open door.

The storage room was...unlocked.

At first, no one moved. No one spoke. Then the three of them let out a collective whoop. Leonard tossed the table leg onto the ground with a clatter. Ollie rushed forward to prop up Laszlo, who was starting to sway.

"Stairs?" Leonard asked.

"Stairs," Ollie agreed. He stepped into the hallway, looking and listening for approaching guards, and heard nothing. Then he gave one last look at the lion's foot, already battered almost beyond recognition, before hoisting Laszlo's weight on his shoulders, steadying his breath, and limping through the open door.

Each floor at Herrick's End was marked by a carved wooden sign on the staircase landing. Ollie watched the 40s and 30s pass with every descending spiral. They took turns helping Laszlo, who was fading fast. Ollie's head injury must have been lingering, because he kept seeing shadows of Francie Delgato as he staggered from one step to the next.

They went as fast as they could, as quietly as they could. The Reds, thankfully, seemed to be occupied elsewhere. At least for the moment.

As they rounded down into the 20s, Ollie noted each passing sign with a fluttering sense of dread. He heard his mother's voice in his ear, and he winced. He didn't want to think about it. He had enough to think about. The damn number grew ever closer.

And finally, there it was, practically flashing like a marquee. Floor 20.

Ollie slowed. Then he sped up, and then he slowed again.

"God*dammit,*" he muttered.

Leonard turned. "Here, let me take him," he said, reaching for Laszlo.

"No, it's not that," Ollie said. He let out a sigh that carried the weight of decades. "I have to stop."

"Okay, we can take a break," Leonard nodded, peering down the stairs. "But just for a se—"

"No, I mean, I have to stop here and get something," Ollie interrupted. "Get some...one."

Leonard, obviously confused, didn't reply.

"It's my father," Ollie said.

"What about your father?"

"He's...here. On this floor."

"Oh," said Leonard blankly. Then his eyes widened in understanding. "Oh!"

"Yeah," Ollie said, slumping.

Laszlo looked up in surprise. "Your father is prisoner?"

"Yep."

"And you want to bring him with us? Out of prison?"

"Yes. I mean no, I don't want to. But I..." He paused, struggling for words. Thinking of his mother's plea. "I think I have to."

Leonard scratched his wide nose, considering this. "All right. Let's you and I go grab him, then, I guess."

"No," Ollie said. "You guys need to keep going. Get Laszlo out of here. I'll find you at the bottom."

Laszlo threw back his head and snorted. "Stop with crazy talk," he said. "I am hurting too much for laughing."

"I'm serious!" Ollie said. "You two need to keep moving. This is just... It's just something I have to do." He gritted his teeth. "Please, go."

"Please," the acrobat repeated. "You tell me please, and I tell you no. I will wait here. Is fine. How is it you say... Less talking, more moving? You go now. Fast." He pulled his arm away from Ollie's and leaned against the staircase wall. "What is your father's name?"

Ollie blinked. "His name? Matteo."

Laszlo nodded weakly. "Matteo Delgato, of the North End Delgatos. You will find him. I will wait, and you will go. And then we all go down, together."

Ollie looked at the number on the wall, then at Laszlo. "Okay. Thanks," he whispered.

"No thanking," Laszlo said. "Just walking."

Ollie smiled. The acrobat's blue Lycra suit still somehow sparkled, even here in the dark. There was something poetic in that, he knew, though his muddled and exhausted brain couldn't quite figure out what it was.

He and Leonard walked about halfway down the empty hall to reach Cell 20G, six doors down on the left. It was closed and locked.

"Shit," Ollie muttered, staring at the thick wood door. Of course, it was locked. What did he think, he was just going to waltz in there and waltz back out, hoisting his dad on his shoulders like a conquering caveman? "Well, I guess that answers that," he said, turning to go. Feeling relieved.

"Slow your roll, kid," Leonard said, examining at the door thoughtfully. He looked up and down the hallway, then kicked out his leg in an explosion of almost effortless energy. The door rocked off its hinges and landed with a loud thud on the ground.

The two men looked down at the carnage, and then at other. Leonard shrugged and grinned.

Steeling himself, Ollie walked through the suddenly open doorway and saw exactly what he had expected to see. His father was alone, propped up against the wall. He had the same vacant look on his face; the same dribble of drool falling from the corner of his mouth.

Ollie stood in front of him. "Hey, asshole," he said. "Get up."

No response.

"Papa, it's me. It's Ollie. Can you move?" He shook his father's shoulders, to no avail.

What the hell was he doing here? This was ridiculous. He tried to remember something good about his father. Something bright enough and substantial enough to balance against all the anguish the man had caused. A moment of kindness, maybe. Or paternal wisdom. Nothing came immediately to mind.

Matteo did try to teach him how to play guitar at one point. And poker. Perhaps not the most useful set of skills for a six-year-old, but at least it was something. Come to think of it, Ollie also seemed to recall his father taking him around on neighborhood errands, letting him ride his tricycle. Calling him "my boy" to anyone who would listen. Matteo had sounded proud. That had made Ollie feel pretty good, while it lasted.

Not that any of it made any difference, in the end. Or came anywhere close to making up for the rest.

"We'll have to carry him," Leonard said.

Ollie sighed. "Grab an arm?"

Together, they heaved yet another man on their shoulders and walked out the door of yet another Herrick's End cell. And as he turned to look behind him, Ollie could only hope, fervently, that it would be his last.

Twenty-Six

It was impossible. Not just difficult, but downright impossible. Ollie and Laszlo had too much dead weight to carry, and too much ground to cover. They managed to descend only two more floors before collapsing in the stairwell, propping Laszlo and Matteo against the curved walls as they gasped for breath.

They would never make it all the way to the bottom. Not in time. Not like this.

"The door," Ollie gasped. "The wood door."

Leonard looked confused for a moment, then nodded. "I'll go get it," he said.

A few minutes later he returned, lugging the oversized door he had kicked down at Matteo's cell—and a second one, too. He laid them on the steps like sleds. Ollie sat on one of them, propping his father in front of him and using his own arms like a seat belt around the lethargic man's waist. Leonard sat on the other door and did the same for Laszlo.

And then, they were off: four guys and two doors, sailing down the stairs with the speed of gravity, bumping and spinning in endless, dizzying corkscrews. Ollie's teeth chattered as his butt slammed down hard with every passing step. His hair flew back from his forehead. The scabrous walls scraped flecks of skin off his arm every time he got too close.

They heard voices below: Guards, running up the stairs. Ollie knew he couldn't stop the speeding sled if he tried, and so, instead, they knocked down the guards like bowling pins when they came upon them. Ollie felt the impact, saw the shock on the Reds' faces as they flew

233

through the air. The sledding doors barely slowed. Around and around and down and down they went, leaving the toppled and possibly concussed guards to flounder somewhere in the darkness above.

Finally, the winding staircase came to an abrupt end. The wooden doors hit the landing and stopped; Ollie, Leonard, Laszlo, and Matteo, meanwhile, kept moving. They shot out of the doorway like circus performers from a cannon and landed in the dirt with a wallop.

Ollie somehow ended up on his back, staring up at the vast, open expanse of the tower. In the distance, he could hear roars, shouts. Pandemonium. But here, in the empty courtyard, all was still. Somewhere nearby, he knew, the shards of the broken scoreboard lay scattered on the ground. He squinted, trying to see all the way to the top, to the suspended platform they had been standing on just an hour or two before, but could not. He saw only speckled dust in beams of light, and nothingness. And then, a face.

"That was quite an entrance," Tera said. She was standing above him, staring down.

Ollie bolted upright. His face broke into an astonished smile. "You made it!"

"Of course, I made it. You, I wasn't so sure about." Tera looked around at the others, who were starting to pick themselves up off the ground. "I'm gone for five minutes and you decide to start a bobsled team?"

"Funny," he groaned.

"Looks like you picked up an extra passenger on the way," she added, glancing at Matteo.

"Yeah." Ollie rose to his feet and brushed off his pantlegs. "That's, uh, my father."

"Your—?" She stopped. Her eyebrows lifted.

"Long story," he said.

"I'll bet."

Ollie walked over to stand beside his father's motionless, emotionless figure. "Tera, meet Matteo. Matteo, this is Tera."

"Lovely to meet you, sir," Tera said.

Matteo Delgato lay on his side, dirt now stuck to his cheek. He didn't reply or react in any way.

"That one's not much of a talker," said Leonard, who had hobbled over to stand beside them.

"I can see that." Tera said.

"We must get us out of here, no?" Laszlo said, coming up from behind. He was dragging his bad leg, wincing. Sweating profusely.

"You look like shit, Laz," Tera said.

"Mmm," he agreed with a cringe.

She turned to look at Ollie. "So. Mr. Mastermind. Ajanta mentioned a Plan B?"

He gave a weary nod. "We have to get to the west trash chute." That was the backup plan. He said a silent prayer that the backup hadn't crumbled to pieces, too, because the backup-backup wasn't likely to do anyone any good. "If we can get to the fifth floor, I can find my way from there."

They turned as a unit to look at the staircase the men had just descended. Far-off rumblings from injured guards echoed against the rounded walls.

"Can't go that way," Leonard observed. "Sounds like they're coming back down."

"The kitchen doorway's clear now," Tera said. "I just checked. And I grabbed this." She gestured toward a nearby slop-wench supply cart.

"You are busy," Laszlo said, sounding impressed.

"Yeah, well, I had to do something to occupy my time while you guys went for the gold medal," she smirked. "Laz, I think we can get you under here. Then you don't have to walk anymore." Tera approached the cart and pulled back the hanging fabric to reveal an empty storage area inside.

"Is small," he said dubiously.

"And you're an acrobat," she pointed out. "Can't you twist yourself up into a little ball?"

He considered this, then nodded.

"What about him?" Leonard asked, pointing toward Matteo's inert body.

"Yeah, that's, uh, an unexpected twist," Tera said.

"Sorry," Ollie muttered. "Maybe we can just kind of...flop him. On top. And cover him with something."

Two minutes later, they stood next to the ramp that led back down into the fighting pit. Laszlo was curled up and hidden inside the cart's storage shelf, and Matteo was concealed, just barely, on the top by gathered bits of broken scoreboard and chain links.

"There," Tera said, sounding satisfied as she shoved one last chunk of wood under Matteo's armpit. "If anyone asks, I'm just a servant cleaning up the mess. You guys wait here until I give you the signal."

Ollie and Leonard nodded.

As they watched, Tera lowered her gaze and pushed the cart down the ramp. She approached a set of loitering guards and pointed off to the right, looking concerned. They listened, looked at each other, and then hurried off in the direction of her pointed finger.

Tera waited only a moment before turning around and waving Ollie and Leonard inside. They tiptoed down the ramp. Tera kept her hands on the cart and jutted her chin to indicate a stack of barrels near the wall; the guys jumped behind them. Then she held up a hand in a clear signal: *Wait.*

They did.

Crouched behind the barrel, Ollie dared a look around the cavernous pit. Most of the fighters were back in their birdcages, screeching and flailing and seriously pissed off. A few stragglers were being zapped and dragged by groups of guards. The Mallet's cage hung like a sore thumb among the rest: conspicuously empty.

Ollie turned to watch Tera's path toward the kitchen, ogling in horror as the cart hit a bump and one of Matteo's hands flopped out into plain view. He started to jump up, to warn her, but Leonard held him down. The big man gave a firm shake of his hand.

"She's got this," Leonard whispered.

Sure enough, Tera noticed the dangling hand and moved swiftly to push it under the pile of debris while approaching the double doors. Ollie and Laszlo waited anxiously as she disappeared inside. Finally, she reemerged, darted her eyes left and right, and waved her hands. *Now.*

They stepped out into the shadows and ducked through the doorway. Ollie didn't know what Tera had said or done—maybe some kind of secret slop-wench handshake—but whatever it was, it had worked. The female servants gave them only surreptitious looks as they passed through the kitchen. No one screamed or alerted the Reds. And when the ragtag group reached the far end of the long room, the wenches simply stepped aside and allowed them access to the pully-system elevator in the back. Tera pushed the cart inside, Ollie followed, and Leonard began to yank on the creaking chain, lifting them up, up and away from Floor Zero.

Ollie gave a shudder when they stepped out onto the fifth floor. The familiar sights and smells hit him like a Knockdown one-two.

They pushed the cart and limped through the hallways while keeping an eye out for roaming guards. Ollie led the way, finally stopping in front of a metal sliding-door panel. The trash chute. He had approached this spot more times than he wanted to remember during his days on the Labor Force, usually lugging bags of unspeakably disgusting garbage.

He held his breath. Not just from the stench, but also from the anxiety. This was it. Plan B. If this didn't work, they were truly screwed. Ollie looked at Tera for courage, then slid open the panel. He saw a short but wide slide, and a torch flickering at the other end.

A well of relief rose in his chest.

"Derrin?" he whispered loudly. "You down there?"

A pale face surrounded by blonde, ropy hair appeared below. She looked up at him. "Took you long enough."

At the sound of her friend's gravelly voice, Tera gave a gleeful smile and pushed Ollie aside. She leaned forward into the chute. "Derrin!"

"And me, too!" someone else called out.

Tera pulled her head free and looked up at Ollie. "Kuyu's down there, too."

He nodded. "They've got a boat waiting."

All eyes fell on Laszlo, who had crawled out from his hidey hole inside the cart. His sweat had morphed from drops into rivulets; his eyes were glassy. His face contorted in pain.

Ollie stuck his head back into the chute. "Laszlo's been poisoned," he called out. "You've got to get him to Ajanta."

"Send him down," Derrin said.

Together, they helped Laszlo climb up and into the raised panel opening. "Wait," he said, grasping Ollie's arm. "I get bad feeling now. What are you going to do?"

Ollie's mouth set into a hard line.

"No," Laszlo said, shaking his head. "I know what you are thinking. You cannot do this. You must leave, now. With me."

Ollie didn't reply.

Tera looked at Laszlo quizzically. "What do you mean? What's he thinking?" Then she asked Ollie, "You're not leaving?"

Ollie paused. Then he answered, "Not yet."

"Why the hell not?"

"You know why not."

"Please, enlighten me," she said folding her arms.

"He's going to go after the Warden," Leonard said quietly. "Aren't you?"

After a moment, Ollie nodded.

"What?" Tera yelped.

"Not such good idea," Laszlo said grimly, still hanging on to the side of the chute. "You do not know Warden like I know Warden."

"Oh, I know the Warden well enough," Ollie replied. His eyes narrowed.

"Ollie, this is nuts," Tera said. "I mean, even for you, this is nuts."

She was right, he knew. He also knew that it didn't matter. "Nothing will change," he said. "The Warden will just come after you again. How long do you think you can hide before he finds you? A day? A week? He'll find you, and he'll drag us all back. And then all this..." He waved his arms. "All this will just...go on. The same. And no one will be safe."

"But you have to go," Tera interjected. "You don't have time to—"

"And what about you?" Ollie pressed. "And Derrin, and Dozer, and all the others?"

Tera waved a hand. "We can take care of ourselves. That's not your problem. Your problem is getting out of here while you still can. Like, now. Please. Get in the hole."

Her expression was pleading. Ollie wanted to follow her orders. More than anything. Instead, he shook his head. "It's not right," Ollie said. "This place, this whole thing... Somewhere along the line, it all went wrong. George Herrick knew it, but he couldn't do anything about it. But Tera, we can." He gripped her arm. "We can."

"We?" she asked.

He nodded.

Her face was still stern. But Ollie could see it in her eyes—she was weakening. "Fine," she finally said. "Let's finish this. But we'd better make it fast."

Laszlo watched the exchange warily. "So, what? You want that I just leave you? No," he said, shaking his long black hair. "No! I cannot! You will not make it out of here. You understand that? He will eat you alive, that Warden. I know that man. What he does. At least you must let me—"

"Laz, you know that's impossible," she interrupted. "We've got to get you healed up."

The acrobat looked at each of them. He looked at Matteo, slumped on the ground against the wall. He looked down into the dark mouth of the trash chute. Then he sighed, sounding resigned. "If I do this, you must promise me to get out," he said. "All of you, out. No matter what. That is most important thing, yes?"

"Yes," Ollie smiled. "That is most important thing."

Laszlo reached out and tapped Ollie's forehead with a finger. "Smart behind the eyes," he said affectionately. "All along, I knew it." Ollie held his gaze. "Thank you," he said. "For everything."

"Ah, is nothing," Laszlo answered, running a hand over his lumpy bicep. "This body was meant for greatness, was it not?" Then he turned to Tera with a wink. "You take care of this young man."

"I will," she said.

Laszlo appraised them both. "No time like now, then." He turned and shouted down the chute: "Here I come to you, beautiful ladies!" He gave a short, two-fingered salute before falling away into the darkness.

For a moment, all was quiet. Then Leonard pointed to Ollie's father. "Him, too?" he asked.

Ollie nodded. "One more, coming down!" he shouted into the chute.

The three of them hoisted Matteo's body and placed it at the top of the slide. The old man's arms dangled; Ollie grabbed one of them, ready to fold it over the other, when his father's back inexplicably stiffened. His neck snapped up. His eyes darted left and right, suddenly alert. A whining sound escaped through his nose.

Tera jumped back, stifling a scream with her hand.

"Holy shit!" Ollie breathed. His heart was thudding. "Papa?"

Matteo's eyes were open and active but didn't land on anything. His lips parted in a ghoulish grimace, releasing a sudden, rumbled rush of words: "Message from your mother," he wheezed.

"Wh...what did you say?" Ollie whispered. His limbs had gone tingly.

"Message from your mother," Matteo said again, looking but not seeing. Speaking in a monotone voice that didn't seem to be his own. "Message from your mother. Message from your mother. Message from your mother. Message from your mother. Message from your mother." The words shot out, louder and louder, like bits of jagged shrapnel.

Leonard took a step back, pulling Tera with him.

Ollie, on the other hand, leaned closer. *Mama.* A swelling in his throat threatened to choke him. "What...message?" he asked.

"Message from your mother! Message from your mother! Message from your mother!" Matteo was shouting now, a demented, animated robot. His head bobbled. His gaze spun then stopped abruptly, landing on Ollie's face. "Message from your mother. Rivers do not freeze."

"Rivers...?" Ollie gripped the man's arms. "Wait, what? What does that mean?"

But Matteo's stare, once again, was empty. His muscles had gone slack.

"What does that mean? I don't understand!" Ollie shook his father's shoulders, his arms, his face. "Look at me! Tell me what it means!"

Tera reached out, gently pulling him away. "It doesn't mean anything," she said. "He's just...somewhere else, Oll. He's already gone."

Tears stung his eyes. Of course, she was right. His insane, barely conscious father was not carrying messages from his dead mother. His father had dementia, or something worse. His brain was dying, or dead, or stuck watching a ceaseless firework display of neuron explosions inside his skull. Nothing he said would make sense, ever again. He pressed his hands against his face, trying to erase the image of his father's ghastly outburst.

"Ollie," Tera pressed. "We have to keep moving."

"Right," he nodded, lifting his head. "Right. Let's go." He cleared his throat and yelled into the hole: "Here he comes!"

They pushed and let go. Matteo slid like a sack of rice all the way to the bottom.

"Get them out of here and then come back," Ollie called down to Derrin. "If you can."

She gave him a thumbs up and disappeared. He stared for a disquieting moment into the suddenly empty chute, then slid the panel shut.

Leonard turned. "You know it's impossible, right? This Warden thing?"

"Not necessarily," Ollie said, reaching into his pocket and closing his hand around the small package Ajanta had given him. He had been rolling the vial between his fingers for the past 20 minutes. Knowing, instinctively, what it was. "Not if you come prepared."

"Prepared with what?" Tera asked.

Instead of answering, he rubbed his chin. A strange and giddy anticipation was pulsing through his chest. "We'll need the cart," he said, turning to examine it. "Can you get some cups and bowls, too? Serving stuff?"

"Probably. Sure."

"What about me?" Leonard asked. "I hope you don't think I'm jumping down that damn chute."

Ollie grinned up at him. "Actually, I was hoping you could round up some of my old coworkers."

Leonard raised an eyebrow.

"It'll be fine," Ollie told them, rising up onto his tiptoes. "It'll be good."

"I'm getting the feeling that your idea of good and my idea of good are two very different things," Tera said warily.

Ollie laughed. "Forget good," he said, a mischievous light glinting in his eye. "Guys, if we do this right, it might even be great."

He gathered them close and told them the plan, there in the dark hallway. And as Tera and Leonard listened, their frowns inverted slowly into cautious, surprised smiles.

Twenty-Seven

Twenty minutes later, Tera's feet were shackled together—or at least made to look that way, thanks to a rope connecting the two clamps that still constrained her ankles. Her cart squeaked as she pushed it down the small incline toward the Warden's island fortress.

Ollie stayed a few feet behind, hiding in the shadows. He didn't see any guards, and didn't expect to. Given the boss's tendency to shoot the messenger, they were probably drawing straws to decide who had to come down here and tell him about their colossal and baffling blunder in the fighting pit. If they told him at all.

When Tera reached the moat, Ollie looked left and right, then ran to stand beside her. They stood like that in silence for several seconds, trying to absorb the grotesque, if not entirely unexpected, sight before them.

The zombified children were at their guard posts. They kneeled at equal intervals around the circular island, facing out over the moat. At first glance, Ollie thought they were drinking from straws—oversized, clear plastic straws, stretching from each child's mouth into the liquid below. And then, with a shiver, he realized: The children were not drinking. Not voluntarily, anyway. The fat tubes stretched their mouths into unnatural widths, probably extending all the way down their throats, carrying the liquid in a thick, yellow, sparkling stream. Force-feeding.

Hollowskin juice, he thought, not willing to say the words out loud.

"This must be how he keeps them powered-up," Tera said, her voice low.

Indeed, a hum was emanating from the moat, with a low frequency that reminded Ollie of the electric crackle of city powerlines back home. The sound thrummed in the air all around them. The children's eyes were closed. And as before, they were all linked together by the deadly, yellow fog. It created a ring around the island and encircled the Warden's office in an unbreakable seal of protection.

Tera took a few steps forward; the children didn't react. "There's something down there," she said, pointing.

Ollie followed her finger. All the freakish feeding tubes converged into one spot, deep below the water. They seemed to be connected to...a box? A gadget? Another tube? From this distance, he couldn't say.

"I think we have to unplug them," Tera said.

"Unplug the kids?" Ollie asked. "How?"

She pointed into the depths of the moat again.

There was just one problem with her idea, and they both knew what it was. To demonstrate, Ollie approached the water and tapped it with his foot. His sneaker didn't sink, but instead bounced: The water was not water at all; not entirely. It had a hard-shell coating across its entire surface, thick and clear, like the glaze on a fruit tart.

"No diving in there," Ollie said.

"No," Tera agreed, her face contorting with displeasure. "So how, then?"

He thought for a moment. "Maybe just...walk across? Walk across and pull the tubes. Right out of their mouths." He pantomimed a forceful tug.

Tera shook her head. "It's everywhere," she said, gesturing at the fog that surrounded each young body. "We'd never get close enough."

Ollie frowned. He took a closer look at the tubes. Each somehow emerged from the moat, popping through the surface effortlessly as though it was made of liquid. But it wasn't liquid. It was solid. Wasn't it?

Ollie got down on one knee and bent forward. Through the hard shell, he saw movement. Flow. Deep below, the water was moving. Swirling.

He stood, swaying on his feet as a barrage of words and memories assaulted his senses with a sudden, mighty slap.

He remembered Laszlo, way back at the Freedom Trail: *You must trust this...and this,* the acrobat had said, tapping Ollie's forehead and chest. *Only those. Forget your eyes. Your eyes do not know as much as those. Yes? All right?*

And Tera, bringing him to Herrick's End for the first time: *You have to think in opposites down here,* she had told him. Up, down. Light, dark. Solid, liquid.

And of course, he thought about Matteo's bizarre and insistent stutter: *Message from your mother. Message from your mother. Message from your mother.*

Rivers do not freeze.

"It's not there," Ollie murmured. He looked at Tera, wide-eyed, and said it again. "It's not there."

"What's not there?" she asked.

"The surface. That!" He pointed down. "The coating. The shell. It's not there. It's an illusion. Protection, for whatever's down below."

"How do you know?"

"Because rivers don't freeze," Ollie said, his voice quaking. "My mother... She used to tell me her 'frozen river' story. It's about a choice, about a kid drowning in the—" He shook his head. "Anyway, that doesn't matter. What matters is, *rivers don't freeze.* A river, by definition, is flowing. Moving. It can be cold, yes, and icy, and all that. But it can't freeze. Not all the way through."

"So...what?" Tera asked, looking flummoxed. "This isn't a river. It's a moat."

"Look down there," Ollie said. "That's a flow. It was there the last time I was here, too. It's strong, and fast. River, moat, whatever you want to call it—the Warden doesn't want anyone down there. He's hiding something, and he's using an illusion to do it."

Tera considered this, then asked, "So, what are you going to do?"

He looked down at the point where all the tubes joined, its appearance obscured by distance and refraction. "You think we should unplug the kids?"

Tera nodded.

"Okay, then, that's exactly what we're going to do," Ollie stared down at the solid surface. "I'm going to jump in and unplug them."

Tera gave him an incredulous look. "That's ridiculous," she said. "You can't do that. It's too thick. You'll break your neck."

"On what?" he asked. "It's just water." He sounded more confident than he felt.

"Ollie—"

"What's the worst that can happen? If I can't get through, I can't get through. I bruise my butt and we try something else."

"Or you break your neck and slide into the path of the death fog, which slices you in half and leaves your guts strewn all over that pretty glass coating. Which doesn't exist. Even though it does."

"Yes," he nodded, feeling queasy. "I guess one of those two things could happen."

"Or, let's say you do break through. Then what? Then you're swimming in toxic Hollowskin juice. Which may or may not turn you into a Hollowskin yourself. Does that sound like a good idea?"

"I don't think the moat itself is the power source," Ollie argued. "I think it's just *concealing* the power source."

She folded her arms. "And you're basing that on what? Your vast institutional knowledge of moat security?"

No, he wanted to say. *I'm basing it on my mother's message from the afterlife, delivered to me by my stark-raving-mad father right before I shoved him down a trash chute.* Instead, he mumbled, "It's a...hunch."

Tera harrumphed. "No way. It's too dangerous."

"Probably," he agreed. "But what choice do we have?"

She stared at him, not answering. She knew as well as he did: There was no getting to the Warden without getting past those kids. There was no getting past those kids without freeing them from the Hollowskin source. And there was no freeing them from the source without doing something stupid.

"When I was kid, my mom used to take me to the community pool," Ollie said, starting to walk backwards. "I wasn't much of a swimmer. But I did okay."

"What are you doing?" Tera asked, a warning note on her voice.

"I couldn't dive. And I never did laps or anything. No swim team." He chuckled, still walking. "I was big, even then. But did you know, there's one thing that us fat kids are really good at? One thing that actually makes the other kids applaud?"

"Ollie..."

"They used to beg me to do it," he continued. "They would chant my name. Oll-ee! Oll-ee!" He heard it, somewhere in the recesses of his memory. Saw them thrusting their fists into the air. He smiled. Then he started to run. Faster and faster as he approached the moat, its glossy, solid surface glinting.

Two last steps, then one, and then...he was airborne. Ollie leapt fast and far, flinging his body with abandon. He resisted the urge to shout "Cannonball!" as he tucked his legs into his chest, curled his head downward, and squeezed his entire frame into a tight sphere.

When gravity pulled him down, he feared, for just a moment, that he had been wrong. His tailbone hit the hard surface, sending a temporary shock of pain up his back. Then, just as suddenly, it was gone. Not just the pain, but the surface. It didn't melt, or shatter, or loosen. It just...disappeared. As though it had never been there at all.

Instead of a thud, he heard a splash. *Oll-ee! Oll-ee!* He disappeared under the surface, swallowed by the press of liquid all around. He held his breath and waited. He opened his eyes. The water, if that's what it was, was perfectly clear. Nothing burned his skin or his eyes.

The current, though, was strong. Too strong. By the time Ollie fought his way to the surface, he was already twenty feet or so from where he had started.

Tera was waving at him, gesturing her arms in a wild circle. *Go around*, she was saying.

Ollie let the current sweep him around the island. As he struggled to keep his head above the water line, he wondered: Where was the current originating from? The moat was a circle, with no inlet or tributaries that he could see. There was no beginning and no end. Was it manmade, or magic? *The Warden probably drowns trogs in here for fun,* Ollie thought. *Or people.*

When he made it back around, he saw Tera's outstretched hand and grabbed it.

"Can you get all the way down there?" she asked.

"I think so," he spluttered. "But the current's pretty strong."

"Just do your best," she told him. "And don't drink any!"

He turned his head to try to locate the convergence point of the tubes down below. When he spotted it, he gave a nod. "Okay. Ready."

Tera hesitated for a moment before letting go. Ollie took as deep a breath as he could manage, then dove. He saw it clearly now, huge and octagonal, with multiple tubes protruding out of each side. It hummed and throbbed like a beacon.

Ollie swept his arms through the fast-moving stream, flailed his legs, and lunged. He grabbed hold of one tube, using it like a tow rope to pull himself closer. His sucked-in breath was running short. Panic rising, he yanked one of the tubes out of its socket. Then another, then another. They released easily, but there were so many... Ollie kept pulling, feeling the pressure rising in his lungs. Three more tubes. Two more. One last... It was out. Ollie shot to the surface, bursting into the open air, gasping and choking. The current swept him away, sending him to bob around the island once again.

Had it been enough? Did he get them all?

He spluttered and splashed, trying in vain to wipe the water from his eyes. Tera was calling out; he spotted her hand, outstretched as before, but this time he didn't reach for it. Instead, he propelled himself toward the opposite bank. Toward the children.

Even through his watery vision, he could see that the fog had thinned. Indeed, in one spot it seemed to have dissipated entirely. He aimed his head in that direction and swam, clinging to the bank as he reached it.

Ollie looked up. He saw a young boy, maybe eight or nine years old, hacking. The sparkling liquid in his tube had been replaced with what looked like clear moat water; the boy was pulling at it. Yanking it from his throat. When the tube was out, the boy collapsed onto his hands and knees, coughing up the liquid. His back heaved with the effort. Then the boy looked up at Ollie, eyes still somewhat clouded with cataracts, and collapsed onto the ground.

To the boy's left, a young girl was enduring the same ordeal. She pulled the tube from her throat and vomited onto the ground. Another girl next to her did the same.

The fog lifted. The circle of children staggered and fell all around the small island, none straying too far from their original posts. Ollie hoisted himself onto the bank and flopped onto his belly, eventually managing to climb to his feet. He rushed to the closest boy. "Are you all right?" he asked.

The boy nodded, weakly. He tried to answer but made only a breathy sound.

"Don't talk," Ollie insisted. "It's okay. You're going to be okay."

He checked on the next child, and the next. All of them were wobbly but breathing. Their eyes seemed to be shedding the awful, milky coating. Most importantly, they were fog free.

He had to get them out of there. Fast.

The bridge, the bridge... Ollie hurried toward the outside wall of the rectangular building and spotted the only protrusion: a lever with a rubbery orange handle. He yanked it down, then ran back to look into the moat. Something was moving, deep below. Rising. He barely had time to register the shift when the bridge appeared, lifting silently out of the water and connecting the two shorelines with perfect, elegant accuracy.

Tera hurried across to join him on the island, her shackles making her gait awkward. She brought the cart with her. Together, they began lifting the children off the ground and gathering them into a group.

"Hurry, now," Tera told them, herding them to the bridge. "Go. Wait for me in those shadows, right over there. Do you see them?"

The children followed her pointed finger to look across the water.

"There's a small alcove in there. Empty. You wait there, just a few minutes, and then I'll meet you there. Can you do that?"

One of the girls clung to Tera's leg, looking up at her with plaintive, terrified eyes.

"It's all right," Tera assured her. "I promise. He can't hurt you anymore. Can you trust me?"

With effort, the girl nodded.

"Good. You hide, and I'll be there just as soon as I can. Go on, now." She gave the girl a gentle nudge.

The children made their way across the bridge, gripping each other in a tight pack.

When they reached the other side, Tera tore her gaze away from the tiny group and looked back up at Ollie.

"That was..." For once, she seemed to be at a loss for words.

"Yeah," Ollie agreed, scowling.

Together, they turned to look at the Warden's office door. It was tall and heavy, painted olive-green.

"You ready?" he asked.

"Yep. You?"

"More every second," he said, thinking about the kids. And the tortured, screaming inmates. And the Labor Force. And the shackled slop wenches. And the fighters, forced to pummel each other in the ring for this man's pleasure. "You have everything?" he asked her.

"Not quite everything," Tera said, holding out her hand.

"Oh, right." Ollie fished around his deep pocket and pulled out Ajanta's small, burlap-wrapped package. He handed it to Tera.

"What if he stops me?" she asked, a note of fear in her voice.

"He won't," Ollie answered. "He won't even notice you."

"But how do you know?"

"Because I've known guys like this my whole life. He's an arrogant prick. You're the help, nothing more. You're invisible to him. You could lick his shoe and dance a jig and he wouldn't bother to look up from his paperwork."

She nodded but didn't look convinced. Then she gestured at the doorknob. "So, how do we get in?"

"Easy," Ollie said. "Just turn the knob and go."

"C'mon," Tera said. "Be serious. It has to be locked."

"It's not."

"Why wouldn't the Warden lock his own door?"

"I already told you," Ollie said, dropping his voice to a whisper. "Because he's an arrogant prick." He reached for the knob and turned it, enjoying her look of surprise when the door popped open without a sound.

Twenty-Eight

Ollie leaned against the wall. He cracked his knuckles. *Pop, pop, pop.* He paced. Still, the time ticked by.

What was taking so long?

Tera had disappeared through the office door five minutes ago, or maybe longer. Her eyes purposefully downcast. Her ankles still shackled. Her cart stacked with cups, a pitcher, cloth napkins, assorted handmade crackers, and some kind of thick, brown spread. It shouldn't be taking this long, he knew. In and out. That was the plan.

So, where was she?

Every second she stayed in there was a second too long.

He had just started scratching the skin on his arm, digging into the flesh with painful acuity, when she emerged. Ollie let out a rush of breath.

"All set?" he whispered, watching Tera step out onto the landing and close the door behind her.

She nodded, smiling.

"And he...?"

She nodded again. "The whole damn thing."

They grinned at each other. Ollie felt a hit of buoyancy trip through his veins. "You're incredible," he said.

"Eh," she waved away the compliment with faux modesty. "I get by."

"So," he said.

"So."

"I guess that means I'm up."

"Like a Butcher to a slaughterhouse," she agreed, a smile still curling her lips.

He gave her an unamused look.

"What?" she asked. "You're gonna go in there and filet the guy, right? Ground up the chuck? Trim the fat?"

"Tera, this is serious."

"You're right," she said, covering her mouth with a hand. "I'll stop."

"Listen, if this goes wrong..."

"It won't," she interrupted. "The hard part is already done."

"But if this goes wrong," Ollie continued, staring into her brown eyes. This was important. She had to hear him; she had to understand. "I want you to know...it was all worth it. And I'd do it again."

Just to find you, he wanted to add.

Tera's smile dissipated. "Yeah," she whispered. "Yeah, me, too."

They stood like that for several seconds, neither speaking. There was nothing left to say.

Ollie squeezed her tiny hands. He could swear he felt the moxie vibrating through her skin, seeping into his own. Eyes closed, he let the sensation linger. He remembered the things he had seen. The things he had suffered. He felt every inch of it, letting it all simmer and come to a boil. Then he let go, faced the doorway, and plowed his big body right on through.

The Warden was sitting at his desk, right where Ollie expected him to be. He didn't even look up.

"Not now," the man grunted, sifting through various papers with a pinched expression. The office looked much as Ollie remembered it from his last visit: streamlined and tidy. The wastebasket was empty. The shelves displayed generic containers, unlabeled folders, and books without titles. Tera's cart sat abandoned near the back wall.

Ollie took a few steps closer. He studied the Warden with a distant, almost impartial lens. Wire-rimmed glasses. Spindly, long limbs. Did the man own twenty gray suits? Or did he always wear the same one? That day's tie—silk, from the looks of it—was emerald-green. Slicked-back reddish hair, with a thin combover. His real name was probably Clark, Ollie guessed. Or Fisher. Or Cooper. One of those preppy monikers meant to evoke an old-timey profession. His last name would be something equally at home on a Yale application: Whittington. Calloway. McMoneybags. Or maybe Ollie had it backward. Maybe the

Warden was an imposter—a scrapper who had inflicted all kinds of pain during his long, uphill climb out of the trailer park, and now expended all of his energy trying not to fall back down. That was the most dangerous kind of asshole, Ollie knew. The kind with a secret to keep.

It took a minute for the Warden to notice that his command had been ignored, but when he did, he pulled off his glasses and looked up at the intruder with annoyance.

"I said, not now," he repeated. It was more of a growl than a request.

Ollie gave an apologetic smile. "I'm afraid now's all we've got, Mr. Warden." An unfamiliar feeling rattled throughout his body. It tasted like the first few sips of an orange soda: bright, sweet, and invigorating. His consciousness was drowning in carbonation.

The well-dressed man stared at him, clearly shocked by the impudence. "Who let you in here?" he asked.

"I let myself in," Ollie said, wandering over to the desk. He took a seat in the chair facing opposite. The same chair Axel the Axe Man had sat in just a few days earlier, watching his friend get bludgeoned to death. "I've been curious..." Ollie continued. "Do you kill them yourself? Or do you have one of your men do the heavy lifting?"

The Warden laid his glasses on the desk. His eyes narrowed. "I don't know who you think you are, young man, but—"

"Oh, right. Sorry. I'm Ollie," he interrupted, holding out a hand jovially. "Formerly of the Floor Five Labor Force. Oh, and the Knockdowns. You might know me better as The Butcher. Went down hard against Dozer in match three?"

The Warden ignored Ollie's outstretched hand. Barely contained fury spread across his features. "Young man, you are making the biggest mistake of your life," he hissed.

"Oh, I doubt that," Ollie said. "You obviously didn't see my try-outs for the track team." He pulled his hand back. "Well, in any case, it's great to meet you. Officially, I mean. Heck of a job you're doing here at Herrick's End. Really whipping the place into shape. Literally, in some cases. Am I right?" He gave an exaggerated wink, then lifted his right foot and propped it up on his left knee.

"I'm going to suggest you walk out of here, now," the Warden said through gritted teeth. But confusion was starting to register. Something else, too. His eyes slid to the doorway.

"Looking for the kids? Yeah, sorry. They're taking a little break. And the guards are pretty busy, too. Seems there's been a bit of a commotion down in the fighting pit. It's just you and me, Mr. Warden."

Ollie stopped and pointed his finger in the air, as though remembering something. "Oh, wait. That's not quite right. I should say, it's just you, me, and a few of my new friends." He got to his feet, walked to the door, and opened it.

Tera walked in first. Then Leonard. Then a long row of filthy, haggard, brown-suited men and women. Leonard, it seemed, had managed to break out and gather up nearly every resident of the fifth floor Labor Force, including Collins, Milowka, Eduoard, Alfred, Martel, and even poor Jumar, now sporting a bandaged shoulder stump where his arm used to be. Their stink and girth filled the room almost to its edges.

With each new arrival, the Warden's eyes opened just a bit wider. By the time they were all inside, the bald spot under his combover was moist with sweat.

"Just what do you think you're doing?" he asked.

"Great group, isn't it?" Ollie said, turning to admire the line of agitated, angry prisoners. "Cream of the crop. Sorry to say, though, I think they might have a tiny little bone to pick with you."

The Warden didn't immediately respond. His Adam's apple bobbed as he started to realize: Something was terribly amiss. His anxious gaze jumped from the door to the gathered group and back again to Ollie. "Look, we can work this out," he finally said. "I understand the working conditions...can be improved. Of course, they can." A thin smile spread across his lips. "You guys are my heroes, really. My favorites. You're the rock stars of this place! What is it you're looking for? Let's talk." He leaned back in his chair, folding his hands on his desk. They were shaking.

"Whoa!" Ollie exclaimed. "You hear that, guys? Rock stars! What do you think?" When no one answered, Ollie turned back around. "Ouch. Sorry. They don't seem to be in a talking mood. I guess that's what happens when you're wrongly imprisoned in a cursed dungeon for like, all of eternity." He smiled.

The Warden tried to nod, but only managed a small, awkward jerk. "It's okay. That's fine. It's... We can... I mean, there's always a way to..." He seemed to have trouble finding his words. Or making his mouth cooperate. He looked at his hands, his arms, confused. Then he looked at Ollie with desperate, dry eyes. "Please, don't kill me," he whispered. "Don't let them kill me. We can work this out."

Ollie sat back down in the chair. He looked across the desk with a tilt of his head. "Kill you?" he said. "Warden, we're not going to kill you."

"You're not?" The man's reply came out as a whisper. His suit seemed too big, suddenly, like a costume for dress-up.

"No! Of course not. We're not even going to hurt you," Ollie said. "Are we, Tera?"

He glanced at her, and she shrugged.

"Your fate is in your own hands, Sir. It always has been."

"Wh...what do you mean?" the Warden asked, looking fearfully from face to face.

Ollie sighed. "You recognize Tera? Right there. The one with the apron, and the shackles. Indentured servant? I think her official title down in the pit was Slop Wench Number Eight."

The Warden looked at Tera, then back at Ollie.

"Of course, you don't. Why would you? She was only here five minutes ago, serving you that lovely selection of crackers and—" He looked at the cart. "What is that stuff, exactly?"

"Loosemeat spread," Tera piped in.

"Ah, yes, crackers and loosemeat spread," Ollie said. "Huh. Not what I would have chosen for a last meal, but to each his own. In any case, all that brown mush must have made you thirsty, which is why you also drank a full cup of that nice refreshing wine, there."

The Warden eyed the empty container.

"And as you're probably guessing now, it wasn't just wine. Your cup also contained a tasteless, dissolving powder called—what's it called, again, Tera?"

"Dark Heart," she supplied.

"Yes, right." Ollie snapped his fingers. "Dark Heart. A reactive powder. I had it myself, once. Nasty stuff. Apparently, it has the ability to peer right inside your soul. Can you imagine?"

"The darker the heart, the more it reacts," Tera added.

Ollie nodded. "And the harder it works, the harder you get. And not in the good way, I'm afraid," he added, chuckling. "In a very bad, very permanent way. But you know all this already, don't you, Warden? If I had to guess, this is the very same powder you snuck into George Herrick's wine, back in the day."

The Warden fumbled and sputtered.

"No need to deny it," Ollie said, tapping the desk. "You had no choice. Everyone knew ol' George was in good with the witches. Sure, he had screwed them over once. Carted their friends off to the gallows after those sham trials in Salem. But George had learned his lesson. He had repented. The witches forgave him and worked with him to create the Neath. And just like that, the heartless enforcer became 'a friend to witches,' as the sign says. Boom. Blessed with a ridiculously long life. Good for him. But bad for you, am I right?"

Ollie leaned closer, staring the wiry man down, and continued. "George was never going anywhere. The witches had seen to that. And if the boss never leaves, the underling never moves up. You were never going to have a shot at running things the way you wanted. You had different ideas for the Neath. You dreamed of vengeance, and torture, and power. *Your* power. Am I getting warmer? What happened, Warden? Did someone hurt you, a long time ago?"

The Warden stayed tight-lipped.

"I get it, believe me," Ollie said. "The whole eye-for-an-eye thing... It has its own appeal, no doubt. But George wanted nothing to do with any of that. He was a new man, turned over a new leaf, blah, blah, blah. George wanted a peaceful sanctuary. And you couldn't kill him, because the witches had blessed him with all that damn long life. He was in your way. So what's a young, ambitious upstart to do?"

Ollie pointed at Tera, who was holding up the small vial.

"George Herrick was trying to change his life. Change his heart. But you knew that he had done bad things in his past. And you knew the powder would know it, too." Ollie held out his hands. "He had shown no mercy to those victims in Salem. So many innocent people, accused, hung, or rotted in jail. Terrible, terrible stuff. George had played his role. And the powder would see it all."

The Warden didn't reply.

"I think it was the paralysis that tipped me off. After all, a man doesn't just freeze, does he? Even a really old man. He'd wrinkle, sure, and maybe take some extra naps. But he wouldn't just freeze into stone. Something caused it. *You* caused it." Ollie sat back in his seat. "You know, right before he died, George Herrick told me something strange. He said, 'As I am, so he will be.' At the time, I didn't know what he meant. But now that I've had time to consider it... I think, Sir, that he was talking about you."

The Warden's fingers twitched on the desk. His eyeballs darted in panic.

Tera stepped closer. She leaned in to peer at his face. "Our Warden is looking a little...stiff," she said.

Ollie nodded. "Yes, he is."

"No hiding a dark heart, I guess," she added.

Ollie looked at the Warden's expensive watch. The shine of his smooth lapel. The thin, slicked hair. Then he looked at his face. "I just have one more question, before we go," he said, resting his hands on his lap. "Where are they?"

"Wh—who?" the man asked. Even the one word was garbled, as though his mouth was stuck together with a spoonful of loosemeat spread.

"You know who," Ollie said wearily. "I'm going to need you to tell me. Where are the witches?"

Tera looked at Ollie in surprise. A murmur of confusion spread throughout the room.

When he got no reply, Ollie sighed. "C'mon, now. There's no way they would have let you get away with any of this. Not if they had any power left. What did you do to them? Did you kill them? Banish them? Did you freeze them, too? What did you do?"

But it was too late. The Warden's mouth, like the rest of him, was already tight. The powder had spread like a contagion, fast and fierce. Only his eyes still had free range.

Shit. Ollie balled his hands into fists, frustrated.

Behind him, Leonard and the line of prisoners stood with their arms crossed, silent and seething. Tera, meanwhile, had turned her attention to rooting through the drawers and shelves. When she came across a key, she tried to fit it into the keyhole of her still-locked shackles. With each failure, she tossed the discards onto the desk. One of them, a particularly large ring holding multiple keys, landed with a loud thwack. Ollie looked at the rusted ring, then noticed that the Warden was looking at it, too. Staring, actually. And Ollie wondered why.

He reached out to pick it up. The ring felt heavier than it should have. Bigger, somehow. He dangled one end, letting the keys jingle. The sound hit his ear like a summons.

The Warden was still watching him, and the keys, blinking rapidly.

Tera gave up on the attempt to unlock her shackles. With a sweep of her arm, she pushed all of the remaining keys onto the floor. "What do you think, boys?" she asked, straightening. "I think we're done here."

The group agreed. They whooped and advanced like a wave, surrounding the desk, lifting the Warden out of his seat, hoisting him into the air. They kicked boxes and scattered papers, making a path to the door.

"Hold up, hold up!" Ollie said, waving a hand.

The brown-suited crew stopped and turned, still holding the Warden aloft like a particularly well-dressed store mannequin.

"We still need a Warden, right?" Ollie asked.

Murmurings spread throughout the group. Nods. A few agreeable shrugs.

"I nominate Leonard!" Ollie pointed to his friend, who was standing near the bookshelf with an open mouth of surprise.

After a moment of stillness, Tera stepped forward. "I second that motion."

Ollie spun to face his former fifth floor colleagues. "All in favor?" he asked.

A cheer broke out, nearly deafening inside the small office.

"I think that makes it official," Tera said, reaching for the big man's arm and leading him to the now-empty chair behind the desk.

"This is—" Leonard stammered. "I'm... No. There's not—"

"Don't worry," Ollie said with a grin. "We'll find a bigger chair. Will you consider it?"

Leonard hesitated. He ran his hands along the smooth, wooden desktop. "Maybe," he finally said.

Ollie gave him a wink. Then he looked up at the former Warden, who was darting his eyes and dripping with terrified sweat. "As for you, Sir, it seems the shareholders have spoken. Time to clear out. No two-week's notice necessary. In appreciation of your years of service, the company will provide a generous severance package that includes food, water, fresh air, and a lake view. No torture, no imminent death. Pretty generous, I'd say, under the circumstances." He gestured at the assembled, impatient group. "Our friends here will get you where you need to go."

Tera reached up and patted the Warden's arm. "Lucky for you," she said, "ol' George saved you a seat."

Twenty-Nine

Leonard and the freed prisoners carried the Warden on their shoulders like marching ants from a picnic bonanza. Out the door, onto the island, over the bridge. Some chanted, some cheered, and some just stuck to vague, celebratory howls.

On the other side, Tera found the group of children huddled in a dark alcove; she gathered them to her. Then she looked up at Leonard. "All right, let's get out of here," she said. "If anyone gives us trouble..."

"They won't," Leonard interrupted. He looked, for once, like he might be happy to kick down a few doors. Or people.

The scruffy men and women grunted their agreement and then they were off—heading down the dark hallway for the nearest exit. Ollie didn't worry that the ragtag group would find their way out. He watched Tera as she reassured the frightened children. Then he fingered the heavy key ring, which now rested in his pocket. He still heard the humming, like a song playing on a speaker far, far away.

Tera threw her arm over a little girl's shoulder. Then she called out to the group: "Okay, everybody, let's go. It's going to be all right. Stay together now. C'mon, this way. Good job."

They shuffled as one into the hallway. Tera paused in her herding to look back at Ollie. He hadn't moved.

"C'mon!" she said.

He didn't respond.

"Ollie? Let's go!"

"Can you do it?" he asked.

"Can I do what?"

"Can you take them? By yourself?"

"Why would I have to do that?" she asked, her eyes closing to slits.

"I'm...not finished," he said. The words seemed to come out of nowhere, as if someone else was speaking them. "I have to stay."

"Stay?" Tera looked at him like he was deranged, which he knew might be an accurate reading of the situation. "What the hell are you talking about? We have to get these kids out of here. We have to get *us* out of here."

"I know," he nodded. "I'll meet you. Can you get them out?"

"Well, Krite, I guess so," she said, flummoxed. "I mean, yes. Of course, I can. But why?"

"I... I don't know," he admitted. An idea was growing like a beanstalk in the back of his mind, but he didn't quite know how to share it. Not without looking even nuttier. "I won't be long. I promise."

Tera's lips pursed. He didn't want to know what she was thinking. She looked down at the two small boys flanking her legs, then back at Ollie. "Fine," she sighed. "Fine. But...be careful."

"I will. You, too."

"I hope you know what you're doing."

"Probably not," he admitted.

"But you're going to do it anyway?"

He shrugged helplessly in reply.

What was the matter with him? Was he certifiable? He should just go with her, now. Leave this wretched place. Get these poor kids to safety. Ollie's vision swam. Suddenly, he saw not her face, but her paintings: Hundreds of them, splayed out in a riot of technicolor. He saw toothy grins. Heart, and happiness, and courage. He saw what she wanted for herself, and for her found family. All the things he wanted to give her.

Ollie looked at Tera and he saw what was missing. He saw where he had to go. And he knew, with sudden, unmistakable certainty, what would be waiting on the other side.

The gathered children watched as he kissed her. A few of them giggled; one of them gasped.

Tera pulled away. "Maybe save that for later," she said. Even in the darkness, he could see that her cheeks had turned pink.

"Right," he said with a grin.

"See you on the outside, then?" she asked.

He squeezed her hand, the lump in his throat making speech impossible. He was infinitely glad she hadn't used the word "goodbye."

Tera gave him one last penetrating look before turning, reluctantly, to leave. The children fell into a neat line behind her. As Ollie watched them go, he couldn't help but think of the famous Mrs. Mallard and her eight obedient ducklings back up on the Brickside—bronze statues waddling in perpetuity inside Boston's Public Garden. People liked to dress them up throughout the year: bunny ears at Easter; Santa hats at Christmas; tiny yellow raincoats in June. But mostly they stayed the same. Dependable. Determined. Never wavering from their course, with Mrs. Mallard always leading the way.

A mama protecting her ducklings, and the whole damn city protecting her. Not that she realized it, of course. Poor Mrs. Mallard thought she was all alone.

Alone.

He felt the weight of it, there in the empty tunnel, but not in the way he had felt it before. Alone by choice. Alone with purpose. Not lonely, for once, but simply alone.

Ollie pulled his sleeves down past his wrists and started walking.

Left, left, right, straight. Around the corner. One flight of stairs, left, straight. Muscle memory dictated the route. He moved at a steady pace, not stopping to think. When doubts appeared, he ignored them.

Two guards approached; Ollie ducked behind a corner until they were gone, suddenly realizing he was standing close to the spot where he had first laid eyes on the Warden. *Step aside! Warden coming through!* Arrogance and vanity. Sauntering around the corner with a troop of zombified, weaponized children. A yellow fog, reducing a man's arm to pulp on the ground.

Then Ollie passed the infirmary, where he had nearly collided with a giant man he had known only as The Mallet. A shared moment, passing between them. An understanding, over almost as soon as it had begun.

He passed the tunnel that led to the water trough, where a girl, a stranger, had appeared out of nowhere. Turning a miserable, torturous day into an extraordinary adventure. Giving wholly of herself and asking nothing in return. Risking everything. Deserving revenge, yet choosing forgiveness. Seeing beauty where others saw only pain.

He passed the bend in the tunnel where a cellmate named Dozer had answered his whispered questions. Carried him through the darkest of days. Shown kindness, in his own gruff way, in a place where no kindness could be reasonably expected.

He passed the off-limits tunnel, pitch-dark. The place where, it was said, "top-level," worst-of-the-worst inmates were housed. Where even the cleaning crew was forbidden from entering. The "solitary" wing. *One crime is worse than all the rest,* Dozer had told him: *Pissing off the Warden.*

The hallway vanished into nothing. A black hole of emptiness. Ollie stopped. He pictured George Herrick's ancient, flaking skin. Saw his mouth fall open like a broken hinge. Heard his final words: *The rightful ones tarry in the place that is not a place.*

The key ring was in his hand, though he could not remember taking it out of his pocket. It vibrated against his skin. The sensation made Ollie think of that long-ago day on Henchman Street, when he had first set out to look for Nell. He had stopped at the Women's Resource Center, only to be turned away. Then he had walked back up the hill to find that the street sign was fading, swirling. Letters, rearranging themselves. Disappearing, and reappearing. Vibrating in the air around him. At the time, he had not believed his own eyes.

Now, he looked at the inaccessible tunnel with the same hesitancy. It was barricaded by a steel gate. A gate with a lock. Ollie stepped closer to find that the lock was marked with a picture. He squinted: He couldn't be sure, but it looked like a rudimentary drawing of a sun.

Ollie lifted the key ring and noticed that each key, too, was adorned with a picture. About two dozen in total. Had there been that many keys on the ring when he first picked it up? He could swear they seemed to be...multiplying. He searched through them for a matching sun but found none. He saw a frog, a square, something that looked like a baseball or basketball, a flame, a flower, a little house, and lots of others. But no sun.

Ollie frowned. Maybe these were the wrong keys. Maybe he was in the wrong place. Maybe the pictures had nothing to do with anything. If that was the case, then he should just try all of them in the hole and see which one, if any, fit.

He chose a key at random and lifted it. But before he could reach the keyhole, the entire ring flew from his hand and landed on the ground with a clatter.

What the...?

He tried once more. Again, something prevented him from making the attempt. A blast of air, or energy, or...something. As before, the ring fell to the ground.

Ollie gritted his teeth. What the holy hell? He couldn't even *try* the keys? How was he supposed to find the right one if he couldn't get near the damn thing? He stared in frustration at the crude drawing of the sun, wavy lines emanating from a central circle. Then he looked back down at the pictures on the keys.

One of them was similar to the sun, at least: The flower. Fat petals emanating from an oval-shaped middle.

He looked at both pictures again and chewed the inside of his cheek.

Sun, flower.

Sunflower.

A compound word. Two individual words combining to make one new one.

Tera had called him a sunflower, back at Blackstone Park. *A flower so nice, they named it twice,* she had said.

Compound words? Could it be that simple? It wasn't a particularly clever cipher, as these things go. Then again, the Warden wasn't a particularly clever man.

Pressing his lips together, Ollie lifted the key emblazoned with the picture of the flower. As he got closer, he waited for the ring to fly from his hand. But nothing happened. Instead, Ollie gently inserted the key into the lock, turned it, and removed it. He held his breath. A quiet buzzer sounded, and the gate began to lift.

The heavy barrier disappeared all the way into the ceiling, accompanied by the steady clatter of moving chains hidden somewhere in the wall. Moments later, the path into the tunnel was clear. Ollie looked over his shoulder, saw nothing and no one, and stepped inside.

He was only ten or twenty feet down when the darkness became almost total; soon, Ollie was reduced to feeling his way along the rough walls. The hallway bent to the right, then the left, before he saw a distant, flickering torch.

When he reached it, he found another gate, and another lock. He held up the flame to get a closer look and discovered that this one featured a tiny picture of an eye.

He flipped through the keys and stopped at the circle with hatched lines. A ball?

Eye, ball.

He inserted the key, turned it, and removed it. The gate began to rise.

The pattern prevailed through more gates and locks. Five, then ten, then eighteen. *Sail, boat. Cave, man. Bull, frog. Rain, bow. Candle, stick. Fish, bowl. Light, house.* And on and on. The keys continued to multiply on the ring, making it harder to find a match as he went along.

Finally, only one barrier remained. This one was not a gate like the others, but a door. A massive, hulking, metal door. Its keyhole featured the unmistakable image of a fire-breathing dragon.

Ollie looked down at the keyring and searched through the etchings. The original six or so keys had replicated into four or five dozen; at that point, the ring was so heavy that he struggled to hold it. He searched picture after picture, sweating. Trying to make sense of the scribbles. Finally, he stopped at an image that looked like a bird, flapping its wings.

Dragon, fly. Dragonfly.

Ollie inserted the key. A series of popping and whizzing sounds echoed in the darkness around him. He took a step back and watched as the door swung inward with a groan.

Slowly, the scene beyond began to reveal itself. It was a cell, not unlike so many others at Herrick's End, lit by the glow of several small torches. The room was round, with scattered, tattered furnishings. Three people sat cross-legged near the center. As the door creaked open, they climbed to their feet. Two women, one man. The man had a beard that stretched all the way to the floor; the women's hair was almost as long. They all appeared to be middle-aged. Or old. Or possibly ageless. From this distance, and in this dim light, Ollie couldn't say for sure.

The door finished its loud, sluggish journey and stopped against the cell wall. For just a moment, the silence was absolute.

The three witches looked at each other. Then one of the women smiled. Her teeth were stained, but intact. "Hello, Ollie," she said. "We've been waiting for you."

"You have?"

"We have."

"Oh," Ollie nodded. Of course, they had. That made perfect, Neath-like sense. Before he could say anything else, he became aware of a pressure in his chest. It slithered in like a snake, wrapping around his lungs and squeezing until all the air was expelled. He tried to cough, then tried to gasp, failing at both attempts. *No air.* He fell, landing hard on his back.

The witches surrounded him, three faces looking down from above. Ollie could read the concern, and the understanding, in their eyes. They knew already, like he did.

It was over. He was out of time.

Ollie slipped in and out of consciousness like a wave lapping and retreating from the shore. There, and gone. There, and gone again.

He heard things, occasionally. Mostly muffled words.

"...have to get him to the..."

"Is it...?"

"...all waiting..."

Was he flying? Yes, definitely flying. The fact didn't interest him, particularly. Nothing did. The questions fell away. The flying, and all the movement, seemed to stop for a while. He smelled familiar scents. Fish in a pan. Burning wood. He heard more voices. Tera's voice? Yes, Tera. The sound of it woke him, if only for a moment.

"...exit pass," he heard her say. He forced his eyes open, saw the flash of yellow. "Take him. Please, hurry!" She kissed his cheek. *No!* he wanted to scream. *I need to say goodbye! I can't go like this!* But it was no use. His eyes wouldn't open. Every breath was a ragged, torturous effort. Other voices, the witches, talking around him. Someone breathed air straight into his mouth, like a resuscitation. And then, suddenly, the pain was lighter. His chest expanded. The relief flooded him, making the waves of consciousness retreat once again.

He was flying, as before. Away. Definitely flying. Over the green lake, over the smoke curls rising from tiny houses. A patch of brown, hard and grainy. That's where they landed, setting him down gently on his feet. Ollie struggled to keep his balance. To keep his vision from spinning. He saw a round door, in a cavern wall. An attendant in a blue suit. Ollie swooned, swayed. The witches held him up. Carried him to the blue-suited man. Moving, moving, moving. *No!* he wanted to yell. *Not like this!*

But it was too late. His body was too weak. He was merely a prop on this stage. Soon, he'd be shoved through the porthole-shaped door and he'd have to—what? Climb? Levitate? Ride another death-defying chairlift, this time going up instead of down? The thought of it exhausted him. Any thought, about anything, exhausted him. His body was shedding itself. And all he wanted to do was give in.

"Ollie?"

The voice was familiar, but far.

"Ollie? Jesus, is that you? What are they doing to you? What are you doing to him?"

He focused his eyes in the direction of the voice. He saw, vaguely, a shape. No, a girl. Long brown hair. Hands on hips. His eyes widened as he struggled to put the various pieces together. It couldn't be. He was seeing things.

"Nell?" he croaked.

"Yeah, Oll, it's me," she said, rushing forward to grab his arm.

"Wh—what are you still here?" He wasn't making any sense. He knew that. But the garbled sentence was the best he could do.

"They won't let me go, Ollie. Can you believe that?" Nell's voice was pained, desperate. "They said I stayed here too long. I waited too long. But I'm fine! Look at me, I'm fine. I can breathe, and talk, and all that. I told them, it's different for everyone! Some people can last a little longer, that's all. That's what they told me, back up top. They said it's different for everyone. *About* three weeks, that's what they said. *About*. But they took away my pass! They took it, and now I can't get out. I'll never get out of here. Please, Ollie, tell them! Tell them! I'm fine! I need to go home! I can't stay here, Oll. I'll die. I swear it, I'll die."

Her words continued to hammer, pummeling his dim consciousness. He grasped the basics of what she was telling him, but not much more.

"I'm so sorry!" she continued. "I'm sorry you got stuck down here, because of me. Because of what I did. It's all my fault. Jesus, Oll, this is all my fault! I'm sorry!"

He heard his mother's voice in his head: *Forgive me, Bambino.*

There is nothing to forgive.

The witches were pulling him away. Moving him further from Nell and closer to the hatch.

He saw her more clearly now: Her hair hung heavy and thick. Her black tank top was stained with...something powdery. Her hazel eyes blinked in rapid-fire desperation. "What are you people doing to him? Let go of him!" Someone was holding her back.

They had reached the blue-suited attendant.

"Number for exit?" he asked.

"One," someone said. It was the long-bearded witch. Warlock? Ollie turned to look at him, noticing with hazy, detached interest that part of the man's beard was tangled in Ollie's sleeve.

The attendant glanced up. "Exit pass?"

"Right here," another witch said. One of the women. She handed the blank, yellow card to Ollie. He took it from her and stared at it, thinking about lemon méringue pie. And canaries in coal mines.

The attendant extended his hand.

Still, Ollie didn't move.

"Oliver, dear," the third witch said kindly. "I'm afraid it's now or never."

She was right. The tightening in his chest had returned. The temporary breath, or whatever it was they had given him, was running out. His body was transforming. If he didn't make it through that hatch and up to the Brickside in the next few minutes, he'd never see the North End again. He'd never hear Mr. Bonfiglio singing *Arrivederci Roma* as he folded bakery boxes. Never lay pink carnations on his mother's grave. Never feel the rumble and the majesty of the Pops concert on the Fourth of July. He'd never again see the falling snow, or the procession of St. Lucia, or the workaday boats chugging in and out of the harbor. The images swam like a nebulous fairy tale. A vision of timeless, abstract perfection.

"Dear one, you know what you have to do," the middle witch said.

Did he?

Ollie looked at the exit pass, and he felt a sharp pain in his heart. Tears stung like campfire smoke in his eyes. He did know what he had to do.

He had to go home.

Thirty

"Hey, come on in. Have a seat. Welcome to Lighter Tomorrows."

The group shuffled in slowly. The chairs were arranged, as always, in a wide circle. A few of the more nervous participants rubbed sweaty hands onto their pantlegs, while others sipped from cups. They shared uneasy smiles. All had been there before and knew what to expect. But that never made it any easier.

"Thanks for coming. Everybody in? Great." Ollie looked around the circle with a smile. "All right, I'll start us off with today's quote. This one is from Buddha, who said, 'Our sorrows and wounds are healed only when we touch them with compassion.' That's a good one."

Various heads nodded. Some kept their eyes on the cups on their hands.

"You've taken a big step just by coming here today," he added. "And of course, we're all here to support each other, and to listen. Does anyone have anything they'd like to share?"

For a moment, no one spoke. Ollie resisted the urge to fill the empty space; instead, he waited. Finally, a hand went up.

"I'll start," Dozer said.

He still wore his eye patch, though his skin had been shaved of stubble.

"Great!" Ollie responded, leaning forward in his seat. "How has the week been for you?"

"Okay, I guess," Dozer said. "I tried to do what you said about...remembering." His eyes went to the floor.

"And did you? Remember anything?"

"Yeah. I remembered the smell."

"The...smell?"

"Whiskey." Dozer cleared his throat. "Now this was Alabama, so you know damn near everybody drank whiskey. But my old man drank enough to fill two barrels twice a day, and then roll on up for more. Whiskey and cigarettes. He didn't love nothing else." Dozer's gaze had traveled to the wall, where he stared at some far-off point.

"And when he drank, what happened?"

"Nothing good," Dozer said gruffly.

"But what happened...to you?"

He stared back down at his cup. "'Bout what you'd expect."

"You mentioned last week that you thought there might be a connection between that, what happened to you, and the things you did later. The things that you regret."

"Yeah," Dozer said again. His gaze was still on the ground. "I just wish...I had learned different, you know? I mean, there ain't no excuse for nothing I did. But it's just..." He stopped and sighed. "I just wish it could've been different, that's all."

Silence settled on the group. Then Ollie said, "Thanks, Dozer. Does anyone else want to share?"

A small woman two seats down from Dozer raised her hand. Petra. She was one of the newer members. Originally from St. Louis. As Petra shared her week's progress, he listened, and nodded, and, as always, stole glances around the room.

Ajanta was there, hands folded in her lap. And Derrin, and Kuyu, and some newer faces he was still getting to know. A few of the former fifth floor laborers, including Collins and Milowka. Cellmates Edouard, Alfred, and Martel, sat beside each other. Even Nikki was there—minus Floyd, so far, but Ollie was working on that.

In the end, he had handed over his exit pass to Nell. Of course, he had. The decision had been remarkably easy. One pass, two people. And only one of them belonged here in the Neath.

Then he had started a new kind of Lighter Tomorrows. The kind focused on losing a heavier sort of weight.

Leonard had come to the first few meetings but had to take a break soon after due to a busy work schedule at Herrick's End. The witches had given their blessing to his appointment as the new Warden. Much to everyone's surprise, he had taken to the job with gusto—abolishing all torture at the prison, ending the Knockdowns, and temporarily banning new admissions. He had also improved the living conditions, though there was a still a long way to go.

Leonard had even established a tentative system of parole, in which Widow Hibbins, the Reader, would perform her job in reverse: Instead of reading past crimes, she was now assigned to read future intention. One by one, she touched each inmate's hand and looked for two things projected on her big white wall: remorse, and a lack of malicious intent. If she saw both of them, the prisoner would become eligible for release. And, just possibly, for membership in Ollie's support group for survivors of abuse.

No one had passed her test yet. But Ollie remained hopeful that someday, someone would surprise him.

Petra finished her story. Another participant, a young girl named Lalibelle, took the opportunity to share her week's progress. Ollie was making eye contact with Lalibelle—"actively listening," as his old LT leader Lorraine would have said—when he felt a hand squeeze his thigh. He smiled.

For just a moment, he let his eyes dart to her face. Ollie didn't normally look at Tera during the meetings; she was too distracting. Today was no exception. Her new jumpsuit was more form-fitting than her old one. Her grin was lopsided. Her hair, still shaved on the sides, was even longer at the top, and still purple. And her brown eyes... They had that look about them. The look that told him she was proud of him, and loved him, without saying a word.

Tera had converted her art studio into a small house, just for the two of them—well, three, if you counted Meatball. They had even added a private barn next door for Mrs. Paget. Tera wanted to make the house bigger, but for Ollie, it was plenty big enough. It was perfect.

He kept busy most days at the Tea Party, where he and Ajanta had opened a food stall. Ollie liked to think of it as "Italian-Indian fusion"— rhizers, blindfish, and other local delicacies prepared with Ajanta's seemingly endless spice blends and Ollie's equally endless quest for deliciousness. They jokingly called it "Ollanta's." One of these days, he would make it official with a sign. A big one, carved into wood.

Tera had started selling her paintings, with a little help from Nikki and Floyd. Soon, she might even have a gallery of her own. *No,* he corrected himself—Soon, she *would* have a gallery of her own. Tera could do anything, after all. Hell, she had already done the impossible.

As for his father... The old man hadn't woken up. Not yet, anyway. Ollie couldn't help but feel a little relieved about that, since he didn't know what the two of them would say to each other if his dad did somehow make the jump back to coherence. Would there be apologies? Forgiveness? Or just more of the same? Ollie couldn't say for sure.

J.M. Blanchet

The girl named Lalibelle ceded the floor to brawny Edouard. After he finished speaking, Kuyu shared a quiet story, which was followed by another one from a crow-boat driver named Dixie. Former laborer Alfred was just finishing up his own tale when a voice called out from behind.

"Knock, knock."

Ollie turned to see Laszlo poking his head through the doorway.

"I am sorry to be interrupting," the acrobat said. "But I bring special delivery from Brickside!" Something dangled from his fingers: blue-and-white string, tied around a white box. A stamp on the side read, simply, "Bonfiglio's."

Ollie's breath quickened. Every time, the excitement was the same. "Come in, come in!" he said, holding out his hand. "What is it today?"

"You see for yourself," Laszlo said, sounding mischievous. Since Ajanta's remedies had cleared the poison from his system, he was looking like his old self.

Gently, reverently, Ollie untied the string and opened the top. The smell hit him first: Powdered sugar. Chocolate chips. Sweetened ricotta cheese. Crispy, bubbled shells. "Cannoli," he said, as if in prayer.

"Enough for everyone," Laszlo added, producing several more boxes from behind his back.

A cheer went out through the group. On his shoulder, Meatball snuffled and wiggled. Ollie broke off a piece of pastry and dropped it into his palm; the trog slurped it into his bill and began waddling down Ollie's arm, looking for more. The sound of animated murmuring filled the room as everyone beheld this new, wondrous decadence.

"I think you've lost them," Tera said, giving his side a nudge.

"All right, all right..." he said, smiling. "I know when I'm beat. Great job, everyone. I guess we can break early today. But before we go, let's hear our motto..." He cupped a hand to his ear.

"Here today, lighter tomorrow," the group chanted.

"Here today, lighter tomorrow," he repeated. "See you all on Tuesday."

Tera wiped powdered sugar from her mouth and gave him a wink.

Ollie looked at her, and at his friends, and at his cannoli. Grief and joy pierced him in equal measure. *I am the luckiest person in the room,* he thought. *The very luckiest.*

Epilogue

By the time Ollie found the note, it was faded and frayed almost beyond repair. He wasn't sure what had made him notice it. There was nothing particularly colorful or interesting about the tattered sheet; nothing to make him think, *Well, would you look at that!* Nothing at all that should have given him the urge to pick it up. And yet he did.

Meatball had been using the note as bedding in his nest on the floor—just one of many treasures gathered and piled into a lump of colorful, comfortable mush. Ollie reached down, scratched the trog's fuzzy head, and tugged the piece of paper free.

The handwriting was shaky and faint. Dancing with inscrutability. Where did Meatball find it? When did he find it? And how long had it been sitting undiscovered in his nest? If Ollie hoped to find answers in the note itself, he was disappointed. All he found there was a single letter "O" written at the top, swirling in wide black ink, followed by a rhyme:

> *Hows and abouts*
> *Souls and mates*
> *Find him his,*
> *Seal your fate.*
>
> *Water green,*
> *Three on high.*
> *Air and breath,*
> *Truth and lie.*

Good is bad,
Beast will bite.
Steer the course,
Bend the light.

Mud to brick,
Dark to sun.
Soon, you choose:
All
     or
          one?

Ollie stared down at the verses. He blinked, then read them again. There was nothing particularly ominous about them; nothing to make him think, *Danger is rising. Worse than before.* Nothing at all that should have made him clench his abdomen with a sharp prickle of fear. And yet he did.

No, he thought. *No, no, no, no, no.*

Angry tears stung his eyes. He was done, dammit. He had already accomplished more, far more, than anyone could have reasonably expected. And now he was proud, and exhausted, and *done.* His boat was moored, his sail was down. No more surprises. No more danger. No more sinister prophesies disguised as nonsensical, ridiculous riddles.

Besides, the note could be anything. A child's poem. A love letter. A practice sheet from someone's calligraphy lesson, faded by a dozen urine storms and swept here by fickle breezes blowing over the dark, green lake. Anything at all.

Ollie held the paper gingerly between his thumb and forefinger as though it might give him a rash. He wanted, suddenly, to be rid of it. To forget about it. To pretend that he had never stumbled across it. Yes, that seemed like the best solution. Clenching his jaw, Ollie crumpled the note in his fist. Then he bent forward and shoved it back into the trog's pile of debris.

There. It was gone. Out of sight, out of mind, and out of his life.

He wanted to believe it. Part of him valiantly did. But the other part, the bigger part, knew that hiding the words would make precious little difference. They were already in him and around him. He could feel the letters and phrases burrowing tunnels through his consciousness like eager voles. Memorized, almost against his will.

Air and breath.

Truth and lie.

He slammed his eyes shut. Covered his ears. And still, they came.

Soon, you choose:

All, or one?

Denial began its slow retreat as a wave of dread advanced. It was no use. He could still see the letter "O" at the top of the page, beckoning like a deep, black hole. He recognized the handwriting, thin and quivery. Of course, he did. He knew who had written the note, and who was supposed to find it. Worse, Ollie knew exactly what it meant.

He had escaped the walls of the prison, but he was still not free.

George Herrick wasn't done with him yet.

As if sensing a disturbance, Meatball woke and sniffed the air. He nudged the note with his beak, pushing the crinkled paper deeper into the mound of collected moss, discarded socks, empty paint tubes, and wadded-up balls of dust. He gave a grunt of satisfaction, or maybe annoyance—Ollie wasn't sure which. Then the trog flipped over onto his back, splayed both webbed feet in the air, and began to snore.

End of Book 1

Be sure to pre-order Book 2,
Herrick's Lie!
(Out 2023)

Acknowledgements

This book was inspired by my time spent working at The Center in Danbury, Connecticut, where I met the most dedicated group of staff and volunteers toiling around the clock to help survivors of domestic violence and sexual assault. Thank you to the courageous pioneers in the movement and to everyone who continues to strive each day to end the stigma, break the cycle of abuse, and strengthen our communities. We are all in your debt.

Thank you to my agent, Julie Gwinn, for plucking *Herrick's End* out of that pandemic fog and seeing the possibilities. Your guidance, savvy, and unwavering support has made all the difference. Thank you also to Grace Smith at The Seymour Agency for being Ollie's first champion and fan. (He owes you a few cannoli.)

Thank you to my editor, Jennifer Wallace, whose talent, patience, and thoughtful suggestions gave this rough diamond a brilliant sparkle. I couldn't have asked for a better partner on this journey. Thank you also to Galen Surlak-Ramsey, Madison Holler, Markella Wagner, and the whole team at Tiny Fox Press for following me down into the weird and wild depths. If I were stuck in the Neath, I'd want you all driving the crow boat.

Thank you to the team at Damonza for designing a cover as beautiful and imaginative as anything Tera could have created in her studio.

There is only one author's name on this book, but there should, by all rights, be many more. Thank you to my merry band of workshop writers, and to our inimitable leader Jenna Blum, for finding the good, fixing the bad, and just generally being the best damn group of cheerleaders and friends a girl could wish for: Hillary Casavant, Mark Cecil, Tom Champoux, Jennifer De Leon, Chuck Garabedian, Julie Gerstenblatt, Kimberly Hensle Lowrance, Edwin Hill, Alexandra Hoopes, Sonya Larson, Kirsten Liston, Joseph Moldover, Jenna Paone, Jane Roper, Whitney Scharer, Adam Stumacher, and Kate Woodworth. Getting to know each of you and your writing has been one of the great pleasures of my life.

Thank you to Mark Cecil, Julie Gerstenblatt, Kimberly Hensle Lowrance, and Zakariah Johnson for your wisdom and honesty on all those beta reads.

Thank you to the team at Operation Delta Dog, who inspire me every day (operationdeltadog.org). This nonprofit organization rescues shelter dogs and trains them to work as service dogs for disabled veterans: The dogs get the homes they need, and the veterans get the help they deserve! And none of it would be possible without an insanely dedicated and brilliant group of staff and volunteers. We all say we want to make the world a better place—they are actually doing it.

Thank you to the entire gang at A Mighty Blaze, who didn't let a little thing like a global pandemic keep writers and readers from finding each other (amightyblaze.com). Your ingenuity, humor, and camaraderie helped me survive lockdown with my sanity (somewhat) intact, and I will be forever grateful.

Thank you to Tricia Chamberlin and Susan Arapoff for a lifetime of support and friendship. "Make new friends, but keep the old. One is silver and the other is gold."

Thank you to Don Blanchet for all the great advice, and to Ginger Blanchet for sharing an infectious love of books.

Thank you to Don Voner for being the best big brother this little sis could ask for.

Thank you to Mom and Dad for giving me the kind of safe and loving home that allowed me the freedom to explore the dangerous and wacky worlds of my imagination. Because of you, I jump first and worry about wings later. Every kid should be so lucky.

Thank you to Lucy for all the brainstorming sessions (and writing time with horses).

Thank you to Ian for always being my first, and best, reader.

And thank you to Scott, for believing in me. I wrote the book, but you made it possible. You are all the magic I need.

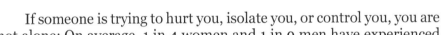

If someone is trying to hurt you, isolate you, or control you, you are not alone: On average, 1 in 4 women and 1 in 9 men have experienced violence or abuse from someone they know well. If you're under 18, this is often called dating violence or parental abuse. If you're over 18, it's usually called domestic violence. No matter what your age or gender, no one else has the right to physically or mentally harm you.

If you want to seek help, you can reach out to the National Domestic Violence Hotline at thehotline.org or 1-800-799-SAFE (**United States**), the Ending Violence Association of Canada at endingviolencecanada.org or the Kids Help Phone at 1-800-668-6868 (**Canada**), the National Domestic Abuse Helpline at nationaldahelpline.org.uk or 0808-2000-247 (**U.K.**), and 1800Respect.org.au or 1-800-RESPECT (**Australia**). Resources are also available at sites like ncadv.org, womenshealth.gov, domesticshelters.org, and loveisrespect.org.

About The Author

T.M. Blanchet is an award-winning humor columnist, a former reporter and editor, and a producer at A Mighty Blaze (AMightyBlaze.com), an initiative created in 2020 to help writers and indie bookstores reach readers during the Covid-19 pandemic. T.M. is also the host of A Mighty Blaze Podcast, which features weekly interviews with authors like John Irving, Cheryl Strayed, Anna Quindlen, and Yaa Gyasi.

In 2013, T.M. founded Operation Delta Dog (OperationDeltaDog.org), a nonprofit with a mission to rescue shelter dogs and train them to work as service dogs for disabled veterans. The organization has since placed more than 50 trained dogs with New England veterans suffering from Traumatic Brain Injury, PTSD, and related conditions.

Website: tmblanchet.com

Twitter: @ TM_Blanchet

About the Publisher

Tiny Fox Press LLC
5020 Kingsley Road
North Port, FL 34287

www.tinyfoxpress.com

CPSIA information can be obtained
at www.ICGtesting.com
Printed in the USA
LVHW111923290422
717575LV00003B/14

9 781946 501479

OYSTER BAY - EAST NORWICH PUBLIC LIBRARY
OYSTER BAY, N Y

MAY 2 4 2022